**She thought about moving closer and, um, what? Kissing him? That could be awkward.**

If he kissed her back, then what? She didn't do casual relationships, and it wasn't as if Desmond had been secretly pining for her.

It had been over a decade since their prom date. If he'd been so interested, he could have easily asked her out a thousand different times. But he hadn't. So making a move would be stupid. He would be way too nice in his refusal and she would feel like an idiot.

And just like that, whatever vague fantasy she'd been harboring disappeared with a nearly audible poof.

"All right, then," she said with a forced smile. "Good night."

She closed her door behind her, then leaned against it.

No more Desmond-is-handsome-and-sexy thoughts, she told herself. She was going to live here for two months, and she needed to remember that and act like a polite but disinterested roommate. Anything else was a slick, steep road to disaster, and no one wanted that.

u

#1 *New York Times* Bestselling Author

# SUSAN MALLERY

## Before Summer Ends

## &

## A Little Bit Pregnant

Recycling programs
for this product may
not exist in your area.

ISBN-13: 978-1-335-47480-3

Before Summer Ends & A Little Bit Pregnant

Copyright © 2021 by Harlequin Books S.A.

Before Summer Ends
Copyright © 2021 by Susan Mallery, Inc.

A Little Bit Pregnant
First published in 2003. This edition published in 2021.
Copyright © 2003 by Susan Mallery, Inc.

This edition published by arrangement with Harlequin Books S.A.

For questions and comments about the quality of this book,
please contact us at CustomerService@Harlequin.com.

Harlequin Enterprises ULC
22 Adelaide St. West, 40th Floor
Toronto, Ontario M5H 4E3, Canada
www.Harlequin.com

Printed in U.S.A.

# CONTENTS

# BEFORE SUMMER ENDS

For Nissa—thanks for lending me your name

# Chapter 1

"Darling, we're pregnant!"

"We are?" Nissa Lang asked, somewhat confused by the "we," as well as the news of the pregnancy.

Mimi was in her midforties and as far as Nissa knew, Mimi and her husband hadn't even been trying. Not that Nissa could be sure about that. Her relationship with Mimi was casual at best. Nissa was going to house-sit Mimi's grand mansion while the happy couple spent the summer in a different mansion in Norway. Not only would Nissa get paid a princely sum for things like flushing the many toilets and making sure the gardeners (yes, plural) did their thing, the money was going directly into her I'm-turning-thirty-and-to-prove-my-life-isn't-a-disaster, I'm-taking-myself-to-Italy-for-three-weeks-next-summer fund.

Knowing she had a place to live for July and August,

Nissa had rented out her own small condo, to add even more money to her fund. Only the sinking feeling in her stomach told her that maybe she was about to get some bad news in that department.

Mimi laughed. "I know it's a shock. We're stunned. We didn't think we were ever going to be able to have children, but I'm pregnant and it's wonderful. I'm calling because the baby means a change in plans. Between my age and the previous miscarriages, I'm a high-risk pregnancy, and travel is out of the question. So we'll be staying home this summer. I hope you understand."

Yup, there it was. Disappointment on a stick, stabbing her right in her travel dreams.

"Of course," Nissa said politely, because that was how she'd been raised, but on the inside, she was pouting and stomping her feet. "Congratulations. You must be thrilled."

"Thank you. We're beyond happy. Take care. Bye."

With that, Mimi hung up and Nissa sank onto the sofa. She looked at the open boxes scattered around her small condo, the ones she was filling up with personal items so the charming young couple who had rented her place for two months would have room for their own things. She glanced at the calendar she'd tacked on the wall, with the date she was supposed to be out circled in red.

"This is bad," she breathed, letting the phone drop onto the cushion next to her. "What am I going to do?"

She didn't have a summer job lined up, the way she usually did. As a fourth-grade teacher, she had summers off and used the time to get a job to supplement her income. It was how she'd managed to scrape together the down payment for her small condo. She'd moved in nearly a year ago and loved every inch of the place.

She was going to use the Mimi house-sitting money and

the rental income for her condo to pay for her Italy trip next year. Postponing it was not an option. Two years ago she and her fiancé of three years had broken up. Before that, her best friend had been diagnosed with kidney disease— the kind that would kill her if she didn't eventually get a transplant. Nissa had firsthand knowledge that life didn't always turn out how you expected or wanted, so putting things off was taking a serious chance of losing out. Something she wasn't willing to risk.

She'd been dreaming about going to Italy since she was fourteen years old. She'd devoured guidebooks, watched travel videos on YouTube and had planned and replanned her stay. Next year, she was spending her thirtieth birthday in Italy.

The problem was, she'd just lost her funding.

Oh, she was putting aside a little every month, but living in the Seattle area was expensive and it wasn't as if she had a six-figure salary. The summer money was how she was going to make the trip happen.

She leaned back against the cushions and considered her options. Obviously, she would have to get a different job. It was already late June, so she might not have a lot of options, what with competing with high school and college students for the best ones. Regardless, she would find something. The more pressing problem was where she was going to live for the next two months.

Her parents would happily welcome her for the summer, but they lived in a small town in Eastern Washington. There wouldn't be many job opportunities if she stayed with them. Plus Nissa didn't want to be that far away from Marisol and her kids. Not when a transplant could show up at any time.

Crashing at Marisol's place wasn't going to work. While

her best friend would welcome her, the house was tiny and already overcrowded. Which left one option.

She grabbed her phone and scrolled through her contacts. Shane picked up on the second ring.

"Hey, kid."

She smiled. "You think you're such a big brother, don't you?"

"It's kind of my thing."

"I'm surprised I caught you. Why aren't you slicing and dicing?"

"I just got out of surgery. Knee replacement. The patient is going to be very happy with the outcome."

Shane was an orthopedic surgeon in a busy sports medicine practice. Four years older and definitely the smarter of the two children in the family, he'd always been driven to be the best. Nissa knew she was much more in the "average" category and was comfortable there. She didn't need to change the world, just improve her small part of it.

"I'm glad for your patient," she said. "I need to come live with you for the next two months. And don't you dare say no. You have that extra bedroom. I know you do— I helped you decorate it."

She explained how her house-sitting job had fallen through.

"I'd love to help, but I can't." Shane's voice dropped nearly an octave. "I've met someone."

She resisted rolling her eyes, mostly because he couldn't see her doing it. "Shane, I refuse to accept that as an excuse. You've always met someone. You spend your life 'meeting someone.' It's the sticking with them for longer than three weeks that doesn't work for you."

"This is different. No can do, kid. I can't have you hanging around when I'm trying to…you know."

"Seduce a perfectly nice woman who doesn't know you're going to be a hit-and-run lover? While that sounds great, I'm in trouble. It's serious and I need your help. I have people showing up in three days to move into my place. I need somewhere to go."

"Stay with Desmond."

"What?" she asked, her voice more of a yelp than she would have liked. "No. I can't."

What a ridiculous suggestion. Desmond? As if.

"He has a giant house and he's practically family."

The key word being *practically*. He was, in fact, her brother's best friend from boarding school. Because Shane had gotten a scholarship to the fancy place when he'd been thirteen, and he and Desmond had been close ever since.

Desmond was great. Nissa liked him just fine. He'd taken her to her senior prom when her boyfriend had dumped her at the last minute. She'd warned him not to marry his now ex-wife and she'd been right.

"It's a perfect solution," Shane said cheerfully. "I'm going to text him right now."

"What? No. You can't. I'm not—"

The rapid *beep, beep, beep* told her she was talking to herself. Shane had already hung up.

"I'm not comfortable staying with him," she muttered to no one in particular.

Not that she could explain exactly why to her brother. Or herself. In truth, the thought of living with Desmond made her insides get all twisty. It would be too strange.

Besides, what were the odds of him agreeing? He wouldn't. Why would he? People didn't generally enjoy having unannounced roommates for months on end. He would say no. She was sure of it. Practically sure. Mostly sure.

For the second time in less than ten minutes, she dropped

her phone onto the sofa cushion and knew she was totally and completely screwed.

## DESMOND

Stilling Holdings, Inc., or SHI as everyone called the company, was a multinational conglomerate with interests in everything from rare element mining to biofuels to construction to infrastructure. The different divisions were managed as separate companies, each division president reporting directly to CEO Desmond Stilling.

Three years ago, Desmond had moved the company headquarters from San Francisco to just north of Seattle. A new ten-story building had been constructed, SHI had adopted six elementary schools, two middle schools and a high school as their local charity projects, and on most days Desmond managed to stay on top of everything work related. Every now and then circumstances bested him. An airport strike in South America had delayed shipment of needed parts to a plant in Germany, leaving road crews in Eastern Europe without crucial equipment. Every day of delay was a problem in a part of the world where there was a season for construction.

In the end, he'd had his people charter two planes out of a private airfield forty kilometers away. By Tuesday of next week, the completed machinery would be on its way and the road work could continue. The cost of the chartered planes would chew up any profit, but he knew the road was more important. He would make up the money elsewhere. He always did.

Shortly after eleven, his personal cell phone buzzed. He pulled it out and smiled when he saw the name and picture displayed.

"No, I can't take off the rest of the day and go hiking with you," he said by way of greeting. "Some of us have to work for a living."

"I work," Shane protested with a laugh. "I save lives, my friend."

"You replace joints, not hearts."

"I improve quality of life. What do you do?"

"I build roads and feed the world. This is me, winning."

The familiar banter was a welcome relief from the fast-paced, business-only rhythm of his day. Much to the chagrin of his staff, Desmond got to the office early and stayed late. When he'd been married, he'd had something to go home to, but these days, there wasn't much waiting for him in his big house, so he stayed at work later and later.

He knew he would have to make a change at some point—just not today.

"You think you're such a powerful CEO," Shane said.

"I *am* a powerful CEO."

"You're talking but all I hear is a buzzing sound." Shane chuckled. "Okay, enough of that. I need a favor."

"Done."

"You don't know what I want."

Desmond knew it didn't matter. Shane was his best friend and he would do anything for him or a member of his family. Desmond had grown up the classically clichéd lonely, rich child. The first ten years of his life, he'd been homeschooled with excellent tutors. When he'd finally been sent off to boarding school, he'd had the education of a college freshman but the social skills of a pencil. The transition had been difficult.

Two years later, he'd been sent to a college prep school where Shane had been his roommate. They'd quickly become friends. That first Christmas, Shane had dragged him home for the holiday. Inside his friend's modest house, Desmond had experienced what a family was supposed to be. For the first time in his life, he'd seen parents hugging their children and had felt warmth and affection. The presents had been chosen with care and love rather than ordered by staff. For those two weeks, he'd been just like everyone else and it had been glorious.

Ever since then, the Langs had been a part of his life. He would do anything for any of them, regardless of what they needed. His parents were still alive, but the Langs were his real family.

"Nissa needs a place to stay for a couple of months. She had a gig house-sitting but that fell through. She's rented out her condo. I'm guessing backing out on that contract could be a problem. Plus she wants the money for her trip to Italy next summer."

Technically Nissa wanted to go to Rome and Florence, rather than generically visit Italy, but Desmond didn't correct his friend. Nor did he mention he was the one who had introduced Nissa to Mimi and her husband when Mimi had said they were looking for a dependable house sitter. Of course Mimi's unexpected pregnancy would have changed their plans. He should have realized that himself.

"She can stay with me," he said. "There's plenty of room."

"That's what I said. You have what? Twelve bedrooms?"

"Eight."

At least he thought there were eight. Maybe it was ten. After his initial tour of the house before he'd bought it, he'd never much gone exploring. He used his bedroom, his home office and the media room. The rest of the house didn't interest him.

"So that's a yes?" Shane asked.

"It is. I'll get in touch with her today and find out when she wants to move in, then I'll let my housekeeper know and she'll get a room put together."

"Thanks, bro. I appreciate it. You're doing us both a big favor. So let's go out on your boat sometime soon."

"I'd like that."

"I'm on call for the next two weekends, but after that."

"Let me know what days work for you. We'll have fun."

"Thanks for helping with Nissa."

"Anytime."

They talked for a few more minutes, then hung up. Desmond glanced at his computer. But instead of rows of numbers, he saw Nissa in her prom dress, earnestly thanking him for offering to take her to the dance at her high school. He'd been in the first year of his MBA program then, having finished his undergraduate degree in three years. He'd flown up from Stanford to be her date.

At the time, he'd been doing a favor for a friend, but the second he saw her, everything changed. Gone was the preteen who had tagged along whenever he'd visited. In her place was a beautiful woman with big eyes and a mouth he couldn't stop staring at, and later kissing.

But nothing more. No matter how much he'd wanted to take things to the next level, he'd known he couldn't. She was the only daughter of his surrogate family. He loved and respected the Langs too much to betray their trust in him. So he'd done the right thing and had firmly put Nissa in the friend column, where she had stayed. And would stay.

He shook off the memories and quickly sent a text.

Shane says you need a place to stay. I have plenty of room. Just tell me when you want to be there and I'll get a room ready.

There was a pause, then he saw three dots, followed by her reply.

Really? You will? I seriously doubt you know where the spare sheets are kept.

He chuckled. You're right, but I'll have it done. Hilde will be thrilled to have someone else to care for. I disappoint her with my boring lifestyle.

Desmond, you're nice to offer, but I couldn't possibly impose.

I insist. There's plenty of room. He hesitated, then added, It's not your parents' house. Whoever you're seeing is welcome to stay over.

As in a boy? LOL That part of my life is a disaster. Kind of like yours. Can I LOL twice in a text without seeming like I'm getting weird?

You can if you'd like. When do you want to move in?

Gulp. Is Friday too soon?

It's not. I'll let Hilde know. Text me when you have an approximate time so I can make sure I'm home to give you a tour and a key.

Thanks, Desmond. You're the best. I promise to be the perfect guest. You won't even know I'm there.

He studied her words, thinking that he very much wanted to know she was there. He would have offered his place, regardless, but he'd always liked Nissa. She was easy to be around, and he felt comfortable in her presence. With her, he didn't feel as much the heartless bastard the women he dated always ended up claiming he was. Plus she'd been right about Rosemary and he'd been the fool who hadn't listened.

See you Friday, he texted.

Thanks again.

He sent a quick text to Hilde, telling her about Nissa's stay. When his housekeeper sent back questions about the types of foods Nissa liked and which bedroom would be best, he gave Hilde Nissa's number so the two of them could work it out. Once that was done, he returned his attention to his computer, because work was the one place where he had all the answers.

*NISSA*

Friday morning Nissa got up early to finish getting ready for her move-out. She'd packed her personal things, along with a few breakables she didn't want to leave out. All that was left was her grandmother's china and her clothes. She would take care of the clothes first thing, then wait for Shane to arrive to help her with the china. Once that was done, she would give her place a final clean, then head over to Desmond's house.

So far she'd done a good job of ignoring her upcoming living situation. If she didn't think about moving into the big house on the Sound and, you know, living with *him*, she didn't get nervous. But if she allowed herself to dwell on the reality of sharing a roof with a guy she'd had a crush on for over a decade, she got a little queasy.

Not that her crush meant anything, she reminded herself as she got dressed before heading for the bathroom. It was just a funny quirk, left over from when she'd been a teenager. Desmond had been older, fantastically good-looking and sweet to her. Of course she'd liked him. Now, as a grown-up, she knew those feelings were just remnants of happy memories. These days they were friends. Good friends. He'd been married, for heaven's sake, and she'd been engaged. They'd both moved on. Or at least she had—she doubted he had anything to move on from. So there was nothing to worry about or any reason to be nervous. Really.

That somewhat decided, she finished getting ready, then put together several boxes and got out packing paper. She set everything on her dining room table. Shortly after eight, her doorbell rang.

She let in her brother, smiling when she saw the to-go tray he carried.

"Morning," he said, giving her a quick kiss on the cheek. "I brought breakfast."

"I see that. Thank you."

She took the coffee and breakfast sandwich he offered, then led the way to the sofa in her living room. They set their food on the coffee table. Shane glanced around at the bare side tables and nearly empty floating shelves.

"You were robbed."

She sipped her coffee before smiling at him. "You know how I am. I have stuff everywhere. No one wants to live with that. So I put it all away. It's very clean looking, don't you think?"

"I don't know. It makes me feel as if you've been taken

over by aliens." He nodded at the small hutch in the dining alcove. "We're just wrapping up the china?"

She nodded. "It's a full set for twelve. I don't want anything to get broken. I made space in my storage unit, so we can take the boxes down there."

"Sounds like a plan. You're moving in with Desmond after that?"

"This afternoon." She wanted to protest that she wasn't moving in with him—not in the traditional sense. But saying that would cause her brother to start asking questions and there was no way she wanted to explain about her crush-slash-fluttery stomach.

"So what's with the new girlfriend?" she asked, hoping to distract him. "Who is she and what makes her 'the one'?" She made air quotes with her free hand.

"Her name is Coreen and she's an ER pediatrician."

"A doctor," she teased. "Mom and Dad will be so proud."

He grinned. "I know. I'm the favorite for a reason, kid."

"Oh, please. They so love me more."

The joking was familiar. Shane might be more brilliant but she was no less adored by her parents. They hadn't had a lot of money for fancy things when she'd been growing up but there had been plenty of attention and affection.

"You didn't answer my question," she pointed out as she picked up her breakfast sandwich. "Why is she special?"

"I don't know. She's smart and pretty and I like her a lot." He took a bite of his sandwich. "There's something about her. We'll see how it goes. I'm optimistic and I don't want to mess up anything."

"Why would you think you mess up your relationships?"

"I'm not like you," he said. "I've never made being in love work."

That surprised her. "Not with any of the women you've dated?"

He shook his head. "There's always an issue." One corner of his mouth turned up. "Unlike you and Desmond." He made kissing noises. "You've always had a thing for him."

She willed herself not to blush, then socked him in the arm. "I had a crush on him when I was a kid. So what?"

"You followed him around like a puppy."

"He was dreamy."

Shane scowled. "Please don't say dreamy before I've finished my breakfast."

"Deal with it, brother of mine. So when do I get to meet the magical Coreen?"

"Not for a while. I want to make sure it lasts. What about you? Who's the new guy?"

"There is no new guy." Her love life was sadly lacking.

"You haven't been involved since you broke up with James. Come on, Nissa. That's been what? Two years? It's time to move on."

"I know and I want to. But it's hard to meet people. My luck with online dating is nonexistent and all the guys I meet through work are married."

"There have to be a few single dads with kids in your class."

She looked at him pityingly. "I don't date students' fathers. It's tacky and against policy."

"That makes sense. What about when you go to Italy? You can meet someone there. A handsome Italian with a nice accent."

She laughed. "Technically if we're in Italy, I'll be the one with the accent." She was less sure about a vacation romance. Not that she would object to being swept off her feet for a week or two but she doubted the affair would last past her time there.

"Want me to ask around at my practice? See if any of my work friends know of a single guy."

"No. Absolutely not. I shudder at the thought." The last thing she needed was her brother finding her guys to date.

"Hey, I have good taste."

"You've never set me up, so we don't actually know that." She tempered her words with a smile. "But thank you for thinking about me."

"I always think about you. You're my baby sister and I want you to be happy." He grinned. "And safe. Why else would I have told Desmond to walk away after your prom date?"

She'd been about to take the last bite of her sandwich. Instead she stared at her brother, her mouth hanging open.

"What?" she managed, trying to make sense of his words.

Shane winked. "I know. You're impressed, right? Like I said, I look after you."

She put down the sandwich. "Wait a second. Are you saying Desmond wanted to go out with me after prom?"

"Sure. He had a great time and was all into you, but I pointed out that he was too old and too experienced. He was in grad school and you were a senior in high school. No way that was happening on my watch."

The adult side of her brain could appreciate what her brother had done. He was right about both the age and experience difference between them. But the teenaged girl that would be with her always nearly shrieked in protest. She'd liked Desmond—she'd liked him a lot. When he'd disappeared after their one date, she'd been devastated.

"Besides," Shane added, obviously unaware of what she

was thinking, "he's a part of the family. I reminded him that he owed my folks for taking him in and stuff, and he shouldn't repay them by going after you."

"You're pretty proud of yourself, aren't you?" she asked, reaching for her coffee.

"I am and you should thank me."

She held in a sigh. He'd done what he thought was right, and at the time, it had been. Her broken heart was her own business. But the information did leave her with some interesting questions, such as if he'd liked her, why hadn't he tried dating her later, when she'd been all grown up? And most important of all—what did he think of her now?

# Chapter 2

*DESMOND*

Desmond had brought home work but couldn't seem to focus on it. Normally he enjoyed getting lost in whatever business project he was involved in. Even the things that most people considered boring—reading contracts or reviewing financial statements—were pleasurable for him. The business was rational—at any given moment he knew exactly where things were and how to improve them. He might not like the answers he came up with, but he knew he could count on them. His business was a place where he excelled. Relationships, particularly the romantic kind, had never been one of his strengths.

Oh, he could get a woman into his bed in a couple of hours. Sex was easy, but anything involving the heart was nearly impossible for him. Probably because he was too much like his parents, he thought, admitting defeat and closing his spreadsheet program. They had raised him to use his head and ignore his emotions, telling him that feelings weren't to be trusted and caring too much made a person weak. They'd certainly demonstrated their philosophy time and time again with him and with each other. There had been no hugs in his family, no displays of affection. Being told he'd done well at something was about as personal as it got when he'd been growing up.

Given the choice between reaching out and holding back, he learned to always hold back. It was what he knew and it was safer. The only place he was different was with Shane and his family. They were the people he trusted.

He remembered when his marriage had ended. Rosemary, who it turned out, hadn't married for much more than a lifestyle, had told him he was the coldest and most heartless man she'd ever known. When he'd protested that he'd been a good and kind husband, she'd laughed at him, telling him he had a chunk of ice in the space where his heart should be.

The end of his marriage had been disappointing—not so much because he missed her but because he didn't. He was supposed to have wanted to spend the rest of his life with her. Shouldn't he have mourned the loss? The fact that he hadn't reinforced her supposition. He was a man without a heart.

He tried to shake off those thoughts and return his attention to his work, but quickly realized that wasn't happening. He obviously wasn't going to get anything done until Nissa arrived and got settled. For some reason, he was more focused on that than the Asian sales report.

He got up and crossed to the large window in his study. The late-June days were long and sunny, and the garden flourished. The grass was dark green, flowers provided plenty of color in the planting beds, the trees looked healthy.

The gardeners did a good job, regardless of the seasons, but in the summer, their hard work paid off.

He turned at the sound of the vacuum cleaner being turned on somewhere upstairs. Hilde had been in a state since he'd told her Nissa was coming to stay. There had been cleaning and washing and other tasks he couldn't begin to imagine. The refrigerator overflowed with food and there were fresh flowers everywhere in the house.

Her burst of happy activity made him feel guilty. His housekeeper obviously didn't have enough to do in a day. The house was large, but there wasn't anyone to make a mess. He rarely ate dinner at home, so she wasn't spending much time cooking. He would guess she was bored working for him—a problem he didn't know how to solve. If he'd stayed married to Rosemary, they would have had kids by now. That would have increased the workload. Of course if they'd stayed together, he and Rosemary would have been living in different wings of the house, barely seeing each other, except when they passed in the hallway.

His phone buzzed. He pulled it out, then smiled when he read the text.

I'm here. Just giving you a heads-up because the house is so big, I thought you'd need an extra minute or five to walk to the door and I really don't want to be kept waiting.

He was still chuckling when he heard the doorbell ring a few seconds later.

He walked through the entryway and pulled open the large front door. Nissa stood on the wide, covered porch, her long red hair pulled back in a ponytail. She had on cropped jeans and a T-shirt. Her lack of makeup meant he could see all her freckles—the freckles he'd always liked and that she claimed to hate every time they were mentioned. Her big blue eyes crinkled as she smiled at him.

"Are you out of breath from the long trek? Should I pause until you're able to speak?"

"I can manage a sentence or two," he said as he held open his arms.

She stepped into his embrace easily, as she always had. He hugged her, telling himself not to notice the feel of her body against his. Nissa was his friend, nothing more. And if a part of him wanted to breathe in the scent of her hair or enjoy the way her breasts felt nestling into his chest, he only had to play the "she's Shane's sister" card to make it all go away.

She stepped back. "Again, thank you for taking me in. I'm really happy for Mimi. Of course I am, but wow did it upset my summer plans." She smiled. "Which makes me a horrible person, so don't think about that too much. As I bring in my stuff, I'll work on repairing my character."

"There's nothing wrong with your character, and I'm happy to have you here for as long as you want to stay." He looked past her to the very full car. "Why didn't you ask me to help you move?"

"I was fine." She waved a hand in dismissal. "Shane carted boxes into my storage unit. Those were heavy. This is nothing. I'll just take a few trips to get it all inside."

"*We'll* take a few trips," he told her. "Let me show you to your room, then we'll bring in your things."

She tilted her head. "You didn't have to say yes, you know. Are you sure you're comfortable with me invading your space? I can be messy and I'm not sure we like the same music."

"Stop," he told her, stepping back to wave her inside. "I'm glad you'll be here. I'll enjoy the company and Hilde needs someone to fuss over."

"Hilde was so nice when we texted." Nissa leaned close

and lowered her voice. "She asked me what kind of cheese I like. No one's ever asked me that before. I honestly didn't know what to say. I was afraid I would disappoint her if I didn't ask for something fancy, but all I could think of was cheddar."

He thought about the contents of the refrigerator. "She bought more than that. You can try them all and tell her which ones you like best."

"I can't wait." She paused in the foyer and looked up.

He followed her gaze, taking in the two-story entry, the large windows and elegant chandelier. Desmond had lived in the house long enough that he no longer saw any one part of it, but he knew it wouldn't be the same for Nissa. While she'd been to the house a few times for parties and barbecues, she'd never lived here.

She looked at the wide staircase and the long hallway, then back at him.

"Is there a map?" she asked, her eyes bright with humor.

"It's an app."

"I almost believe you."

Hilde, his housekeeper from the day he'd moved in, appeared. She was in her mid-to late-forties, with short dark hair and a warm smile.

"Miss Nissa," she said, her hand outstretched. "Welcome to Mr. Desmond's home. Please let me know if I can do anything to make your stay more pleasant."

"I'm thinking you've already done so much," Nissa told her. "It's nice to meet you in person. I hope you didn't go to too much trouble."

"No trouble." Hilde glanced at him. "Did you want to take her on a tour, Mr. Desmond, or should I do it?"

"Go ahead," he murmured, thinking she knew the house better than he did. But instead of retreating to his office, he joined the two women as Hilde led the way.

"The formal dining room," Hilde said, pausing inside the doorway. "The table expands to seat twenty." She glanced at him. "Mr. Desmond doesn't have any dinner parties. Maybe while you're here you could talk to him about that."

A dinner party? Why would he want to do that?

Nissa glanced at him, her mouth curving into a smile. "I will happily talk to Mr. Desmond about a dinner party. Who should we invite? Ex-girlfriends?"

"Only if your ex-boyfriends come, too," he told her.

"Hmm, I'm less excited about that."

They followed Hilde into the large kitchen. She showed Nissa all the appliances and the pantry. Nissa seemed taken with the six-burner stove and the contents of the refrigerator, especially the cheese drawer.

"Does Mr. Desmond ever come in here?" she asked.

"He does," Desmond told her. "I make my own breakfast every morning and if I'm eating at home, I eat in the kitchen."

There was a very nice table by the window. Or he took his meal back to his office. He was by himself—it made no sense to go sit in the big dining room.

"You can cook?" She pressed a hand to her chest. "I'm genuinely impressed."

He smiled at her. "Gee, thanks."

They toured the rest of the downstairs. The family room and formal living room both had views of the Sound. Nissa stuck her head into his office, and gasped at the size of the laundry room. Upstairs, Hilde showed her the large, well-appointed media room. Nissa stared at the drawer full of remotes, then looked at the giant TV on the wall.

"I could never manage this," she said, shaking her head. "It's too much equipment."

"You can never have too much equipment," Desmond

told her. "It's easier than it looks. There's a notebook with instructions in with the remotes."

"Uh-huh. Good luck with that. I'll just livestream on my tablet."

Their last stop was her room. Hilde had prepared one of the suites, with a small living area attached to the bedroom. Both had a Sound view. His housekeeper had done a great job with everything. There were plenty of plush towels in the oversize bathroom and fresh flowers sat on the desk.

Nissa looked around. "This is really nice and much bigger than my condo." She hugged Hilde. "You did far too much work for me, and I want you to know how much I appreciate all of it." She turned to him. "You're being really nice. Thank you."

"Happy to help."

Hilde showed her the laundry chute tucked in the closet. "Just send your clothes down and I'll take care of them."

Nissa shook her head. "I'm going to do my own laundry. You don't have to do extra for me."

Hilde's expression turned stern. "I'll do your laundry."

Nissa raised her eyebrows. "If it's that important to you."

"It is."

She moved next to him. "She's determined."

"Best not to mess with her."

They all went downstairs and outside to Nissa's car. With the three of them working together, it didn't take long to get everything unloaded and delivered to her suite. On the last trip up the stairs, Desmond carried an armful of her hanging clothes. The action felt oddly intimate, as if he were seeing into something private. Silly, really, he told himself. So what if a few of her dresses were draped over his arm?

Once they'd dropped off everything, Hilde excused herself to go start dinner. Desmond hesitated.

"You have the Wi-Fi code," he said, pulling a house key out of his pocket. "Here's this."

She took it. "What about an alarm code or something?"

"It's only set at night. I'll get you the instructions to de-activate it. Or you can ask me."

"But what if you're out on a hot date?"

"I'll probably be home."

"Not seeing anyone these days?"

"No."

She sighed. "Me, either. I'm focused on growing my Italy fund." She waved her hand. "Which you are contrib-uting to by helping me out. Did I say thank you already?"

"Fifteen times."

She grinned. "You'd better get used to it, then. I plan to thank you a lot more."

"You're family, Nissa. And always welcome here."

He chose his words as much for himself as for her. That was what he had to remember. That while she was a beau-tiful, sexy, smart woman and there was just something about her that got to him, he was not to go down that path. She was someone he needed to look out for and protect, even from himself.

"Thank you." Her gaze met his. "So how does the whole dinner thing work? Is there a bell? Or does a butler show up and escort me?"

"Dinner's at seven. In your honor, we'll be eating in the dining room. After tonight, just let Hilde know if you're going to be home or not. She'll plan meals accordingly."

"You have a great life, Desmond. Next time, I'm going to remember to be rich."

He thought about telling her that his life wasn't what she thought and there were times when he felt isolated and alone. That she was the one with the warm, loving family and to him, that was priceless. But he knew saying the words would be to admit something he wasn't ready to face.

"I'll see you tonight," he told her instead.

## NISSA

Nissa got settled quickly. Putting away everything she'd brought with her turned out to be easy, what with the giant closet with built-in drawers, actual shoe shelves and more hanging space than any three closets in a normal house. The bathroom was equally spacious. There were two sinks, drawers between the sinks and a floor-to-ceiling cabinet for whatever items she might have left over. Oh, and the toilet not only had a remote control, it lifted the lid when she walked into the room, as if giving her a weird toilet greeting.

"I am so out of my element," she murmured as she plugged in her tablet to charge while she was at dinner. She wasn't totally sure she could find her way back to her room after she left, but she was determined to make the effort. Hilde had promised a special dinner. Given the luxuriousness of the house, Nissa had no idea what that meant, but she knew it was going to be good.

By six, she was starving, what with having missed lunch. She showered and changed into a dress because it seemed that she should. She debated curling her hair, but that felt like too much, so she settled on a little makeup, then used up the time until seven by flipping channels on the TV in her bedroom. Fortunately for her, there was only a single remote and no fancy equipment to worry about.

At six fifty-eight, she left her room and only took two wrong turns before finally making it to the stairs. Once on the main floor, she found her way to the family room where she saw Desmond standing by a built-in bar that had previously been hidden behind concealed doors in the wall.

In the second before he saw her, she used the opportunity to take in his tall, lean body and broad shoulders. Desmond had always been good-looking. Quiet in a confident kind of way, with a thoughtful expression that had made her feel he was really listening when she spoke. A heady occurrence for the younger sister used to being dismissed by her older brother.

Later, as a teenager, she'd thought of Desmond as her brother's cute friend. Interesting and nice, but not, you know, swoon-worthy. That hadn't happened until he'd taken her to prom. A topic she planned to discuss with him, as soon as she found a casual opening.

He saw her and smiled. "You made it."

"I did."

"All settled?"

"Yes, with closet space to spare." She held up a hand. "Before you ask, I have everything I need. Hilde was very thorough in her preparations. I'm telling you so you can put it in her employee evaluation."

"Good to know." He motioned to the bar. "May I fix you a cocktail?"

"Yes, you may."

She moved closer to the bar and looked at all the bottles on the shelves. "I don't know what most of those are."

"You probably don't want to try them at once. Do you have a favorite drink or may I make a suggestion?"

"Suggest away."

When she went out with her friends, she usually just had a glass of wine or a margarita. Nothing fancy. At her place, she had the obligatory bottle of red wine in her tiny pantry and a bottle of white in her refrigerator and that was it.

As she watched, Desmond pulled out a bottle of rum, along with cranberry juice, a small, unlabeled glass container and a bottle of champagne.

"What's in there?" she asked, pointing at the container.

"Vanilla simple syrup. Hilde made it earlier today." He expertly opened the bottle of champagne.

"So you planned the cocktail you're serving me?"

"I gave it some thought."

"That's so nice. Thank you." She smiled at him. "You're making me feel special. What if I never want to leave?"

"You're always welcome here, Nissa."

The man had a very nice voice, she thought, his words wrapping around her like a hug. She'd always enjoyed listening to him speak. There was a formality to how he put his sentences together—no doubt the result of a very expensive prep school education.

He mixed the first three ingredients in a shaker, then strained them into a glass and poured champagne on top. After handing her the glass, he waited while she took a sip.

"It's nice. Thank you." She liked the combination of flavors and the fizz from the champagne.

He poured himself a scotch, then they sat across from each other, each on a large, comfy sofa.

She tasted her drink again. "How did you happen to choose this particular drink?"

"I thought you'd like it."

"You have an entire cocktail menu selection handy in your brain?"

"Something like that. Just one of my many skills."

"Because your parents made sure you were prepared for any social situation?"

He nodded.

"So a formal dinner? Meeting the queen?"

He smiled. "Easy."

She raised her eyebrows. "You've met the queen? And we're talking the actual Queen of England, here. Not Bert, who does a drag show on the weekends?"

He chuckled. "Who's Bert?"

"Don't avoid the question."

He leaned back in his seat and rested one ankle on the opposite knee. "I have met the Queen of England. Twice."

"OMG! And you didn't think to mention me to Prince Harry before he met Meghan?"

"No, I didn't. Did you want me to?"

"Not now! He's married. But before would have been nice. I could have been a princess."

"Technically she's a duchess."

She waved her hand. "One and the same. You disappoint me."

"I apologize for not making your duchess fantasies come true." He studied her, a lazy smile tugging at his mouth. "I wouldn't have taken you for the princess type."

"Nearly every girl is, and let's face it. I'm pretty ordinary."

"I wouldn't say that."

"You're always so nice to me. Thank you. Even when I was an annoying teenager, you made me feel special."

Before she could say anything else, Hilde came into the family room with food on a tray. She set fried zucchini and a luscious-looking dip on the coffee table between them.

"Thank you," Nissa said, eyeing the appetizer. "That looks delicious."

"I hope you enjoy," Hilde said before returning to the kitchen.

Nissa set down her drink and reached for a napkin and a piece of zucchini. "Does she always stay this late?"

"No. Tonight is special. She wanted to be around for your first dinner. She's excited to have someone to fuss over."

Nissa appreciated the sentiment, but felt badly that Desmond's housekeeper was staying late on her account.

"Can you tell her to go home and that we'll serve ourselves?"

"I can try, but it won't work. I've already mentioned that to her. She's not listening."

"If I'm the highlight, you must be a really boring client."

"I think I am. She would be much happier with a family who had a couple of kids and a dog."

"But she doesn't leave you?"

"No. She's loyal."

She took a bite of the zucchini and had to hold in a moan. It was crisp and tender at the same time. The breading flavors were perfectly savory, but when combined with the slightly spicy dip, they were even better.

"This is amazing," she said, reaching for a second slice. "Can we have this every day?"

"If you'd like."

"You're very accommodating. So I'm going to thank you again for letting me stay."

"Will you stop after that?"

"Is it important?"

"Yes. I'm happy to contribute to your Italy fund in this small way."

She laughed. "All right. Thank you and now I'm done. At least for today."

"Good. Have you planned out your trip?"

"A little. I'm hoping to take three weeks. One in Rome, one in Florence and one in Tuscany." She picked up her drink. "And yes, I know Florence is the capital of Tuscany, but it seems as if it's the kind of place that deserves its own week."

"I agree. You should take the trip you want. You've been dreaming about it since you were fourteen."

She had been. A school report on Italy had sparked her interest. Her mother liked to tease her that for an entire year, she'd talked about nothing else.

"How could you possibly remember that?" she asked.

"You found out I'd been there and asked me questions. A lot of questions."

"Was I obnoxious?"

"No. Even then you were charming." He studied her. "You know I could—"

"No," she said firmly. "Just no."

"You don't know what I was going to say."

"I do. You were going to offer to pay for my vacation and while that's very sweet, the answer is no. I want to earn this myself, because that way it's meaningful."

"All right. Too bad you lost the income from Mimi's house-sitting job."

"I know. I'm sad about the money, but happy for her about the baby." At least she tried to be, because it was the right thing to do. But the cash would have been nice, too. "I'll find another job. There's a temp agency I've worked for before. They have very eclectic clients, so that should be interesting."

"You're comfortable having people renting your condo?"

"I wouldn't say comfortable, but they're paying me a lot. I put away everything that's personal, so I'm not freaked about that."

She thought about Shane helping her, which caused her to think about what her brother had said about Desmond and being warned away. Only half a cocktail hadn't given her enough courage to bring up that particular topic.

"What blood type are you?" she asked, reminding herself it was always good to know.

He looked startled by the question. "Ah, A positive."

"Oh, that's not super common. I'm O negative, but I have weird antibodies or something. I can't remember. I'm not a good donor candidate but my blood is very sought after."

"Do I want to know why you know that?"

She grinned. "You forget, I'm a teacher. At my grade level, I teach everything, including science."

Not the reason she'd asked about his blood type, but he would probably accept the explanation. Regardless, she was saved from having to deal with the problem when Hilde appeared and said dinner was ready.

Nissa led the way into the formal dining room where two place settings had been arranged at one end of the table. Desmond poured wine while she admired the beautiful china plates and the fresh flowers. Once they were seated, Hilde brought out tomato gazpacho soup and a basket full of crusty, warm rolls.

"Bread," Nissa breathed, eyeing the temptation. "I love bread." She smiled at the housekeeper. "This all looks wonderful. Thank you so much."

"You're welcome."

Hilde shot Desmond a look that Nissa couldn't interpret. She waited until they were alone to ask, "What was that glance about?"

"I'm sure she was trying to tell me to eat dinner at home more often."

"You don't?"

"Many nights I grab something to-go."

"When you could eat like this?" She took a roll and placed it on her side plate, then tasted the soup. It was the perfect blend of fresh and seasoned with a touch of creaminess.

"I get busy. It's easier than having a set time to be home."

"If you didn't have an empire, you could enjoy your life more."

He smiled at her. "If I didn't have my empire, I couldn't afford Hilde."

"Oh, right. I guess everything's a trade-off. I love my work, but no one gets rich being a teacher."

"Did you want to be rich?"

She laughed and waved her hand at the dining room.

"There are obvious perks. But if you're asking if I wish I'd chosen a different profession, no. I love what I do. The kids are great and I really enjoy my days. Do I wish the school district budgeted more money? Of course. But otherwise, I'm a happy camper."

"You're an upbeat person."

"I am. Some of it is my personality and some of it is the joy of annoying others."

He grinned. "Attitude. I like it."

"It's easy to be brave when there's nothing on the line," she told him, only to remember there was a topic she needed to discuss and that waiting for the false courage of alcohol was a flawed plan. If she wanted the information, she was simply going to have to ask the question.

She cleared her throat. "So Shane helped me pack up my grandmother's china."

"You mentioned that."

"Right. While we were doing that, he teased me about living with you and during that discussion he mentioned that back when I was in high school and you took me to prom, that he warned you about me. I mean he warned you to not plan on going out with me. Later. After prom. Obviously we went to prom. Together."

She pressed her lips together, wondering how much of a mess she'd made of that.

Desmond studied her for a second before saying, "He's right."

Was he being difficult on purpose? "About what part?"

"All of it. I enjoyed our evening together and when I mentioned that to him, he reminded me you were a lot younger and less experienced than I was."

"So you should leave me alone?"

"Exactly."

"Which you did."

His dark gaze met hers. "Yes."

"I'm perfectly capable of making my own decisions about who I date," she reminded him.

"Now. Back then you were barely eighteen and I was in grad school. We were in different places."

True, but still. "You had a good time with me, didn't you?" she asked.

One corner of his mouth turned up. "I did. Very much."

"Me, too." She thought about how attentive he'd been, and the slow dancing. And the kissing. The kissing had been spectacular. "You were a great date."

"You, too."

They stared at each other, then his gaze lowered to her mouth. She wondered what he was thinking and if he had any regrets about listening to her brother. If they'd started dating back then they would be... She wasn't sure exactly what, but something. Maybe they would have stayed together all this time.

Desmond looked away. "They say we're in for a warm summer," he said.

Was it just her or was the man the tiniest bit flustered? "Do they?" she asked, hoping she was right and not indulging in a little too much wishful thinking.

# Chapter 3

*NISSA*

After a dinner of pan-grilled chicken with fresh plum salsa and green beans, followed by coconut layer cake for dessert, Nissa and Desmond lingered over decaf coffee. She'd always found him easy to talk to, and tonight was no exception.

"When will you find out about your first temp job?" he asked.

"They'll text me tomorrow, telling me where to be and when. If there's a uniform, I'll swing by the offices and pick it up."

One eyebrow rose. "Uniform? Like at a fast-food place?"

"I don't work in food service. I've tried, but I'm not good at it. A lot of businesses have a shirt they want employees to wear. Even temporary ones. Oh, a few years ago I sold hot dogs down by the aquarium, so that's food. I did okay.

There weren't a lot of choices, so that helped." She smiled. "To be honest, I have no idea how servers keep the orders straight. Or carry so many plates at once. Or those big trays. If it were me, everything would go tumbling."

"Then we'll clear the table one plate at a time."

"Probably a good idea."

Hilde had left after she served the main course, telling Desmond she would take care of cleanup in the morning. But Nissa and he had already put everything in the dishwasher and wiped down the counters. All that was left were their dessert plates, forks and the coffee mugs.

He glanced at his watch. "It's getting late. I should let you turn in."

They finished up the last of the dishes, then started up the stairs. She had to admit, it felt strange to be in Desmond's house, going to their bedrooms. She'd only been here a few times for parties and those had all ended with her going home.

"Thanks for dinner," she said when they reached the landing. "It was amazing."

"That's all Hilde," he told her.

"I'll thank her in the morning."

They stared at each other. He had a nice face—all strong lines and chiseled features. She thought about moving closer and, um, what? Kissing him? That could be awkward. If he kissed her back, then what? They went to his room and had sex? She didn't do casual relationships and it wasn't as if Desmond had been secretly pining for her.

When she thought about it, she realized it had been over a decade since their prom date. She'd graduated from college and everything. If he'd been so interested, he could have easily asked her out a thousand different times. Before he met Rosemary, after the divorce. She'd been right here—there'd been plenty of opportunity. But he hadn't. Not even once, which was a pretty clear indication that the man wasn't interested at all. So making a move would be stupid. He would be way too nice in his refusal and she would feel like an idiot. Worse, he might ask her to leave and it wasn't as if she had a bunch of places where she could go.

And just like that, whatever vague fantasy she'd been harboring disappeared with a nearly audible poof.

"All right then," she said with a forced smile. "Good night."

She turned and walked determinedly toward her bedroom. Lucky for her, she'd picked the right direction and managed to find her way to the familiar space. She closed her door behind her, then leaned against it.

*No more Desmond-is-handsome-and-sexy thoughts*, she told herself. No more anything, where he was concerned. She was going to live here for two months and she needed to remember that and act like a polite but disinterested roommate. Anything else was a slick, steep road to disaster and no one wanted that.

.*NISSA*

Saturday morning Nissa drove to North Seattle. She stopped for donuts on the way and arrived at her friend's house a little after ten.

The neighborhood had seen a revitalization over the past few years. Rather than tear down and start over rebuilding, most residents were sprucing up their older homes with new windows and roofs, and the occasional second story over the garage. Nissa found parking right in front of the house and looked at the unmown lawn. Before leaving today, she would make a point to run the push mower over the grass.

She hesitated before getting out of her car. She loved her friend, but sometimes the visits were emotionally challenging. A few years before, Marisol had been diagnosed with kidney failure. Everyone had been shocked, Marisol and her daughters most of all.

Nissa had known the family since Marisol had been assigned to be her mentor when she'd first started teaching. They'd become close quickly. Nissa had been there when Marisol's husband and the girls' father had been killed in a car accident. Marisol had helped Nissa when she'd decided to end her engagement. They were best friends who depended on each other.

Nissa got out of her car and walked onto the front porch. She knocked once, then waited. Seconds later the door was flung open as Rylan and Lisandra, ten-year-old twins, greeted her enthusiastically.

"Nissa! You're here."

"Are those donuts? Did you get the maple ones?"

"And chocolate. They're my favorite."

"Yes, yes and yes," Nissa said with a laugh, hugging both girls with her free hand. She stepped inside and saw Marisol on the sofa.

Despite the fact that it was already in the low seventies, her friend had a blanket draped across her lap. Her face was pale, and there were dark shadows under her eyes. The toll of her kidney disease was becoming more and more visible.

"Hey, you," Nissa said, handing the donuts to the girls and crossing to the sofa. She hugged her friend. "How are you feeling?"

"Today's a good day," Marisol said. "Thanks for coming by."

"I haven't seen you in a couple of weeks. I want to catch up." She looked at the empty mug on the coffee table. "Let me get you some more tea. I'll make myself a cup, as well. Two donuts each for the girls?"

Marisol nodded, then leaned back against the sofa and closed her eyes.

Nissa went into the small kitchen. The house was clean and bright, but on the small side. It could do with a spruce-up of its own, but she knew that wasn't in the budget. So far the insurance was covering all of Marisol's medical bills, but she'd had to stop working at the end of the semester and unless there was a kidney transplant, she wouldn't be returning to work in the fall.

Nissa helped the girls choose their donuts, then put a couple more on a plate and carried them and Marisol's tea back to the living room. She got her own drink and joined her friend on the sofa. The girls finished their donuts and retreated to their room.

"How are you really feeling?" Nissa asked when she had taken a seat.

Marisol shook her head. "It's not bad today. I'm tired, but that's to be expected." Exhaustion was just one of many symptoms she endured.

Marisol reached out and squeezed Nissa's hand. "I don't want to talk about being sick. What's happening with you?"

Nissa smiled at her. "I will accept the change in topic, but only because it's what you want. I'd rather talk about you."

"I'm boring. Tell me about living with Desmond. You've had a thing for him for years. How is that working out? Are you plagued by illicit thoughts?"

Nissa laughed. "Illicit thoughts? Have you been reading Jane Austen again? His house is wonderful and he's the perfect host. I'm doing fine."

Marisol leaned close. "And the illicit thoughts?"

"Fine. One or two. I can't help it. He's very appealing."

"Maybe you living with him is a sign."

"Or God having a sense of humor," Nissa pointed out. "I

was just thinking about this last night and if the man had wanted to date me, he would have done something about it before now. So he doesn't and I'm fine with that."

"If you're sure."

"I am. We're friends. That's all."

Marisol sighed. "But I need to live vicariously through you. It's hard when you're not dating. Do you know what your first temp job is going to be? Maybe you'll meet someone there."

"I'm going to be at a doggie day care for a couple of weeks. I'm not sure about that being a hotbed of dating activity."

Marisol wrinkled her nose. "I'm afraid you're right. Oh, unless one of the dogs has a cute dad. You could date him. It wouldn't be like at school where dating a parent is against policy."

The girls came into the room. Lisandra had a board game in her hand.

"We decided on Monopoly," Rylan announced.

Nissa smiled. "One of my favorites. I'm in. We'll do that, then I'll take you two to Kidd Valley for lunch."

Marisol was on a special diet that was designed to not stress her body. Nissa would fix that before she took the girls out. After lunch they would go to the park to run off some energy while Marisol rested.

As they set out the game and Marisol counted out the money, Nissa asked, "How's day camp?"

"Good," Lisandra told her. "The other kids are nice. We've been doing a lot of craft projects. In a couple of weeks, we're going to learn how to make movies."

"That sounds like fun."

"It is."

They were good girls, Nissa thought, and they'd already been through so much. First losing their dad, then having their mom get sick. She knew they were scared for her. Without a kidney transplant, she wasn't going to survive a year. When she was gone, Nissa would step in. She'd already agreed to be the girls' guardian.

But that wasn't going to happen, Nissa told herself. Marisol would get her kidney and everything would be fine. It had to be. And if it wasn't, she would be there for the twins, partly because she'd given her word, but mostly because she loved them.

## DESMOND

Four days after Nissa moved into the house, Desmond found her presence everywhere. Several pairs of athletic shoes and sandals clustered by the door to the garage. A sweater, a hoodie and a light jacket hung on the coat rack. Magazines and books were scattered throughout the family room. Instead of turning on the television in the kitchen and finding it was tuned to his favorite financial channel, he instead saw *House Hunters International* on HGTV.

She had invaded and while she lived with him, nothing would be the same. A truth that he found strangely appealing. His life was too predictable and boring. While he liked the quiet, he also enjoyed knowing there was someone else under the same roof. And if that someone was as lively and appealing as Nissa, then he was a lucky man.

He walked into the kitchen and found her sitting at the kitchen table, a bowl of cereal in front of her. She had on jeans and a T-shirt from the doggie day care center where she was working. She'd pulled her long hair back into a braid and she wasn't wearing any makeup.

For a second, he remembered her at seventeen—fresh-faced and beautiful enough to make him ache. He'd enjoyed how she always had something funny to say and that her first instinct was to be kind and thoughtful. Even now, when she saw him, she picked up the remote and hit several buttons.

But instead of landing on the financial channel, the TV changed to a cooking show.

"That's not right," she murmured, before looking at him. "I can't remember the number."

"Or where you put your keys."

She winced. "You heard that yesterday morning?"

"They heard you in New York."

She laughed and handed him the remote. "I was panicked. I didn't want to be late on my first day. I can keep track of my phone and my purse and everything else in my life. Just not my keys. It's a curse." She flashed him a smile. "Good morning."

"Morning. How did you sleep?"

"Great. The bed is super comfortable and it's much quieter here than at my place. It's all the land you have. No noisy neighbors getting in at three in the morning."

He walked to one of the cupboards and pulled out a bowl. "There's a shelf in the mudroom. I'm going to put this right there. When you walk in the house, put your keys in the bowl. That way you'll know where they are."

"Isn't it early to be that sensible?"

"It's a solution. Unless you enjoy the drama of nearly being late every morning."

She took the bowl from him and set it next to her place setting. "I really don't. I've always thought it's because I have three bubbles and the keys push me into four."

He poured himself coffee. "Three bubbles?"

"You know, above my head. Like thought bubbles. I can keep track of three things or follow three instructions. But the fourth one pushes out the first one. There's only three spaces. So the work I brought home, my purse, my phone, my keys." She shrugged. "One bubble too many."

"Use the dish. Then the keys don't need a bubble."

"That is really smart. Thank you."

He glanced at her breakfast. "What are you eating? The liquid is gray."

She wrinkled her nose. "It's a protein-enriched cereal with almond milk. Want some?"

"Based on the look on your face when you describe it? No, thank you."

"I'm trying to eat healthy."

"There are better ways to do that."

She put down her spoon. "What are you having?"

"Greek yogurt with fresh berries and granola. Toast with almond butter."

She immediately pushed away her bowl. "Is there enough for two?"

He grinned. "There is. Drink your coffee. I'll make you breakfast."

"I can help."

"Not necessary."

He got out the ingredients and put four slices of bread into the toaster.

"What do you do about lunch?" he asked.

"Hilde made me something to take. I feel guilty, but I'm not going to say no. The woman's an amazing cook."

"She is." He scooped the plain Greek yogurt into two bowls. "How's the job going?"

"I like it. The dogs are great. They each have a different personality. The weather's been nice, so they're outside a lot."

He rinsed fresh blueberries and raspberries. "What about cleanup?"

She laughed. "Okay, yes, that's a part of it, but you forget. I work with kids—I'm used to smelly messes. It's not that big a deal. We run around and play ball. I was with the big dogs yesterday and they get along great. When there's a new dog, the day care has a whole process of getting acquainted. There's a group of dogs that are more shy, so the new ones start there and get to know everyone before moving into their size group."

She sighed happily. "In the afternoon, after a rousing play session, we all relaxed in the shade and took a nap for a couple of hours."

"Even you?"

"I didn't sleep, but I did get to cuddle. It's fun. Makes me think about getting a dog." She shook her head. "Don't say it. I know I can't. I work all day. The poor thing would be trapped in my condo and that's no life. But it's fun to play with everyone else's. I wish I could bring Rylan and Lisandra with me. They would love it."

He set her yogurt in front of her and returned to finish the toast. "Who are they?"

"Oh, my friend Marisol's kids. Ten-year-old twins. They're turning eleven in a few weeks and going into middle school in the fall. I can't believe how fast they're growing. Marisol was my mentor when I first started teaching. We became friends and now we hang out all the time. That's where I went on Saturday."

He'd wondered where she'd gone, but had known he had no right to ask. Funny how quickly he was getting used to having her around.

"They're so strong," she added, dipping her spoon into the yogurt. "Marisol lost her husband a few years ago. She was devastated, as were the girls. It was a hard time."

"How are they doing now?"

Nissa hesitated. "They're dealing. It's always something, isn't it?"

There was something she wasn't telling him, he realized, setting the toast in front of her and taking a seat at the table. Not that he would ask. Her friends were her business.

"They're in summer camp, which they really enjoy. But I was thinking I'd like to plan a couple of activities with them this summer. Something more fun than just lunch and going to the movies."

He could see her freckles and the various colors of blue that made up her eyes. Her mouth was full and soft and there wasn't any part of him that didn't want to kiss her. No, not just kiss. In a perfect world, he would slide her onto his lap. She would wrap her arms around him, maybe straddle him while they kissed. He could already feel the weight of her body and the feel of her mouth as she—

He slammed the door on that line of thought. No and no. But heat had already begun to burn, starting a chain reaction that would end with him hard and unable to stand without revealing his serious lack of control. He needed a distraction.

"Let's take them out on my boat," he said.

Nissa took a bite of her toast. "You have a boat?"

"Yes. On Lake Washington. We can spend the day going around here, or head out through the locks and explore the Sound."

"When did you get a boat? I love boats. Why haven't you invited me out on it? I thought we were friends!"

He held in a smile. "My apologies. I thought you knew. You are welcome out on my boat anytime you would like. Bring your friends. We'll make a day of it."

"Is it a nice boat?"

He raised one eyebrow. "Have you met me?"

She laughed. "Right. Let me rephrase that. How nice is it?"

"It's about fifty feet long with three guest cabins, a

good-sized salon. The area up by the flying bridge is covered, so you don't have to worry about too much sun."

"Fifty feet? I have no idea how big that is, but I'm going to assume I couldn't drive it."

"No. There's a captain."

"Other than you?"

"It's big enough that it requires a skill set I don't have time to develop."

"What about getting a smaller boat you could drive yourself?"

"I've thought about it."

But the larger boat was better for parties. Something smaller would mean just him and a couple of friends and somehow that never seemed to happen. He'd thought when he and Rosemary moved up here, they would have a boat for the two of them, but then they'd split up and he'd relocated by himself.

He paused, telling himself he wasn't as pathetic as that all sounded. He couldn't be.

"So you'd have two boats?" she asked.

He smiled. "There's a dock right here on the property. I could keep the smaller boat close."

"Because the big one is too, um, big to be here?"

"Exactly."

She looked at him. "I keep forgetting about the rich thing. I mean I know it in my head, but I don't think about it when we're talking and hanging out."

"That's a good thing."

"Because you know I'm not in it for the money? Is that a real problem?"

"What do you think?"

"I guess it must be, but even without the money, you're still dreamy." She nibbled on her toast. "If you're serious about the boat, I'd love to ask Marisol if she and the girls would want to come out. But you have to be sure."

He would rather talk about her thinking he was dreamy. What did that mean and did being dreamy mean he could nudge her toward his bedroom?

"I'm sure."

"Thank you. That's very nice. And while you're in a giving mood, may I please have a bit of the garden to play with?"

"I have no idea what you're asking." His garden? For what?

"I miss gardening. My mom and I used to garden all summer long, but she and Dad have moved and I live in a condo, so I never get to dig around in the dirt anymore. I thought while I'm here I could plant some flowers, do a little weeding. You know, play."

"You're welcome to dig away," he told her, not sure why she felt the need to ask.

She didn't look convinced. "One of us should probably talk to your gardener. The landscaping is very beautiful, but formal, and I'm not sure anyone will be happy with me claiming space for random flowers and a tomato plant."

"I'll speak to Hilde," he told her. "She oversees the gardeners."

"Thank you. I love Hilde. She's so good at her job."

"She is. I'd like more Hildes in my life, especially at the office. The person who usually coordinates the company summer party is out on maternity leave and her second-in-command is having trouble handling everything." More than once, he'd thought about bringing Hilde in to manage the project.

"Do you need help?" Nissa asked. "I'm available. I don't know anything about a big corporate party, but I could run errands or help with setup."

Which was exactly like Nissa, he thought. "Thank you. I'll let you know if things spiral out of control."

"If that happens, ask Hilde and I'll be her assistant."

She smiled as she spoke, looking impossibly beautiful, sitting there at his kitchen table. James had been a fool to let her go, he thought.

"Would you like to go to the party?" he asked, surprising himself and, based on her wide eyes, her, as well.

"Sure, if it's okay." She smiled. "I guess if you're the boss, you get to say."

"You might want to recall your acceptance when I tell you my parents will be there."

She brushed away the warning. "I've only met them a couple of times, but they seem perfectly nice. Besides, I've never been to a real office party before. Are there rules? A dress code? Can I wear a hat?"

"Did you want to wear a hat?"

"I don't know. Is it a thing? Like the Kentucky Derby, where all the women wear hats?"

"Your mind is a confusing place. You may wear a hat if you'd like. I'll text you the particulars. In the meantime, I'll let Hilde know about the garden and speak with the captain about some dates to take out the boat." He smiled. "I'm leaving breakfast with a to-do list."

She fluttered her eyelashes. "Then my work here is done."

# Chapter 4

*NISSA*

Nissa drove out onto the street. Despite the heat, she had the windows rolled down, mostly because even she could smell the dog on herself. She loved her doggie day care job, but wow, did she get stinky. She desperately wanted a shower and a change of clothes, but she had a more pressing problem to deal with.

Thirty minutes later, she parked in front of the large building that housed Desmond's company. Right now she needed someone to talk some sense into her and he was the most sensible person she could think of.

She walked inside and was immediately aware of the fact that she was dressed completely wrong. While everyone else had on business attire, she was wearing jeans and a purple T-shirt with a dog logo on the front. Her athletic shoes were grass-stained, her face had smudges, plus the whole smell thing. But she'd come too far to turn back now.

She walked up to the security desk and gave her name. "I'd like to see Desmond Stilling please."

The uniformed man looked doubtful. "Do you have an appointment?"

"No."

She thought briefly about explaining how she and Desmond had been friends forever and that she was currently living with him, but decided against it. The "living together" comment might be misunderstood.

"Maybe you could get in touch with his assistant and give her my name," Nissa suggested.

The security guard did as she requested. Seconds later, his eyes wide with surprise, he allowed her through the security gate and led her to an elevator that whisked her to the top floor.

When the doors opened, an attractive forty-something woman in an elegant suit greeted her.

"Mr. Stilling is in his office. If you'll follow me, Ms. Lang."

"I can do that."

The floors were hardwood, the walls a neutral color. There were a lot of plants, big windows and a general air of business. Everyone was hurrying or talking or busy on a computer. A few glanced up at her, then turned away before making eye contact. She wasn't sure if that was good or bad.

She and her escort walked through a series of open doors before finally passing an anteroom and a final set of double doors. Nissa stepped inside and saw Desmond behind a large desk. All that was really impressive, but what totally got her attention were the floor-to-ceiling windows.

Desmond had an incredible west-facing view of the water and Blackberry Island and the Sound beyond.

He came to his feet. "Nissa. I wasn't expecting you. Everything all right?"

She pointed to the windows. "Did you know you had this? How do you work? It's so beautiful. In the winter, you'll be able to watch the storms blowing in. Wow. Just wow."

Desmond nodded at the woman waiting next to Nissa.

"Thanks, Kathy. I'll take it from here."

Kathy left, closing the door behind her. Nissa shook her head. "This is great. I love it. I'm not really an office kind of person, but if I could work here, it wouldn't be so bad."

"Sadly, most of my employees don't get this kind of view. But the break room is on the floor below mine and it faces the same direction."

"It was very nice of you to give everyone that space." She rubbed her hands up and down her jeans, then exhaled. "I want a dog."

She took a step toward him. "It's been four days and they're so fun and sweet and affectionate. Dogs are the best. They love with their whole heart and they're so happy to see you and I want one. Or all of them. I need you to talk me down. I keep telling myself what we talked about before. I'm gone too much and my condo is small and this isn't a good time, but it's hard. Just one fluffy dog. Is that too much to ask for?"

He smiled at her. "You don't need me here for this conversation, do you?"

"Yes, I do. That's why I came here. So you could be sensible. It's just I think about going hiking with a dog, or camping, and it would be fun."

"You could take it out on my boat."

Her eyes widened. "Could I? Oh, we could buy one of those doggie life jackets." She shook her head. "No. Stop it. You're not helping."

He sat on the corner of his desk. "You're not getting a dog. Once you move on to another temp job, the need won't be so intense."

"You're killing my dream."

"Your dreams are too big to kill and you know I'm right. You will probably get a dog eventually, but this isn't a good time."

"I know. But I want one."

"Deep breaths. It's just a couple more weeks."

"I feel pouty."

"What can I do to help? Would you like a hug?"

She would. A nice, squeezy, Desmond hug with her body pressing against his. Of course he was offering comfort and she was hoping to get a little hug action, which wasn't fair of her. Plus, you know, the smell.

She took a step back. "Don't get close to me. I have doggie stink on me. I need to go home and shower. Thank you for reminding me to be sensible. It's just they're so sweet. We never had pets when I was growing up. I should ask my mom about that. Did you?"

"Have pets? No. My parents wouldn't have allowed them in the house. Too much mess. They barely tolerated me."

She smiled as if she got the joke, but she knew in some ways, he wasn't kidding.

"Want me to scold them when I see them at the office party?" she asked. "I will. I have a great scolding voice. It comes from years of being stern when the situation requires it at work."

One corner of his mouth turned up. "While I would pay money to see that, I would never ask you to do that. Besides, that was a long time ago. These days they're far more interested in getting me married."

"Why?"

"They want an heir."

"Because of the empire, right? That makes sense. My parents want me to get married and have grandchildren for them. So it's kind of the same thing."

They looked at each other. She knew he was thinking it wasn't the same thing at all, but he was too nice to say that.

An unexpected and unpleasant thought occurred to her.

"Is me living with you getting in the way of a relationship?"

"I'm between women right now."

Whew. "Is there a waiting list? Or an application process?" she asked, her voice teasing.

"There's a form they fill out online."

She laughed, knowing she liked him a lot. She always had.

"I'm going to go while I'm feeling strong about not getting a dog," she said. "Thank you for your help."

"Anytime. I'm always here for you, Nissa."

She nodded and let herself out of his office. On her way back to her car, she told herself while the words were nice, he only meant them as a friend and not anything remotely more than that.

## DESMOND

Unless he had plans to do something with Shane, Desmond usually worked on the weekends. He did so in his home office, but still, there was work. Without interruptions from phone calls and meetings, he could get through a pile of paperwork, review reports and generally get caught up. Not the healthiest decision for himself personally, he acknowledged, but excellent for the company.

But on this particular Saturday, he had trouble concentrating. The cause was obvious—Nissa. Despite the fact that he could neither see nor hear her, he knew she was around. Out in the yard, to be exact, doing whatever it was she planned to do in what she referred to as her "temporary plot of earth."

As he'd suggested, Hilde had talked to the gardeners, who had given Nissa a section of the garden to do whatever it was she wanted to do. Her interest in planting flowers wasn't anything he could relate to, but it was obviously important to her, which meant it was something he would make sure got done.

As long as she was happy, he told himself. While she was living here, she was his responsibility.

He turned his attention back to the spreadsheet on his computer. Three minutes later, he swore softly, saved his work, then closed the program. He wasn't making any progress on the work he'd brought home. Better to admit defeat and let it go than to keep staring unseeingly at the screen.

He got up and walked through the house to the back door and stepped outside. Typical to the Pacific Northwest, the warm weather had given way to several days of cool temperatures and lots of rain. Today it would barely reach seventy degrees, as they transitioned back to something more summerlike.

The backyard was about an acre of manicured lawn and tidy plant beds. There was a huge pool off the rear deck and beyond that, a stone path led the way down to the dock and Lake Washington. Tall, thick hedges provided privacy on either side of his property.

He glanced around but didn't see Nissa anywhere. He

started to circle around the house and found her on the south side, on her knees, using a spade to dig out roots.

She had on jeans and a T-shirt. Her long hair was pulled back in a braid and a big hat covered her head and shaded her face. Gardening gloves protected her hands. Nothing about her was the least bit provocative, but he still found himself moving more quickly as he approached—as if he couldn't get there fast enough.

Just the sight of her made him feel better about the day. He waited for her to look up and smile when she saw him— as she always did—looking forward to the sense of anticipation her smiles always produced.

Before she saw him, she rose gracefully to her feet, then reached for a shovel. He hurried over and took it from her.

She looked up at him and grinned. "Checking up on me? I'm in demolition mode, so don't judge. Later, when the new plants are in, you'll see a riot of color."

"Why didn't you ask for my help?"

She frowned. "For what?"

He waved the shovel. "The heavy work."

"Desmond, I can dig out a few plants. I'm stronger than I look."

"I have no doubt about that, but I'm stronger than you. Tell me what you want dug out."

She shook her head slowly. "I don't know. Are you capable of manual labor?"

"Very funny. Which ones?"

She pointed to a couple of bushes and a few flowers. "Those, please. I don't want to dig out too much. Come September, everything I plant will be taken out and the garden returned to its former glory. I kind of feel bad for your gardening team. There were actual tears when I told them what I wanted to do."

"I doubt any of them cried."

"It was pretty close to that. They weren't amused by my request to have some yard."

He stepped on the shovel, pushing it under the first bush. With the recent rains, the soil was damp and he dug in easily.

"Do you want me to talk to them?" he asked, lifting the bush out of the ground.

"What? No. I was sharing, not hinting. Come on, Desmond. Look at your yard. It's beautifully designed and maintained. These guys take pride in their efforts and here I am, messing with it. I'm being incredibly self-indulgent. But I can't help it. Digging in the dirt makes me happy." She paused, then laughed. "Actually watching you dig in the dirt isn't bad, either."

"Glad to help."

He made quick work of the plants she wanted removed. Once he was done, they tossed them into the composting bin.

"What's the next step?" he asked, helping her sweep up the path.

"I go buy plants. I talked to my mom earlier this morning and she gave me some good ideas. Because it's already July, I'm not going to be able to grow anything like vegetables, so I'm sticking with pretty flowers that make me happy."

"How is your mom?"

"She's good. She and Dad are going to come over to this side of the mountains in a few weeks to hang out with me and Shane."

"They're welcome to stay here," he said, thinking it would be nice to spend time with Shane and Nissa's parents. They had always been kind to him, drawing him into the family and including him in their traditions. Around her family, he'd always felt…normal.

"They were going to stay with Shane, but I'll make the offer," she said. "I'm sure he'll be excited." She gave him an impish smile. "Apparently he's still dating his new lady friend. We're talking about four weeks' worth of relationship. You know how rare that is for him. Having my parents bunking in his place will cramp his style."

Desmond chuckled. "I'm happy to help the cause."

She looked at him. "Do you think he's going to get serious about her?"

Desmond hesitated before saying, "Shane hasn't said much to me about her," which was the truth. What he didn't say was that Shane had his reasons for not wanting to commit to anyone. Reasons Nissa didn't know about and that Desmond wasn't going to mention. Shane was his best friend and Desmond would never betray a confidence.

"When are you going to buy plants?" he asked, hoping she didn't notice his attempt to change the subject.

"Right now. Fred Meyer is having a sale," she said, naming a popular local superstore chain.

"Or you could tell the gardener what you want and he could get them from the nursery he uses."

She sighed. "Wow, you really have led a sheltered life. I don't know exactly what I want. I'll wait to see what looks good and appeals to me. Plus, buying the plants is part of the fun. It's satisfying to bring them home and then plant them myself."

"If you say so."

She pulled off her gloves. "You sound doubtful and that makes me feel challenged. All right, you're coming with me to the store. You obviously need to experience the thrill of plant buying." She paused. "Unless you have plans or something."

"No plans." And if he'd had any, he would have canceled them. He would much rather spend the rest of the morning with Nissa.

"Great." She glanced at the tools scattered around. "Let's leave these here. We'll need them for planting later."

Five minutes later they were in her car, heading to Fred Meyer. There had been a brief discussion about which car to take, but she'd insisted on hers, claiming putting plants in the back of his expensive Mercedes would make him weep and she didn't want to be responsible for that. Which was how he found himself in the passenger seat of her Honda CRV.

She chatted as she drove, mentioning the change in the weather and how she was still trying to be strong about not getting a dog. He tried to pay attention to her words but kept getting caught up in his awareness of her. They were sitting close in her car. It would be easy to slide his arm across the console and settle his hand on her thigh.

Or not, he told himself firmly. Nissa was a friend. She was too important for him to mess with that way. Besides, he owed her family. The last thing they would want was her hooking up with some heartless guy.

They pulled into the crowded parking lot. Desmond was surprised at the number of people at the large store. Nissa had to circle a couple of times to find a spot near the nursery.

"Why so many people?" he asked as they got out.

She looked at him over the vehicle. "It's Saturday. People do their shopping on Saturday. Fred Meyer sells food and clothes and home goods, as well as plants. It's a popular and convenient one-stop shopping spot."

He glanced around. "I didn't know that."

"Have you ever been?"

"I don't shop much."

"Or ever. Do you at least buy your own clothes?"

"My suits are custom-made, and my tailor has my measurements." At her look of incredulity, he quickly added, "I have a shopper at Nordstrom who takes care of the rest."

She stared at him. "I forget who you are. To me you're just Desmond whom I've known forever." Something flashed in her eyes that he couldn't name, but then it was gone. "You're a friend and a part of my life. But there's so much more to you, isn't there?"

He walked around the car until he was standing in front of her. "No. I'm exactly who you think I am."

"With a billion-dollar fortune and a multinational company."

"It's not a billion dollars."

She smiled. "But you're closer to a billion than to a million, right?"

"Maybe." He brushed a bit of dirt off her cheek. "It doesn't change anything."

"Except if you weren't rich, you'd be shopping at Fred Meyer, like the rest of us."

"I'm shopping here today."

She leaned in for a hug. Desmond pulled her close, wrapping his arms around her. She felt good, leaning against him. Warm and feminine. He wanted to do more than hug. He wanted to have her look up at him so he could kiss her. A long, lingering kiss, totally inappropriate for a store parking lot. But she didn't and he knew better than to go anywhere near that sort of thing.

"All right you," she said stepping back. "Let's go buy plants."

She went in through the nursery entrance, pointing at a flatbed cart. "You get to push that, but be careful. No bumping into people. It's not nice."

"Yes, ma'am."

Once they were in the fenced area, she started walking along the aisles of plants, choosing pots of flowers as she went. While he didn't know any of the names, he recognized a lot of them from her mother's garden.

He put the plants on the cart and was mindful of the other customers. But when he saw a small display on the other side of the nursery, he excused himself and went over to study the beautiful plants.

Long, elegant stems supported creamy flowers with purple centers. Nissa joined him.

"Do you like orchids?" she asked.

"Yes. Because of your mom."

"My mom didn't grow them. She loved getting them, but they seemed to be the one plant she couldn't keep alive."

He looked at her. "Your dad brought one home for her the first time I came to visit. Shane and I had just arrived when he walked in with the orchid. Your mom was surprised, but happy, even as she told him it was too expensive and he shouldn't have."

Nissa stared at him. "How do you remember that?"

"I remember everything about my visits to your old house."

He could walk it blindfolded. He knew which stairs creaked and how to jiggle the handle when the toilet got fussy. On Christmas, stockings were opened first thing, followed by breakfast, then the real presents.

"I'd never been in a house like that," he added.

"Small?" she asked with a laugh.

He shook his head. "Normal. You all loved each other. I

could see that. Your parents made me feel welcome, maybe for the first time ever. Your mom made me a stocking. I'd never had a Christmas stocking before. Those were the best Christmases of my life."

He hadn't meant to admit all that, but it was too late to call the words back. Besides, he didn't mind Nissa knowing how he felt. Being with her family had always been the best part of his year. He was accepted as just another kid in the house. Her mother had looked out for him and her father had talked to him about life in a way his own father never had.

She reached past him and picked up one of the orchids. "We'll put this in the kitchen and see what happens."

"I'd like that."

Their gazes locked. He felt something pass between them. A connection, he supposed. Shared memories of good times.

She looked away first. "This Christmas you need to hang your stocking. Otherwise, how is Santa going to fill it?"

He chuckled. "Is that what I've been doing wrong? Thanks for the tip."

"Anytime."

# Chapter 5

*NISSA*

By late afternoon the plants were in the ground and watered. Nissa and Desmond put away the last of the tools. She'd expected him to simply drop off the plants by the path and disappear back into the house, but he'd stuck with her through all the hard work.

"I couldn't have gotten through all this today," she told him. "I would have had a bunch more to put in the ground tomorrow. You were great."

He flashed her a smile that made her insides a little quivery. "I had a good time."

They picked up the last of the tools and put them in the shed before heading into the house. She was hot and sticky, but satisfied. She was on her way to having fun flowers for summer—temporarily, but that was good enough for now. One day she might be able to buy a house and then she'd have a real garden with vegetables and maybe a cherry tree or two, and all the flowers she wanted.

When they reached the kitchen, Desmond glanced at her. "Hilde left chicken marinating and a few salads. I was going to barbecue. You're welcome to join me if you'd like. Unless you have plans. It's Saturday, after all."

Plans as in a date? Yeah, not so much these days. In fact she hadn't been in a serious relationship since she and James had broken up over two years ago.

"I don't date," she blurted before she could stop herself. "I mean I can, but I don't. Or I haven't been. Um, lately."

She consciously pressed her lips together to stop herself from babbling like an idiot, despite the fact that the damage was done.

"So dinner?" Desmond asked, rescuing her without commenting on her babbling.

"I'd like that. After I shower. Meet back down here in half an hour?"

"Perfect."

There was an awkward moment when they both tried to go through the kitchen door at the same time. Desmond stepped back and waved her in front of him. She hurried out, then raced up the stairs and practically ran for her bedroom. Once there, she closed the door and leaned against it.

"Talking isn't hard," she whispered to herself. "You've been doing it since you were two. You know how to do this."

But when it came to being around Desmond, knowing and doing were two different things.

She headed for the bathroom, trying to decide what to wear as she went. It was a casual dinner at home. She shouldn't worry about dressing up. But hanging out with her host was anything but casual, which left her in a quandary.

After a quick shower, she discovered that her wardrobe

had not become sophisticated or elegant since the last time she'd checked. She'd packed away her work clothes, leaving her with an assortment of jeans, cropped pants, shorts and tops. Oh, and two summer dresses, one of which he'd already seen.

Shorts were way too casual, she thought. Plus, she wasn't as confident about her thighs as she would like. So she settled on cute cropped pants and a coordinating tank top, both in bright apple green. She gave her hair a cursory blowout and put on mascara, then decided to call it a win.

She made her way downstairs and found Desmond already in the family room, opening the secret bar.

"What are you in the mood for tonight?" he asked.

"Did you have a suggestion?"

"I thought we'd go old school tonight and have gimlets."

She'd heard of the drink but had never tasted one. "I'm in."

She watched him while he collected botanical gin, limes, a few basil leaves and what she'd come to recognize as simple syrup.

He worked quickly and with a confidence that she envied. No matter the situation, Desmond always seemed to fit in. She did well with friends and in her classroom, but in new situations, she was awkward.

He added ice to a shaker, then measured and poured in ingredients. He'd showered, as well. He had on jeans and a polo shirt. Both showed off his muscled body. The man obviously worked out. She would guess there was a gym in the house—probably in the basement.

He capped the shaker and shook it, then put a strainer on top of each of their glasses and poured. After handing her a glass, he led the way to the sofa.

She kicked off her sandals before sitting down and tucking her feet under her. She sipped her drink. "This is nice," she said. "Very refreshing." She liked the lime with the botanical gin and the hint of basil was unexpected.

"I'm glad you like it." He leaned back against the sofa. "I texted with your mother. She and your dad are going to stay here when they visit."

She grinned. "And you're okay with that?"

"Of course. I enjoy their company and I'm happy to repay their hospitality."

"Will your parents also be staying here when they come to Seattle?"

A muscle in his jaw jumped. "No. They prefer to stay at a hotel. Separate hotels."

She stared at him. "They're not at the same hotel?"

"No. They haven't been together for a few years now. They were never close but recently they've stopped pretending. My mother spends most of her time in Paris while Dad lives in New York."

"Are you all right with that?"

"My opinion isn't relevant. If you're asking if I'm worried they'll get a divorce, the answer is no. They won't. There's too much at stake. Besides, they each have their lives."

"But not with each other."

"You're thinking they were once in love and now they're not. It wasn't like that with them. They had a merger. It was a sensible decision that grew both businesses. Romance wasn't part of the package."

"That's sad."

"Why? It's what they expected and it's what they got. Even when I was little, they rarely saw each other. They took separate vacations, sometimes bringing me along, sometimes leaving me with my nanny."

She'd known the basics of his past, but not any details. Certainly not that his parents had been so estranged. Or maybe that was the wrong word, because it implied that at one time there'd been a connection.

"I can't understand how anyone would do that," she admitted. "Marry for business reasons."

He looked at her. "Marrying for love is a relatively new idea. For hundreds of years marriages were arranged with economics in mind."

"I wouldn't have liked that. I'm not sure I could go through with an arranged marriage simply for the sake of the family fortune."

"Back then, you wouldn't have had a choice."

"Did your mom?"

"I don't know. She doesn't talk about it. When I've tried to ask questions, she'd always told me she's perfectly content with her life. She also pointed out that her way was far more sensible. Emotions were messy and unnecessary." He raised one shoulder. "Neither of my parents has much interest in feelings. They don't see the point of love and affection. It comes with not having a heart. It's sort of a family trait."

"They have hearts."

"They're not mean or cruel, but they don't believe in love. Duty, yes. That makes sense to them. But to do something just out of love isn't their way. Or mine."

She finished her drink and put the glass on the table. "I don't accept that, Desmond."

"You should. I've been told I'm quite the heartless bastard more than once."

"Whoever said that was wrong. You care. You love me and my family. I know you do."

His gaze locked with her, making her aware that using

the *L* word might have sent the conversation in a direction she didn't want to go.

She cleared her throat. "What I mean is you love us the way you love family. Regular families, not your family. I didn't mean romantically. You're not in love with me or anything. You love us the way we love you."

His mouth twitched as if he were trying not to smile. "Would you like me to change the subject?"

"Yes, please."

"And pretend this never happened?"

"That would be great."

"The Mariners are doing well."

Baseball, she thought with gratitude. There was a safe topic.

"They are. I wonder if they'll make the playoffs this year."

Later, as she put together a green salad and Desmond cooked the chicken, she thought about his comment about not having a heart. He couldn't really believe that, could he? Desmond was kind and generous—of course he cared about people. But she understood why he might want to hold back. His marriage to Rosemary hadn't ended how he'd wanted, and that sort of thing left a mark. She knew she was still dealing with James scars and they'd never even been married. That kind of pain could change a person.

That had to be it, she told herself. Because if Desmond thought he was heartless like his parents, he was the wrongest of wrong.

*NISSA*

Wednesday after work, Nissa walked into the kitchen to find Hilde at the island, several cabinet doors spread out in front of her.

"What are those?" she asked.

Hilde waved her closer. "We're remodeling the kitchen. Mr. Desmond approved the budget and hired a decorator, but he won't help me make decisions about what to order."

Nissa turned in a slow circle, studying the huge kitchen. She was pretty sure her entire condo would fit in here with plenty of room for a deck or two. The mid-tone cabinets went up to the ceiling and the island was in a good location, but the stove seemed old and the hardware on the cabinets was dated.

"Was anything done to the kitchen when Desmond moved in?" she asked.

Hilde shook her head. "No. Mr. Desmond had his bathroom remodeled and the house painted. New carpet was put upstairs but nothing else. This kitchen is about twenty years old."

"Then it's time. What do you have so far?"

Hilde opened a cabinet and pulled out several appliance brochures, along with paint swatches and three different floor plans.

"I have all this, but it's not my kitchen," Hilde said, sounding stressed. "Mr. Desmond needs to decide and he won't."

Nissa grinned. "Then I'm going to have to explain to him how that's totally unacceptable. Is he in his study?"

"Yes, Miss Nissa. He's been home about half an hour."

Nissa walked down the long hallway that led to Desmond's private study. The door was open and he was sitting at his manly desk, his attention on his computer.

His gaze was intense, she thought as she paused in the doorway. Desmond was the kind of guy who focused on one thing at a time. She allowed herself a few seconds of wondering what it would be like to have all that attention focused on her, then softly cleared her throat.

He looked up and smiled when he saw her.

It was a good smile, the kind that welcomed and told her he was pleased to see her. As if she were important to him. Telling herself not to read too much into his reaction, she leaned against the doorway and folded her arms across her chest.

"You are needed in the kitchen," she said.

"Am I?"

"Yes. You need to make some decisions on the remodel and today is the perfect time."

The smile disappeared. "It's not my thing. Hilde's handling it."

"It's your house and you get the final say. Whether or not it's your thing, it's your responsibility. Come on, Desmond. Look at a few samples. Wave imperially at one of them and we will all rush to do your bidding. You'll like that part of it."

His mouth stayed straight but she saw humor flash in his eyes.

"People do my bidding all day long," he told her. "I don't need it at home."

"Then indulge me." She dropped one arm to her side and raised the other as she pointed down the hall. "Kitchen. Now."

"You're so bossy."

"I can be and that should frighten you."

He got up and followed her back to the kitchen. Nissa held up both hands.

"Ta-da! I bring you Mr. Desmond."

Hilde motioned to the cabinet samples on the island. "We

have to pick which one. They're going to be custom-made, so the trim can be changed to how you like."

Desmond studied them. "Any of them is fine."

Nissa moved close. "Don't say that. You have an opinion. Door style. Simple? Ornate? Something in between?" She pointed to a Shaker style. "I think that's too plain, but you don't want anything really fussy. This is a big kitchen and there are going to be a lot of cabinets."

Desmond looked at the doors, then out the big windows toward the backyard.

"This part of the house faces more north than east, so there isn't as much natural light. So nothing too dark."

He moved closer to the cabinets and studied them.

"This detail," he said, pointing at quarter-round trim. "No inlay."

They discussed other possibilities before Desmond chose the ones he liked best. From there the discussion moved on to appliances. Hilde made a case for a warming drawer.

"I've always wanted one," she admitted. "They're so nice for entertaining, and in the winter. It's no fun to put hot food on a cold plate. My mom bought me a silly plug-in plate warmer. It's like a folded heating pad. While it works, a warming drawer would be pretty amazing."

Desmond nodded at Hilde. "A warming drawer it is. What else?"

"The stove." Hilde fanned out several brochures. "I like this one best. It's big and a little more expensive but it has two ovens and a grill."

Desmond nodded. "I like the grill. I can barbecue in the winter."

"Yes, and it changes out to a griddle. I would use that a lot."

He refused to weigh in on which refrigerator, so Hilde

and Nissa discussed options. When it came to the layout, all three plans worked, but one involved a lot more construction, basically turning the kitchen ninety degrees.

"I don't think it's worth it," Nissa said. "It's a lot more work and money, and for what? To me, everything is where it belongs right now." She smiled at Hilde. "But your opinion is more important than mine. You're the one who works in this kitchen."

Hilde tapped one of the other designs. "Yes, I agree. Why make so many changes? I like how things are now. It just has to be refreshed."

Hilde and Desmond studied the other options before picking one. After that they moved on to paint colors and made their choices very quickly. When they were done, Hilde made a final list of their choices.

"Thank you, Mr. Desmond. I'll call the decorator in the morning."

"You're welcome, Hilde. I shouldn't have waited so long to get involved."

Nissa walked him back to his office. "That was fun. I love spending other people's money."

"I appreciate your help." He walked into his office, then turned back to her. "I was wrong to push that all on Hilde. She wasn't comfortable making the decisions herself."

"Plus you're her boss, and she has to think about that. I, on the other hand, am free to annoy you whenever I want."

"You're never annoying."

"Really? Because sometimes I try to be."

He smiled. "No, you don't. You're easy to be around. I like that."

Was that the same as liking her? Like as in like-like? Because she knew Desmond liked her as a friend, but was there anything else she should know about?

He started for his desk, then paused. "Are you still up for the company party?" he asked. "My planner was asking about my plus-one."

"I'll be there. I'm looking forward to meeting your staff and telling them what you were like as a teenager."

He chuckled. "I'm not worried. There are no secrets in my past. Besides, if there were, I would trust you to keep them."

"I totally would. Except for the embarrassing ones." She paused, not sure what to say next. It seemed like they were almost going somewhere, but maybe that was wishful thinking on her part.

"Dinner at seven?" she asked instead.

"I'll be there."

Two weeks into living with Desmond, Nissa had settled into a routine. She went to work—she was still at the doggie day care—came home, showered, had dinner with Desmond and then retreated to her spacious room where she relaxed with an audiobook or watched something on one of the streaming services he made available to her.

She'd gone over to see Marisol and the girls every weekend and kept in close touch with her friend. Shane kept talking about getting together, but so far he claimed to be too busy with work, which she took as code that he was still involved with his mystery woman. If the relationship went on much longer, she was going to have to do some serious investigating. In the meantime, she had a party to get ready for.

Mid-July meant summer sales, so she'd indulged in a mini shopping trip. She'd bought a new summer dress for the event—a pretty black fit-and-flare style that fitted perfectly. She already had fancy sandals and a cute evening bag she'd bought years ago.

She took the time to curl her long hair. Actual curls didn't last, but she ended up with waves that looked great. Exactly at six, she went downstairs to meet Desmond.

His summer office party didn't start until seven, but he'd said he wanted to get there early and she'd been fine with that. They would drive there and back together—something that made sense, given their living arrangement. It wasn't a date, she told herself as she reached the main floor. It was convenience. Kind of like carpooling. There weren't any—

"You look beautiful."

She turned toward the voice and saw Desmond in the archway by the dining room. He had on dark pants and a dark gray shirt—nothing special and yet the sight of him made her heart beat just a little faster than usual.

"Thank you," she said, her gaze locking with his. "I wanted to look nice for your work friends."

"Mission accomplished." He motioned to the door. "Shall we go?"

Her nerves continued to be on edge, even as she settled next to him in his fancy Mercedes. Her throat was dry and her skin felt hot, which didn't make sense. This was Desmond. She *knew* him. They were friends. She would trust him with her life. More important, she would trust him with her family, so what was the big deal?

Rather than answer the question, she decided to distract herself with conversation. "Hilde's very excited about the party. You were sweet to invite her and her husband."

"I thought she would enjoy the event."

"She said last year's party was wonderful. Apparently there's dancing."

He glanced at her, his mouth curving into a smile. "I heard that."

"Do you dance with the office staff?"

He returned his attention to the road. "No. But they often dance with each other."

"You must have to balance issues like that," she murmured, watching him merge into traffic as they headed south on I-5. "Being a concerned boss, but not getting too involved. Being in charge without being a mean boss."

"Maybe I am a mean boss."

"I don't believe that. You wouldn't be. You care about people."

"I try to be fair."

She smiled. "See. You can't help it. I'm excited about seeing your parents."

He spared her another glance. "Are you sure about that?"

"Okay, excited is strong, but they've always been really nice to me. Plus, it's fun to see what your mom is wearing. Evelyn has amazing fashion sense and the jewelry is spectacular."

"I wouldn't have thought of you as the jewelry type."

She laughed. "Why would you say that? I don't have much because I can't afford it and if I have extra money I want to save it, but that doesn't mean I don't like sparkly things as much as the next girl."

She thought about the last time she'd seen Desmond's mother. It had been at his housewarming party a couple of years ago.

"That diamond necklace she wore," she said, thinking about how it had glittered. "I doubt I could afford the insurance on it."

"It's probably heavy and uncomfortable to wear," he teased.

"I would be willing to suffer. See how much character I have?"

They talked easily for the rest of the drive. As they approached Seattle, the traffic got heavier. Desmond drove into the city and made his way to the Chihuly Garden and Glass, where the party would be held. He pulled up to the valet parking he'd arranged, then helped her out of the car.

"I've never been here," she admitted, looking at the building in front of them. "I should have come. I always meant to. I'm a huge fan of his work. Did you know there's a massive Chihuly installation in Montreal? It's made of all these individual pieces and every year they have to take it apart and bring it in for the winter."

"I didn't know that, but I'm not surprised. His work is all around the world."

They walked toward the entrance.

"I'm going to stay up front so I can greet everyone as they arrive," he told her. "You're welcome to explore the museum, if you'd like. It's closed to the public for the party, so you'll pretty much have it to yourself."

"I'd love to look around. Thanks for the suggestion."

She really did want to explore and she knew standing with him while he welcomed his guests would only invite a lot of questions. It wasn't as if she and Desmond were a couple. She was just a family friend.

They went inside. He excused himself to go talk to his staff while she collected a brochure on the museum and prepared to be dazzled. But just before she stepped into the first room, she glanced back at Desmond. He'd gone out of his way to make the evening special for those who worked for him. Not exactly the actions of a man who had no heart.

# Chapter 6

*NISSA*

Nissa spent over an hour admiring the various installations. While she'd started out as the only admirer, by the time she entered the outdoor garden the party was in full swing and there were people everywhere. Several smiled at her, but no one came over to talk to her, making her realize that except for Hilde, she didn't know anyone who worked for Desmond. Not that it mattered, she told herself. She was capable of starting a conversation herself.

She took a glass of champagne from a server and looked around, searching for a likely prospect. Her gaze settled on a familiar older couple. Evelyn and Charles Stilling looked like what they were—wealthy, cultured and well traveled. She knew that each of them had inherited a part of what had become Stilling Holdings, forming the bigger company when they'd married. What she hadn't known until recently was that marriage had been about business rather than affection.

Now she studied them, wondering how they could survive so many years in a loveless marriage. She wouldn't like that at all. For her, marriage was about giving her heart to one man for the rest of her life. She wanted a traditional family with kids and pets and camping.

Evelyn turned toward her and the light caught the spectacular sapphire necklace she wore. Nissa smiled. Okay, maybe she would add a few jewels to her wish list.

She was still smiling when Evelyn glanced in her direction. The older woman studied her for a second before heading in her direction. Nissa moved toward her, as well.

"I don't know if you remember me," she said, holding out her hand. "We've met a few times. I'm Nissa Lang, Shane's sister."

"Yes, of course."

Evelyn had dark hair and eyes. She was tall, slim and moved with a grace that Nissa envied. Maybe she'd studied ballet or maybe she was blessed with natural grace. Nissa wasn't exactly clumsy, but she didn't have anything close to Desmond's mother's style.

"How was your trip to Seattle?" Nissa asked.

"It was commercial travel. One does the best one can, under the circumstances." Evelyn sipped her champagne. "Are you here with Desmond?"

"You mean as a date?" Nissa tried to ignore the sudden surge of nervousness. "No. I came with him because it was easier. I'm staying with him for a few weeks while my condo is rented out." She held in a groan. Really? She'd had to say *that*? "It's not anything romantic. We're friends. Just friends. We have been forever. Desmond would spend

Christmas with my family, which, um, I guess you knew because he wasn't with you."

She forced herself to stop talking and offered a tight smile.

Evelyn's expression sharpened. "You're living with him."

"I'm staying at the house. In my own room. Not, you know, *with* him." She made little air quotes, then wished she hadn't.

"So, have you seen the exhibit?" she asked brightly, hoping to change the subject.

"I don't need to. Dale and I are friends."

Dale? As in Dale Chihuly? Sure. She wasn't even surprised.

"Do you think you're right for him?" Evelyn asked bluntly. "You're hardly his type and you bring nothing to the table. How will you help him with business? Be an asset when he travels? What kind of a hostess will you be?"

Nissa went cold. "What are you talking about?"

"It's obvious you have feelings for him. I'm not sure what your ridiculous charade is about staying with him, but not *with* him." Evelyn copied her air quotes. "Desmond always does the right thing. He made a mistake with Rosemary, but he rectified it immediately and he never looked back. She begged for a reconciliation, but he wouldn't have any part of her, once he recognized her for what she was. The same thing would happen with you, Nissa.

"You're the kind of girl who expects love when you marry. Desmond's incapable of that. I consider that a point of pride, but I doubt you'd agree." Desmond's mother offered her a cold smile. "He knows what's expected from him and he will do as we ask. Silly girl. I almost feel sorry for you."

With that, she turned and walked away, leaving Nissa

feeling embarrassed and exposed, although she couldn't begin to say why. Although she knew it was her imagination, she felt as if everyone was staring at her, judging her. She felt awkward and out of place and wished that she could be anywhere but here.

She glanced around, looking for an exit and if not that, at least somewhere to hide. She'd barely taken a step when Desmond appeared in front of her.

"Are you all right?" he asked, sounding concerned.

"I'm fine."

He stared at her. "I saw you talking to my mother. What did she say?"

"About what?"

"Nissa, you went white."

Oh no! She couldn't tell him what Evelyn had said—she couldn't talk about it with anyone. "That must be a trick of the lighting. I'm fine."

His dark gaze never wavered. "You don't usually lie to me."

Obviously he got his bluntness from his mother, she thought, wishing she could see humor in the moment, rather than feeling uncomfortable.

"Maybe just this once you could let it go," she told him.

He surprised her by nodding. "Are you hungry?"

"Not really." Her stomach was too upset for her to eat.

"Then come with me."

He took her hand in his and drew her back inside. There was a large dance floor set up under the glass roof. A band played and several couples were dancing.

He took her half-empty champagne glass from her and set it on a table, then pulled her into his arms and started moving them to the music.

At first she could barely follow his movements. She was

acutely aware of everyone around them, and worried that his mother was watching. But gradually the heat of Desmond's body, the feel of him holding her, made her relax. She told herself she would deal with her conversation with his mother another time and that she should simply enjoy the rest of the evening.

One song became two and then three. Finally Desmond drew her to the side and found a couple of empty chairs. They sat down.

"That was nice," she said, smiling at him.

"It's like prom."

"Yours?"

He looked at her. "No. Yours. Everyone is dressed up. You look amazing."

"Look at you with the compliments." She tried not to think about what his mother had said—that Desmond was incapable of love and she was silly. "It was a long time ago."

"But still a good night."

"Yes, it was." She'd been so crazy about him, she thought, remembering how the evening had gotten better and better. The best part had been him kissing her at the end. Wonderful sexy kisses that had made her think a future was possible.

"And then you walked away from me," she added softly.

"You know why."

"Imagine where we would have been if you hadn't."

She hadn't meant to say the words, but somehow she had. Desmond's gaze sharpened.

"You mean if we'd kept seeing each other?"

She nodded. "I think about that sometimes."

"So what happens?"

"We'll never know."

He started to speak, then suddenly looked away and came to his feet. One of his assistants walked over.

"A few of the guests are getting ready to leave," she told him. "You wanted me to let you know when that happened so you could say goodbye."

"Thanks, Brittany."

The woman nodded and retreated the way she'd come. Nissa stood. "Go play the host. I'll be fine."

"I won't be long." He pointed to the buffet. "Eat something. You have to be hungry."

"I will."

He turned away, took a step, then spun back to her. Before she knew what was going to happen, he pulled her close and kissed her. The brief contact seared her skin and sent liquid desire pouring through her, but before she could react in any way, he was gone, following Brittany to where his guests were leaving.

Nissa stood there for a couple of seconds, not sure what had happened or how she felt about it. She smiled. Scratch that last thought, she told herself. She knew exactly how she felt about Desmond kissing her. She felt good. And if it happened again, she was going to enjoy every second of it.

*DESMOND*

Desmond left work nearly two hours earlier than usual. There was no reason—no pressing appointment or phone call. Instead he went home because he knew Nissa was there and he wanted to spend time with her.

He tried to tell himself she would still be there when he left at his usual time, but for some reason the words had no effect. Normally he was disciplined to the point of annoying his friends, but not today. Not with her.

He arrived home a little after four and walked into the house. Nissa was in the family room, the TV on and tuned to a local news show, although the sound was off. She was sitting on the sofa, her hair still damp from her shower. She was reading something on her tablet, wireless headphones on her head.

She was wearing shorts and a T-shirt. Conventional clothing that shouldn't have stirred anything inside of him, and yet did. Or maybe the problem wasn't the bright yellow T-shirt, but the woman wearing it.

He wanted her. Knowing it was a mistake, that he shouldn't cross that line did nothing for the need that lived inside of him. He wanted her and the brief kiss the night of the party had only made that wanting increase.

He thought of crossing to her, of tugging her to her feet and then pressing his mouth to hers until she wrapped her arms around him and begged him to take her to his bed. Assuming Nissa begged. He wanted to know. Was she quiet or did she moan? Was she shy or adventurous? He wanted to learn every inch of her body and discover all the ways he could pleasure her, then he wanted to do it all again, simply because he could.

And then what? He could imagine taking things that far, but the next step always eluded him. What if she fell in love with him? She would want roses and a happily-ever-after. While he could give her the former, the latter wasn't possible.

He remembered when he'd been twelve or thirteen. His parents had sat him down for what they'd billed as "an important conversation." He'd been horrified they were going to talk about sex, but instead they'd explained about his responsibilities to the company. How he was expected to excel at business and build upon what he would inherit.

To that end, he was expected to marry appropriately.

A young woman of note, perhaps with a small fortune or another firm worth acquiring. Love was for others, not for him. He could date whomever he wanted, but to take things further was unthinkable. He was to always make the sensible choice, to leave emotions for those who lived smaller lives. He remembered his mother turning to his father and smiling.

"We don't have to worry about Desmond. He doesn't feel things very strongly. He hardly has any friends and no real connections."

She'd said it with such pride. He remembered thinking the reason he didn't have friends was because he was tutored at home. He wanted to be like the other boys he saw through the mansion windows.

Then he'd been sent to boarding school where he'd discovered making friends was harder than he had thought. He'd never fit in, until he'd met Shane. Even though they'd stayed close for the past twenty years, he couldn't help wondering if his mother was right. If there really was something wrong with him. An inability to connect the way everyone else did.

He hadn't wanted that, but no matter how he tried, he couldn't seem to feel the things others did. He might put on a decent show, but the truth was, he was more like his parents than he wanted to admit and in the end, his lack of heart would destroy Nissa. And that was the one thing he refused to do.

So instead of acting on his need, he forced a smile and walked into the room, loudly calling her name. She looked up and smiled at him.

"You're home early," she said.

"I ran out of work."

"I doubt that." She put down her tablet and removed

her headphones. "Why don't you go get changed and I'll make tonight's cocktail? I looked online and think I found a good one."

"I look forward to it."

Ten minutes later he was back downstairs. She was in the kitchen, muddling mint in a shaker. As he watched, she poured in simple syrup, rum, lime juice and some kind of puree. After shaking, she added club soda, then poured the drink over ice.

"A pear mojito," she said proudly. "I know it's not your usual thing, but it got great reviews."

"I'm sure I'll like it."

They touched glasses. Nissa pointed to the deck.

"Let's sit outside. The temperature is perfect. Hilde made enchiladas for dinner. We only have to heat them in the oven. There's a delicious salad, too. I'm super excited."

"About Mexican food?"

She grinned. "It's my favorite. I think I was born in Los Angeles in a previous life."

He chuckled as he followed her outside. They sat next to each other on the lounge chairs in the shade. The temperature was in the low eighties and the lake beyond was calm with only a hint of shimmer from the sunlight.

"Tell me about your day," he said, sipping the mojito. It was surprisingly refreshing.

"It was good. I miss the dogs, but delivering flowers doesn't leave me so stinky at the end of my shift. Some of the arrangements are really heavy, which I didn't expect." She flexed an arm. "I'm getting a workout."

"Are they too heavy?"

She raised her eyebrows. "Do not even think about trying to rescue me," she told him. "I'm perfectly capable."

"I know you are, but I want to make sure—"

*Before Summer Ends*

She held up a hand to silence him. "No. I can do this."

"All right. You delivered heavy flowers. Anything else?"

She laughed. "I'm discovering I don't know the area as well as I thought. There are little streets I've never heard of. But I have GPS on my phone and that makes it easy. Siri loves telling me to make a U-turn because I've gone the wrong way."

"She does have attitude. Do you want to become a florist?"

She looked at him. "Why would you ask that? I love being a teacher."

"I know but when you were working at doggie day care, you wanted to get a dog. I wondered if the trend would continue."

"I might want to plant more flowers in the garden, but I'm going to stick with my current profession." She paused and took a sip of her drink. "What else? Oh, I talked to my friend Marisol today and mentioned the boat thing again. She said she was excited about it. Assuming you're still willing to play host."

"I am. When would you like to go?"

Nissa hesitated. "She hasn't been feeling well for the past couple of weeks, but she's better now. Still weak, but better. How about Thursday? I know it's a weekday, but I have it off and the girls don't have camp that day."

She looked so earnest, he thought, meeting her gaze. Like she was worried about asking for too much. How could she not know that he would give her anything?

"Let me text the captain and see if he's available then," he said, pulling his phone out of his pocket and typing. When he was finished, he looked up. "How old are her daughters? Do you know how much they weigh? We'll want the right size life jackets for them."

She gave him the information and he texted that, as well. Seconds later, Captain Pete wrote back saying he was available and looking forward to it. They settled on a time. When Captain Pete asked about lunch, Desmond suggested the usual picnic fare.

"We're set," he said. "Let's leave at ten and stay out until two or so. Remind everyone to wear sunscreen and bring a hat. We'll have lunch on the boat. The weather is going to be good and the winds will be calm, but if there are any upset tummies, we'll just head back."

She looked at him. "You're very good to me, so I spend all my time thanking you."

"No thanks necessary. I'm looking forward to it." Not just spending time with Nissa, but meeting her friend. He knew a person could learn a lot about someone by how they were with their friends.

*NISSA*

Nissa tried to relax as she drove to Marisol's house. After several really bad days, Marisol was finally feeling better, but Nissa knew that could change at any second. Happily, when she got to the house, her friend was up and dressed, looking pale but determined.

Lisandra and Rylan practically danced around her, asking questions, one after the other.

"Is it a really big boat?"

"Does it go fast?"

"Mom says the toilet is different—more like an airplane toilet, but we've never been on an airplane, so will we know how to flush?"

"Will we eat lunch on the boat? Can I have a soda?"

Nissa gathered them close and hugged them. "I'm glad

you're excited. I am, too. I've never seen the boat, so I can't answer your questions, but we're on our way to the marina right now, so you can see it for yourselves."

Marisol laughed. "They've been like this for two days. I'm amazed they got any sleep last night." She looked at Nissa. "Thank you for arranging this. It's a great distraction for all of us."

"I'm excited, too. Apparently the boat is very fancy."

Marisol raised her eyebrows. "I'm more interested in meeting Desmond. I've been hearing about him for years."

Nissa tried not to flush. "Yes, well, he's a good guy and we're friends."

As Marisol knew about Nissa's ongoing crush, the post-prom debacle and pretty much everything else on the Desmond front, she wasn't likely to buy the whole "friend" thing, but the girls would and that was what mattered.

It didn't take long to collect their tote bags and confirm everyone was protected with sunscreen. They all piled into Nissa's car and she headed for the marina.

She carefully followed the instructions Desmond had given her and was soon entering a code to unlock the big gates that protected the parking lot of the fancy boat section of the marina. There was a big clubhouse, a bar with plenty of outdoor seating and dozens and dozens of boats. Maybe hundreds of them, neatly pulled into slips, bobbing slightly in the water.

She wanted to say there were big boats and small boats, but there weren't. Everywhere she looked were massive seagoing vessels that had to be multiple times bigger than her condo, or Marisol's house.

In the back seat, the girls went quiet and next to her Marisol sucked in a breath.

"He owns one of those?" her friend asked.

"I guess so."

She pulled in next to Desmond's Mercedes, then texted him that they had arrived. He replied that he would be right out. Everyone got out of her car and collected their bags as she saw a gate open and Desmond walk toward her.

She looked at the man multiple times a day—they were living together, so she shouldn't be surprised by his appearance. But there was something about his casual dress— board shorts, a Hawaiian shirt and boat shoes—that made her shiver just a little.

Marisol stepped close. "You didn't say he was so handsome."

"I did."

"You weren't specific enough. The man is hot. How do you resist him?"

Nissa sighed. "If he ever asked the question, I wouldn't, but so far, he's showing amazing self-control."

"Men can be so stupid."

Nissa smiled. "Tell me about it."

When he had joined them, she made introductions. He insisted on carrying their bags as they went inside the gate and onto the ramp that led down to the boats. Marisol went slowly, hanging on.

"Is the walk too much?" Nissa asked anxiously.

"The exercise is good for me."

They passed several boats on their way to the end of the small pier, stopping in front of the one on the end. It was big and sleek, with a dark blue hull. There was a huge covered deck up what felt like three stories, and a bigger open space out back. Large windows allowed them to see a living room and dining area. Smaller windows were darkened so she couldn't see in. Those were probably the bedrooms, she thought, unable to take in how incredibly massive and beautiful the boat was.

"Welcome aboard," Desmond said, waving toward the five stairs that led to the side of the boat. "I'll give you a tour, then we'll get everyone fitted for life jackets and have a quick safety talk before we head out."

Marisol was still hanging on to the pier railing. She looked at the narrow stairs and the gate on the side of the boat, then shook her head.

"I don't think I can do that," she said quietly. "I'm feeling better, but I'm not sure it's possible." She glanced over her shoulder. "Why don't I wait at the clubhouse?"

"Mom," Lisandra and Rylan said together, their voices thick with disappointment. "You have to come. It won't be fun without you."

"I have to agree with them," Desmond said, passing the totes to Nissa and walking over to Marisol. "Do you trust me?"

Marisol's brown eyes widened. "I'm not sure what that means."

"Do you trust me?"

Marisol's expression turned doubtful. "I guess."

Before she could say anything else, Desmond swept her up in his arms. Marisol shrieked and wrapped her arms around his neck.

"What are you doing?"

"I would have thought that was obvious."

He moved to the stairs and took them easily, then stepped over the side of the boat and set Marisol on the deck, before turning to the girls and waving them onboard.

"Come on. We don't want to leave without you."

The girls scrambled after him. Nissa followed, taking the stairs before stepping through the gate and onto the boat.

She immediately felt the movement of the boat—a physical reminder that they were on water. Excitement blended with anticipation as she wondered how great it would be when they were actually moving!

Desmond kept his attention on Marisol. "You doing all right?"

"I am." She studied him. "Now I know what Nissa was talking about."

Nissa didn't know what her friend meant, but decided to go with it. She set their totes on a padded bench as Desmond started the tour.

As she'd seen from the outside, there was a very large living area, a "salon," Desmond called it. The kitchen or galley was much bigger than she would have thought and there were three small bedrooms and two bathrooms onboard.

They returned to the rear deck and were introduced to Captain Pete, a small, wiry man in his fifties.

"Welcome aboard," he said cheerfully. "Who might these young mermaids be?"

Both girls giggled as they introduced themselves.

"Nice to meet you both." Captain Pete leaned close. "So I have some work to do before we can get underway. It would go a lot faster if the two of you would like to help me."

The twins nodded eagerly. Pete led them to the finger pier and started explaining about the lines holding the boat in place. Desmond looked at Marisol.

"I thought we'd spend the day on the upper deck. There's plenty of cover so the girls will be out of the sun. There's a nice breeze and the view can't be beat."

Marisol put her hands on her hips. "You're about to tell me you're going to carry me again, aren't you?"

"I was going to ask rather than tell, but yes."

Marisol glanced at Nissa and mouthed, "He's a keeper," before turning to Desmond. "You're a good man. Thank you."

Desmond carried her upstairs. Nissa followed and found herself on a big, covered deck with plenty of seating, and tables to hold food and drinks. There was a sink, a refrigerator and a stack of towels.

"This is really nice," she said, looking around. "I think I'm in love."

Desmond settled Marisol on one of the bench seats, making sure she had plenty of pillows.

"It's a good boat."

"It's a luxury yacht. How far can it go?" she asked. "Could we sail up to Canada?"

"Probably not today, but she's capable of making the trip."

Nissa thought about what it would be like to spend a few days on the yacht. From what she'd seen, everyone would be really comfortable. Of course the quarters might be a little tight with Captain Pete along. Assuming she and Desmond went as more than friends.

Not that he'd made any moves on her. There had been one brief but mighty kiss and nothing since. A fact that left her confused and wondering if it had simply been a friendly kiss and she'd been wrong to read more into it.

"We have to work on our communication skills," she murmured to herself.

The girls raced up the stairs to the upper deck.

"We saw the engine room and got fitted for our life jackets," Lisandra said.

"The ropes are called lines and the bathroom is called a head," Rylan added. "Captain Pete said once we're underway, we can both steer!"

Captain Pete joined them and made sure the adults knew where their life jackets were, then gave a brief safety lecture. After that, Desmond joined him on the main deck. The powerful engines roared to life and shortly after that, they were off.

The day was perfect—warm and sunny. The girls spent part of their time upstairs with their mom and the rest of it with Captain Pete who was more than patient with their endless questions.

Marisol and Desmond talked as if they'd known each other for years. Nissa listened as her friend expertly extracted information on Desmond's childhood and business. When it was time for lunch, he carried Marisol down to the dining area in the salon.

There were different kinds of sandwiches and salads, cut fruit with dip and potato salad, along with pitchers of lemonade and ice water. Marisol admitted she had an appetite, something that didn't happen much these days.

"It must be the fresh air," Marisol said with a laugh. "I haven't felt this good in a long time."

Rylan put down her sandwich and pulled her hair back in a ponytail. "Look how long it is," she said to Nissa. "Fourteen inches from my fingers." She turned to Desmond. "I need to get to sixteen inches before it can be cut off."

"Me, too," Lisandra added. "My hair's that long, too."

Nissa leaned toward him. "They're growing out their hair so they can donate it. There's an organization called Wigs for Kids. Fourteen inches is good, but sixteen is better."

"That's a big commitment," he told the girls.

"Donations are important," Rylan said. "We want to help."

Nissa wondered if she would say more and confess how

Marisol was waiting for a kidney. Nissa still hadn't ex-plained why she was sick—it wasn't her secret to tell—and so far Desmond hadn't asked.

"I know you're doing a good thing," Marisol said, fin-gering her daughter's hair. "But I'm probably going to cry when they cut it off."

"I'm not," Lisandra said proudly. "I'm going to be brave."

"You already are."

*NISSA*

After lunch they continued their journey around Lake Washington, then went through the Montlake Cut to Lake Union in the center of Seattle. They dodged paddleboarders and saw a seaplane take off. By two, the girls were sleepy and Marisol looked ready to go back. Captain Pete turned the boat so they were headed for the dock.

Nissa moved next to Desmond on the benches.

"This was wonderful," she said. "We've all had a great time."

"Me, too," he said, gazing into her eyes. "I don't get out on the water enough."

"You should do it more. It's fun."

"That could be the company as much as the boat," he told her.

Which sounded great but made her wonder if there was one person's company he meant in particular, and if so, hopefully that person was her.

# Chapter 7

*NISSA*

Nissa couldn't remember the last time she'd had such a busy social life. Normally she was a stay-at-home kind of person. Once she'd finished at work, she tended to like going to her condo and settling in for the evening. Oh, there were the occasional drinks out with girlfriends or dinner at Marisol's place, but for the most part, she lived a pretty quiet life.

Lately, though, she was going and doing. Just in the past week there had been Desmond's work party, then a day out on the water, and now she was once again curling her hair and pulling out her new party dress for dinner with Desmond, Shane and his girlfriend.

Maybe she wasn't as much of a homebody as she'd assumed. Maybe her quiet lifestyle was more about a lack of things to do. Something she should consider. Maybe when the summer was over and she moved back into her condo, she should think about expanding her social horizons. Maybe start taking a class or join a volunteer group. She'd been considering getting one of those foreign language apps to brush up on what she would guess was her very rusty college Italian. Instead of that, she could take a class at the community college and be with people.

After she finished applying her makeup, she added "check out Italian classes" to her calendar so she wouldn't forget, and then stepped into her dress.

It was the same one she'd worn to the Chihuly event, but it wasn't as if she had two "nice dinner" dresses. Her social events tended to be more casual. But when Shane had suggested dinner and named a restaurant, she knew that casual wasn't going to cut it.

As she pulled the hot rollers out of her hair, she wondered about the mystery date her brother would be bringing. He hadn't said much about her, beyond that he liked her. As she rarely met anyone he was dating, tonight was going to be fun.

She fluffed her hair, put in the pair of pearl earrings her parents had given her for her twenty-first birthday, then went downstairs.

Even though she was braced, she still had to consciously keep her mouth from falling open when she saw Desmond. The man could wear clothes. Once again he had on dark trousers and a dark shirt. Nothing overly special, yet he looked sexy and strong and more than a little tempting.

He smiled at her. "You look beautiful."

She waved away the compliment. "I know this is the dress I wore last weekend, but I wasn't prepared for all the fancy dinners and parties. My teacher's wardrobe isn't up to your level."

"You always look perfect."

She raised her eyebrows. "Perfect? Really? Don't you think that's pushing it just a little?"

"Not at all."

She sighed. "You are a great date. Do you know that, because you are." She shifted her wrap to her other arm. "I can't wait to meet Shane's girlfriend. He's been going out with her at least five weeks. Mom and I don't have the original start date of their relationship, so we can't be sure. Even if it's just five weeks, that's like a personal best for him. She's given me a list of questions to ask. I hope I can remember them all."

Desmond shook his head. "Does it occur to you that conversations like this are one of the reasons your brother keeps his private life to himself?"

She grinned. "Of course, but who cares about him being uncomfortable? We need information!"

"You'll have a whole dinner to ask your questions."

"Oh, because you don't want to know anything? You have to be just as curious as I am."

Desmond glanced away, as if hiding something from her.

"What?" she demanded. "You know something. What is it? Tell me!"

He returned his attention to her. "Shane is my friend and anything he and I have discussed will stay between the two of us."

"That's so unfair. Not even a hint? Tell me something. You have to!"

He took her hand in his, brought it to his mouth and lightly kissed her knuckles. "As I said before, you look beautiful and I'm looking forward to spending the evening with you."

While she appreciated the compliment and the feel of

his mouth on her skin, she knew he was trying to distract her from her interest in her brother's personal life.

"You're very loyal," she grumbled, snatching back her hand. "It's disappointing."

"I would be just as loyal to you."

An interesting concept, she thought. She suspected he was telling the truth. From what she'd observed, Desmond would be an excellent boyfriend. Attentive, kind, funny, charming.

"Rosemary was never good enough for you," she told him. "You should have listened to me."

"Yes, I should have. Shall we go?"

They drove to the restaurant where he handed off his car to the valet. Nissa looked around at the waterfront setting. Despite the fact that they were meeting at seven, it was plenty light. Sunset in this part of the country was still after eight thirty.

As they walked toward the entrance, Desmond put his hand on the small of her back. She instinctively moved closer to him, trying not to get too caught up in the heat from his touch. He was being polite, nothing more.

Once inside, he gave Shane's name and they were immediately shown back to a table by the water. Her brother was already there, and next to him was a petite, dark-haired woman. She was pretty, with an air of quiet elegance Nissa immediately liked.

They both came to their feet when she and Desmond approached the table. Shane engulfed her in a big bear hug before kissing her cheek.

"Hey, munchkin."

"Hey, yourself." She gazed into his eyes. "You good?"

His smile was happy. "I am." He turned. "Nissa, this is Coreen. Coreen, my baby sister, Nissa."

They shook hands, then Shane introduced Desmond. The four of them took seats across from each other. Nissa told herself not to stare but it was hard not to be interested in her brother's date. She couldn't remember the last one he'd introduced to anyone in the family. There had been Becky back in high school, but they'd known her for years before she and Shane had started going out.

"It's wonderful to finally meet you," Coreen told Nissa. "I've heard so much about you."

Nissa glanced suspiciously at her brother. "Is that good or bad?"

He grinned. "I only told her the good stuff. It didn't take long."

"Ha!" She pointedly turned away from him and looked at Coreen. "Shane said you're a doctor?"

"I am." Coreen smiled. "I'm an emergency room pediatrician at the hospital."

Nissa smiled at her brother. "Like I said before, Mom will be so proud."

"That's the least of it. I know she's going to grill you later."

"She won't have to grill me. I'm giving up everything I know for free." She smiled at Coreen. "Shane has been pretty quiet about you, so we're all curious. I'm here representing the entire family, but don't worry. We're a friendly bunch."

"That's what I've heard. Shane told me you're a teacher. That's a wonderful profession. You must have a lot of patience."

"So speaks the pediatrician."

"I like kids."

"Me, too."

Shane leaned toward Desmond. "They don't need us here for the conversation."

"Apparently not."

Nissa ignored them both. "I usually get a summer job but this year, for an assortment of reasons, I've been doing temp work. It's been interesting. I spent a couple of weeks at a doggie day care. That was fun, but made me want to have a dog. Then I delivered flowers for a few days. Now I'm working for some big international company that is doing a very large mailing. They've brought in people to stuff envelopes and apply postage. I keep reminding my boss about the existence of email, but so far she's not listening."

Their server appeared and they all ordered drinks, then discussed the menu. Coreen was pleasant and obviously crazy about Shane, which made Nissa like her more.

Coreen talked about how long she'd been at the hospital and how she'd moved up from Los Angeles where she'd done her residency at the UCLA Medical Center.

Nissa listened attentively, enjoying the information and how approachable Coreen seemed, only to be distracted by Desmond and Shane having some kind of silent communication. It wasn't anything overt—more subtle eye contact and a quick head shake on Desmond's part, as if he didn't want to do whatever Shane expected.

"I've only ever lived in the Pacific Northwest," Nissa admitted. "Born and raised. Our dad was a ferryboat captain for years. In the summer we would tag along on his trips." She looked at Desmond. "So his boat is way bigger than yours."

"Thank you for putting me in my place."

The server appeared with their drinks. Shane raised his glass.

"To finally getting together," he said.

"And meeting Coreen," Nissa added.

"Desmond and I met at boarding school," Shane said. "I was there on scholarship, but he got in the old-fashioned way. His parents paid the bill."

Nissa looked at her brother, trying to figure out why he would say such an odd thing.

"I was nervous about having him as my roommate," Shane continued. "But we got along right away. I used to drag him home with me every holiday so he didn't have to rattle around alone in his massive estate."

"I came willingly," Desmond said mildly enough, but there was something in his tone.

Nissa couldn't place it. Not annoyance or even resignation. Concern, maybe? Exasperation?

"We liked having him around," Nissa said, still confused about what was happening between the two men. "I had a huge crush on him when I was a teenager."

"I didn't notice," Desmond murmured.

Nissa laughed. "You knew about it, but of course you didn't do anything about it. Such a gentleman."

"How long have you two been going out?" Coreen asked.

"They're not dating," Shane said, his voice a little loud. "You thought they were together?" He laughed. "They're just friends. Have been for years. The crush thing is long over."

Okay, this was too strange, Nissa thought, unsure of what to do or say. She glanced at Desmond, but he was too busy watching Shane to notice her.

Not sure if she should say something or ask to speak to her brother alone, she decided to try changing the subject.

"Anyone know what's good here?" she asked, picking up her menu. "I would guess the seafood is delicious."

They each studied their menus. The server came by and

told them about the specials, then took their orders. Conversation took a more conventional turn and Nissa started to relax enough to enjoy herself. But between the salads and the entrees, Shane surprised her by asking to speak with her outside.

"Family business," he said to Coreen and Desmond. "We won't be long."

Family business? What family business? Nissa followed him out onto the deck and turned on him.

"What has gotten into you? You're acting strange, even for you, and it's freaking me out. If you're this weird on your dates, it's no wonder you've never gotten married."

Instead of laughing at her or getting annoyed, Shane surprised her by apologizing.

"I should have warned you," he said. "About what was happening."

"I have no idea what you're talking about. You'd better tell me or I'm calling Mom."

Shane grinned. "That's your best threat? You'll call Mom?"

"You don't think she and Dad will get in the car and drive over the mountains to check on you?"

His humor faded. "Oh, right. They will. Okay, so none of this is about you. I'm testing Coreen."

"Testing her how? And why?"

He shuffled his feet, as if buying time. "Look, I like her."

"Yes, I can see that. For what it's worth, I like her, too. In a totally different way," Nissa added. "So what does that have to do with anything?"

He looked at her. "I don't like women."

Nissa laughed. "Since when?"

He groaned. "I mean, I don't get involved. I don't do serious. But with Coreen, I'm tempted to take things further and I want to make sure she's interested in the right things."

She poked him in the chest. "You're not making any sense."

"Desmond is a rich, good-looking guy. Coreen knows who he is and that he's single. Will she hit on him while we're gone? That's what he's going to let me know."

She felt her mouth drop open and had to consciously close it. "You're setting a trap for your date?"

"It's not a trap if nothing happens."

"And Desmond agreed?"

"He wasn't happy. He told me I was a jerk for doing this to her, but he said he would help me out."

Nissa had no idea what to say to that.

"But I like Coreen," she complained. "I don't want to find out she's icky and I don't want you to lose her because you're a moron."

"Better I find out now than in a year."

"Or you could just talk to her and ask the question."

"If she's who I hope she is, the question will break her heart. If she's not, she won't tell me the truth." He glanced at his watch. "They've had enough time. We can go back in."

"And say what? If she asks what we've been talking about, what should I say?"

"Tell her we were discussing Mom's birthday present."

"I'm not a good liar."

He put his arm around her. "One of your best qualities, Sis."

## DESMOND

"You're quiet," Desmond said, thinking that it was better to simply state the obvious than to try to talk around it. "Are you angry?"

"About what Shane did to Coreen?" She looked at him.

"No, but I am confused about why he felt he had to test her that way. I asked him why he didn't just ask what was going on with her and he pointed out that someone who would go after you wouldn't be honest with him, which I guess is right… But the whole situation makes me sad. Why isn't my brother more trusting of women?"

"You'll have to ask him that."

"Oh, like he'll tell me anything." She sighed. "Someone, somewhere really broke his heart."

"Yes."

She understood that was a big admission for him. As for the details, she would work on getting them from Shane.

"You weren't happy playing along," she said. "He told me you thought he was being a jerk."

"I was just hoping he was wrong to worry about Coreen. I don't want to have to tell my best friend that the woman he's dating just tried to pick me up."

"Is that an ongoing problem?"

He thought of the women who had been thrilled to be alone with him, regardless of who they were with. How they'd moved closer, running their hands along his arm or his thigh, offering their number and anything else he might want. They knew he was rich and for some people, money mattered more than anything.

"Sometimes. Not with your brother's dates."

"But Coreen was good, wasn't she? Tell me she didn't do anything, because I really like her."

"She wasn't the least bit interested in me. She talked about how great Shane is and how much she had wanted to meet you. I think she's the real deal."

"That makes me happy."

He smiled. "I thought it might."

"I'm just surprised. I just thought Shane had it all together, but he doesn't. Sure, he's a gifted surgeon and he has a great house and stuff, but inside, he's just as broken as everyone else."

She looked at him. "I know you didn't want to help him, but you did anyway. You're a good friend."

"I'd do anything for him."

"I know. You love each other." She smiled. "In a very manly, friendship kind of way."

Some of his tension faded. "We do."

He pulled into the garage and they both got out. When they walked into the kitchen, Nissa came to a stop and faced him.

"Do you miss Rosemary?" she asked.

Her eyes were the most perfect shade of blue, he thought, meeting her gaze. Clear and deep, with long lashes.

"No."

She smiled. "You don't want to elaborate?"

"She married me for my money and when I told her the marriage was over, she walked away. There wasn't much to miss."

"I told you not to marry her."

"Yes, you did, and next time you give me that kind of advice, I'm going to listen."

"Do you think it's going to work out with Coreen and Shane?"

"I hope so. She seems crazy about him. Any other questions?"

Like did she want him to come upstairs with her and make love all night? Because if she did, he was more than willing.

But instead of asking that, or teasing him or mentioning a snack, she simply said, "I'm tired and I'm going to bed. Good night, Desmond."

And with that, she was gone, leaving him alone with the sense of having blown something important. Not that he could, in any way, say what it was.

*NISSA*

Nissa kept to herself for the next few days. The dinner with her brother had unsettled her—no, not the dinner. The testing of a perfectly nice woman because Shane didn't want to trust her.

His need to do that surprised her, and made her wonder what else she didn't know about him and about Desmond. She felt foolish—like the country mouse seeing the big city for the first time, and it wasn't a happy view. She felt sad that Shane felt the need to go so far to protect himself, which meant something really bad had happened to him and she had no idea what.

The evening had also opened her eyes about what Desmond's dating life must be like. How could he know if someone was in it for him or for the money?

Monday after work she drove back to his big house, determined to shake off her mood. If Shane wanted her to know the details of his personal life, he would have told her, so she was going to have to let that one go. As for Desmond, she could only be herself around him and draw comfort from the fact that he knew she liked him for him. The rest of it was just a part of who he was, but not important to her.

After showering and changing her clothes, she went downstairs and talked with Hilde about the progress being made on the decisions for the remodel. Construction was due to start in mid-September and would take about four weeks. She would be long gone by then, but promised to come back and view the finished kitchen.

She checked her email and social media, texted with Marisol, all the while listening for Desmond's car. When she finally heard him pull into the garage, she got up and walked through the kitchen to wait for him.

He stepped into the house and saw her. His immediate warm, welcoming smile made her feel all tingly down to her toes.

"I'm ready to talk," she told him. "Because I know you've been missing my sparkling conversation."

"I have. Let me put my things away and I'll join you in the family room."

She went to wait for him. He returned in about ten minutes. He'd changed out of his suit and looked casual and relaxed in jeans and a T-shirt.

"The young executive at home," she teased. "It's a good look."

"Thanks." He crossed to the bar and started pulling out ingredients. "Why are we speaking again? I ask the question out of curiosity and not to annoy you. I missed having you to talk to."

"I needed to work things out," she admitted. "The money thing is so strange to me. Although in Shane's case, it's not about money. I suppose that's what upset me as much as anything. Someone damaged him and I don't know who it was or when it happened."

"He was gone a lot," Desmond reminded her. "He went off to boarding school when he was thirteen, and then to college."

"Meaning there are many parts of my brother's life I don't know about?" She nodded. "I figured that part out. I was just surprised by all of it. And sad for both of you. It must be hard to be so afraid to trust someone you want to care about. I don't think I could do that." She smiled. "I do tend to just put it all out there."

"That's part of your charm."

"It's a different view of the world."

He held out a lemon drop for her and picked up his scotch.

"Don't stop trusting people," he said. "I've always admired how you embrace the world, flaws and all."

They took their usual seats on the facing sofas.

"You make me sound foolish."

"No." He looked at her, his gaze intense. "I said I admire you, Nissa, and I mean that."

He did? "You do?"

"Yes. You have the purest heart of anyone I know. I only want good things for you."

There was something in the way he spoke the words, as if there was a secret message in them. One she couldn't decipher.

He smiled. "I want you to marry for love."

"Why else would I get married? Giving someone your heart, accepting theirs in return, that's the point of marriage. Knowing that for the rest of your life, this is the one person you can count on to care about you, no matter what."

His dark gaze was steady. "Did you have that with James?"

"No, and that's why I didn't marry him. Something was missing. It took me a few months to figure that out, though. He kept pressing me to set a wedding date and I kept resisting. Then one day I knew what was wrong. I didn't love him enough to want to marry him."

"I'm sorry you had to go through that."

"Me, too. It was hard on both of us." She thought about how angry James had been when she'd ended things, but the fury had quickly turned to hurt. He'd told her he would love her forever. She hoped that wasn't true.

"Do you ever hear from him?" Desmond asked.

"No. I gave him back his ring and that was the end." She looked at him. "Do you hear from Rosemary?"

"No." He smiled. "Let us remember, she wasn't in the marriage for me. Once she realized she wasn't getting any money, she was ready to move on."

"That makes me sad."

"Why? Marrying her was a mistake, but a recoverable one."

"Yes, but she reinforced all your ideas about women only being after you for money. That's not right and it's not true. Not everyone is like that."

He surprised her by smiling. "That's true. Some of them are after me for the sex."

Despite the emotions churning inside of her, she laughed. "You are such a guy."

"Women like sex, too."

"They do," she admitted, thinking that she found him very sexy and that she'd enjoyed every fantasy she'd ever had about him. Based on what she knew about him as a man, it wasn't a giant leap to think about how he would be as a lover. He liked to see a job through—an excellent quality for a sexual partner. Not that they were going there.

"Life is complicated," she said, picking up her drink.

"It can be."

"I remind myself that a year from now, I'll be in Italy. That helps."

She caught a slight tightening around his mouth.

"What?" she demanded. "You were thinking something."

"I wish you didn't have to work at a job you don't like to pay for it."

She stared at him. "What are you talking about?"

"You hate stuffing envelopes."

"Of course I do. It's not the sort of thing anyone likes, but it's no big deal and totally worth it."

"If you'd just let me give you the money," he began.

She set down her glass and glared at him. "Stop, Desmond. We've talked about this. No and no. This is *my* trip and I'm happy earning the money. This is my dream and I want to make it happen. I want the satisfaction of having earned it. Why can't you understand that?"

"I do understand that you're being stubborn. We're friends. I care about you. Why won't you let me do this for you? Then you could take off the rest of the summer and enjoy yourself."

"Life doesn't work that way."

"Sometimes it does. Sometimes good things happen. If you let them. It makes me feel good to help you. Why is that bad? Why can't you accept that? Why do you always have to be so stubborn about everything?"

"What?" she said, her voice rising slightly. She wasn't mad—not yet—but she was on the road. "You're the one who totally expects to get his way. Why does it annoy you that I want to do the work? Most people have to."

"I agree and I wish I could change that, but I can't. However, I can give you a trip to Europe." He leaned toward her. "You're being ridiculous. If we were married, you'd have no trouble letting me pay for the trip or anything else. Why is this different?"

The absurdity of the statement propelled her to her feet. "You didn't just ask that. If we were married, we would have agreed to spend the rest of our lives together. It's totally different from being friends." She put her hands on her hips. "Not that it matters because we're never going to *be* married, or anything other than what we are, mostly because you're never going to ask me out. Heaven knows we're certainly never sleeping together. What if my brother disapproves? What if he tells you not to? So don't talk to me about—"

The reality of what she'd just said sank in slowly, but when it was fully absorbed, she stopped talking midsentence.

*No*, she thought in horror. *No. No. No.* She hadn't just said that. About them being married or more than they were or the sex thing. She couldn't have because if she had, Desmond would assume some or all of it was what she wanted. He would think she'd been hoping for more all this time, and then he would, well, she didn't know what, but it would be bad.

His dark gaze locked with hers. She saw questions in his eyes and tension in his body. She didn't know which was worse—the comment about marriage or the hint about sex. Were they equally bad or should she rank them somehow?

The silence between them lengthened. Nissa wasn't sure what to do. Running away seemed the most logical next step, but to where? Her room upstairs? Once she closed the door behind her, she was going to have to stay there forever, slowly starving to death. Once she was dead, she wouldn't care about facing him.

"Did you want me to ask you out?" he asked, coming to his feet.

She held in a high-pitched keening sound she could feel building up inside of her chest. "Um, back in high school? After prom? Yes, I did. I called you and you never called me back."

"I meant now."

Crap. Double crap. Did he really expect her to answer

that? To bluntly say what she thought of him and hoped would happen? Not that she'd ever put her hopes into words, but she was fairly clear on the fact that she—

"Nissa?"

She cleared her throat, careful to keep her gaze fixed on a point just over his shoulder. "You're very attractive and we have fun together. Going out would be, you know. Nice."

"So you like me."

She groaned as she returned her gaze to his. "Of course I like you. We've been friends for years. Why are you doing this? Why all the questions? Why don't you tell me how *you* feel? I get why you didn't ask me out back in high school. Shane was right. I was too young for you. But it hasn't been that way for a while and it seems to me if you were the least bit interested, you would have done something, so I don't get why you feel the need to drag all this information out of me when you have no intention of—"

He circled the coffee table and reached for her. One second she was feeling confused and embarrassed and the next she was in his arms and his mouth was on hers and she was remembering how glorious his kisses had been so many years ago and discovering they were just as delicious now.

# *Chapter 8*

Desmond gave as much as he took, kissing Nissa with a need that fed her own desire. No matter how tightly he held her, she wanted to be closer. His hands stroked up and down her back, then dropped lower to cup her rear. She instinctively arched toward him and was both surprised and happy to feel the hard ridge of his erection against her stomach.

She pulled back and stared at him. "You want me!"

One corner of his mouth turned up. "Why are you surprised?"

"You're always so controlled. I believed you about just being friends and you were lying the whole time."

"I wasn't lying. I was doing the right thing."

"And now?"

"You seem willing to go in another direction."

This conversation had more twists and turns than a

round of Candyland, she thought. "So you want to sleep with me."

"That's more blunt than I would have put it, but yes. I would very much like to take you to my bed and make love with you."

The words sent heat pouring through every part of her. A faint tingling began to radiate out from her midsection. She felt her breasts getting heavy and a telltale ache settling low in her belly.

"That's very clear," she said quietly.

"Nothing has to happen," he told her. "I mean that. You're too important to me to want this relationship messed up. We can go back to what we've always been. I won't ever push you."

She believed him. Not only did she know his character, Desmond had never lied to her.

She thought about how much she liked him and how good they were together in every other way, then she put her hands on his chest.

"I'm on the pill but I don't have condoms with me. I'm hoping you do."

His eyes dilated. "Upstairs."

She smiled. "I've never seen your bedroom."

"Would you like to?"

"Very much."

They stared at each other for another two heartbeats, then he took her hand and led her toward the stairs. They went up faster and faster, until they were racing to the top.

Laughing together, they ran down the hall and into his bedroom. Nissa had a brief impression of high ceilings, a large fireplace and a view of the Sound before she saw the massive bed against the far wall. Then Desmond was kissing her and nothing else mattered.

While his lips claimed hers, his hands were everywhere. She understood his desire to touch all of her because she felt the same way about him. She stroked his back, his shoulders and his chest. He tried to pull off her T-shirt while she attempted to work the buttons on his shirt.

They bumped hands and arms and nothing was accomplished. Finally they stepped away from each other and quickly stripped off their clothes. Then they were holding each other, skin against skin. He retreated again, just long enough to fling back the covers from the bed, before lowering her down and joining her.

He explored every inch of her, with his hands and his tongue, teasing her into an arousal that had her panting as she strained toward her release. Kissing her deeply, his skilled fingers between her legs, he eased her over the edge, then drew out her orgasm until she was boneless.

Only then did he enter her, his dark eyes locked with hers. He filled her over and over again, exciting her until she had no choice but to soar a second time, with him only seconds behind.

*NISSA*

Satisfaction and happiness battled for dominance. Nissa, still naked and wrapped in Desmond's arms, her head on his shoulder, was willing to let them decide on the winner. She would be content with either or both emotions. Her breathing had returned to normal and her mind was starting to clear, but none of that changed the fact that she and Desmond had just made love.

She shifted so she could look at him. When his gaze met hers, he gave her a slow, sexy, "I'm the man" kind of look that told her he had zero regrets.

"That was nice," she murmured, her tone teasing.

"Very pleasant," he agreed.

They smiled at each other. He propped himself up on one elbow and stroked her bare shoulder.

"You're really all right?" he asked.

"Very."

"Good."

He moved his finger from her shoulder to her breast. Sparks immediately began to light inside of her. They got more intense when he reached her nipple and lightly stroked the tight peak.

"So next time, I was thinking you could be on top," he said, looking at her. "If that's all right."

"I can do that." Straddling him, arching into his thrusts. Yup, she was a firm yes.

He used his thumb and forefinger to gently pinch her nipple, before leaning close and taking it in his mouth and sucking. Pleasure shot through her, making a bee line for her core.

"That's really good," she breathed, her eyes sinking closed.

He got to his knees and shifted to her other breast, drawing it in and—

Somewhere in the distance she heard a high-pitched ringtone. At first she didn't recognize the insistent clanging noise, but then the meaning of it sank in and she pushed him away before scrambling out of his bed and diving for her shorts.

It took her two tries to answer, then she gasped. "It's happening?"

On the other end of the call, Marisol's voice was thick with tears. "They just called. They found a donor. Everything checks out and I'm scheduled for surgery tonight."

"I'm on my way." Nissa felt her throat tighten as she

fought tears of her own. "I'm so happy for you. Tell the girls to hang tight. I know they're scared, but I'll be there for them and for you. Don't you worry."

"Thank you. I love you so much."

"I love you, too."

She hung up the phone and reached for the rest of her clothes. Desmond had gotten out of bed and crossed to her. She gave herself a second to admire his strong body before pulling on panties and picking up her bra.

"What's going on? Who was that?"

Because he didn't know. She'd told him Marisol was sick, but not the particulars.

She fastened her bra and pulled on her shorts. "Marisol has terminal kidney disease. We've been waiting for a donor kidney so she can have a transplant. One just came through." She pulled on her T-shirt. "I'm sorry the timing isn't the greatest, but I have to go be with the girls. Marisol is having surgery tonight so they need me. I hope you understand."

*DESMOND*

Desmond had no idea what Nissa was talking about. He'd known Marisol was ill, but it had been obvious that Nissa hadn't wanted to go into detail, so he'd never asked. A kidney transplant? Wasn't that a dangerous surgery? Of course if her disease was terminal, then not having the procedure wasn't an option.

All those thoughts were pushed aside when he realized Nissa was going to be leaving. He quickly pulled on his own clothes and followed her down the hall to her room. She darted into her closet and pulled out a small suitcase.

"My to-go bag," she said with a shrug. "Because I'll need to stay with the girls."

"I'll go with you."

She was already starting for the stairs. "You don't have to. I know this is sudden, but I have to get to her house and drive her to the hospital. I'll call. I promise."

He was on her heels. "I know you will, but that's not the point. You're dealing with a lot. I'll drive. My car will be more comfortable for Marisol and the girls. We can recline the front seat for her."

They'd reached the main floor. Nissa hesitated only a second before nodding.

"Thank you for the offer. I'll admit, my head is spinning."

They got into his car and he backed out of the garage. Once they were on the street, she gave him Marisol's address and told him the quickest way to get there.

"Tell me about Marisol's disease," he said quietly. "There's no other treatment?"

"No. Her doctors tried everything before deciding a transplant was her only hope of survival. Until then, she's kept alive by dialysis. I volunteered to be a living donor, but while our blood types would work—I'm considered a universal donor—we didn't pass the cross-matching test. Basically she has antibodies against my cells. You can only donate to other A or AB positive people."

"That's why you asked my blood type."

"I ask everyone," she said. "Just in case. I wanted to talk to her about doing a paired exchange. That's when you have a donor who is willing, but can't give to you. So you find someone else in the same position, but who can give to you. So far we haven't found anyone."

"You would have given her a kidney?"

A stupid question. It was obvious she would. Nissa loved her friend and she was simply that kind of person.

"Of course. She needs to live. She's got the twins and they've already lost their dad." Tears filled her eyes. She shook her head and inhaled. "I'm not crying. I'm not going to cry. I have to be strong for the girls."

"You'll be taking care of them," he said, starting to understand what was happening. "You're going to what? Move into their house?"

"Yes." She turned to him. "I'm sorry, Desmond. I wanted to tell you all this before, but Marisol didn't want people to know. Things got weird when some of her friends realized she might die. Plus, she's protective of the girls."

"Are you their guardian?"

"If something happens to Marisol?" She nodded. "Yes. If she dies, I'll step in and raise them."

She spoke so calmly, he thought. As if she was simply going to water houseplants for a few weeks. But it wasn't that.

"What about your trip to Italy?"

He realized it was a ridiculous question as soon as he asked it, but couldn't call it back.

She smiled. "Marisol is going to be fine. That's what I believe. But if she's not, I guess I'll save a little longer and the three of us will go together in a few years. It's not like my dream trip is going away. Italy will still be there."

She was willing to turn her life upside down, he thought, stunned by her acceptance of such massive responsibility. He didn't know anyone else who would be willing to take on two children the way she was.

"Rylan and Lisandra must be terrified," he said. "This is a lot for anyone to deal with but they're only ten."

"They've been very brave, but it is a burden. They don't

like seeing their mom sick and I know they're scared about the possibility of losing her. They've both been in counseling, which helped." She shook her head. "I wish I could take her disease from her. I don't have the responsibilities she does. It would be easier for me."

His gut clenched at the thought of her facing death or transplant surgery, but he didn't say anything. Instead he focused on getting to Marisol's house as quickly and safely as he could.

When they arrived, Marisol was sitting on the sofa. She looked more pale than she had, but there was hope in her eyes. Her daughters were on either side of her, clinging to her. They had both been crying.

Nissa rushed over and knelt in front of the three of them, holding out her arms. "We're going to get through this," she said firmly, hugging them. "We're going to be strong and pray and come out the other side."

"You're a blessing," Marisol said.

Desmond felt out of place, and moved toward the small dining room to give them more privacy. He still couldn't completely absorb what was happening. Marisol was facing a terrifying procedure and there was nothing he could do to help. For once, his ability to write a check was meaningless. Not a feeling he enjoyed.

He circled the small table, part of him listening to the low rumble of voices in the other room, and part of him noting the battered table and rickety chairs. He moved into the kitchen and saw it was a decent size, but the cabinets needed replacing and the appliances were practically antiques.

"Desmond?" Nissa called.

He hurried back to the living room.

"We need to go," she said, standing.

The girls each picked up a tote bag, then Marisol struggled to get to her feet.

He immediately moved close and helped her up. "I can carry you to the car."

Marisol gave him a smile. "While that's the most action I've seen in years, how about you just help me walk there?"

"Whatever you want."

When they arrived at the hospital, someone was waiting with a wheelchair. Marisol had already preregistered so only had to sign a few forms before they took her upstairs. Nissa and the girls led the way to where they would wait out the surgery.

The waiting area was filled with comfortable sofas, a table and chairs and lots of books and board games. Nissa had brought blankets and pillows for when the twins were ready to try to sleep.

"They'll get to see Marisol before she goes into surgery," she said. "Just for a few minutes."

To say goodbye, he thought grimly. In case something went wrong. Because if Marisol died, Nissa would suddenly be both mother and father to two ten-year-old girls.

How had he not known that? Why hadn't she been talking about it, worrying and making plans? But she hadn't. She'd simply agreed to a life-changing possibility. Who did that?

A few minutes later, a nurse came and got them. Desmond stayed behind, wishing there was something he could do to help. The surgery was beyond him and Marisol already had a donor, but maybe something with the girls.

When the three of them returned, Rylan and Lisandra were both crying. Instinctively, he held out his arms and they surprised him by rushing to him and throwing themselves against him. He hung on tight.

"I know you're scared," he said. "But we need to think positive thoughts. Why don't we pray together, then decide what we want to do next? It's going to be a few hours until we hear anything."

"We're supposed to get an update every two hours," Lisandra told him. "That's what the doctor said."

"Good to know."

Nissa sat next to him and the girls knelt on the carpet. They all joined hands and prayed for Marisol's safe recovery, then asked for blessings for the family of the person who had passed away, thereby donating the kidney for the transplant.

When they were done, Desmond watched while tears filled the girls' eyes and knew they were seconds from a very understandable meltdown. What they needed was a distraction.

"Is the plan for you to go live in Marisol's house?" he asked Nissa.

She nodded, looking a little shattered herself. "Yes."

"I have a suggestion. Why don't the twins come stay at my place while their mom is in the hospital?"

Both girls stared at him.

He smiled at them. "I have a very big house that might be fun for the two of you. You could each have your own room, but with a bathroom in between, so you're close."

Nissa brightened. "He's right. It's called a Jack and Jill bathroom. I'm not sure why. But it's very cool. Oh, and Desmond has a pool. And the house is right on the Sound."

The twins looked at each other, then at her. "You'll be there?" Rylan asked, her lower lip quivering.

"Of course. I've been staying there while my condo is rented out. It's very nice there. Hilde, the housekeeper, would love to spoil you both. She's a fabulous cook and she makes cookies and brownies."

He was glad Nissa was onboard with the idea. Everything had happened so quickly. Two hours ago, they'd been in his bed and now they were at the hospital, dealing with Marisol's surgery and her children.

The twins looked at each other and slowly nodded.

"That sounds nice," Lisandra said, wiping away tears. "But not until we know about Mom."

"Of course not," Desmond said quickly. "We're going to stay right here and wait to hear the good news."

Nissa shot him a grateful look, before pulling tablets out of the tote bags. "Okay, let's get comfortable and find something to entertain ourselves."

Time passed slowly. Two hours in, a nurse came and said the surgery was going as well as could be expected. Eventually the girls fell asleep on one of the sofas. Nissa rescued their tablets before they slid off onto the floor, then pulled him into a far corner of the room.

"Are you sure about all of us staying with you?" she asked, searching his face as she spoke. "It's going to be a lot to take on."

He gave her a gentle smile. "Have you seen my house? There's plenty of room. Hilde will love it, and I think being somewhere else will be a distraction for the girls when they need one."

He waved his phone. "I've been doing some research on kidney transplants. After Marisol is out of the hospital, she's going to need to take it easy for a couple more weeks."

Nissa bit her lower lip. "She's going into a skilled nursing facility until she can come home."

"Or she could move into the house. There's a guest room downstairs and we can get a nurse in."

Her eyes widened. "Desmond, you can't do all that."

"Why not? I like Marisol and her kids. They've been through enough. You know the money doesn't matter to me." He chuckled. "I do like to write a check to solve problems."

"Don't say that. You're being so nice." She blinked several times as if holding back tears. "Having her come to your house would be wonderful, but it's a lot to take on."

He waved away the comment. "We'll have a nurse in to help. It will be easy. And she'll feel better knowing her daughters are right upstairs."

What he didn't say was that part of his motivation was that he didn't want Nissa to move out. Not now. After last night, things were different between them. He wasn't sure what was happening, but he liked it. He wanted to keep her close for as long as possible.

"I'll talk to her in a few days, when she's feeling better," Nissa told him. "I'm sure she'll agree, but I can't say yes for her."

"Understood."

She shifted her weight. "About what happened earlier."

"You mean getting the call from Marisol?" he asked, pretending he didn't know what she was talking about.

"No, before-before. Us."

"Oh, that. Regrets?"

"No! Of course not." She blushed. "It was wonderful."

"Good. Me, too."

Her gaze locked with his. "I want to be with you again, but with the girls around, I can't. At least not at first. Because they're going to need me."

"I know. I thought that for the first couple of nights, they'd share a bed and you could sleep in the other room, so they could easily get to you if they need you."

"That's a great idea. I'll do that. Should I go back to the house and get the rooms ready?"

"I've already texted Hilde. She's taking care of it right now."

"You've thought of everything."

"I hope so." He drew her close and wrapped his arms around her. "We're going to get through this. Whatever happens, the girls have you and you have me."

"Thank you for understanding how important this is to me."

"Anytime."

He kissed the top of her head and released her. She returned to the sofa closest to where the girls slept. He would guess she was going to watch over them all night, if necessary. And he would watch over her.

## NISSA

Marisol's surgery took four hours. The surgeon was pleased with the outcome and told them there hadn't been any complications. Now the real waiting game began. They had to get through the first twenty-four hours, then the second, and so on. With each passing day, she would get stronger.

The girls cried when they heard the news and fought leaving the hospital. Nissa knew they had been through so much—they had to be exhausted. She convinced them to get a little sleep at Desmond's house before they returned in the early afternoon. They wouldn't be able to see their mom until after lunch sometime.

Despite the late hour, Hilde was there to greet them when they arrived at the house. She showed the girls their room and the adjoining bathroom. Nissa took Desmond's advice and suggested they share a bed, with her right next door. The twins were relieved by that idea and quickly got ready for bed.

Nissa stayed with them until they were asleep, then went into her own room where she found Desmond reading in the chair in the corner. He put down his book as she entered, then crossed to her and pulled her close.

As he held her tight, all her emotions seemed to crash in on her at once and she started to cry. Tears quickly changed to sobs that shook her body and made it impossible to get control. But he seemed unfazed, continuing to stroke her back and murmur quietly that she would be fine.

After several minutes, she managed to calm down enough to catch her breath and slow the flow of tears.

"I don't know what that was," she admitted. "I think I scared myself."

He smiled at her as he wiped her cheeks. "You've been dealing with a lot. It's good to get it out." He leaned in and lightly kissed her mouth. "I finally got Hilde to go home. She'll be back first thing to make breakfast. She can't decide between pancakes and waffles, so be prepared to have all the food on your plate."

Nissa managed a shaky smile. "She's been so wonderful."

"Having kids in the house is her dream. She's thrilled to have people to take care of."

He kissed her again, lingering just long enough to make her aware of the fact that about eight hours ago, she'd been naked in his bed. A situation she'd like to repeat—just not tonight.

As if reading her mind, he said, "Go to bed. You're exhausted. I'm right down the hall if you need me."

She looked into his dark eyes. "Thank you for everything. You've been amazing."

"I was happy to help."

With that, he walked out of the room.

She watched him go. She'd always known that Desmond was a great guy, but she hadn't known how dependable he was in a crisis. He'd calmly taken charge of the situation and had made everyone feel safe.

Funny how everything she learned about him only made her like him more and wonder what would have happened if he hadn't listened to her brother, all those years ago.

# Chapter 9

*DESMOND*

Desmond didn't get a lot of sleep that first night. He'd called to check on Marisol every hour. Her condition was unchanged, but the ICU nurse had said she was resting comfortably and her vitals were good. Now it was just a waiting game.

He got up early and showered, then headed downstairs. Hopefully the girls would sleep late. Getting some rest would make the stress easier to deal with. He'd told Hilde not to come until after eight, but of course his housekeeper was already at work in the kitchen.

When she saw him, she started to pour him coffee.

"So you don't listen to me anymore?" he asked, his voice friendly.

She smiled. "I want to be here when the girls wake up.

To make breakfast and show them around the house. They need to feel safe here."

"Thank you."

"You're welcome."

He drank his coffee and chugged the protein drink Hilde made for him as he tried to decide if he should wait for Nissa to get up before heading to the office or instead write her a note. She made the decision for him by walking into the kitchen.

She looked pale, and there were shadows under her eyes. When she saw him, she crossed to him and wrapped her arms around his waist.

"I didn't sleep," she admitted, leaning against him. "I kept worrying and checking on the girls. But everything is good at the hospital and the girls slept through the night."

"I'm glad on both accounts."

She straightened and greeted Hilde, then walked over to the coffee. His housekeeper stared at him, her eyebrows raised. He stared back, not saying anything. Finally Hilde simply smiled and went back to work prepping for breakfast.

"What's the plan for today?" he asked. "Don't the girls have camp?"

"Yes, but they're going to stay home with me. We'll go to the hospital this afternoon. Seeing their mom is the best thing for them. She's already explained that she's going to look terrible, but that she'll be on the mend, so they're prepared."

Nissa grimaced. "As prepared as you can be, considering what's happening. I've already called in to work and told them I quit."

He stared at her. "Your job?"

"Uh-huh. I'm sure eventually the girls will want to go

back to camp, but I'm not going to push them. I'll stay close. It's better for them."

"What about your Italy fund?"

She smiled. "It's doing okay, and if I have to put off my trip for a year, then I will. This is more important."

He knew enough not to (once again) offer to pay for everything. Although that argument had had a fairly stellar outcome. Still, the trip was important to her.

She took the cup of coffee Hilde handed her. "I thought it might be fun for the girls and me to go to their house and paint their bedroom. They're a little older now and the bright pink is getting to be a bit much."

He thought about the worn furniture in the living room and dining room and how the kitchen needed updating. The girls' room was probably in the same shape.

"Marisol's going to be in the hospital for ten or twelve days, then staying here for another couple of weeks. That's almost a month. Let's redo her house."

Nissa stared at him. "What are you talking about? Redo what?"

"All of it. Paint, refinish the floors, put new carpet in the bedrooms, fix up the kitchen."

"You can't do that."

"Why not?" He leaned against the island. "I give tens of thousands of dollars away every year to charities because I think it's important to help out where I can. Marisol has been to hell and back. Why can't I help her? I know her and I like her. Unless you think she'd be upset."

"I don't know what to think." She looked at him. "Just like that?"

"Wouldn't you do it if you could?"

"Sure. In a heartbeat." She sipped her coffee. "It would

be a great project for the girls, but we'd have to come up with a kitchen design and what about contractors?"

"Desmond has people," Hilde said quickly. "I could help, too."

"You're outnumbered," Desmond said with a grin. "I'd like to do this for Marisol and her daughters. Let's give them their dream house."

"You're going to make me cry again," she said, turning away.

"Happy tears?"

She nodded. "Thank you, Desmond. I'm overwhelmed by your generosity. Yes, let's do it. Let's fix up Marisol's house."

## NISSA

Three days after Marisol's surgery, Nissa stood in the middle of her friend's small house and stared at the petite woman with glasses. Erica was the architect Desmond had hired to take on the remodel. Nissa had told him they were just doing a remodel and no architect was required, but he'd only smiled at her and now she knew why.

"You want to what?" Nissa asked, trying to keep her voice from rising to a shriek. Lisandra and Rylan were staring at her with identical expressions of confusion, which made her feel better. At least she wasn't the only one wondering what on earth they were talking about.

"It's being done all over the neighborhood," Erica said with quiet confidence. "Adding a second story onto the house is time-consuming and expensive, but adding a second story to the garage is much easier. Many of these older houses are well constructed, with strong foundations that can take the weight. I've already confirmed that."

She unrolled large sheets of paper and put them on the kitchen table.

"This is only a two-bedroom house," Erica said, pointing to the drawing of the original floor plan. "With a single bathroom. The master is a decent size, which gives us a lot to work with."

She flipped to a second drawing. "We take the current full bath and make it an en suite with the master and take a little from the second bedroom to give Marisol a walk-in closet. The new staircase goes here, and we put a powder room under the stairs. A toilet and sink will fit just fine."

She smiled at the twins. "For you two, we take the whole space over the garage. You each get a large bedroom with a Jack and Jill bathroom. The toilet and tub-shower combo are shared, but you'll each have a sink with a long counter and plenty of storage. The closets are about the size you have now, but you'll each have one so that doubles what you're used to." She flipped to yet another page to show the upstairs.

"As for the kitchen," Erica continued, pointing to the room next to them. "The layout works great. I suggest we just do a quick update. New cabinets that go to the ceiling to provide more storage. New flooring and new appliances. Quartz countertops." She looked around. "Fresh paint throughout the house, and that's pretty much everything."

Nissa told herself fainting would cast a pall on an otherwise happy day, so she rested her hand on the back of a chair and did her best to keep breathing.

"How long would all this take?" she asked.

"Four weeks." Erica's voice was firm.

"That's not possible. Won't we need a permit, and won't that take a while?"

Desmond smiled. "I know a guy."

"Of course you do." Nissa turned to the girls. "This is a lot to take in. You'll want to think about it, but do you have any initial thoughts?"

The girls exchanged a look.

"We want to do this," Lisandra said firmly. "Mom's been talking about wanting to update the kitchen. She was saving for it before she got sick."

The girls disappeared into their mother's bedroom, then reappeared with a folder. Inside were pictures from magazines showing different kitchens.

"Excellent," Erica said. "This will give us a sense of her style. Oh, that's a beautiful farm sink." She pointed to a picture. "And I like these cabinets very much. They'll go perfectly."

Erica began rolling up her drawings. "I'll have a preliminary design to you by this afternoon. We'll meet tomorrow to choose finishes and the work will start the day after."

"So fast?" Nissa asked, barely able to breathe.

"Why wait?" Desmond looked at the girls. "We want to get this done, don't we?"

The twins nodded.

"It's like a TV show," Rylan added. "Where they do the work and later the family gets to see their new house!"

Erica smiled at the twins. "You two are going to have to think about paint color. We'll be putting in nice durable carpeting, so I'll have samples for you to look at tomorrow, along with fixtures for your bathroom. So you have homework."

Nissa's head was spinning. "We have to pick out bedroom sets."

"I'll have ideas for those, as well," Erica told her. "Not to worry. My office is going to be one-stop shopping."

The rich really did live different lives, Nissa thought. Not that she was going to complain. The house was going to be amazing and something that Marisol would have forever. But it was a lot to take in.

"All right," she said, going for cheerful, rather than panicked. "We're going to leave Erica to work her magic and go visit your mom. How does that sound?"

"Excellent," Lisandra said. Rylan nodded.

They thanked Erica for her help. Desmond said he was going to stay with the architect to go over a few details and would meet her at home. As she and the girls walked to the car, the twins couldn't stop talking about the house remodel.

"I hope we can get storage under the bed," Lisandra said. "And lots of shelves."

"I want one of those bunk beds where the bottom bed is a full size and the top one is a twin bed so we can have sleepovers."

"Oh, that's a good idea. And we need desks." Lisandra waited while Nissa unlocked her car. "Mom needs a little desk in her room, too. Or maybe the cabinet kind so it can be closed up and look nice when she's not using it."

"We'll have to email Erica when we get back from the hospital." Nissa smiled at them. "Are you both going to be able to keep a secret?"

The girls nodded.

"Mom deserves a good surprise," Rylan said. "And so do we."

Later that night, Nissa read to the girls until they fell asleep. At first they'd complained they were too old to hear a bedtime story, but the ritual allowed them to relax and doze off.

Nissa made sure the bathroom night-light was on, then

quietly left the room. As long as they were sharing a bed, she was in the room next door. She was sure that once Marisol was released from the hospital, the twins would feel better about everything.

She went downstairs and walked into Desmond's study. He was behind his desk, typing on his computer. As always, the sight of him made her heart beat a little faster. His appeal was more than how good-looking he was. She liked that he was strong, and being around him made her feel safe.

He looked up and saw her. His intimate smile did nothing to calm the fluttering.

"Are they asleep?" he asked.

She nodded. "They're exhausted. Between staying up most of the night of their mom's surgery and dealing with everything else, not to mention the excitement of the remodel, they were ready to crash."

"What about you?" he asked, coming to his feet.

"I'm a little tired."

"I bet."

He walked to the sofa in his office, grabbing her hand on the way. He sat and pulled her down next to him, then put his arm around her so she could rest her head on his shoulder.

He was warm and just the right height to be the perfect pillow, she thought, breathing in the scent of him.

"You smell good," she said, snuggling closer.

"So do you. How was your visit with Marisol?"

"Good. She's alert and feeling better every day. The doctors are thrilled with her progress. She should be released right on time." She raised her head to look at him. "Is it still okay for her to come here?"

"Of course. I have a hospital bed and table being delivered on Monday. Marisol will have twenty-four-hour-a-day nursing care for the first few days, then a night nurse until she goes home. A physical therapist will be here to help her recover the muscle tone she will have lost by being in bed so much and Hilde has already consulted with the hospital's dietitian to get meal ideas."

"I'm impressed." She smiled. "I shouldn't be—this is how you roll—but I'm still impressed."

"How I roll?" His voice was teasing.

"You know what I mean."

He kissed the top of her head. "I do."

"The twins said they're ready to go back to camp," Nissa told him. "Tomorrow we have our meeting with Erica, but the day after, they'll return to camp."

"You sure they're ready?"

"I think they're the best judge of when that happens. I'm going to stay home so if they start to get upset and want to leave, I can go get them."

"You're a good friend."

"I love them."

"That's very clear," he said.

"You're being incredibly generous. Thank you for that."

"I'm happy to help, and you can stop thanking me. Helping Marisol and her family makes me happy."

"So you have a selfish motive," she teased.

"Very."

She laughed. "I know that's not true. You're a good guy, letting the girls stay here, and then taking care of Marisol when she gets out of the hospital."

"There's plenty of room in the house."

She sat up and slid back a little so she could see his face. "Why this house? It's huge and while it's beautiful, you buying it isn't intuitive."

"I wanted a home for a family."

"Sure, if you're going to have seventeen kids."

He chuckled. "I was thinking two or three, but I've always had a big house. I like the location and the size of the lot. The view. I felt comfortable here."

"You're right about that," she said. "The place is huge, but also homey." She cleared her throat. "Did Rosemary like it?"

One eyebrow rose. "Asking about the ex-wife?"

"Apparently."

He shook his head. "She didn't like anything about it. She didn't want me to relocate the company headquarters. She was happy there." He paused. "Some of it was Shane, I think."

"My brother? What does he have to do with anything?"

"She and Shane didn't get along. Neither of us could figure out why, but his theory is that Rosemary was afraid Shane could see through to the real her."

"If he had been able to, he could have saved you a disastrous marriage. Or maybe not. Maybe you were determined to marry her. I warned you off her and you didn't listen."

"Something I still regret."

"Was the divorce difficult?"

"Not legally, but I felt as if I'd failed. My parents weren't happy, more because they wanted an heir than they cared about Rosemary."

Nissa remembered what Desmond's mother had said to her at the party and wondered if the other woman would be happy with anyone he chose.

"Rosemary tried to convince me not to give up on the marriage," he added. "When she figured out I was done, she stopped trying. She accused me of never loving her."

"That's not true. You married her. Of course you loved her."

"I didn't," he admitted. "I married her because she was what was expected. Love never entered into it."

Given what she knew about his parents and how his life was different from hers, she shouldn't be surprised, but she was.

"I'm sorry," she told him. "That makes me sad."

He touched her cheek. "I never want to make you sad."

"You're not responsible for how I feel." She deliberately lightened her tone to lighten the mood. "I hope you've learned your lesson, young man. Next time marry for love."

"Yes, ma'am."

Nissa studied him. "You gave her a generous settlement, even though you didn't have to, didn't you?"

"Why do you ask that?"

She smiled. "You so did. It's your style."

"I didn't want her to end up with nothing. The money didn't matter to me."

She again thought about what his mother had said at the party.

"I don't get marrying for money," she admitted. "Marriage is about love and connection and being together always. That's what I want—solid, steady love. I want kids and a dog and maybe a couple of cats and a regular life."

"Did you think you'd find that with James?"

The unexpected question made her wince. "No."

He stared at her. "I don't understand. You were engaged to him."

"I know." She shifted so she was sitting cross-legged, facing him. "Okay, I'll tell you but you have to swear to keep it to yourself."

"Who would I tell?"

"Shane. My mother."

"Ah, good point. You have my word."

She thought about the day James had proposed. "He and I were fighting. I had been complaining about your engagement to Rosemary because you wouldn't listen to me. James was frustrated. He said I talked about you all the time and if he didn't know better, he would think that I..."

*Was in love with you.* That was what James had claimed but Nissa wasn't comfortable blurting that out, so she searched for a slightly less embarrassing description.

"He felt I was too involved in your engagement," she amended. "He wanted to know if he mattered at all. I said of course he did. He wanted me to prove it. Then he asked me to marry him."

Desmond frowned. "That's not exactly romantic."

"It wasn't and now, looking back, I can see that even then I wasn't sure if I loved him the right way. I mean I loved him, but not enough to want to spend the rest of my life with him."

At Desmond's look of confusion, she added, "My mom walked in right then. She'd heard him propose and had assumed I said yes. She was thrilled and immediately told my dad and then it was kind of a done deal."

"You never said yes."

"Technically, I didn't. The next day he showed up with a ring and we were engaged."

"But you didn't get married."

"I kept putting off setting a date." For an entire two years, she thought, feeling guilty about how she'd handled the situation. "I told him I wanted to save the down payment for my condo first. He wanted to know why I was so determined to buy a place on my own instead of saving for a place for the two of us."

His dark eyes gave nothing away. "What did you tell him?"

"I didn't have a very good explanation. Eventually he

got tired of waiting for me. He said I either had to pick a date for the wedding or the engagement was off. I gave him back the ring."

"He was a fool," Desmond told her. "He should never have let you go."

"I'm not sure keeping me was an option."

"I'm sorry for my part in it."

She touched his arm. "Don't be. If we hadn't been fighting over you, we would have been fighting over something else. We weren't right for each other. I just wish he'd understood that. I'm afraid I hurt him."

"You're too softhearted."

"That's not possible."

She was going to say more, but just then he leaned over and kissed her. The feel of his mouth on hers had her shifting toward him. He pulled her onto his lap and deepened the kiss. Heat immediately burst to life, making her tingly all over. She wrapped her arms around his neck and kissed him back, enjoying the feel of his tongue against hers and his strong hands moving up and down her back.

When he drew back, she was breathless and hungry.

"I know you can't stay the night," he began. "But maybe you could spare an hour."

Anticipation made her smile. "An hour is very doable."

# Chapter 10

*DESMOND*

The remodel of Marisol's house moved forward relatively smoothly. Desmond received daily updates from Erica, letting him know that the team was sticking to the aggressive schedule. He'd been forced to pay a premium for some of the work to be done so quickly, but the extra money was worth it. He wanted the house done on time.

Late Saturday morning, he took the girls out to see the progress. Nissa was working with Erica, picking out light fixtures and door pulls. While the twins were excited to talk about paint colors and bedding, they lost interest when it came to the details. He'd offered to keep them busy for a few hours. Nissa had looked doubtful but had agreed.

They arrived at the house to find workmen swarming all over the place. The second story was already framed and the new roof was nearly finished.

"Good thing it's not raining," Lisandra said as she scrambled out of his car.

"Summer's the best time to replace a roof," he agreed, making sure Rylan made it safely to the sidewalk. They walked in through the open front door and found themselves in the middle of a huge open space.

The kitchen had been gutted and the flooring had been pulled up. All the draperies were gone and shiny new windows replaced the old ones. Several patches covered the walls.

They made their way to the rear of the house. The master was empty, the windows were new and the carpet had been torn up. They could see the framing for the new closet and half bath under the stairs.

"It looks so different," Rylan breathed. "Mom's gonna love it."

They admired the kitchen cabinets stacked together in the center of the garage. Behind them were the new appliances. While the front yard was untouched, the backyard had been torn up. New sprinklers were being installed and most of the old, tired plants had been ripped out. Desmond knew that next week a new covered deck would be installed.

"This is really nice," Lisandra told him. "Thank you for being our fairy godfather."

He chuckled. "You're welcome."

"Can we get our hair cut?" Rylan asked. "It's long enough. We measured."

Desmond held up both hands. "No way. I'm not allowing you to cut your hair while your mom's in the hospital."

"Can we go to the mall?" Lisandra asked. "And then out to lunch?"

He eyed them suspiciously. "You're playing me, aren't you?"

The twins grinned at him, then each took one of his hands.

"It will be fun," Lisandra promised. "We can go to the Lego store. Boys like that."

"I haven't been to the Lego store before," he admitted. "I would like that."

An hour later, they were at the mall. The place was crowded with Saturday shoppers, but the girls stayed close. As promised, they took him to the Lego store where each of them chose something to put together. He promised to help with any of the tough parts, but suspected they would do fine on their own.

They went to the Cheesecake Factory for lunch. The twins sat across from him in their booth, each of them studying the very impressive menu. Once their orders were placed, they turned their attention back to him.

"When are we going to tell Mom about the house?" Rylan asked.

"I don't know. When do you think we should?"

The girls considered the question.

"We should wait until the very end," Lisandra said firmly. "So it's a super big surprise. Like on TV. So we shouldn't say anything now."

He looked at Rylan. "Do you agree?"

"Yes, but it's hard not to tell her when she asks what we've been doing. Plus I know the house is going to make her really happy."

"I hope it makes you happy, too."

The girls looked at each other.

"It will," Lisandra said. "We love our new rooms. They're so big and they're going to be beautiful and we can have friends over and everything. Plus the new kitchen. We can make cookies and help with dinner."

He didn't mention that Erica was replacing their mismatched cookware and dishes with new.

"I'm ready to go home," Rylan said quietly, then looked at him. "Does that make you mad? Your house is nice, but we miss our mom."

"It doesn't make me mad, at all. You've been through a lot. First waiting for her to get a transplant, then the surgery itself. That's a lot to deal with."

Their server came and took their orders. When she'd left, Desmond smiled at them.

"I have liked getting to know you both. You've been really brave and strong."

"Mom told us we had to be," Lisandra admitted. "Sometimes it's hard. But Nissa's always there and now you're part of the family, too."

Rylan nodded. "It's like having a dad, only different." She brightened. "Like a stepdad."

The unexpected turn in the conversation made him uncomfortable. He'd never been good with people thanking him and hearing he was a part of the family was so much worse. Not that he didn't want to be—he liked the twins and enjoyed having them around. It was more that he wasn't sure he was up to the responsibility. What if he let them down?

"Are you Nissa's boyfriend?" Rylan asked.

"I, ah…"

Lisandra leaned toward him, her long hair swinging across the table. "Mom needs a boyfriend, so if you know any good ones, you should tell her."

Desmond did his best not to bolt for the exit. "You want your mom to start dating?"

The twins nodded. "It's time," Rylan told him. "We still miss our dad and we'll always love him, but our mom needs someone in her life. Someone who will love her and bring her flowers and make us all feel safe."

He was in over his head, he thought grimly, not sure

what to say. Asking for a moment to text Nissa for help seemed inappropriate.

"You don't feel safe now?" he asked instead.

The twins exchanged a glance.

"We do," Lisandra told him. "Most of the time. Not while Mommy was sick, though. That was hard. We cried a lot. Now she's getting better so we can think about other stuff, like a stepdad."

Why him? Why couldn't they talk to Nissa about this? Or their camp counselor?

"Your mom might not be ready to start dating," he said with a shrug. "Hearts are tricky things. With being sick and then having the surgery, she's probably not ready to think about getting a boyfriend right this second."

"That makes sense," Rylan said. "But if you see a good one, you'll tell us?"

"I will."

He would also be letting Nissa know about the conversation so she could tell him if he'd screwed up anywhere and she had to step in and repair the damage. He liked the girls a lot—they were brave and smart and funny. But taking them on full-time? He couldn't imagine it. Yet Nissa had been willing to do just that. If Marisol hadn't pulled through the surgery, Nissa would be their legal guardian. He had no idea how she was so brave. He couldn't have done it, not for anyone. Kids needed so much, including someone who could love them back. And that person wasn't him.

*NISSA*

Nissa tried not to bounce in the front seat of Desmond's car, despite her growing excitement.

"I can't believe they're releasing her today," she said.

"I knew it was going to be this week, but it's a day earlier than we'd thought. She's got to be so happy to be taking the next step of getting out of the hospital."

She looked at him. "Thank you again for letting her stay with you and arranging everything."

"Happy to help."

They'd gotten a call the previous evening from one of the nurses on Marisol's team. She was progressing so well, they were ready to release her, assuming things were ready at home. Nissa knew that the hospital bed and table were in place, along with a comfortable recliner.

She'd confirmed that he was good with the earlier date, then had let the nurse know they were ready to welcome Marisol home.

"Did we do the right thing with the girls?" she asked anxiously. They'd made the decision not to tell them what was happening. Just in case something went wrong and Marisol had to go back to the hospital.

"They'll find out when they get home," he said easily. "Let them have the fun day at camp. There will be plenty of happiness to go around tonight."

"You're right." She leaned back against the seat. "My stomach is fluttering."

"You're a good friend."

"So are you. This isn't what you signed up for when you agreed to let me stay with you for a couple of months. Desmond, are you all right with the invasion? First me, then the twins, now Marisol and her nurses. There will be a physical therapist in and out, and my parents are planning to show up in a couple of weeks. It's too much."

He glanced at her. "Do you hear me complaining?"

"No, but—"

"Let it go. The house is happy with everyone running around and so am I."

"I want to believe you."

"Then you should."

He parked in the hospital lot.

"Once we know she's ready, I'll pull around front," he said.

Nissa nodded and got out.

"Let's go get Marisol so she can get started on the rest of her life."

Most of her transplant team showed up to say goodbye. Marisol hugged everyone, then waved as she was wheeled to the elevator. Nissa stayed close.

"Both your nurses have been in touch with the team," Nissa told her. "They understand where you are in your recovery and what the medication regimen is going to be. Once you're feeling better, we'll cut back on the nursing hours, but there's no rush on that."

Marisol grabbed her hand. "You're a good friend and I love you."

"I love you, too."

They left the elevator and moved toward the wide glass doors. Nissa could see Desmond was already in place, the car parked and the doors open.

As they went outside, Marisol raised her face toward the sun and took a deep breath. "This feels good," she said with a smile. "I'm a blessed woman."

Despite the recent surgery and her time in the hospital, she looked good. Her color was coming back and the faint gray cast to her skin had faded, along with the dark circles under her eyes. She was starting to look healthy again.

The drive home was uneventful. Marisol couldn't believe her beautiful room with the view of the Sound and a private patio. There were comfy chairs for her to rest in and the stone deck was smooth enough that she could use her wheelchair if she wanted.

"My goal is to get up and around as quickly as possible," she said. "I'm looking forward to my physical therapy. It's the only way to get strong again. I need to be in fighting shape to start my life!"

"We'll get you there."

Nissa and Marisol's nurse got her settled in bed. Nissa unpacked all her things, then sat in the chair next to her bed.

"The girls are going to totally freak when they find out you're here."

Marisol grabbed her hand. "Thank you so much for taking care of them."

"Of course. I was happy to step in while you had your little miracle."

Marisol yawned. "Sadly a car ride is too much excitement for me, but later, I want to talk to you. How are things with you and Desmond? Was he okay having the girls around? Anything going on that I should know about?"

Nissa thought about how she and Desmond were now much more intimate than they had been and the giant remodel waiting for Marisol, but kept quiet about it all. Her friend needed to rest.

"There's really not that much to share, but we'll definitely talk later." She kissed her cheek. "I promise."

"Good." Marisol released her hand and closed her eyes, then immediately opened them again. "Go back to work. I know you quit to take care of the girls. I'm here now, so you can go get another temporary job to help with your Italy fund."

Nissa hesitated. "I'm not sure I should."

"You absolutely need to. I already feel guilty about the

time you've spent with them when you could have been earning money. Believe me, if I had any extra money, I would insist you take it."

"Marisol, no! I'd never accept it. You're my friend. I love you and the girls and I'm honored to have been able to help. You have to believe me."

"I'll believe you when you go back to work, then."

"You're kind of bossy."

"You know it."

Nissa smiled and rose to her feet. "I'll call the temp agency right now."

"Good." Marisol closed her eyes. "See you in a bit."

"Yes, you will."

*NISSA*

Thirty minutes into her shift, Nissa knew she'd made a horrible mistake. Sign dancing was way harder than it looked. Her arms ached and her back wasn't happy, but the worst part of her job was the unsolicited advice people yelled as they drove by. Apparently a large percentage of drivers felt she lacked rhythm, which was kind of insulting.

She'd thought the job would be easy—it was over a four-hour shift and the pay was decent. She'd watched several videos online to get an idea of how to twirl, dip and spin the sign. Again, it looked soooo much easier than it actually was.

Part of the problem was she kind of did lack the whole rhythm thing, and she wasn't much of a dancer. The big chicken tail she had to wear didn't help, either. It kept messing with her balance.

A pickup truck slowed and the driver's window rolled down.

"You gotta work it, lady. Put some heart into it."

The driver continued through the intersection.

She supposed being told to put some heart into it was better than other, less civilized comments she'd heard. Thank goodness she only had a half hour left on her shift. Once she got home and her body stopped hurting, she was going to have to reconsider her employment options. She was starting to think she wasn't sign-dancing material.

She tried to focus on the upbeat music playing in her earbuds, but it wasn't enough to distract her from the horn honks and the searing pain in her shoulders and upper arms. No one had warned her that the sign got really heavy in hour three. Obviously she was in much worse shape than she'd realized. She should take advantage of living in Desmond's house and use the gym there. Hadn't he mentioned it was in the basement somewhere? And while she wasn't a fan of basements in general, she had a feeling his was much less creepy than most.

"Nissa?"

She turned toward the sound of her name and saw a dark blue sedan pulling up to her corner.

"Nissa, is that you?"

She lowered the sign and walked toward the car, only to come to a stop when she saw James step out onto the sidewalk.

No, she thought, fighting humiliation. No, no, no! She was not just about to come face-to-face with her former fiancé while she was sign dancing and wearing a chicken tail.

He, of course, looked perfectly normal in suit pants and a white shirt with a blue tie. The sleeves were rolled up to his elbows—always a good look on a guy.

James was tall and handsome, with soft brown hair that was forever falling onto his forehead, and glasses that made him look smart and kind.

He moved toward her, smiling. "What are you doing?"

She held up the sign. "Working one of my crazy summer jobs."

"As a sign dancer?"

"I just started today." She rotated her free arm, feeling the pain shooting into her back. "It might not have been my best decision, but I'm—"

"Saving for something," he said, finishing her sentence. "Of course you are. You're the best saver I know." He studied her. "How are you? You look good."

"So do you."

He did. Not in any way that tempted her, but he seemed… happy.

She smiled. "Of course you're lacking a chicken tail, so obviously I look better."

He grinned. "Yeah, that tail is really something. How are you doing?"

"Good. On summer break, so that's fun, although I'm missing my kids. I've started counting down to the start of school. Oh, Marisol has a new kidney. She got a donor a couple of weeks ago and came through the surgery great. She's home recovering right now."

She and James had been together when she'd found out about her friend's illness.

"That's great news. I'm glad for her. How are the girls?"

"Excellent. They've been so brave. They're ten now."

"No, really? They're growing up fast."

They stared at each other. Nissa wondered how they'd reached the awkward part of the conversation so quickly. At one point she and James had been planning their lives together.

"What's new with you?" she asked.

His expression turned sheepish. "I'm engaged."

"What? You are? That's amazing. Who is she? When's the wedding?" She dropped the sign, flung herself at him and hugged him. "James, I'm so happy for you."

He hugged her. "I'm happy for me, too. Her name is Cami and she's an office manager for a doctor. She's beautiful and funny and sweet and I'm crazy about her." He stepped back. "You were right about us, Nissa. When you said we weren't in love enough. I fought you on that, but you were right."

He shrugged. "What happened with you and me was kind of driven by circumstances. I always felt Desmond was between us in a way. Like he had a piece of your heart that no one else could touch. I wanted all of you."

"I'm sorry you felt that way," she said, careful not to say it wasn't true. Because sometimes she thought the same thing. That Desmond had always had a piece of her heart, and if that was true, she wasn't sure what it said about her future happiness with someone else.

"I shouldn't have proposed the way I did," he continued. "And I shouldn't have just gone along with everything when your mom overheard it. You never wanted to marry me."

"I'm sorry, James."

His smile returned. "I'm not. Because of what happened, I found Cami. It's what you talked about. The rightness of it. She and I get along much better than you and I ever did. And when she walks in the room, I know I'm the luckiest man alive."

Envy collected in her belly, but she ignored it. She was determined to be the kind of person she should be rather than pouting like a spoiled brat because James had found his one true love and she hadn't.

"Good for you," she said. "I'm so happy for you."

"Me, too. You seeing anyone?"

"No," she said, thinking she wasn't sure what she and Desmond were doing but traditional dating in no way described it. "Things are kind of crazy right now."

"You'll get there," James said kindly. "I know you will."

He reached for her again, hugging her. She returned the embrace, delighted for him and the knowledge that she didn't have to feel guilty about their relationship anymore.

Still hanging on to him, she drew back enough to see his face.

"So when's the big day? Tell me everything."

*DESMOND*

Desmond stared at Nissa as she smiled at James. Even from across the intersection, he could feel their connection. He'd left work to come by, not liking the idea of her dancing on a street corner. Not that he was checking up on her so much as making sure she was all right. But instead of finding her dancing around and shaking her chicken tail, he'd discovered her talking to James, of all people. Worse, she'd been hugging James, and he didn't know what the hell that meant.

The light turned green and he drove through, trying not to watch as Nissa laughed at something James said. Desmond returned to his office, planning to get buried in work, but once he got to his desk, he found he couldn't concentrate—not the way he should. Every time he looked at his computer he saw Nissa with James.

He stood and crossed to the window, staring unseeingly at the blue water of the Sound. In the distance were the San Juan islands, with Whidbey and Blackberry Islands the closest. Normally the view got his attention, but not today. All he could see was Nissa smiling up at James.

What had happened? Was it a chance encounter or were they really seeing each other? And if it was the latter, when had they gotten involved in the first place?

His phone buzzed. He walked over to his desk and saw the text was from Shane.

Sorry, man. Should have warned you earlier, but I didn't know things had changed until this morning. Hope you can handle it.

He swore silently. Shane knew? Things were serious enough that Shane knew? How had that happened? She'd told her brother about getting back together with James.

No, Desmond told himself. She wouldn't do that, not without saying something. He and Nissa were sleeping together. Okay, they'd never discussed their relationship or any expectations. Their transition from friends to lovers had been unexpected, and then Marisol's surgery and the arrival of the twins had kept them from talking, but he knew Nissa. She wasn't the kind of person who was involved in more than one relationship at a time.

Except he'd seen her with James himself. He knew that part of it was real. And Shane knew about it, so it was more than his imagination.

He dropped the phone onto his desk and collapsed in his chair. There was only one solution. When he got home, he was going to insist he and Nissa talk. There was no way he was going to waste time speculating on the situation when he didn't have all the facts. It was the logical solution. Until then he would get his mind back on his job.

Which, as it turned out, was much easier said than done.

# Chapter 11

*NISSA*

Nissa didn't consider herself a quitter, but when she returned to the office, she turned in her sign and chicken tail for good. She simply wasn't sign-dancer material. As she made her way to her car, she wondered how long her back and shoulders were going to ache. She'd always assumed her active lifestyle was good enough in the exercise department, but obviously not. She was going to have to start some kind of regular workout. Maybe a little jogging and certainly lifting weights. Her upper body strength was pathetic. And while she was at it, maybe she should look for a dance class. The world at large had not appreciated her moves.

She drove to Desmond's house, working on her plan, but as she pulled into the driveway, all thoughts of exercise and everything else fled when she saw a familiar silver Ford

Explorer parked by the garage. She barely turned off her engine before grabbing her purse and flying into the house.

"Mom? Dad? You're here?"

"In the family room," her mother called.

Nissa raced into the large room and saw her parents sitting on a sofa, Marisol across from them looking happy, with good color and an easy smile.

"Look who turned up this morning," Marisol said with a laugh.

Roberta, Nissa's mother, stood and held open her arms. "I know, I know. We weren't supposed to be here for two weeks, but when you told me Marisol was out of the hospital, I said to your father that I just couldn't wait that long to see her and know she was healing."

Her mother hugged her and kissed her cheek. "Plus, we miss you, little girl."

Nissa laughed. "I think Marisol is the real draw, but I'm glad to have you here." She hugged her father. "Does Desmond know you've arrived?"

"Shane said he would text him." Roberta smiled. "That poor man is going to feel invaded."

"There are plenty of bedrooms," Nissa said, squeezing Marisol's shoulder. "The girls are going to be thrilled."

"They are," Marisol agreed. "They should be home from camp any second."

"I'm going to run upstairs and shower," Nissa said. "Don't go anywhere. I want to hear everything that's been going on."

Barry, her father, gave a mock sigh. "You two talk almost every day. How much could you have to share that the other doesn't know?"

"You know it doesn't work that way, Dad," Nissa told him with a grin.

She walked into the kitchen and found Hilde prepping for dinner.

"Your parents are so nice," the housekeeper said when she saw Nissa. "I knew they would be. Your mother said Shane and his girlfriend will be joining everyone for dinner."

Nissa winced. "That's a lot for you to get ready. Let me go take my shower, then I'll come back and help."

Hilde shook her head. "It's an easy menu and I'm happy to do the work. Desmond is alone too much. It's good to have the house full of love."

"I agree," Nissa said, before heading upstairs.

She made quick work of her shower, then blew out her hair and put on crop pants and a sleeveless shirt. Her shoulders and back were still sore, but hopefully that would get better in the next couple of days.

She went back downstairs, hoping Desmond would be home soon. She wanted to see him. Not that there would be any sneaking around tonight, what with her parents just down the hall. Still, she always felt better when he was nearby.

She could hear conversation from the family room. The happy squeals told her the twins were back from camp. They'd always loved Nissa's parents, who acted as surrogate grandparents to the girls.

She'd just started for the family room when she heard the garage door open. She hurried to the mudroom where she waited until Desmond walked into the house. She rushed to him.

"Shane told you, right? You're not totally shocked my parents are here, right? They came early because of Marisol. They wanted to know she was all right. But this really makes for a houseful. Is that okay?"

Instead of smiling at her and reassuring her, he gave her a quizzical expression. "I saw the Explorer so I knew they'd arrived, but Shane didn't tell…" He frowned. "He texted me earlier."

"That's what my mom said. He warned you they were here."

Desmond's mouth tightened. "That wasn't exactly what he said. I thought he was talking about something else."

She studied him, aware of a tension in his body. "What's wrong?" she asked. "There's something. Did you have a bad day at work?"

Before he could answer, her mother joined them.

"Desmond, there you are. I hope you're not too upset that Barry and I have rudely shown up with no warning."

He smiled at her as he hugged her. "Roberta, you're always welcome here. You know that."

"Thank you for saying that, even if you don't mean it." Her mother laughed. "We just couldn't stand to wait to see Marisol. She looks amazing. So much better than anytime in the past couple of years. The surgery was a blessing. I'm praying for the other family, who lost their loved one. Praying they'll find comfort in the organ donation."

She linked arms with him. "Now come join us, Desmond. We've taken over your family room. The twins are telling us about their day and Barry is going on about the Mariners. You know how that man loves his sports."

"I do."

Nissa trailed after them, hoping she was wrong about Desmond. But even as he chuckled and joined in the conversation, she couldn't help thinking there was something lurking in his eyes. Something she couldn't quite define, but knew in her gut the source wasn't anything happy.

## DESMOND

Desmond escaped from the group in the family room long enough to go upstairs and change his clothes. In the few minutes he had to himself, he tried to figure out what was going on. Obviously Shane's text hadn't been about James at all, but had instead been a heads-up about Roberta and Barry showing up a couple of weeks early.

Based on his brief conversation with Hilde, he knew that Shane had also warned her, so another guest room was ready and his housekeeper was hard at work on dinner.

More pressing for him was the question about James and Nissa. Obviously Shane didn't know about them, assuming there was a them. Once again he knew he had to talk to her to get clarity on the situation, but given the crowded house, he wasn't sure how that was going to happen.

He went downstairs in time to answer the doorbell. Shane and Coreen stood on the wide porch. Shane grinned, but Coreen looked a little apprehensive.

"You got my text?" Shane asked. "I wanted to let you know you were being invaded."

"I did. And having your parents here isn't a problem."

"You say that now, dude," Shane teased. "Wait until they decide they never want to leave."

"I'd be okay with that."

He liked Roberta and Barry and in the past couple of weeks, he'd discovered he liked having people in his house. Nissa, most of all, but everyone else was welcome, too. After years of solitude, he enjoyed the conversation, the shrieks of the girls playing.

He greeted Coreen, then said, "There are a lot of people. The good news is you won't be the center of attention."

Coreen shot him a grateful look. "Thanks for saying that. I hope it's true."

Shane pulled her close and kissed the top of her head. "She can be shy. What can I say? She's charming."

As they walked toward the family room, Shane released Coreen. "You'll want to stay out of the line of fire for the next few minutes," he said quickly, before raising his voice and calling, "Do I hear my best girls?"

There was a heartbeat of silence followed by yells of, "Uncle Shane? Is that you?"

The twins raced into the foyer and flung themselves at him. Shane managed to pull them both up into his arms and squeezed them tight while giving them kisses on the cheek.

"You're so big! When did you get so big? How old are you now? Five?"

"Uncle Shane, you know we're ten," Lisandra said with a laugh.

"One day we're going to be too big to pick up and then what?" Rylan asked.

"You'll always be my best girls."

They all walked into the family room. While Shane introduced Coreen to his parents, Desmond pulled one of the sofas back a little so he could drag in a few club chairs scattered around the room. Nissa helped, tugging a small side table close.

"If you keep having this much company, you're going to have to reconfigure your family room," she teased, smiling at him.

Her expression was open and affectionate. There wasn't any guilt, no hint of her keeping secrets. But the knot in his gut said he still wasn't sure about what he'd seen.

"Who wants a drink?" he asked when there was comfortable seating for everyone.

"Do we get something fun?" Rylan asked.

Nissa headed for the kitchen. "I'm sure we can find something good for you." She glanced at Desmond. "I'll have whatever you make for my mom and Coreen."

He poured scotch for Shane and got a beer for Barry, then got out vodka, cranberry juice and the lavender simple syrup Hilde had left in the small bar refrigerator.

Nissa returned with glasses of watermelon lemonade for the girls.

"Dinner is going to be spectacular," she announced, handing the girls their drinks. "Caprese skewers to start, then pulled pork tacos with guacamole, and rice."

Lisandra rubbed her stomach. "I can't wait. I'm hungry."

"Me, too," Nissa told her, moving toward the bar. "Lavender cosmopolitans. Very fancy."

"Only the best for my ladies."

As he poured ingredients into the shaker, he felt her lightly brush his arm. Just a quick touch, to connect them. Once again he looked into her eyes and saw nothing there but happy affection. So what the hell had been going on earlier?

Once everyone had their drinks, they all took their seats. Hilde brought out a couple of bowls of tortilla chips with regular salsa and pineapple salsa.

Roberta took a chip and scooped up pineapple salsa, then took a bite.

"That's delicious," she said before turning to Coreen. "So, dear, how long have you and Shane been going out? And where did you meet?" She glanced at her son. "Some people keep their personal life far too quiet for my taste."

Coreen blushed and ducked her head. "We, ah, met at the hospital where I work."

Shane put his arm around her. "I'd seen her a few times

but she was always so busy. I couldn't figure out how to approach her. Then I saw her at the Starbucks, so I waited until they called her name and I reached for her coffee at the same time."

Roberta pressed a hand to her chest. "That's so romantic. Was it love at first sight?"

Coreen blushed harder. Desmond saw Nissa straighten, her expression sympathetic.

"So I had an interesting day," she said, holding up her drink. "Maybe interesting is the wrong word."

"What happened?" Shane asked quickly in what Desmond would guess was an attempt to distract his mother from grilling Coreen.

"It turns out I'm a terrible sign dancer."

"A what?" her father asked.

Nissa laughed. "Sign dancer. You know, those people who wear a costume, hold a sign and dance on street corners."

Roberta looked concerned. "Nissa, we love you so much but you don't have much rhythm. Why would you be a sign dancer?"

"Just a temporary job, Mom. But you're right. I was terrible at it, plus it's really hard to hold a sign like that for hours and hours. I kept getting all kinds of comments." She grinned. "Some of them weren't very helpful. Even though I did my best, it wasn't a good fit for me, so I quit. I'll find something else. It's just for a few weeks, until school starts."

Desmond listened intently, waiting to see if she would say what else had happened while she was sign dancing.

"I would have loved to have seen that," Shane said.

"Oh, you would have just mocked me and driven on." She picked up her drink, then put it down. "But I did get to talk to someone really unexpected. James saw me and stopped to talk for a few minutes."

Her parents looked at her. Shane's brows drew together and Marisol tensed.

"James?" Marisol asked. "What did he want?"

Her protective tone told Desmond that Nissa hadn't said anything about James to her best friend. That had to be good news.

Nissa waved. "It was fine. Don't worry. I'm glad we got to speak. He wanted to let me know that he's found someone special and they're engaged. Her name is Cami and he seems really happy."

Her mother didn't look convinced. "Anything else?"

"Nothing." Nissa smiled. "I was happy for him and relieved. I always felt guilty about not wanting to set a date for the wedding when we were engaged."

"It was a sign," Roberta said firmly. "You weren't thrilled to be getting married. I was so sad when you broke up but it's obviously been for the best."

"That's what I said," Nissa told her. "I'm glad James and I got the chance to talk about what happened. I was happy to see him and to hear about Cami. They're getting married in about six weeks and going to Tahiti for their honeymoon."

"Tahiti?" Barry shuddered. "That's a long flight."

Roberta patted his leg. "For you, dear. Some people don't mind flying."

"I don't want to go anywhere I can't get to by car or boat," Barry grumbled. "Planes fall out of the sky."

"Ignore him," Roberta told Coreen. "Barry's a retired ferry captain. Given the choice, he would always go by boat. The only way I got him to Europe was to drive to New York and take a cruise ship across." She sighed happily. "But it was the trip of a lifetime. Every day was magical."

Conversation shifted to other forms of transportation and who had been to Europe, but Desmond kept his attention on Nissa. She was listening and laughing, completely relaxed and happy. As if nothing had happened. Which it apparently had not.

He'd been an idiot, worrying about Nissa seeing James. While they had never defined their relationship, she wasn't the type to be with two men at once. He knew that because he knew her. So why had he worried? Why had he immediately thought the worst? And perhaps most important of all, if he was so sure he didn't have a heart, then why had he cared in the first place?

*NISSA*

Nissa enjoyed visiting with her parents and having Shane and Coreen hang out. Everyone stayed up too late, not wanting the fun evening to end. It was after midnight when they called it a night.

While Coreen was saying good-night to Barry and Roberta, Nissa pulled her brother aside.

"You seem happy," she told him, careful to keep her voice low. "Things still going well?"

"They are." He glanced over his head toward his date. "She's pretty amazing."

"She is. So no more games?"

He looked at her. "No more games," he agreed. "I kind of freaked out that night. I feel dumb about what happened."

"What did happen? Who hurt you so badly that you weren't willing to trust Coreen?"

"The who doesn't matter, but obviously someone betrayed me. It was a long time ago, Nissa. I was in medical school."

"Why didn't I know?"

He touched her cheek. "Because I was played for a fool and I didn't want to talk about it. I promised myself I would never trust again. But that's a lonely way to live."

"You men and your absolutes. What is it with that?"

He grinned. "We're quirky."

Coreen joined them along with Nissa and Shane's parents, cutting off any further chance for conversation.

Once Shane and Coreen had left, Nissa made sure her parents were settled. When she checked on the twins, they were already in bed and asleep. She hesitated outside of Desmond's room, but then didn't knock or go inside, instead retreating to her own. Sneaking around didn't seem like a safe bet with the house so full. Getting caught with Desmond would raise a lot of questions that she wasn't prepared to answer which, sadly, meant sleeping alone.

On the bright side, whatever had been bothering him when he'd first gotten home had worked itself out. By dinner, he was his normal friendly, charming self. Plus, now she understood her brother a little better. She was grateful he was letting himself fall for Coreen.

She took off her makeup and brushed her teeth, then crawled into bed, grateful that she could sleep in if she wanted.

She drifted off instantly only to be awakened two hours later by the night nurse shaking her.

Nissa sat up and stared at her. "What's wrong?" she asked, knowing there was no good reason for Marisol's nurse to be in her room at—she glanced at the clock on her nightstand—two thirty in the morning.

"I'm sorry to bother you, but Marisol is running a fever. It came on quickly and it's still climbing. I'm worried her body is rejecting the transplant. I've called her doctor and he wants her to come to the hospital right away."

Nissa was already moving. She got out of bed and flipped on the overhead light.

"Is she responsive?" she asked, ignoring the fear that exploded inside of her. She had to stay focused. She could give in to terror later.

"She's getting less so. I'm about to call an ambulance."

"Don't. At this time of night, we can get her there faster by driving her ourselves. Go wake Desmond, please. Tell him we need to take her to the hospital. I'll be downstairs in two minutes."

Nissa bolted for the bathroom. She splashed water on her face, then quickly pulled on clothes. She grabbed her purse before hurrying to her parents' room. Her mother woke up as soon as she entered.

"What's wrong?" Roberta asked.

Nissa quickly explained about Marisol. Her mother got up at once, pulling a robe on over her nightgown.

"Are you going to tell the girls?"

Nissa shook her head. "Let's get her to the hospital first and find out what's happening. If it's bad…" Nissa swallowed against rising dread. "If it's serious and she's in danger, I'll call and you can bring the girls. It might be nothing." She prayed it was nothing, but didn't know if that was possible.

"I'll stay in touch," she promised. "Try to go back to sleep."

"I'll sleep later," her mother said firmly. "I'll go watch TV in your room. That's where the girls will go if one of them wakes up. I don't want them to find your room empty."

Her father had slept through the entire conversation. As they moved into the hall, her mother hugged her.

"I'll be praying," Roberta promised.

Nissa hugged her before running down the stairs. Desmond was already there, carrying a nearly unconscious Marisol out to the car. Nissa followed. The nurse was on the phone, letting the hospital know they were on their way.

Desmond drove quickly, obeying the stoplights, but speeding where he could. The lack of traffic meant the trip was made in half the usual time. Nissa watched her phone, waiting for instructions from the nurse. When the screen lit up, she read the message.

"We're to drive up to the emergency entrance," she said. "Don't park. A team will be waiting."

She glanced over her shoulder. Marisol was still in the back seat. Breathing, but her eyes were closed, and she seemed unaware of what was happening.

"I'm scared," she whispered, fighting tears.

"Me, too."

She saw the hospital up ahead. Desmond followed the signs to the ER and drove directly to the entrance. As soon as he stopped the car, medical personnel swarmed the vehicle. Marisol was lifted onto a gurney and rushed into the hospital. Desmond pulled away to go park the car.

Nissa waited for him just inside the entrance. When he walked inside, she rushed to him and let him pull her close. They hung on to each other.

"We can't lose her now," she whispered against his shirt. "We just can't. She's come through the surgery. She's getting better. I don't want her to die."

"Me, either. Let's wait and see what the doctor says. Maybe it's no big deal."

She looked at him and saw the worry in his dark eyes. "You don't believe that."

"I'm trying to convince myself."

They settled in the waiting room. A few patients came and went. An ambulance pulled up with victims of a car crash. It was close to five when Marisol's doctor walked out looking exhausted but relieved. Nissa gripped Desmond's hand, telling herself not to read too much into his expression.

He sat down across from them and exhaled. "She's all right. There's no sign of rejection, which is our biggest worry. She has a virus—nothing you or I would find difficult to shake, but it's more challenging for her. She was a little dehydrated and she admitted she's been doing too much over the past few days…"

He smiled. "Something about a party going past midnight?"

Nissa winced. "That's my fault. My parents came into town and my brother and his girlfriend came over and we stayed up late."

"She can't do that right now. She needs her rest and plenty of fluids. I made that clear to her. This was a scare, but she'll be fine. She just has to be careful and take things easy for a few more weeks."

Nissa nodded, tears filling her eyes. "I'm so sorry. I didn't mean to hurt her."

Desmond put his arm around her. "It wasn't your fault."

"It's my family. I should have thought to tell her to go to bed."

Marisol's doctor shook his head. "That's on her. She needs to read her own body's signals. She was feeling good and did too much. It happens, Nissa. It's not on you. But everyone needs to keep her condition in mind."

He stood. "You can see her if you want. We're going to keep her on fluids another hour or so and then she'll be ready to go home. Where she needs to rest." His voice was kind but stern.

"We'll make sure that happens," Nissa said. "Thank you so much."

"You're welcome. We all care about Marisol. She's been through a lot. No way we're going to lose her now."

When he'd left, Marisol texted her mother to let her know what was happening. They agreed to let the girls sleep in. Hopefully by the time they were up, Marisol would be back home and asleep in her own bed. Seeing her there would make them less scared when they heard what had happened.

They made their way back to Marisol's room. An IV dripped steadily, nearly in time with the up-and-down line of her heartbeat on the monitor. As they moved close to the bed, Marisol opened her eyes and smiled at them.

"Hey, you two. Sorry if I scared you."

Nissa squeezed her hand. "You nearly gave me a heart attack. I'm glad you're feeling better."

"Me, too. I guess I got too wild last night." She grimaced. "I should have listened. My nurse came and told me I was doing too much at least three or four times, but I ignored her." She glanced around the small room. "Next time I'll do what she says. I don't want to end up here again."

"Next time she needs to force you to obey her," Nissa said firmly.

"I'm not sure dragging me across the living room is in her contract." She looked at Desmond. "You carried me to the car, didn't you?"

He nodded. "Happy to do it."

"I really do intend to start walking everywhere on my own."

Desmond moved around the bed and took her other hand.

"You're fine. You have a virus and you need to rest and stay hydrated. Those are easy things to do. In a couple of days, you'll feel better. It was a cheap lesson."

"You're right. I'm lucky that's all it was." She smiled at them both. "Thank you for being my friends."

"We love you," Nissa said. "We'll always be here for you."

"I know that. It gives me strength." She cleared her throat. "All right, you two. You look terrible. I'm going to be about an hour. Why don't you get some breakfast and then come back? By then they'll be ready to release me and we can all go home and get some sleep."

"You sure you'll be all right?" Nissa asked.

Marisol waved to the door. "I'm fine. Go eat and have coffee. You'll feel better."

Nissa looked at Desmond, who nodded.

"Text me if you need anything," Nissa said. "We won't be long."

Marisol said she would and they left. In the hallway, Desmond put his arm around her.

"You doing okay?" he asked.

"Yes. She looks good and hearing from the doctor was very reassuring."

"You know what would make you feel even better? There's a fast-food place down the street. We could go get a breakfast sandwich."

She smiled at him. "You know I love a breakfast sandwich."

He chuckled. "Yes, I do."

# Chapter 12

*DESMOND*

Desmond was relieved when life quickly returned to normal. Marisol got plenty of rest and fluids and within a couple of days was feeling much better. The twins had been spared the worst of the ordeal. As everyone had hoped, they slept until after their mom was back home. They'd been told what had happened, but seeing their mom right there, looking better than she had, helped them deal with the information.

Late Saturday morning, he stepped onto the deck to join Marisol. Nissa and her parents had taken the girls to the Woodland Park Zoo for the day.

He set down two glasses of lemonade and sat in the lounge chair next to her. The temperature was perfect—midseventies, with only a few clouds in the sky. They were out of the sun and Marisol had a blanket across her legs.

"You're spoiling me," she said, picking up the glass and smiling at him. "Don't stop. I really like it. I'm just pointing out the fact that I've noticed."

"You're feeling better."

"I am. I'm seeing my doctor on Monday, but I'm sure he's going to tell me the virus is gone. I'm sleeping through the night and my energy is coming back." Her humor faded. "Sorry I scared everyone. I'm being more careful."

"Screwing up is how we learn."

"I know I learned my lesson. I'm going to do everything my doctor tells me. I don't want another trip to the ER. I'm also ready to go home. Not that you haven't been a welcoming host."

"You can stay as long as you'd like, but I do understand wanting to be in your own place. Just a few more days."

Not only because she needed to recover, but there was still work to do at the house. The kitchen was finished, as was the upstairs addition, but they were waiting on a few fixtures and a couple of pieces of furniture. The plan was for Marisol and the girls to go home next Friday.

"I'm ready to be there now, but it makes sense to wait. I need to be a little stronger to manage on my own."

"You'll have a night nurse for the first couple of weeks."

She looked at him. "Desmond, no. That's ridiculous. You've already paid for too much. I don't need a nurse."

He picked up his lemonade and smiled at her. "Too bad. One's going to be there regardless."

"You're a difficult man."

"So I've been told."

"And a generous one. You've been very good to me and I don't know why."

"I'm in a position where I can help. It makes me happy to do so. Besides, we're friends."

"We are." She smiled. "Thank you. Being here rather than in a skilled nursing facility has been a blessing. And you've been so kind to the girls."

"Not being kind," he told her. "I like them. They're fun to be with. We're all going out on the water tomorrow, and Captain Pete is going to start teaching them how to drive the boat."

"That's a terrifying thought," she said with a laugh. "They are relaxed and happy. That makes my heart glad. They've been so worried about me when they should just be worried about being kids."

She frowned. "Oh, I've been meaning to ask. What's the deal with my house?"

The unexpected question surprised him. He wasn't sure what she meant or how to answer.

"I don't know what you're talking about," he said, hoping he didn't sound evasive.

"I heard the girls mention something about a new sofa and how they hoped it was comfortable. You did something, didn't you?"

He swore silently, not sure how much she knew or how to misdirect her. Perhaps some version of the truth was the easiest solution.

"I bought you a new sofa. It's a sectional with a built-in chaise. I thought you'd need something like that to help you recover. That way you don't have to go lie down every time you want to rest for a few minutes. You can sit with the twins on the sofa and be a part of things."

Tears filled her eyes. "That's so thoughtful. You're a good, good man."

"It's a sofa, Marisol. Nothing to get too excited about."

He thought she might push back on that, but she surprised him by saying, "You don't like me saying you're kind or nice, do you?"

"I, ah, it makes me uncomfortable."

"Because you're supposed to be a badass?"

He chuckled. "I have never thought of myself as a badass."

"You know what I mean. Macho and tough."

"I lean more toward contained and self-sufficient."

She sipped her drink. "Given that, how are you dealing with the house invasion? It's hard to be contained with two ten-year-old girls running around, not to mention nursing staff and Nissa's parents."

"I like having people around."

"Then why don't you make that happen on a permanent basis?"

He smiled. "Invite random strangers to move in? That would be awkward for all of us."

"Not strangers. Regular people. Why aren't you married?"

The blunt question surprised him. "I was. It didn't work out."

"Yes, I know about Rosemary the Awful." She smiled. "That's what Nissa and I call her. It's the marrying for money thing. I don't get it. There's an old saying that if you marry for money, you're going to earn every dollar. Marriage is supposed to be about loving someone."

"The way you loved your husband?" he asked, then shrugged. "Nissa mentioned you lost him a few years ago."

"Yes, like I loved him. He was a good man and we were devastated by the loss. If I hadn't had my girls, I'm not sure I would have been able to go on. But they needed me so I had to at least pretend to keep it all together. After a while, I wasn't pretending anymore, but I still miss him every day."

He believed that. Life had been hard for her—first losing her husband, then fearing for her life as she waited for a transplant. He didn't want to think about what might have happened if one hadn't come through.

"I don't miss Rosemary," he said.

"I should hope not. But that doesn't answer the question. Why haven't you fallen in love with someone else and gotten married again?"

Not a question he wanted to answer.

"I'm not the marrying kind."

She pointed at her face. "Do I look like I believe that?"

"That doesn't mean it's not true."

"What about having children? Don't you need heirs?"

He did—for the company. His parents had certainly been on him about that during their brief visit. And he wanted children in his life. Having the twins around had only confirmed that.

"I don't have a heart."

He hadn't meant to say that, but somehow the words had slipped out. He expected Marisol to roll her eyes or tease him, but she didn't. Instead she nodded slowly.

"So that's the problem?" she asked. "You don't think you're capable of love?"

"Yes. I keep people at a distance. I've done it all my life. It's what I know. Rosemary married me for the lifestyle and the money, but I've realized I married her because she checked all the boxes. I never loved her. I don't get close to anyone."

Marisol laughed. "Uh-huh. Sure. We'll ignore how you feel about Shane and his parents, but I can't not mention Nissa. You care about her. Plus, there's all that fun stuff you're doing behind closed doors. I'm guessing there's not a lot of distance there."

"How did you know?"

"I might be recovering from surgery, but I still have eyes. I've seen the way you two look at each other. There's some naked business going on for sure. So not that kind of distance?"

"I'm talking emotionally."

"You're telling me you don't let people get close and you don't want to be close to them. But you're right there with my girls and you're letting me stay here for as long as I need. Not to mention Nissa and her parents. You've opened your home to all of us, and you're taking care of everyone. Those are not the actions of a man who doesn't have a heart. Are you in love with her?"

There was no need to ask who the "her" was. "No."

"Just like that? You don't want to think about your answer first?"

"I don't love her. I can't. She needs a good man in her life, someone who can love her with his entire heart. I can't do that and I won't hurt her."

He thought Marisol might push back, but instead she simply smiled at him. "That's a whole lot of worry for a man who claims he can't care."

"I'm not a monster."

"No, you're not, but you are hiding from the truth, Desmond. You care more than you think and I can't help but wonder if that's the real problem."

She was wrong, he knew that, but saying that wouldn't convince her. The easier path was to let her believe what she would and let the rest take care of itself.

## NISSA

Nissa pressed her hand to her stomach. Nerves had been growing for the past couple of days and now they were just plain acting out. For the past two days, she'd been questioning the decision to surprise Marisol with a remodeled house. They hadn't ever talked to her about it—what if she didn't want a bunch of strangers messing with her stuff? What if she hated everything they'd done? What if she blamed Nissa for all of it and stopped being her friend? And perhaps most important of all, why hadn't she thought about all this *before* the work had begun rather than after?

"It seemed like a good idea at the time," she whispered to herself as she finished getting dressed. The twins were excited and had been bursting to tell their mom what had happened. Her parents had been to the house a couple of times already and were thrilled with the changes. But none of that mattered if Marisol wasn't pleased.

Nissa went downstairs. Her parents and Desmond were sitting at the table, finishing breakfast. She took one look at the food on their plates and felt her stomach lurch. No way she was eating anything, she thought, pouring herself a cup of coffee.

"Are you all right?" her mother asked, eyeing her. "You're really pale."

"I'm fine. Just a little apprehensive about what's going to happen today."

"Second thoughts?" her father asked. "You should have considered them before you ripped off her garage roof and built a second story."

"Barry!" Roberta glared at him. "That doesn't help."

"I'm teasing." Her dad flashed her a grin. "The house is great."

Nissa glanced toward the doorway. "Where's Marisol?"

"She's already eaten," Desmond told her. "She's getting in an early therapy appointment before we load up the cars and take her home. She can't hear us."

"Good." Nissa sat at the table, doing her best to avoid looking at any of the food. "We've kept the secret this long. I don't want to ruin that now." Besides, if Marisol was going to yell at her, Nissa would prefer to put that off, as well.

"She's going to love it," Desmond told her. "The twins were very clear about what she likes and doesn't like. We didn't push back on that."

"I'm less concerned about elements of the design than the entire project." She drew in a breath. "There's no going back now. It's done." She tried to smile. "Thank you for taking the day off work."

When the time came, they would load up his car and her parents' Explorer to transport everyone to the house.

"I wouldn't miss the big reveal," he said, his voice teasing.

"I hope it goes okay," she murmured, also hoping that at the end of the day, she and Marisol were still friends.

Two hours later, everyone pitched in to carry suitcases, clothes and toys to the two vehicles.

"We've accumulated way too much stuff," Marisol said, watching the loading process from a bench in the foyer.

She'd been instructed not to carry anything heavier than a throw pillow, and Roberta was keeping an eye on her to make sure she complied. Between Nissa, Desmond, Barry and the twins, it didn't take too many trips to load the two vehicles.

"I'll bring over anything you've forgotten," Nissa told her friend.

Marisol studied her. "You feeling all right?"

Nissa faked a smile. "Never better."

"You don't look right."

"It's my stomach," Nissa admitted, thinking it was the

truth. The writhing was still there, and getting more violent by the second. "Maybe something I ate."

"You sure you're up to this move?" her friend asked. "You can stay behind if you'd like. It's not as if you haven't seen my house before."

Nissa managed a slight laugh. "I want to get you settled at home." Once that happened, however the situation played out, she would feel better…or possibly worse. Either way, there would be a change.

Marisol slowly walked to Desmond's car. The twins got in the back and Nissa rode with her parents. As they'd discussed in advance, Barry left first with Desmond fake forgetting something in the house so his car arrived about five minutes later. That way Barry, Roberta and Nissa could be waiting in the driveway and not miss Marisol's reaction.

Nissa did her best not to throw herself across the back seat and beg to be put out on the side of the road. They'd done what they'd done and if Marisol was upset, she was going to have to deal with it like a grown-up.

Quicker than she would have liked, they arrived. As they got out of the SUV, she looked at the house and thought whatever happened, the place looked fantastic.

The railings had been replaced, and the front door was now a deep blue. The new windows gleamed in the perfect summer morning. The old shrubs had been replaced with bright green hedges and the grass had been fertilized and reseeded. The second story over the garage blended seamlessly with the house's roofline.

Her mother hugged her. "You did a good thing for your friend."

"It was mostly Desmond. He paid for it all and his team did the work."

"However it happened, she's going to be delighted."

Desmond's car pulled into the driveway. Nissa kept her gaze on Marisol, waiting for the moment her friend noticed all the changes. But Marisol was busy unfastening her seat belt. She climbed out of the car.

"I can't believe I'm finally home," she said with a laugh, turning around to help the girls out of the back seat. "Not that you weren't a gracious host, Desmond, but home is where—"

She stopped talking and stared at her house, first at the porch, then at the lawn and hedges.

"What did you do?"

The twins each grabbed a hand.

"Mom, you have to come see! Everything's different and it's so beautiful." Rylan practically danced in place.

Lisandra pulled her toward the porch. "It's like on TV!"

Marisol looked from the house to Nissa and Desmond. "What did you two do?"

"It wasn't just them," Lisandra told her. "It was us and Erica and everybody."

"Who's Erica?"

"Perhaps not the point," Desmond said drily, and walked to the front door. "Shall we?"

He opened the front door, then stepped back. The girls led Marisol inside the house. Nissa followed, hoping it was going to go well.

Light spilled in through the new windows, and the hard-wood floors gleamed. There was a big overstuffed sectional in a pretty blue-green fabric and lots of pillows and a few throws. A couple of club chairs provided additional seating, and on the wall above the refurbished fireplace was a new big-screen TV.

To the right was the dining room. Marisol's big table was still there, but a new hutch filled the long wall, providing tons of storage. New linens and dishes were in place on the table and on the living room side of the huge two-level island.

Marisol pressed a hand to her mouth as tears filled her eyes. "You redid my house."

Nissa bit her bottom lip, not sure if that was an informational statement, a complaint or happiness.

"It's so beautiful," Marisol added, turning to Nissa. "Everyone did this for me?"

"Who else?" Nissa asked, moving close and hugging her. "You're not mad?"

"Mad? You've made this my dream house. I can't believe you did this."

She held out her arm to Desmond, who joined them in a three-way hug. The twins danced impatiently around them.

"There's more," Rylan said eagerly. "You have to see it all."

They went into the kitchen where Marisol ran her hands along the stunning quartz countertops. The girls pointed out the new appliances and the pull-out drawers in the lower cabinets. Marisol admired the new pots and pans and agreed she liked the dishes very much.

They went out back. New outdoor furniture sat on the new covered deck. A stainless steel barbecue stood in one corner and all the plants had been replaced with hardy, regional favorites.

Returning to the house, the twins took her down the short hall that had led to the two bedrooms. Marisol came to a stop as she pointed.

"There are stairs." She spun to face Desmond. "You gave me a second story?"

He grinned. "You didn't notice it when we drove in?"

"No. I was too busy looking at the yard and my front

door." She pressed a hand to her chest, as if trying to catch her breath. "No wonder my physical therapist has been pushing me to work on my thigh strength. She knew about the stairs."

Nissa opened the door to the half bath tucked under the stairs, then pointed to the door leading to the master.

"You might want to check that out."

Marisol began to cry again when she saw her refurbished bedroom. The furniture was all new, as was the area rug over the hardwood floors. The girls showed her the remodeled bathroom and the new walk-in closet.

Nissa's throat tightened a little as she watched her friend's happy reaction.

"I was terrified she would be mad," she admitted to her mother.

"You did everything with love. She knows that."

They all returned to the base of the stairs. Desmond picked up Marisol and carried her to the second story. Once on the landing, he put her down.

"I'm going to get busy building up my strength," she said firmly. "I want to be able to get up here myself."

"You will," he told her, nodding at the two doors. "Take a look."

The girls' rooms were mirror images of each other. There was a big window, one overlooking the front of the house and the other overlooking the back. A comfy chair was tucked in the corner by the window and a desk was next to it. Bookshelves stood on either side of the closet door.

Against the north wall stood the loft-style bunk bed, with a full bed on the bottom, a built-in chest of drawers at one end and a twin bed up top. Rylan had done her room in shades of blue, while Lisandra had chosen purple as her main color.

Barry looked around. "Good use of space," he said. "Quality materials."

"It's lovely," Roberta added.

Marisol nodded, wiping away tears. "I can't take it all in." She looked at Desmond. "I don't know how to thank you."

"Be happy and healthy. That's all I need."

"This is so wonderful," Marisol murmured. "It's like a dream."

"Except it's real!" Rylan shouted.

Everyone laughed, then started downstairs. Marisol insisted on going on her own. She went slowly, but made it to the main floor.

"Let's unload the car," Nissa said.

Marisol pointed to the stairs. "I'm going to start practicing while you do that. Five stairs today, six tomorrow, until I can make it upstairs on my own." She laughed. "My physical therapist will be so proud of me."

Nissa wanted to say she didn't have to push herself, but knew that Marisol would want to be able to reach her kids in case something happened.

They brought in all the suitcases and tote bags. It didn't take long to get it all put away. By then Marisol had finished her five stairs and was exploring the kitchen. Nissa showed her where the manuals had been stashed.

"You'll need to learn how to use your fancy new appliances," Nissa teased.

"I will. And I'm having you both over for dinner, just as soon as I'm comfortable standing long enough to cook."

Desmond leaned against the island. "Don't worry about that. I set you up with a meal delivery service through the end of September." He glanced at his watch. "You should already have an email from them telling you about the program. Nissa and Roberta picked out the first two nights' choices, but after that, you can choose from a wide selection."

"So much for not having a heart," Marisol said before hugging him.

Marisol looked at Nissa. "Thank you. It's the most wonderful surprise ever."

Nissa looked around at the beautiful new house and knew her friend was right. Not because of the things that had been purchased, but because of the love that would always live here.

# *Chapter 13*

A few days after the fantastic house reveal, Nissa found herself feeling oddly restless. She had no idea of the cause, but she couldn't shake the sense of something being not right. She liked her temp job—she was working in a small bakery where the owner's daughter had to unexpectedly go on bed rest for the last two months of her pregnancy. Nissa was learning all about decorating cakes and cookies, not to mention working the front counter. The money was good, the owners warm and friendly. So her problem wasn't the job.

And it wasn't missing Marisol. She'd already been over to the house several times. The twins were settling in to their new rooms and her friend could make it up the stairs on her own. Everyone was happy and healthy, so they weren't what was making her feel almost itchy inside her skin.

She wandered through Desmond's large house, as if

she'd left the answer in one of the beautiful rooms, but there was nothing to be found. Finally, she went into her parents' room. Her father was out golfing with Shane while her mother packed them up for their trip back home.

Nissa knocked once on the open door before walking in and sitting in the chair in the corner. Her mother looked up from the pair of jeans she was folding.

"You're troubled," Roberta said, putting down the jeans and settling on the bed. "What's wrong?"

"I don't know. I can't seem to settle."

Her mother nodded. "I know the feeling. Restlessness with a vague sense of dread."

"That describes it, but I don't know the cause, so I can't fix it. Maybe I should start a regular exercise program."

Her mother laughed. "While that would be healthy, I doubt it will solve the problem."

"I know, but it might be a distraction. I just can't figure out what's wrong. I'm ready for the new school year and I'm excited about my students. The temp job is fun and interesting. I'm saving plenty of money for my trip next summer. My renters have sent a couple of emails saying what a good time they're having. Marisol's doing great, you and Dad are healthy. So what's my problem?"

"You really don't know?"

Nissa shook her head. "Do you?"

"You're in love with Desmond."

Nissa half rose out of the chair, only to collapse back on the seat. Her mind went completely blank as she momentarily forgot how to breathe. It was as if her entire being had to reboot.

"What? No. In love with him? I can't be."

Her mother watched her with that "I'm going to be patient because I love my child, but wow is she dumb" look.

"Why would you think that?" Nissa asked. "It's ridiculous. We're friends."

Friends who slept together, Nissa thought, wondering if her mother had figured out what was going on the way Marisol had. She wasn't about to ask. Discussing love was one thing, but sex wasn't a topic she wanted to share with her mother.

"Nissa, you've had feelings for Desmond since you were fourteen years old. At first I was sure it was just a crush, but they never fully went away. Now you've been living with him and spending time with him. It makes sense that what you'd had before would grow into something bigger."

"It doesn't make sense to me," she admitted, emotionally poking at her heart to try to find out what was happening in there. In love with Desmond. Could she be? Did she want to be?

"I like him a lot," she said slowly. "He's kind and funny and generous and we have fun together. He's a really great guy. I trust him. But that's not love."

She looked at her mother. "His parents hate me."

"No, they don't."

"His mother does. Evelyn told me that I wouldn't in any way be an asset to him and that he would break my heart." She frowned, trying to remember the exact words. "Okay, maybe not that, but it wasn't good."

"Desmond isn't close to his family. He's not going to care what they think."

"He might care a little. Mom, I can't be in love with him. It would ruin everything."

"How so?"

"He doesn't think he has a heart."

She expected her mother to scoff at the suggestion, but Roberta surprised her by nodding slowly.

"I can see how he would think that. Of course not having a heart isn't the problem. It's that his heart has been broken over and over again."

Nissa raised her eyebrows. "Since when? He's never been dumped. He's the one who ended things with Rosemary."

"Yes, but why? It's not as if he suddenly decided he didn't want to be married to her. Desmond figured out why she'd married him. He saw she was only in it for the money and not for the man. How do you think that made him feel?"

She'd never thought about the situation from that perspective. "He would have been upset." Hurt, certainly. She wasn't sure that he'd ever truly loved Rosemary, but regardless, the end of the marriage would have been difficult.

"Let's go back a little in time," her mother said. "What about all those young women who tried to get his attention because he was rich and not because of who he was?"

"You know about that?"

"It doesn't take a genius to know it happened over and over again. Before them, he was dealing with his parents. They weren't exactly nurturing when it came to their son. He was raised by a series of nannies until he was sent off to boarding school. Who loved him then? It might be easier for Desmond to tell you he doesn't have a heart, but the truth is, his has been shattered and he's afraid to trust."

Nissa tried to take it all in. Her mother's words made sense, she thought. It wasn't about him loving so much as him trusting himself enough to risk caring about someone. About her.

That last thought surprised her. Was that the problem? She didn't know how he felt about her? Oh, she knew he liked her and they were good friends, but none of that would upset her. The real problem was much bigger because there was so much potential for everything to go wrong. Staying friends with Desmond would be easy but falling in love with him would change everything.

"Loving him isn't a good idea," Nissa said, still easing into acceptance.

"Oh, I don't know. You've waited for him for a long time. Don't you think you're due for a little happiness?"

"You're ignoring everything we just talked about. Desmond can't or won't love me back."

"That's what he said," her mother told her. "Let's wait and see what he does. A man's actions often have a lot more significance. He didn't help Marisol just because he's a nice guy, he helped her because he wanted to do something nice for your friend. You're at the center of everything that's happened."

Nissa wished that were true, but she was having a hard time believing Desmond saw her as more than a friend he liked in his bed. As for her feelings...

She thought about how she felt when she was around him and how he'd always been the best man she'd ever known. She thought about his kindness and thoughtfulness, how he made her laugh and how she knew, when something bad happened, that he would be there. She thought about how she wanted to take care of him and be there for him, so he would know, no matter what, that she had his back.

"Oh, no," she whispered. "I'm in love with him."

Her mother smiled. "I'm just so proud. Now what are you going to do?"

"You mean after I throw up?"

"Yes, after that."

"I'm going to tell him." She had no idea where she would get the courage, but she was going to do it. She had to. After everything that had happened to him, Desmond needed to know she loved him fully and truly, with no reservations. Not for the money or anything else, but just for himself.

*NISSA*

Nissa's parents left an hour later. She spent the rest of the morning trying to get her courage together, only to fail a thousand times. It was close to three when she finally got herself downstairs and heading for his office. She was going to do it, she told herself. She was going to confess her feelings. With a little luck he would sweep her into his arms and tell her he felt exactly the same, then whip out an engagement ring and get down on one knee.

Okay, that last bit was unlikely—most men didn't keep a diamond ring in a spare drawer, just in case they needed to get engaged. But having him tell her he loved her back would be great. Or if not that, then at least maybe he could mention he liked her a lot and wanted to go out with her and be in a serious relationship that would lead to love. Any other option was going to be difficult to handle, but she was determined to be mature. Or at least not beg.

She saw his office door stood open. That had to be a good sign, she told herself, not that she could remember a time when it had been closed, but still. She would take all the good signs she could get. She wiped her suddenly sweaty hands on her shorts, then cleared her throat and walked directly into his office.

"Hey, Desmond," she began, only to come to a stop when she saw his expression.

He didn't look happy to see her as he stared at her from across his desk. In fact he looked kind of scrunchy, as if he was upset about something. No, not upset. That was the wrong word. So was mad, but she immediately knew there was a problem.

"What happened?" she asked. "Is everything all right?"

Emotion flashed in his eyes, but was gone before she could figure out what he was thinking.

"I don't want you to be in love with me."

"Wh-what?"

She managed to speak that single word before all her air rushed out and the room began to spin. The only way she stayed upright was by grabbing the back of the visitor's chair and telling herself to breathe.

"I don't want you to be in love with me," he repeated, his voice firm and completely lacking in any feeling. He might as well have been telling her that quarterly taxes were due in two weeks.

"But how did you—"

"I overheard you talking to your mother earlier."

Heat rushed to her face as humiliation swept through her. "You were there?"

"In the hall. I was coming to tell your mother she had several things in the family room. I didn't want her to forget them."

He sounded so formal, she thought as her chest tightened and her eyes burned. So distant. Gone was the man who had laughed with her, kissed her with so much passion and made every day just a little bit brighter.

"I apologize for eavesdropping."

"I hardly think that part matters." She forced herself to meet his cold gaze. "I take it you don't return my feelings."

He opened a desk drawer. For a single second, she thought he would pull out an engagement ring. Only she knew that was wrong and when she saw what he held in his hand, she felt her heart shatter into a thousand pieces.

He stood and placed a hotel room key on the desk be-tween them.

"I've made arrangements for you to stay there for the rest of the summer. It's a suite, so you'll have plenty of room. You can check in now. Hilde will bring you your things."

He was getting rid of her, she thought, ready to go numb anytime now. Because hurting as much as she did was going to be unendurable in the long term.

"You want me gone that quickly," she said, knowing he could hear the pain in her voice.

"You're welcome to pack them yourself," he said stiffly. "I thought you'd prefer to go as soon as possible."

She looked from him to the key and back. "I'm not run-ning from you, Desmond. I'm sorry you feel the way you do about what's happening. Regardless, I think the hotel room is a little dramatic. You could have just said you weren't in-terested in me that way. I would have gotten the message."

She took a step back. "I won't need the hotel room, al-though the offer is generous. I'll get my things together and be out of here within the hour." She looked at him, memo-rizing his handsome face and wondering how long it would be before she saw him smile again.

"I appreciate what a gracious host you've been. Until today, the summer has been amazing and you've been a big part of that. What we had together..." She tried to col-lect her thoughts. The pain was still there, but it was con-tained by a new confidence and a certainty that she'd done nothing wrong.

"I've been in love with you a long time," she said softly. "Probably from the night of my prom. The feelings got bur-ied, but they were still there. James wasn't wrong when he accused me of being too involved in your life, but I couldn't see what he was talking about."

She walked to the door, then turned back. "I'm not sure what you're afraid of. I get that you'd have trouble believing someone loved you, what with your parents and learning Rosemary was only in it for the money. But what about you and Shane? You've been friends for years. You love each other." She managed a slight smile. "In a very manly way, of course."

He didn't react to her words and her smile faded.

"My parents have been devoted to you," she continued. "And even ignoring my recent declaration, I've been very consistent about being your friend. I'm sad after all this time, you still won't trust us."

She paused, only to realize that there was nothing left to say. She'd been honest and had told him everything, and none of it had changed his mind.

"Goodbye, Desmond."

## DESMOND

Desmond saw the determination in Nissa's eyes and the strength in her body. She'd laid herself bare to him and she wasn't afraid. No matter what happened, she was going to be honest to the end and accept the consequences. He wasn't sure he'd known anyone that brave.

"I don't want to hurt you," he said.

"Too late."

"This is short term. If we stayed together, I would destroy you. Everything seems fine now, but eventually you'd figure out that I'm just like my parents. That I don't have a heart and that even if I wanted to love you back, I don't know how. That would eat away at you, over time. I don't want that for you."

She smiled at him. "Really? This is for my own good? It's not like you to lie, Desmond."

"I'm telling the truth. You don't know who I am. Not deep down inside."

"I know you better than you think. I'm going to tell you something that is going to make you angry and you're not going to have anywhere to put that anger, which will frustrate you. You'll want to protect me, even more than you do now, and that will only make this situation more difficult for both of us."

"I doubt it can be much more difficult," he told her.

"Want to bet?" She raised a shoulder. "Remember the Chihuly event? How your parents came?"

"Yes." Although he had no idea how they related to any of this.

"Your mother and I had a little chat. She told me that I shouldn't get my hopes up. That you wouldn't be interested in me because I didn't bring anything to the table, so to speak. I couldn't help you in business or socially and I didn't belong in your world."

Anger erupted. "She had no right to say that."

"But say it, she did."

The anger grew and bubbled, making him want— He swore quietly. He wanted to protect her, just like she'd said. He was furious and frustrated and he wanted to take on the world, only that wouldn't do any good.

"You guessing what would happen doesn't change anything," he told her.

"I didn't guess." She drew in a breath. "You're wrong about all of it, Desmond. You're missing the entire point. If you were like your parents, if you were as heartless as you claim, why would my loving you make a difference in what was happening between us? Me loving you should only enhance the lovemaking, so in theory, you should be taking advantage of me. So what if I get my heart broken? It doesn't matter to you. Heartless people aren't moved by that sort of thing. But you do care about me, perhaps more than you want to. I'm not the problem. You are."

She shook her head. "I didn't see that before now, but it's true. You find it easy to write a check because that's safe. But giving of yourself, that's the hard thing. Because when you give, you take a risk that you'll be rejected. The only way to know love is to give love, and that's what you've been unable to do. It's not about the money or having a heart. It's about being brave enough to risk it all."

She raised her head and squared her shoulders. "I love you, Desmond, but you're right. I don't belong here. Not anymore. I need to be with someone who's willing to fight for me. I want a man who loves me back, heart and soul. I want to be someone's everything and you can't give me that."

She pressed her lips together. He thought she might say more, but instead she turned and walked out of his office. He stood where he was, listening to her move around his house, then she walked to the stairs. He would guess she'd collected her things and now she was going to pack them and leave.

She was right to go and she was right to tell him she didn't belong to him anymore. She was right about all of it.

Unable to watch her walk away, he left his office and got in his car. When he started driving, he had no destination in mind, but he knew he wouldn't go home for a long, long time.

*NISSA*

Nissa drove to Marisol's house. She'd texted to say she was on her way and her friend had said she would be waiting. She was strong and brave right up until Marisol opened the front door and said, "The girls are at a friend's house, so I'm hoping you're here to see me."

Nissa started to say that was fine, but burst into tears instead. Marisol pulled her close.

"It's that man, isn't it? I knew he was going to be trouble. Want me to call around and see if I can find someone to beat him up? I might know a few people."

Despite everything, Nissa managed a smile. "You don't know anyone to beat him up."

"Not personally, but you'd be amazed what you can find on the internet."

They went inside. Nissa was together enough to look around the house and admire how great it all looked before collapsing on the sofa.

"I'm such a fool."

"No," her friend said firmly sitting next to her. "It's not wrong to love someone. He's single, you're single and you were sleeping together. Love is kind of the next step."

"Not for him."

"Then he's the fool, not you. Tell me what happened."

Nissa explained about the conversation with her mother and her decision to suck it up and confess her feelings.

"Only he already knew," she said. "He'd overheard the whole thing and when I went into his office, he handed me a key for a hotel room. He expected me to stay there instead of with him."

"Like I said, a fool."

Nissa felt her eyes fill with tears. "I'm trying to be brave, but it hurts."

"Of course it does. He broke your heart. You know you belong together, but he's not willing to see that. At least not yet."

"You can't still have hope."

"Of course I do. I'm a romantic at heart."

Nissa supposed that was because she'd loved once. Marisol knew what it was like to give her heart and get someone else's in return. She knew about the ups and downs of any relationship and how good it felt to find the right person, even if that love didn't last as long as she'd hoped.

"Do you ever think about falling in love again?" she asked.

Marisol surprised her by shrugging. "Sometimes. At first I couldn't imagine it. But since the surgery, I'm ready to start imagining the possibility, if that makes sense. He'd have to be very special to step into our lives, but I'm hoping someone like that is out there."

Nissa squeezed her hand. "I hope so, too."

She said the words automatically, but what she was thinking was how incredibly brave her friend was. To have lost her husband, faced a terminal illness, then to have gone through transplant surgery and come out the other side still believing in love was amazing.

"I want to be like you when I grow up," she said.

Marisol laughed. "Aim higher. So what's the plan? Would you like to stay here? The girls could move into one room and you could take the other."

"Thank you but I'm going to head over the mountains. I've already texted my mom and she said they're fine with me staying there until my renters leave in a couple of weeks. I'll use the time to clear my head and get ready for the upcoming school year."

"A wise plan. What about Desmond?"

Nissa didn't want to think about him, but it was impossible. Between the ache in her heart and the fact that she already missed him, there was very little else on her mind.

"He knows how I feel," she said firmly. "What happens next is up to him."

# Chapter 14

*DESMOND*

The house echoed with silence. The Monday after Nissa had left him, Hilde had told him she needed to take a couple of weeks off to visit her family in Estonia. Desmond had bought her a business-class ticket and had assured her that he would survive in her absence. She'd arranged for someone to come in a couple of days a week to do basic cleaning and make sure there was food in the refrigerator. Not that he was eating. Or sleeping.

When he was at the office, he couldn't focus on what was happening and when he was home, he wandered from room to room, listening to the echoes of conversations he and Nissa had had on nearly every topic imaginable.

He stood by her small patch of the garden, filled with random plants and flowers that had been on sale the day they'd gone to Fred Meyer. He waited by the hidden bar in the family room, hoping to hear her footsteps on the stairs so he could fix her a cocktail. He searched for items she might have left behind—a book, a scarf, a pen—anything that he would have to return, as an excuse to go see her. Only he knew he couldn't barge into her life. She'd gotten away from him and wasn't that the point of all this? To let her go live her normal life with a normal man who would love her and cherish her and give her everything she could ever want?

Thursday afternoon, he traced a now-familiar route through the house. He'd yet to find anything she'd forgotten and the quiet no longer comforted him as it had before she'd moved into his house. Instead the rooms echoed with memories and laughter, with words he couldn't quite hear and conversations that seemed to mock him.

He hadn't eaten in days and he couldn't sleep. He would guess both of those conditions were making the situation worse. The solution to the problem seemed just out of reach. Every time he thought he was about to understand all of it, his mind went blank and he started walking the house again.

He'd just returned to the kitchen, more because he'd heard it called the heart of the home than because he was the least bit hungry, when his cell phone rang. He answered it without glancing at the screen, then wished he hadn't when he heard his mother's voice.

"I called the office, Desmond. They said you weren't in. Are you ill?"

"I'm fine, Mother, how are you?"

"I'm doing well. I have some excellent news. Do you remember Pedra Holder? She was such a beautiful girl. A brilliant pianist. She married far too young and of course the relationship failed. But she's divorced now, with two darling little boys. I had lunch with her mother and she said Pedra was asking about you."

"I have no idea who she is."

"Of course you do. You met her several times when you were home on holiday. She's tall and blonde. Oh, I'll text you a picture. You'll recognize her at once. My point is, she's back in San Francisco. I'll get you her contact information. You can fly down and take her to dinner."

"Are you setting me up?"

"Why are you asking that question? Isn't it obvious? I've been patient long enough, Desmond. You decided Rosemary wasn't the one, and all this time later, you're still single. We need heirs and Pedra is a proven breeder. We'll have to be extra careful on the prenup, of course. Make sure the two children she has won't inherit anything, but that's why we have lawyers."

He sat on the bottom stair, not sure which was more shocking. His mother referring to the daughter of a friend as a "breeder" or the assumption that he was single.

"I'm not going to be going out with Pedra or anyone else, so you don't have to worry about the lawyers."

"Why ever not? Don't tell me you're actually involved with that Nissa girl. You can't be. I'll admit she's pretty enough, but Desmond, do be sensible. She's simply not one of us. She would never fit into your lifestyle. She doesn't have the education or the socialization."

His mother lowered her voice. "If you're worried about giving up great sex, then keep her on the side. Marry Pedra to have children and use Nissa for sex. You won't be the first man to solve a problem that way."

He wondered if she thought she was being helpful. He knew she wouldn't be deliberately trying to provoke him. That wasn't her way. For his mother, life was all about position and power and making sure she achieved her desired outcome.

"Have you ever been in love?" he asked. "Truly, romantically, wildly in love?"

He expected her to immediately say no and tell him love was a nonsense word invented by sad people with sad lives as a way to get through the day. But instead she sighed.

"Yes. Once. Many years ago. One of my tutors. He was just out of college, so your grandfather didn't want to hire him, but he was a brilliant mathematician and it was only for a few weeks. His name was Marcus."

He was as surprised by the wistful tone to her voice as by what she was saying.

"You were lovers?"

"Why do men always ask about sex? Fine, yes, we were lovers, but for me it was about so much more than that. Marcus was a wonderful man with a brilliant mind. He went on to join NASA where he worked on the Space Station."

"But you didn't marry him."

"What?" Her voice sharpened. "Marry him? A penniless mathematician with no family, no prospects? And do what? Live in the suburbs in a tract home, popping out babies every three years?" She laughed. "That was not my dream at all."

"But you loved him."

"Yes, and I enjoyed our time together. Then I married your father."

"It was more of a merger than a marriage."

"Call it what you will. We've been together forty years and we've provided a very comfortable life for you. Now it's your turn to do your duty. Have children, Desmond. I've been very patient and it's past time. Call Pedra and set up something, then fly down to San Francisco and dazzle her. If things go as I hope, you can move the company back to where it belongs. Your father and I are getting tired of flying to Seattle. The weather is always miserable there."

He glanced out at the warm, sunny day. "You're right, Mother."

"About the weather, or about the rest of it?"

"About everything. It is time I married and had children. It's time for me to do a lot of things."

"Excellent. I'll text you her contact information right now. And a picture of her boys. They're charming, but as I said, they won't be inheriting. All right, Desmond. Good luck. I'll speak with you soon."

She hung up and seconds later, the contact information was delivered, along with a couple of pictures of two smiling little boys.

He ignored both as he tried to process the fact that his mother had once fallen in love. He wouldn't have thought her capable. But apparently it had happened, not that she'd let her feelings stop her from moving forward with her life. Marcus had touched her heart, but there was no way he was getting his hands on her life or her bank account.

So she *could* love, but she'd chosen not to. Duty came first. Duty and money. He supposed if he were to ask his father the same question, he would get a similar answer. For all he knew, there was a woman somewhere, his father's true love, kept in a lovely apartment. Cherished but never seen in public. It was like something out of a nineteenth-century novel.

He didn't want that, he thought. He didn't want to marry for duty and produce heirs. He didn't want to get in touch with Pedra and fly down to San Francisco to take her out. He wanted to be with Nissa. He wanted a house full of family and friends. He wanted kids running around and a messy garden with plants bought on sale. He wanted Nissa smiling at him, touching him, telling him she loved him. He wanted her so much, he wasn't sure how to survive without her.

But if he went to her and told her that, then what? What happened when she found out that he was—that he was—

"What?" he asked aloud.

What exactly was she supposed to find out? That he could be difficult and moody, that sometimes he got too involved in work? That he wasn't overly fond of his parents, but he tried to be dutiful? That she made everything better and that he'd never once in his life felt about anyone else the way he felt about her?

If he really didn't have a heart, how was it possible to miss her so much? If he didn't love her, why could he so easily see a future with her? If he wasn't a normal person with regular emotions, how could he feel sorry for his parents and the ridiculous choices they'd made?

He stood up and searched through his contacts. When he landed on the right one, he pushed the call button and waited.

"I wondered how long it would take to hear from you," Barry said, his voice a grumble. "You've made my baby girl cry. That's not something a father forgives easily."

"I know. Can you meet me for coffee?"

"You in the area?"

"I'm heading over now."

"It's a six-hour drive, son."

"Not if you charter a plane."

There was a pause before Barry said, "And that's what you're going to do?"

"I am."

"All right, then. After that, we'd best meet for a beer." He gave Desmond the name of a local bar. "See you in a couple of hours."

"I'll be there."

## DESMOND

The bar wasn't much to look at from the outside, or the inside, but Desmond didn't care about that. He glanced around until he saw Barry sitting at a table in the back, a beer in front of him. Desmond paused by the bar and ordered a beer for himself, then walked toward Nissa's father. When the older man looked up and saw him, Barry's expression wasn't welcoming.

"You can't buy your way out of this," Barry told him. "Not with a fancy plane or your big boat. You hurt her. She's been crying since she got here. How do you think that makes us feel? We trusted you, Desmond. We let you into our life and our hearts. We welcomed you and this is how you've repaid us."

Each word was a kick in the gut with a few of them slashing at the heart he'd claimed not to have. As Barry glowered at him, Desmond realized that he'd been more wrong than he'd realized. Shane wasn't taking his calls, and now Barry was looking at him like he'd destroyed something important.

He supposed he had—he'd broken Nissa's heart.

"I'm sorry," he began.

Barry turned away. "I don't want to hear it."

Desmond knew that wasn't true. Barry had agreed to meet him, so he must want to hear something.

"My mother wants me to marry some socialite she knows. Pedra. She already has two boys from a previous marriage, so my mom is concerned about a prenup. The other kids shouldn't inherit any part of the family empire. She pointed out that not only was Pedra a proven breeder—and that's an actual quote—if Nissa was so important to me, I could keep her on the side."

Barry's gaze narrowed. "Don't make me take you down, son. Because I can and I will."

Desmond ignored that. "I asked her if she'd ever been in love. I already knew she didn't love my father. Theirs is a true marriage of convenience. She admitted she had, many years ago, but she wasn't the least bit tempted to stay with the man she loved. She didn't see the purpose."

He looked at Barry. "That's how I was raised. I don't say that as an excuse, but as an explanation. I grew up knowing I had a duty and that the family business was all that mattered. Growing it, being more powerful. I needed to fit in with society." He thought about all those wonderful evenings with Nissa. "How to make a great cocktail. I look good in a suit, I speak four languages, but no one ever bothered to teach me or even show me how to be a good person. No one ever talked about love or respect or treating people with decency. The little I know, I learned from you and Roberta."

"Apparently you forgot the most important lesson of all," Barry told him.

"I didn't forget it, I didn't think it applied to me. I didn't think I had a heart. It never occurred to me I could love anyone, not the way you love Roberta or she loves you. I thought I wasn't capable of those kinds of feelings and because of that, I wanted to protect Nissa from me. If she fell for me, then she would be saddled with a man who could never love her back."

One of the servers put a beer in front of him, then walked away. He moved the glass in a slow circle.

"I told myself I was sending her away for her own good. Better to end things quickly, let her get over me and have a chance at someone better."

"I'm still going to beat the crap out of you," Barry said conversationally. "Just so you know."

"Fair enough." He paused to gather his thoughts. "I was wrong about all of it. About letting her go and thinking it was better for her, about not having a heart, about being incapable of loving. I do have a heart and it's a pile of rubble right now."

He looked at Barry. "I hide behind my money. I write a check instead of getting involved. I keep my distance from people because it's what I know and therefore it's easier. The only place I've ever felt that I could truly be myself was when I was with you and your family. No. Wait. That's not true. I was myself with Nissa. When she was living with me, I was exactly who I was meant to be."

He picked up his beer, then put it down. "I love her. I think I have from the night I took her to her prom. She is an amazing woman and for reasons I don't understand, she loves me back. I don't deserve her or her heart, but she wants me to have both. I'm sorry I hurt her and that I betrayed your trust in me. I want to spend the rest of my life proving myself to both of you, and most importantly to Nissa. And I'd like your permission to ask her to marry me." He paused. "If she'll have me."

Barry took a long swallow of his beer and set down the glass. "No."

Desmond hadn't expected that. He'd thought the older man would lecture him, but the flat-out refusal hit him like a sucker punch.

"You did say you'd take me down," he murmured. "You were right."

"Let me tell you something, Desmond. You've always been like a son to me, but if you want my blessing, I'll only give it on the condition that you grovel before you ask. I mean take full responsibility. No piddly-ass 'I'm sorry if you're upset' crap. Being sorry she's upset doesn't own up to what got her that way in the first place. You need to grovel like you've never groveled before."

"Yes, sir."

Barry threw a few bills on the table. "All right, let's head home. Roberta took Nissa out to the movies. They should be getting back in the next half hour or so. You'll be waiting on the front steps." Barry grinned. "Like a homeless dog."

Desmond would have been happy to wait on the curb, he thought, following the man he hoped would be his future father-in-law outside. The where didn't matter. All that was important was seeing Nissa and telling her how sorry he was and how much he loved her.

## NISSA

"Oh, that movie was so charming," Nissa's mother said with a sigh as they drove back home. "I loved it. Did you like it, dear?"

Nissa faked a smile. "Sure. It was funny."

Or at least the audience had laughed a lot. Nissa hadn't seen the humor in two people thrown together in unexpected circumstances and then falling in love. The romantic comedy had reminded her of what it had been like to be with Desmond, only for her, there hadn't been a happily-ever-after ending. Instead she was heartbroken and he was, well, she didn't know where he was but he wasn't with her.

The pain hadn't faded. She would have thought it would start to get better, but obviously more time needed to pass before that was going to happen. She thought about him constantly. At night, when she managed to fall asleep, she dreamed about him. Every part of her ached for him. She'd lost her appetite and could barely get through the day.

She was giving herself the rest of the week to wallow. On Saturday her tenants were moving out. When they were gone, she would return home and get ready for the upcoming school year. She was going to find a cheap yoga class and take an Italian course. She would hang out with her friends and cook healthy meals and just plain fake it because she knew that after a while, she wouldn't be faking it anymore. She would be healed. Right now that seemed impossible, but she'd seen how strong people could be and she was determined to act just like them.

Exhausted but fairly sure she wouldn't be able to sleep, Nissa leaned back in her seat and closed her eyes. The steady sound of the motor and the movement of the car relaxed her. She opened her eyes when she felt them turn into the driveway. Her mother stopped in front of the garage.

"Would you go around front, Nissa," she said as she got out. "I think I saw a package on the porch when we drove up."

"Sure, Mom."

Nissa slung her handbag over her shoulder and walked around to the front of the house, only to come to a stop when she saw Desmond sitting on the front porch steps. He rose when he saw her.

It was late, nearly ten, and dark. The porch light illuminated the shape of him, but not his expression. She had no idea why he was here or what she was supposed to say to him. The man had broken her heart into so many pieces, she wasn't sure it could ever be whole again and yet she wanted to run to him and hold him. She wanted to feel his body against hers, listen to his voice and tell him how much she loved him and had missed him, which made her the biggest idiot ever born.

"I'm sorry," he said, walking toward her. "I was a fool. Worse, I was cruel and unthinking and I apologize for that, as well."

He stopped in front of her. "Nissa, you are the most warm, giving person I know. You embrace the world and see only the good in people. You are funny and beautiful and there are a thousand reasons why I didn't see what was right in front of me, but I didn't. Until now. I love you. I love you and I'm so sorry for not recognizing that before. I'm sorry I hurt you and I'm sorry for what you've been through. I was totally in the wrong."

She blinked, not able to take it all in. He loved her? He *loved* her?

"What happened?" she asked, not quite able to believe.

"I talked to my mother."

"I know she's not a fan, so she can't be responsible for your change of heart."

He smiled. "She is. She wants me to marry for duty, like she did. I don't want that. I don't want a cold, sterile existence. I want plants on sale and your books everywhere. I want laughter and kids and dogs and a loud, crazy house. I want a life with you. Can you forgive me just enough to let me try to earn my way back into your world?"

Deep inside a tiny spark of hope ignited. It grew and grew until she felt the pain of missing him start to ease.

"Because you love me?" she asked.

"Yes. With all my heart. For always. I love you, Nissa, and I hope you still feel the same way about me."

"I'm not the kind of person to simply fall out of love."

"That's what I was hoping you'd say."

He leaned down and kissed her. At the feel of his mouth

against hers, her heart filled with all the love it had been denied. She flung her arms around him and gave herself over to his kiss and everything it promised.

They stood on the front walkway, wrapped in each other, kissing and whispering their love for several minutes. Then Desmond stepped back and dropped to one knee.

"Nissa Lang, you are the most amazing woman I've ever known. I love you and I promise to love you for the rest of my life. Will you marry me?"

As he spoke, he drew a small ring box out of his jeans front pocket and opened it. Inside was a sparking emerald-cut diamond set in an art deco design.

"I know this isn't traditional, but it reminded me of you," he said. "If you don't like it, I'll get you something else."

She pretended to consider the offer. "Because you couldn't get a diamond solitaire? I just don't know."

He smiled. "Nissa, did you want to answer the question?"

She tugged him to his feet, then stared into his beautiful dark eyes. "Yes, Desmond. I'll marry you. I love you. I want us to be together always."

"And the ring?"

"I love it exactly as it is."

He slid the ring on her finger. It fit perfectly, which she took as a sign.

"I can't believe this is happening," she admitted. "You really came all the way here and you love me."

"I can't believe I almost lost you."

They settled on the porch stairs, his arm around her. "Where do you want to live?"

She looked at him. "We can move into my condo, but you're going to find it a little small."

He smiled at her. "I meant, is the house all right? Do you want to buy something together?"

"I love your house. It's beautiful and big. We can have lots of kids." She grinned. "After we tell my parents, we need to let Hilde know we're engaged."

"And Marisol and the girls, and Shane." He kissed her. "So I was thinking we'd go to Italy for our honeymoon."

"That would be amazing. I'd love that."

His expression turned wary. "Traditionally, the husband pays for the honeymoon. Are you going to be okay with that?"

"Of course."

"Because when I offered to pay for your trip to Italy before, you got really mad at me."

"That was totally different."

He kissed her again. "I'll never understand you."

"I think in about fifty years you'll do just fine."

He grinned at her. "Even if I'm still trying to figure it all out, I know those are going to be the best fifty years of my life."

"Mine, too."

\* \* \* \* \*

# A LITTLE BIT PREGNANT

To my real-life Nicki

# Chapter 1

"Nicki, I'm desperate. You *have* to help me."

Nicole Beauman heard the impassioned plea over her headset. The words gave her a measure of satisfaction, but weren't impressive enough to make her do much more than blink.

"I'm filing my nails, Zane," she said. "Filing my nails and yawning. That's how impressed I am."

Swearing filled her ears. Despite the seven-hundred-plus miles between her and Zane Rankin, the sound was crystal clear. Modern technology was really amazing.

"My butt is hanging in the wind," Zane told her. "Dammit, Nicki, do something."

He wasn't exactly begging, but it was close enough. Sighing softly, she set down her nail file and glanced at the half dozen monitors on the console.

She'd tapped into the impressive security system of the Silicon Valley computer firm Zane was currently trying to break into. Nearly sixty camera positions showed everything from the six entrances to the lobby to the "sensitive" areas. All Nicki has to do was push a couple of buttons to get the view of her choice.

She watched Zane type frantically on a small, portable keyboard that should have unlocked the side door. He knew the sequence of codes to enter, but sometimes these things were tricky, and required a woman's touch.

"Hit clear," she told him.

He nodded, pushing a single key, then waited.

She used her keyboard to reenter the codes. When nothing happened, she used a backdoor entry into the security system and unlocked it from the inside. Zane glanced toward the camera monitoring his position and gave her a thumbs-up.

"You're the best," he murmured.

"You say that now," she told him. "But yesterday you carefully explained to me how you didn't need my help on this job. You said you were perfectly capable of doing it all on your own."

"I am."

"Uh-huh."

She switched camera positions and saw the security guards heading down the main corridor.

"Then you don't need me to tell you that you're about to have a close encounter with your hosts, right?"

Through the grainy security camera she saw Zane freeze. He glanced up and down the long hallway, then ducked into a room. Five seconds later, the security guards turned the corner and walked past the closed door.

"You're clear," she said when they were out of sight. "And if you have this covered, I'm going to head home."

There was a heavy sigh that originated in the northern

California storeroom and made its way to her headset in Seattle.

"What do you want from me?" he asked in resignation.

Nicki grinned at her victory. "Money, but as you're not here to deliver, I'll take an apology."

Zane stepped into the hallway and faced the security camera. "You're the best," he said in a tone of long suffering. "I couldn't do this without you."

She smiled. "You left out the *W* word."

"Wrong. I was wrong. Okay? Now will you get me into the research lab?"

"Of course." She could afford to be gracious in her victory. "It's on the second floor. Take the back stairs and wait on the landing until I give you the all clear."

Five minutes later he was at the door to the research lab. Nicki coaxed the heavy double doors into releasing, then talked Zane through the laser sensors. The safe, hidden in the supply closet, wasn't connected to the main computer system, so she couldn't help with that, but she did temporarily disable the smoke detectors in the lab so the charred smell from the explosion wouldn't set them off.

Zane ducked out of the supply closet and shut the door. Two seconds later there was a *thud-bang* and the door shuddered. He hurried back inside, only to reemerge with a small black box in his hand.

"Got it," he said, slipping the unit into his backpack. "Now get me out of here."

"I should let you get caught, just to teach you a lesson."

He glanced at the camera and grinned. "But you won't."

He was right, she thought as she located the guards. "Okay. Take the north stairs to the main floor. I'll unlock the front door before you get there. Just breeze on through."

When he was safely speeding away from the building,

she reset the security system, cleared the fire alarms and turned them back on, then disconnected from their computer. There was no way to disguise the fact that someone had broken in, but they wouldn't trace the entry back to her. She'd made sure to cover her tracks.

Of course at about nine-fifteen the following morning Zane's partner, Jeff Ritter, was going to review the computer logs for the previous twenty-four hours and find lots of unauthorized searches, entries and activity. To say he would be unamused was putting it mildly. Nicki wondered if there would be an actual explosion of tempers or just fireworks.

"I owe you big time."

Zane's voice came over her headset.

"I know," she told him as she shut down her computer.

He chuckled. "Want me to bring in doughnuts in the morning?"

"That hardly makes up for it, but all right. Don't eat all the glazed this time."

"Promise."

"Ha."

She knew exactly what his doughnut promises meant. She would be lucky to have a glazed crumb to nibble on.

"I'm heading home," she told him.

"Drive safely. And Nicki?"

"Yes?"

"You're the best."

"I know. Night, Zane."

She smiled as she disconnected their call and dropped her headset onto her console.

"I saved you one," Zane said the following morning as he strolled into Nicki's office and placed a glazed doughnut on her desk.

She glanced from it to him and wondered why she'd bothered with coffee. There was no need for caffeine to get her body jump-started—not when she could watch Zane's easy stride and casual smile. The combination always sent her pulse to racing, her blood to boiling and her heart to fluttering. Embarrassing but true.

Being around Zane was nearly as much of a workout as an aerobics class. One of these days she would actually calculate the calorie burn rate. Now if only keeping her crush a secret was a form of strength training, she would be fit enough to kayak around the world.

"What time did you get back last night?" she asked.

"The flight was about ninety minutes. I was sliding into bed shortly before one." He settled on the chair next to her desk and grinned. "Slept like a baby."

"What? No new chickie keeping the sheets warm?"

"Not this week. I need to catch up on my beauty sleep."

Nicki had seen Zane on zero sleep and happened to know he was still way too pretty for her comfort zone. Tall, lean, handsome, with dark hair and deep-set eyes that held too many secrets, he could have made his fortune on TV as the hunk of the month.

He was one of those men women found irresistible. While she prided herself on being unique, in this case she was just one of the crowd. The only difference between her and every other woman mooning over Zane's broad shoulders and high, tight fanny was she kept her foolish dreams to herself. He didn't date women with an IQ larger than their bust measurement and she'd been blessed with plenty of smarts. Unfortunately all the brains in the world didn't seem to be an antidote for his particular brand of charm.

"What about you?" he asked, snagging her cup of coffee and taking a sip. "Did Brad wait up for you?"

She grabbed her mug back. "His name is Boyd and no, I didn't see him last night." She hadn't been seeing much of Boyd at all, lately, but she wasn't going to share that with Zane.

Zane raised his eyebrows. "Why not? All that computer jargon getting boring? Seriously, Nicki, don't you get tired of the guy talking in binary code?"

"Boyd isn't a programmer. He's an electrical engineer who—" She broke off in midsentence and shook her head. "Why do I bother? You make fun of the men in my life because you're embarrassed about the women you date. I mean what about Julie?"

Zane chuckled. "Embarrassed? Julie is a former Miss Apple Festival who is studying very hard to be a dental hygienist."

"Right. She's in year four of a nine-month program."

"Math isn't her thing."

"She's going to clean teeth. How much math could there be? What? She can't count high enough to know how many teeth there actually are in someone's mouth?"

"She's gorgeous."

"She's an idiot. Don't you ever want to have a conversation with these women? I mean when the sex is over for the evening, then what?"

He winked. "I go home and sleep. Besides, when I want to have a conversation with a woman, I come see you."

"How flattering." The good old female best friend, Nicki thought with a combination of chagrin and humor. That was her.

"I'm telling you, Nicki, let go of the smart guy thing," he said. "Find some stud and let him have his way with you."

"No, thanks."

"Why not? You're pretty enough."

"How flattering. Pretty enough? Pretty enough to get a brainless fool who thinks with his biceps? Why would I want to?"

"For the fun."

"I'm into substance, but thanks for the offer."

She would never understand Zane's casual attitude toward the opposite sex. Didn't he want to settle down? But she already knew the answer to that question. In the two years she'd worked for him, she'd never seen Zane get involved with anyone for more than a few weeks. There was always a new airhead on his arm and he didn't seem to care that they were interchangeable.

For her part, she gravitated toward serious men who used their brains. Unfortunately none of them had been appealing enough to get her over her Zane crush. Biceps-Man would be a change, if nothing else.

Oh, like that was going to happen.

"I need to like the guy before I have sex," she said. "Call me old-fashioned, but it's true."

"Fascinating information," Jeff Ritter said as he walked into her office. "Thanks for sharing, but we have more pressing matters."

Nicki winced silently. If she could have picked some part of the conversation for her other boss to overhear, it wouldn't have been that.

Jeff stalked into the glass-enclosed office and slammed the door shut behind him. Nicki braced herself for the explosion while Zane seemed singularly unimpressed. He remained slumped in the chair next to her desk.

"What's up?" he asked.

Jeff tossed him a folder. "What the hell were you thinking? Dammit, Zane, you could have told me what you were going to do."

Zane flipped through the pages of the computer activity report. "You would have told me not to. Technically we're partners and you can't order me around, but you would have tried to convince me it was a bad idea."

Jeff glared at him. "It *was* a bad idea. Do you have any idea how many laws you broke last night?"

Nicki figured she might as well join the fray. "I have the actual count, if you'd like it."

Jeff turned his laserlike stare on her. "You're in enough trouble already."

She sighed. "I know. But just for the breaking and entering, and turning off the security system. And the fire alarms." She considered the number. "Okay, so it was a lot of laws."

Zane shot her a grin. She held in a smile. Jeff wasn't amused.

"I'm glad you two think this is so damn funny, but I don't. Our company has a reputation to uphold. We don't go around breaking the law for our own purposes."

Zane raised his eyebrows. Jeff shoved his hands in his pockets. "Only under extreme circumstances," he amended.

"I was helping out a friend," Zane said.

Jeff's gazed narrowed. "You should have told me what you were going to do."

"I couldn't. If it went bad, I didn't want you or anyone in the company implicated."

"Nicki knew," Jeff said.

"Sure, but she'd never say anything."

Zane's casual acceptance of her loyalty was both gratifying and annoying. She felt like the faithful family retainer…or a favorite dog.

"You could have gotten her in a lot of trouble," Jeff said.

For the first time since swaggering into her office, Zane actually squirmed.

"I couldn't have done it without her," he said.

"That's right," she told Jeff. "Zane's pretty useless."

Now they were both glaring at her. She shrugged.

Jeff started to speak, but Zane cut him off. "My friend had been working two years on the prototype. These guys stole it and he wanted it back. I said I'd help him. I had to, Jeff. I owed him."

Nicki knew a few details about Zane's background. He'd been in the Marines where he'd done a lot of things he didn't talk about. Jeff had the same sort of background. Several years ago the two of them had met up and started the company.

Neither of them talked about their past, nor did they ever sit around telling war stories. But every now and then, something came out. A new piece of information, a whisper of a truth.

It was there now—in the tone of Zane's voice as he said those three words.

*I owed him.*

She didn't know what they meant, but Jeff did. Instead of complaining or continuing the questioning, he simply nodded.

"Next time, run it past me, okay?"

Zane rose and nodded. "Promise."

He walked out of the office.

Nicki watched him go. How had Zane owed the guy? Had he saved his life or something? She knew there was no point in asking. Zane was a master at avoiding topics he didn't want to talk about.

Jeff turned his attention back to her. "You could at least *pretend* to be worried that I'm going to fire you."

"You can't. Not over this. I work for Zane and he needed my help. My job is to provide backup, not to pass judgment on what he's doing."

Jeff sighed. "You're too smart for your own good."

"You like that I'm smart."

"Yeah, well, you're okay. When you're not being a pain."

She grinned. "Is Zane in trouble? Are you going to punish him? Can I watch?"

One corner of Jeff's mouth twitched. "You two deserve each other. I have a meeting with a client. Someone who's going to pay us for protecting him and his family."

"Good luck."

"Thanks."

She turned back to her computer. Zane walked by and stuck his head in her office. "How about lunch? Mexican. You can buy."

"I want Chinese and this one is on you, bucko."

He shook his head. "All right. But only because you're crabby. Brad must not be putting out this week."

"His name is Boyd," she yelled after him.

"Whatever," he called as he headed down the hall.

She considered chasing after him, but then what? It wasn't polite to run down her boss.

Nicki turned in her wheelchair and rolled over to the file cabinet under the window. As she flipped through the folders, she told herself that she simply had to get over her crush and pronto. Boyd was a perfectly nice guy, and if not for her weakness for Zane, she might have fallen in love with him. That was what she wanted—to have one great man in her life, to settle down, get married, do the kid thing.

But until she found a way to get over Zane, she was stuck in limbo—wanting what she couldn't have and having what she didn't want.

\* \* \*

"The Seahawks by three," Zane said over a plate of Kung Pao Beef and rice.

Nicki grinned. "You lead with your chin. You should know better. I'll take those three points, and listen to you whine come Monday morning."

She noted the information on a sheet of paper that listed all the pro football games for the weekend.

Zane knew taking the Seahawks wasn't smart, but he couldn't help rooting for the home team. Nicki had no such loyalty. She studied stats, read the sports section and made her choices based on abilities, injuries and who was on a winning streak. Every now and then she took a team because she liked their uniforms, but not often. What killed him was even when she made her choices on something as stupid as team colors, she often won. They were only two weeks into the regulation season and she was already up by three games.

They didn't bet money. Instead they keep a running total and whoever had the most wins at the end of the season owed the loser a day of slave labor. The previous season he'd had big plans to make her cook, stocking his freezer with homemade dinners. Instead he'd spent nearly eight hours washing and waxing her van. Afterwards, he'd been sore for three days.

"I'm going to have you paint my living room," she said dreamily as she wrote down the rest of their picks. "I'm thinking of a color-wash treatment that's going to take at least three coats of paint."

He shook his head. "Not this time, sweet pea. You're going to be cooking your heart out."

"That's what you said last year. Do we remember what happened instead?"

"I'd rather not."

She grinned. "You've got to start listening to the experts, Zane. They usually know who's going to win the games."

"That's cheating."

"No, that's beating your fanny."

She grinned as she spoke. Laughter danced in her green eyes. He smiled back.

"You're smart for a girl."

She picked up her fork and leaned forward. "You left out pretty. Earlier you said I was pretty enough to get some macho, brainless guy with huge muscles."

He studied her heart-shaped face. With big eyes and a full, sensual mouth, she was more than pretty. Long auburn curls cascaded down her back. Every swaying movement begged a man to run his fingers through them. Put all that on a body that, while not as lush as the women he dated, had all the right curves in exactly the right places and she was a serious contender.

"You're okay," he said.

She laughed. "Wait. I want to pause and savor this moment for as long as possible. The wildly extravagant compliment has gone to my head."

He pointed his fork at her. "Come on, Nicki. You know you're attractive. Half the guys in this place can't take their eyes off you."

"Only half?" She glanced around. "I suppose that's something."

He followed her gaze and saw a couple of businessmen in tailored suits giving her the once-over. There were three college guys in the corner. They practically had their mouths hanging open.

"I rest my case," he said.

"Their attention will last for a long as it takes us to finish our meal and head for the door."

He frowned. "Because of the chair?"

She shrugged. "Well, duh. What do you think?"

"That you're crazy. They're not going to care."

Nicki being in a wheelchair meant that she was faster than him and more likely to run him over if she was annoyed. But it didn't make her any less attractive.

"It doesn't bother Brad," he said.

"Boyd. And you're right. It doesn't. But he's into substance."

"I'm not and it doesn't bother me."

She rolled her eyes. "That's because we're friends. You wouldn't date a woman in a wheelchair."

He considered the statement. "I would if she had really big breasts."

Nicki shook her head. "I don't know if I should thank you or stab you with my knife."

"Technically you work for me. If you tried to stab me it would reflect poorly on your next evaluation."

"You drive me crazy."

He grinned. "I know. Isn't it great?"

When they'd finished lunch and she'd badgered him into paying, he stood and she pushed back from the table. Zane paused to watch the men in the restaurant.

None of them had noticed the sleek wheelchair. Nicki had hers specially made by a guy in California. It was lightweight, made to fit her slender body and more low-profile than most.

The college guys exchanged a look of surprise, shrugged and continued to stare. One of the businessmen turned away, but the other looked as if his eyes were about to fall out. Just as he'd thought. Most of them didn't care.

He followed her into the parking lot. She hit the remote on her key chain, which activated the special motor installed in back. The rear doors of the van opened and a ramp lowered. Nicki rolled onto it and rose to level with the back of the vehicle. While he slid into the passenger side, she secured the back doors and moved in behind the steering wheel. Special grooves locked her chair into place and a custom-built harness acted as a seat belt. She started the engine.

"They were still looking," he said conversationally.

"I'm not," she told him.

"Brad isn't all that."

She sighed. "Boyd, Zane. His name is Boyd. You'll be meeting him in a couple of nights at the Morgans' party. Please try to remember his name by then."

"I'll do my best."

"Who are you bringing? Miss Apple Festival?"

He shrugged. Currently he was between women. Oddly enough, he was in no hurry to find a new one, either. He glanced at Nicki. The two of them had never been uninvolved at the same time. Not that he would ask her out if they were. Nicki was…

He glanced out the window. Nicki was special. She mattered to him and he made it a rule to never get involved with anyone fitting that description. Not again.

# *Chapter 2*

"So the guy says, 'It's only a parrot.'" Rob, one of the burly bodyguards employed by the company laughed as he finished telling his joke.

Nicki rolled her eyes and smiled. Rob loved telling jokes nearly as much as he loved puns. At times conversations with him were physically painful as he went from pun to pun.

"You're not sweating, Nicki," Ted called. "I want to see you sweat."

"Bite me," Nicki yelled back as she picked up the pace on the recumbent bike. Her thigh muscles ached, but in a good way. As for sweat, there was a river of it pouring down her back.

She hated aerobics. Oh sure, they were good for her heart and probably added years to her life, but she loathed them with a cheerful intensity that never faded. Unlike Zane, who thought all forms of physical activity were pure play.

Speaking of which, he chose that moment to stroll into the company gym. The bodyguards called out a greeting. Nicki ignored him because looking at him would spike her blood pressure and set off alarms.

But as he approached, she couldn't resist a quick peek at his long bare legs, the loose gym shorts and cutoff T-shirt that exposed way too much flat, sculpted tummy. The man had a serious body.

She would have accepted that with good grace if she'd been able to study it impersonally. As if he were nothing more than fine art. *Very* fine art. But what she resented most was her visceral reaction to that A set of abs. She *wanted.* Yup, physical cravings set in that made the PMS need for chocolate seem wimpy by comparison.

"Hey," he said as he slumped down into her wheelchair. "You're not sweating."

"That's what I said," Ted told him as he straightened and grabbed a towel. "The girl's loafing."

"The *woman* is busting her butt," Nicki complained.

Zane ignored her. "I called you last night and you were out. How's Brad?"

His hips were narrow enough to allow him to easily fit on her custom seat, but his legs were miles too long. He stretched them out in front of him and rested his heels on the hardwood floor.

"*Boyd* is doing great," she said. "Thanks for asking. But I didn't see him last night."

"So where were you?"

"So why do you get to know?"

He grinned. "Because I'm fifteen kinds of charming and you adore me."

He had that one nailed.

"I was at the bookstore."

"Why not with your computer geek?"

"He's in the middle of a big project right now."

Zane looked anything but convinced. "Sure he is. You're bored. Admit. You think he's tedious."

"I think you're overcompensating because of personal inadequacy."

Rob and Ted finished their workouts and left. Zane glanced at the timer on her bike's program. "Your mom sent me cookies."

"She mentioned she was going to."

Nicki found a certain amount of irony in the fact that her parents were nearly as taken with Zane as she was. Maybe it was something genetic. A weakness in the Beauman family tree.

"So when are they coming up for a visit?" he asked.

"Probably not until the holidays. They're taking off for a cruise in Australia and New Zealand at the end of the month. It's fall here, but spring down under."

"You need to have me over for dinner while they're here. I like your folks."

"Me, too."

He grinned.

What the man could do to her with just a smile.

"Is their remodeling finished?" he asked.

"Just about. Mom promised the guest room would be done in time for my next visit."

Nicki had been a change-of-life baby and a surprise for a couple who had given up hope of ever having a child. As such, she'd been doted on from birth. Despite their devotion, they'd been ready to retire as she finished college. They'd left Seattle for the sunny warmth of Tucson, which gave her a good excuse to flee the incessant rain every winter.

"Maybe I'll swing down and visit them sometime," he said.

"They'd like that."

Her mother especially. While Muriel Beauman would have adored Zane for his own sake, she had a special place in her heart for him because of how he treated her daughter. When her parents had met Zane, her mother had made it a point to tell Nicki that he didn't seem to notice she was in a wheelchair.

Nicki knew that was true. Zane's acceptance was complete. Sometimes she consoled herself that his lack of interest in her had nothing to do with her problems with her legs. Nope, it was her pesky brain getting in the way.

The timer on her bike beeped. Nicki slowed, then stopped and wiped the sweat from her face. Her muscles were comfortably tired, but her workout was just beginning.

Still in the wheelchair, Zane moved next to the bike. "Climb on," he said as he wrapped one arm around her waist.

She relaxed as he pulled her onto his lap and "drove" her to the weight machines clustered at the far end of the room. This was a familiar part of their routine—one she tried not to get excited about. Yeah, he had his arm around her. Yeah, it felt good. So what?

She slid from Zane's lap to the bench. He locked the wheelchair in place and rose.

While she hooked up the elaborate pulley system that allowed her to strengthen her leg muscles without putting too much weight on them, he moved to the treadmill where he punched in his favorite program. The machine started at a warm-up pace that would send most people into cardiac arrest. Zane wouldn't even begin breathing hard until mile three.

She might hate exercise, Nicki thought as she began the leg lifts designed by a physical therapist to keep her lower body toned and flexible, but there were compensations. One was a boss who'd had no problem adding a couple of pieces of equipment to the company gym so she could work out there as well. The other was watching Zane move.

Mirrors covered all four walls so wherever she turned, she saw front and back views of the man. The machine picked up the pace and he eased from a jog into a full-out run. Long, lean muscles bunched and released with nearly balletlike grace. Nicki mentally smacked herself upside the head and returned her attention to her own workout.

"Jeff and I are having a planning meeting later today," Zane called to her. "Any preferences?"

Employees were often allowed to request assignments so those with families could stay close to home and those without could indulge their wanderlust.

"I'd like to winter in Hawaii," Nicki told him.

He grinned. "I don't think we have any clients there."

"Then we should get some. Maybe a pro football player or a surfing champion."

"Maybe a suntan lotion model."

Nicki sniffed. "Not at all my style."

She released the pulleys and turned so her legs hung off the bench. When she was in position, she began to work her upper body.

Strong muscles were essential for a number of reasons. Not only did they help her maneuver and stay fast in her chair, but well-toned arms burned more calories. She might be able to keep in shape with her workouts, but she didn't have the ability to walk from place to place during the day. If she wasn't careful to balance her exercise with her lifestyle, she could pile on five pounds in the time it took most people to sneeze. On her smallish frame, that was hardly attractive. So she did the exercise thing and told herself it was like taking a really sweaty vitamin.

Zane finished his five-mile run and stepped off the treadmill. As she shifted from the bench to her wheelchair, he nodded to the free weights and barbells.

"Want me to spot you on the chest press?" he asked.

Nicki eyed the equipment in question. Did she want to lay on a bench, Zane poised at her head, ready to rescue her if she got into trouble as she raised and lowered a too-heavy weight? The view was spectacular—she could see all of him from knee to chin—but it came at a price. Namely unfulfilled fantasies.

"I'll pass," she said as she headed for the women's locker room and the showers. "But thanks."

"No problem."

He turned to the equipment and began his own weight training. Nicki didn't want to stick around. She'd seen the show countless times. If only she could be like Zane, she thought as she rolled to her locker. If only she could be happy with them just being friends and never consider any other possibilities. If only he didn't bother her so much.

She needed a plan. Or a program. Or an anti-Zane patch. Barring that, she had to find a way to clear her head. Boyd might not be the love of her life, but what if the next guy was? Would she miss her opportunity because she was hung up on Zane? Wouldn't that be a tragedy?

She was going to have to find a way to lick this problem once and for all, even if it meant something as drastic as finding a new job.

"This client is interesting," Jeff said as he tossed Zane a folder.

Zane picked it up and flipped through the pages. "An Italian banker?" He grinned. "Okay. I'll take that one."

Jeff didn't look surprised. "You think you're going to get a trip to Italy out of this."

"Sure."

Jeff shook his head and passed over two more folders. "Middle Eastern oil executives."

"A whole lot less fun," Zane muttered as he looked through their files. "Definitely more work."

Although he wouldn't mind a good distraction—maybe a kidnapping or hostage situation. He felt restless and on edge and he couldn't say why.

"Westron has had a couple of nasty letters delivered to his house," Jeff said. "He annoyed the wrong group of people."

"Death threats?" Zane asked.

"Daily. He's working with local police, but he wants us to come up with a plan to protect the family he has here in the States."

Zane made a few notes in the margin. When the company first started, he and Jeff had shared the work equally. In the past couple of years Jeff had taken over more administrative and sales duties, leaving much of the field work to Zane. The switch had come about because of Jeff's marriage to a single mom and the subsequent birth of his son. Little Michael was nearly eighteen months old.

"How's Ashley?" he asked.

Jeff's expression softened as he smiled. "Great. She's still getting morning sickness, but if this pregnancy is like the last one, it should pass in a few more weeks."

He continued talking, but Zane found himself unable to listen. Instead he fought against ghosts from the past, and the pain they brought with him.

He was happy for his friend, he told himself. As for his own life, it had turned out the way it had and there was not a damn thing he could do about it. Once he'd thought he could have a normal life, then he'd found out he was wrong. End of story.

He returned his attention to his partner's conversation and made notes on the various files. When they were finished, he headed for Nicki's office and found her on the phone.

He leaned against the door frame and waited as she chewed out whoever had annoyed her. Watching Nicki mad was a kick.

"You can't be serious," she said, using both hands to gesture, even though the person on the other end of her headset couldn't see. "If I'd wanted a cheap piece of crap, that's what I would have ordered. Instead I ordered an expensive transmitter that was supposed to have a two-mile radius. The one I received has a radius of about three hundred yards. Now I'm not a math person, but even I can figure out that's not close to one mile let alone two. So what are you going to do about this?"

She listened, sighed impatiently, then rolled her eyes. Her frustration made him grin. Nicki had a lot of great qualities but suffering fools gladly wasn't one of them.

He watched the fire flashing in her eyes and the way her mouth moved as she spoke. As always, he acknowledged her beauty with the same emotional attachment he had to the weather. It was a part of his world. He lived with it, prepared for it when he remembered and had absolutely no control over it. So mostly he ignored it.

"You'd better credit me the shipping cost," she muttered. "Yeah, I know. This is your last chance. One more screwup like this and I'm taking my sizeable budget elsewhere. Uh-huh." She listened for another couple of seconds, then said goodbye and hung up.

She glanced at Zane. "He actually had the nerve to tell me to have a nice day. My day was doing great right up until I found out about the messed-up order. People can be so annoying."

"Maybe it's not people. Maybe it's you."

Her gaze narrowed. "Easy for you to say. You delegate all the annoying stuff to me."

"One of the perks of the job." He waved a folder. "I have some exciting news."

She didn't look convinced. "Sure you do."

"Nicki. I'm not kidding. But I'm not going to tell you until I see the proper level of enthusiasm."

She drew in a breath and clutched both hands to her chest. "Oh, Zane. Exciting news? I just can't wait." Her voice was a falsely high pitch that could have called dogs from three states away. "Wait. I'm all flustered. Let me sit down and recover for a second."

She fluttered her fingers and quivered in her chair.

He chuckled, then sank into the seat by her desk. "It's not the world that's annoying," he told her. "It's you."

"Sell it somewhere else. What have you got?"

He handed her the top folder. "New client. An Italian banker. I'm going to be talking to him about setting up a better security plan for his family."

Nicki's green eyes widened. "Will you be visiting him yourself?"

"I just may. And if I do, I'll need an assistant."

She flipped through the pages and smiled. "I love Italy. It's so beautiful and do they know how to make wine or what? I haven't been in years."

"Did you go with your folks?"

"When I was in high school. Then I went with a bunch of friends while I was in college."

"With a guy?"

She raised her eyebrows. "There might have been a man or two in the group. I simply can't remember."

"Liar."

"Are you inquiring about my sex life?"

"Absolutely."

She pretended to be shocked. "A lady never kisses and tells."

"I'm not interested in the kissing. Do it anywhere interesting?"

"I'm not into public displays of affection, thank you very much." She closed the folder. "My big complaint is that despite promises to the contrary, not one man in Italy pinched my butt."

He shook his head. "Did you ever think it might have something to do with you being in a wheelchair? It's not exactly easy to pinch when the butt in question is planted on a seat. You should have worn your braces a couple of days and given the guys a chance."

"Good point. Honestly, I never thought it would be worth the effort."

"That's because you haven't had your butt pinched by a professional."

"Are you offering?"

"It's not my fantasy, but I could ask around if you'd like."

Nicki pushed the folder toward him. "You are too weird for words. Yes, if asked, I will accompany you to Italy. Now get out of here. Unlike the rest of you, I have actual work that needs to be done."

The Friday morning planning meeting lasted over two hours. As per the usual schedule, the least pressing clients were discussed first, leaving the most time for those with the largest and most imminent problems.

Oil executives stationed in the Middle East should know better than to make political statements, Nicki thought as she listened to Jeff outline the situation. There had been daily threats against George Westron and his family ever since he'd told an AP reporter that most of the area's problems could be solved if people simply practiced Christian values.

But the man being an idiot didn't mean he should be killed by a car bomb or that his family should suffer, either.

Jeff passed Nicki copies of the threats left on the Westron's front porch. She scanned the block letters taken from various magazines and newspapers, then glued into words and sentences.

"Obviously there is an entire international task force working on that," he told her. "But see what you can do."

Nicki nodded. She wasn't an expert, but she had contacts who were. People outside of mainstream law enforcement. Sometimes she got lucky. She also noted a list of information Jeff wanted cross-referenced.

"There are two children," Zane said, when Jeff had finished. "Twelve and ten."

Nicki winced. She hated when kids were in danger. "Tell me they're not still going to school."

He nodded. "It's private. We have two guys with them the entire day."

She shook her head. While she understood the need to keep kids' lives as normal as possible, the knowledge that they were out in the open, *exposed*, put a knot in her stomach.

Zane didn't look any happier than she felt. He shrugged. "I sent in Mathews and Gorson."

Some of her tension eased. Those two were great with kids and seemed to have a sixth sense about danger. Zane would have chosen them for that reason. He sweated when kids were in danger, too. Jeff worried, but he *had* kids of his own so she expected it. The same level of concern from Zane always left her weak in the knees...figuratively *and* literally.

She reminded herself she should be looking for reasons not to like Zane, not more excuses to fall harder for the guy. But it was difficult to dislike him. He was too close to perfect for her comfort.

Jeff finished up his report and asked for questions. When there weren't any, he reminded them that there was a new batch of bodyguards starting training on Monday, so they needed to stay sharp.

Nicki knew that new recruits were often ambushed while walking through the halls of the company. Once a fake terrorism team had invaded and taken hostages. She'd been caught in a standoff for nearly a half hour, which wouldn't have been a problem if she hadn't been on her way to the bathroom in the first place. She made a mental note to be more careful about her water consumption during the next few weeks.

Brenda, Jeff's fifty-something assistant, rose and glared at her boss. "I can't believe you didn't consider my application. *Again.*"

Zane glanced at Nicki and grinned. "Here we go," he murmured.

Brenda's desire to be a real live spy was an ongoing source of humor in the office.

Jeff rose and patted her on the arm. "Brenda, I can't risk losing you. Not only would your husband kill me, but the office would fall apart. You're too valuable for field work."

"That's a crock and you know it," she said, following him from the room. "Come on, Jeff. Just give me a chance."

Nicki watched her go. "I'm always torn," she admitted to Zane as the rest of the staff filed out of the conference room. "On the one hand I know Jeff is right—Brenda does keep things running smoothly. But on the other hand, she should be allowed to live up to her potential."

"She would never pass the physical."

"Fine. Then let her take it and fail. At least she would have had the chance."

Zane didn't look convinced, which made Nicki suspicious. "You and Jeff are afraid she *will* pass and then you'd have to let her into the program. You know she'd kick butt once she was accepted."

"You're a troublemaker."

"I prefer to think of myself as a rebel. Sort of like a freedom fighter for people who are being oppressed by those in power. Those who have never—"

The phone on the table buzzed. "Nicki, you have a call on line three."

"Thank God," Zane muttered. "I couldn't stand another one of those speeches on the oppressed."

"I'm not finished with you," she said as she picked up the receiver.

"This is Nicki," she said, then felt her mood deflate when she heard Boyd's voice. He wasn't the kind of guy who checked in during the day "just because." Which meant there was only one reason he was calling.

"I'm really sorry I can't make it tonight," he told her. "But with Stan quitting, the project is at risk. I don't want it to fall behind."

He went on about some particularly complex problem

that made no sense to her after the first three words. When he paused for breath, she spoke up.

"It's okay, Boyd. Tonight is just a party. Don't worry about it."

"I'll call you in a few days," he said. "After the weekend." He seemed to realize that most couples who were dating actually spent time together on weekends and quickly added, "I have to work."

"I guessed that. It's fine."

More than fine, she thought sadly as she hung up. She didn't feel regret or sadness or anything. For the past couple of weeks she'd been telling herself it was time to end things with Boyd. Whatever potential had been there had obviously been lost. This conversation told her it was *past* time to make a clean break.

"That's the thing," Zane said as he leaned toward her. "Guys like Brad just don't appreciate women. Computer chips and binary code are more interesting. Crazy, but true."

She closed her eyes and counted to ten. When that didn't help, she opened her eyes and glared at him. "*Boyd* isn't a programmer and he's plenty interested in woman and—" She laughed. "Why on earth am I trying to convince you?"

"I have no idea. I don't have a date, either. We can go together."

Nicki told herself that the sudden flash of heat that zinged up her thighs was little more than the beginnings of some kind of rash. Or a food allergy. It wasn't excitement about Zane's offhand invitation. So he was between women. That happened all the time. Just as quickly, he would be involved again with a large-breasted, slow-witted beauty whose most challenging conversational gambit would be to discuss the various shades of teal that went with her eyes.

"I suppose I could hang out with you at the party," she

said with a casual deliberateness she didn't come close to feeling. At this moment in time, her insides were practicing clog dancing.

"Hey, I'll even pick you up," he said.

She thought about his flashy two-seater sports car and grinned. "I think tying my wheelchair to your bumper and dragging it behind would be a really bad idea."

"Don't sweat the details, Nicki. I'll take care of everything." He rose and headed for the door. "I'll pick you up at seven. Wear something sexy."

"You're not picking me up," she called after him. "Don't be silly. I'll drive myself."

He paused in the doorway and stared at her. "I never let my date drive herself."

Her throat didn't just get tight. No, first it twisted up like a spring. "D-date?"

"Uh-huh."

He flashed her the kind of smile deigned to reduce her to a quivering mass. Damn the man—it worked.

"I'm going to show you all my best moves," he said. "You'll be impressed."

Nicki watched him walk out of the room and had a really bad feeling that Zane was right. She was going to be impressed and where exactly would that leave her? The last thing she needed was to be *more* attracted to him.

Then she reminded herself she'd never been the sort of person to walk away from a challenge. Zane thought he could knock her socks off. Well, two could play at that game. He'd told her to wear something sexy. She could do that and then some. Maybe if she surprised him, she could get the upper hand for once. Of course what she would do with it once she had it was another question entirely.

## *Chapter 3*

Nicki stared into the full-length mirror and wondered if she was making a mistake. Yes, she wanted to impress Zane, but maybe she was going about it all wrong. She might be attractive and all that, but there was no way on earth her size-B breasts could compete in the major leagues. Zane dated women who were so top heavy they couldn't walk straight.

She glanced from her reflection to her chest and back. In her closet was a black dress with a neckline that sank nearly to her navel. With some double stick tape and a very straight back, she could dazzle. But in a world of watermelons, who bothered with peaches? Maybe this choice was better. Simple, elegant and classy. Wasn't that better than trying too hard?

Nicki wished desperately for a second opinion, but her mom was in another state and Ashley, Jeff's wife, was busy getting herself ready. Besides, there wasn't much her friend could tell her over the phone.

"You look great," Nicki said in an effort to make herself feel better.

She knew she didn't look bad at all. The shimmering bronze fabric of her dress draped beautifully. The loose boat-style neckline left her arms bare—arms that were toned. Folds of fabric hinted at the curves of her breasts without actually exposing them. Her skin was pale and she'd chosen to leave it bare, even her legs, smoothing on a lotion with a hint of glimmer.

One advantage of her wheelchair was she never had to worry about sore feet so she wore strappy impractical shoes that would have crippled anyone trying to walk. A cascade of curls that had taken nearly twenty minutes to arrange and spray into place tumbled down her back.

Had her date been anyone but Zane, she would have been pleased with her appearance. But seeing as it was him... She pressed a hand to her fluttering stomach and tried to think calming thoughts.

"Not a date," she whispered. "This is not a date. It's two friends hanging out together. But if it were a date..."

She allowed herself a minute or two of pure fantasy. Zane walking in the door, being so swept away that he pulled her into his arms and kissed her senseless. Then their clothes dissolved and they were making love on the rug in front of the fire.

Of course there were several problems with her fantasy. First of all, she was in a wheelchair and pulling her into his arms could be complicated. Second, the fireplace wasn't lit, nor was there a rug in front of it. Somehow making love on a hardwood floor wasn't very appealing.

Maybe she shouldn't have attended that job fair after

college. If she hadn't met Jeff and been intrigued by his Ritter/Rankin Security, she would have pursued a post-graduate degree in psychology. With professional training she would be able to handle her crush on Zane. Of course if she'd gone to grad school she never would have met him and how gray her world would be without his light.

"Decisions, decisions," she murmured as she wheeled out of her bedroom.

The doorbell rang just in time to offer a distraction. She headed in that direction and pulled it open.

She'd known Zane was going to pick her up—he'd insisted. And she'd been aware that by him coming to her house, she would be forced to look at him. She'd even told herself he would look good. Unfortunately she'd underestimated the situation by about forty-five percent.

He didn't look good, he looked amazing. While he usually wore suits at work, the one he had on tonight was more elegant or better tailored or something. The smooth gray fabric brought out the depth of his eyes and made his shoulders look about two miles wide. He'd showered, shaved and wore the burgundy-and-silver tie she'd given him for Christmas the previous year.

Her brain registered all that before she noticed the spray of flowers he held in one hand. And not just flowers. Nothing traditional like roses or carnations. Instead Zane held several stalks of delicately beautiful orchids. The pale creamy petals were alabaster, tinged with muted green.

"Hey, Nicki," Zane said as he stepped into her entryway. "You look beautiful, but I expected that." He handed her the flowers. "I chose these because they reminded me of you."

As he bent toward her, he brushed her cheek with his mouth. Tingles shot through her like out-of-control fireworks.

She couldn't think, couldn't move. Fortunately, it didn't matter if she swayed a little. She was already sitting down and if she collapsed in a heap, the floor wasn't that far away.

"Thank you," she murmured, not sure if she meant the flowers, the compliment or his presence. Maybe she meant it for all of them.

"Shall we put these in water before we go?" he asked.

She nodded and led the way to the kitchen.

The room had been customized with lower cabinets and nothing essential above the countertop. As she didn't get many flowers, the vases were stored in an upper cabinet. She pointed to the right one and Zane got a container down for her. After filling it with water, he retrieved the flowers and set them in the vase.

"They're lovely," she said.

He winked. "Do I know my moves or what?"

"You're a pro," she told him, and meant it. He was a man who knew his way around women. Okay, so they were just friends going out to a work party. But maybe she could allow herself to live in the fantasy for a few hours and pretend this was all real. As long as she didn't get her heart engaged, what could it hurt?

She smiled at him. "You're wearing my tie."

"I know." He touched the length of silk. "Maybe later you could let me tie you up with it." He wiggled his eyebrows as he spoke.

She laughed and tapped her chair. "I'm at enough of a disadvantage already."

"Want to tie me up instead?"

More than he could know. "I'll think about it," she said instead.

He followed her to the front door. When she wheeled out she was surprised to see an SUV parked at the curb.

"You couldn't possibly have traded your car in on that," she said. "Is it a rental?"

"Nope. I borrowed it from Ashley. Pretty slick, huh?"

It was more than slick. It was a regular car, which meant there was no way she could get inside on her own. Before Nicki could worry about the awkwardness of the moment, Zane had opened the passenger door and scooped her into his arms. He lifted her into the seat.

For the moment, they were at eye level. In the overhead interior light she could see the flecks of gold and amber that sparkled in his dark brown irises. There was a tiny scar by the corner of his mouth and shadows hollowing his cheekbones.

All she could think was that she wanted him to kiss her. Which was crazy, so what she said instead was, "You didn't have to borrow her car. I could have driven."

Zane pulled the seat belt around her and clicked it into place. "No way. On a date, guys drive."

"That is wildly sexist."

He winked. "I know."

The door closed and he moved to the rear of the vehicle where he collapsed her wheelchair and slid it into the back. When he sat next to her, he grinned.

"Is this the most fun you've had in weeks or what?"

She knew she should have answered "Or what." At the very least she should have acted bored, mentioned Boyd or pretended none of this mattered. Instead she found herself a quivering mass of Zane-lust weakened female hormones.

"It's pretty fun," she admitted.

His smile turned promising. "There's more."

Nicki had never been much of a drinker, but she was a sucker for the occasional glass of champagne. And when it was expensive and served in an actual crystal glass, how could she say no? So she sat in her chair and sipped, while enjoying herself at the party.

There were about forty people in attendance, half of them the staff from Ritter/Rankin Security while the other half were employees of their host.

A few months ago Al Morgan had come to Zane and Jeff after his firm was targeted by a foreign group trying to steal proprietary technology. A sting had been hatched, the culprits apprehended and all was well. The party was a big thank-you to the security firm.

"More?" Zane asked, nodding at her half-full glass.

Nicki shook her head. "I don't like to get too buzzed. You know what they say about drinking and driving." She tapped the arm of her wheelchair as she spoke.

Zane smiled. "I could be your designated driver. I think you'd look cute drunk." He leaned close. "A few sexy moves in that dress and you'd cause a riot."

His low, velvet voice brushed against her bare skin and made her want to swoon. He'd been at it all night—staying close, teasing in the most delicious way, gazing at her as if she were the only woman in the room. While she liked the attention, even as she knew it was dangerous to see it as significant, she couldn't help wondering *why* he was doing it. Bringing her flowers was one thing, but actually spending the evening in date mode was something else.

"Move over big guy," Ashley Ritter said as she walked up to the sofa.

Zane stood. "I'll grab us some food," he said, then leaned toward Ashley and kissed her on the cheek. "You're radiant as always."

"If you think that shamelessly flattering your partner's wife is going to influence how I talk about you, you're right," she said as she settled on the sofa. "Bring me back anything salty please."

He nodded and headed for the buffet. Nicki frowned at her friend. "Aren't you supposed to be watching sodium? Didn't you swell up like a balloon when you were pregnant with Michael?"

Jeff's wife wrinkled her nose, then brushed back her dark hair. "Thanks so much for reminding me."

"I'm your friend. I worry."

Ashley sighed. "I know I have to watch my diet but in the past couple of days I've been like a cow without a salt lick. Desperate." Her hazel eyes danced with amusement. "But enough about the oddities of my pregnant self. What's going on with you? Since when did Zane start escorting you to parties and hanging on your every word and why didn't you call and tell me he'd finally seen the light?"

Nicki instinctively turned to make sure Zane was safely across the room and not within hearing distance. "It's not like that," she said, her voice low. "Boyd couldn't make it tonight and Zane offered to bring me. Nothing more."

"That's not what it looks like to me, young lady."

Nicki sighed. "He's on date patrol or something, but it doesn't mean anything."

Ashley's expression turned sympathetic. She leaned close. "I know you're convinced he couldn't possibly be interested in you because he only dates bubbleheads, but I think you should tell him the truth about your feelings and give this whole thing a chance. Zane is a lot like Jeff—there's plenty concealed beneath the surface. The difference is Jeff hid himself behind the walls of being a warrior while Zane chooses a more charming facade. But that doesn't change the reality. They're both hiding the real man."

"Who is the real Zane?" Nicki asked. "Sometimes I think

I catch glimpses of him when we're hanging out together. He lets his guard down, which I appreciate. But there's no telling that the inner Zane will be any more interested in me than the outer one."

"You could try to find out."

A good plan, Nicki thought, except she wasn't sure she really wanted to know. Not if the answer was negative.

Ashley read her expression. "So go another route," her friend suggested. "Find out about the secrets he hides. Why does he pursue young women with minimal IQs?"

"Because they're easy."

Ashley chuckled. "Tell him you could be, too. And if you do see him naked, I want a full report."

Nicki grinned. "You always say that but if I ever try to give you details, you can't stand to hear them."

"I know. I get shy."

Nicki thought about the affectionate glances she'd seen between Ashley and Jeff, and the very hot kiss she'd accidentally interrupted one afternoon at the office.

"Not with Jeff," she said.

Ashley sighed. Her expression softened and her gaze sought out her husband. "No, not with Jeff," she agreed.

Zane grabbed a fresh glass of champagne from the server's tray and handed it to Nicki. She took the offered drink.

"Hmm, why do I know this puts me over my limit?" she asked.

He winked.

"You're trying to get me drunk."

"I'll admit the thought crossed my mind," he told her.

"I wouldn't have thought you would have to resort to cheap tricks with your dates."

"I don't," he said smugly. "The women I go out with fall at my feet."

"Easier for me to do that than most, but don't hold your breath."

She grinned as she spoke, then sipped her drink. Zane tucked a loose curl behind her ear.

Laughter brightened her eyes. He'd always found her attractive, but dressed to kill she was stunning.

He'd seen her legs countless times—in the gym, when she wore shorts in the summer. He was used to the long, lean length of thigh and calf. He barely noticed the faint crisscrossing of scars that patterned her right leg. She kept herself in shape and he'd always been man enough to appreciate the curves.

But tonight something was different. Maybe it was the length of her skirt—the way the filmy fabric barely covered the tops of her thighs. Maybe it was the faint glow of her skin, or the fact that when he'd lifted her into the SUV his hand had cupped bare, warm flesh. Whatever the reason, he couldn't stop looking at her legs…or wanting to touch them.

He knew she could feel everything. Her being in a wheelchair wasn't about being paralyzed. So if he stroked his fingers from ankle to knee, then knee to thigh, she would feel every millimeter of contact. And then what? Would she lean toward him, her mouth parting in welcome? Would her breathing quicken as she—

"Zane?"

Nicki's voice called him back to the party.

He blinked and forced his mind away from her body. "What?"

"You had the oddest expression on your face. What on earth were you thinking about?"

He was saved from coming up with a lie by the arrival

of their host. Al Morgan pulled a chair up next to Nicki and sat down.

"How are you doing?" the gray-haired man said as he took Nicki's free hand in his.

She smiled. "I'm great."

Al studied her. "We've been doing some work with various metal alloys. It's all hush-hush stuff for the government, but it will have industrial applications. I was wondering—"

Nicki cut him off with a quick shake of her head. "You're a sweetie for thinking of me, Al, but no."

"Hear me out," he told her. "We're talking very strong but extremely lightweight. You'd barely know they were there."

"Braces are still braces."

"But you'd be walking."

Her smile was patient. "The two-legged thing isn't all it's cracked up to be. Believe me, I've tried it." She released his hand and tapped his knee. "Walking is what you know and I appreciate that you want that kind of freedom for me. But shuffling along in braces is slow and awkward."

Al didn't look convinced. "There are medical advances every day."

"I agree and I have a doctor who keeps on top of that sort of thing. I trust her completely, but despite miracles, some things can't be healed. I learned that when I broke my legs." She smiled ruefully. "The left one was so bad, even one of the ski patrol rescue guys passed out when he saw the bones sticking out. There was no way the bones could heal correctly. Walking was still a possibility because my right leg would be okay."

She paused. Zane knew the story, knew how she'd struggled all those years ago. She'd been fourteen when her world had crashed in on her.

"Then I got a bone infection," she continued. "It took months to heal and when it did, the bones in my right leg had been weakened to the point where they could never support my weight."

"With physical therapy—" Al started.

Nicki cut him off. "With physical therapy I can use braces. I can be upright and so what? It's hard work, not to mention painful. In my chair, I'm completely mobile."

"She's hell on wheels," Zane told Al. "Trust me—I've been run over."

She smiled at him. "Only when you're getting on my nerves." She turned back to Al. "I *can* walk with braces and a walker, I choose not to. A wheelchair beats the step-drag thing in my book."

Al didn't look convinced but he nodded. "If I can change your mind," he said.

"You can't."

She changed the subject to how his oldest daughter was doing at college. When Al was called away to look after his other guests, Zane touched her arm.

"Are you okay with him interfering?"

"Sure. He's doing it because he cares about me." She smiled. "I like that in a man."

Zane had always admired Nicki's courage and temperament. He found himself wanting to say that *he* cared, too.

"If he brings it up again, I'll go into more detail," she said. "Al sees me now, years after the accident. But if he'd been around when it happened, he would understand how far I've come."

She sipped her champagne. "Back then I would have agreed with him. I was determined to walk again, no matter how difficult it was or how much it hurt. When my parents bought me my first wheelchair, I saw it as a defeat. No way

I was going to give in. Then one day I sat in it and I was amazed at how lightweight it was and how easily I could move around. Once I figured out I could outrun anyone and be involved in sports, I never looked back."

Typical, he thought proudly. Nicki wasn't a quitter. "Do you still have braces?"

"Sure, but I rarely use them. A friend from college got married and I was a bridesmaid. I used the braces so I could stand up with the rest of the wedding party, but I didn't try walking down the aisle in them. Back in high school and college I would take them to dances so I could shuffle around the floor with my date." She grinned. "Sometimes I let the guys take them off. That always got them really excited."

Young men unbuckling cool metal from her smooth, warm thighs? He could understand the attraction.

He pretended shock. "You let them feel you up?"

"Of course."

"Did your mother know?"

She rolled her eyes. "Someone with your dating history is in no position to be judgmental. Besides, my prom date didn't get much more than a quick feel. I'm guessing your prom date offered you a chance to score."

He shook his head. "I didn't go to my prom. I was in a high school boot camp, paying my debt to society."

"You're kidding? What had you done?"

He shrugged. "Got caught in stolen truck with a few dozen TVs that didn't belong to me."

"No way."

"I was a wild kid."

She leaned close. "Okay, start at the beginning and talk slowly. I want details."

"No way." He held up his glass. "I'd have to be a whole lot more drunk than this to spill that story."

She raised her arm to flag a waiter. He caught her hand and pulled it down.

"I'm driving, Nicki. One's my limit."

"How annoying. I'm going to have to lure you to my place then, with plans to get you drunk and worm the truth out of you."

He considered all the possibilities that went along with that and knew he should back off. Nicki was a friend—he didn't want that to change. Still he found himself agreeing to her plan, and anticipating the event.

# *Chapter 4*

"You're going to have to invite me in," Zane said as he pulled up in front of Nicki's house.

Refusing to give in to the sudden fluttering in her chest, Nicki pretended a casualness that she didn't feel. "And that reason would be what?"

He grinned. In the dimness of the SUV, the only light came from the streetlamp. She was able to see the outline of Zane's face and the flash of his white teeth.

"You promised to get me drunk. Besides, it's barely ten-thirty. I have a reputation to think of. What would my neighbors say if I pulled in this early on a Friday night?"

"Of course," she murmured. "Your reputation."

There was no reason to refuse his request, she thought humorously. He didn't know about her out-of-control hormones. Nor was he likely to feel trapped if she had a brain hiccup and suddenly made a pass at him. No, the worst that could happen would be unfulfilled expectations on her part and Lord knew she'd been living with those forever.

"Far be it from me to ruin your stellar reputation," she said easily. "Come on in."

He turned off the engine and pocketed the keys. After collecting her wheelchair from the rear, he brought it around to the passenger side and locked the wheels. Then he opened her door and scooped her into his arms.

"Great perfume," he said as he settled her onto the chair's seat.

She could say the same thing except she knew Zane wasn't wearing a scent. That delicious fragrance she inhaled whenever they were close was nothing more than the man himself.

"Want a drink?" she asked when they were in the one-story house.

"Nothing alcoholic."

She tossed her purse onto the narrow table by the front door and wheeled into the living room. "There's an assortment of sodas and juices in the refrigerator. Help yourself."

"You want anything?"

"No thanks."

Zane sidetracked down the short hallway into the modified kitchen. She shifted restlessly in her chair, not sure what to do with herself. Or with him.

She glanced around at the clutter-free living room. She wasn't neat by nature, but she'd long ago learned that dropping items on the floor meant maneuvering around them later. Rather than turning her life into an obstacle course, she'd learned to tidy as she went.

The pale green walls picked up color from the striped green sofa. She'd chosen the scaled-down piece of furniture because the firm back and arms allowed her to brace herself when she moved from her chair to the sofa. She'd placed a tall table behind the couch, rather than in front, and used floor lamps for light. There weren't any rugs to impede her progress, but she'd used prints, cushions and stackable tables to provide spots of color and warmth.

Zane returned from the kitchen with a can of soda in his hand. Instead of flopping down on the sofa, he crossed to her DVD collection and flipped through the movies.

"There's not enough death here," he complained as he held up a DVD with a picture of a couple on the front. "Too many chick flicks."

"Maybe because I *am* a chick."

He frowned. "Seriously, Nicki, there's not a decent car chase in the bunch."

"Amazingly enough, I didn't buy the movies for you."

"You can't tell me Brad enjoys these."

She shook her head. "You know his name is Boyd and *I* know you know, so why do you insist on pretending you can't remember?"

He blinked at her, his face an expression of innocence. "Know what?"

She sighed. "Fine. Be difficult. But I'll have you know that Boyd enjoys romantic comedies as much as I do."

Zane snorted. "He's lying."

"He is not. He likes the kissing."

Zane walked to the table behind the sofa and set down his drink. "Yeah, the kissing is okay, but the rest of it is boring."

As he spoke, he bent over her and pulled her from her chair to the couch. Nicki didn't have time to protest, not that she was sure she would have. She liked sitting somewhere other than her chair, although she usually preferred to get there by her own power. Still, she couldn't complain about a few seconds spent in Zane's strong embrace.

He settled next to her and reached for the remote. "Maybe there's a game on."

"Wouldn't that be special," she muttered.

He glanced at her. "What's wrong? You're into sports."

"I know."

She enjoyed a good football or baseball game as much as the next person, but didn't Zane want to pay attention to her instead of a bunch of sweaty guys?

Obviously not, she thought as he flipped through over a hundred channels in less than two minutes. Note to self—this was not a real date and if she allowed herself to forget that, she was going to get her feelings hurt.

On his second round through the channels he stopped on a familiar scene with Tom Cruise. It took her a second to recognize the movie *Top Gun*.

She laughed. "Okay, so this is the perfect movie, right? Planes, death, macho moments and kissing."

He chuckled. "You're right. Something for everyone."

He angled toward her and reached for his drink. After taking a swallow, he put the can back, but left his arm up on the back of the sofa.

His fingers were less than an inch from her shoulder. The second she realized that, she became painfully aware of how close they were sitting, of how she could feel him breathing. Tension crackled. Unfortunately it was all on her side. She doubted he was the least bit aware of her.

She told herself to pay attention to the movie. Tom and Kelly were having a heated argument, which meant the good parts weren't that far away. But she found her gaze being drawn back to the man sitting next to her. To his strong profile and the stubborn set of his jaw. To the long, dark lashes and the scar at the corner of his mouth.

"You're not watching the movie," he said as he tugged gently on her hair. "You'll miss the kiss."

She knew he was right, but she couldn't turn away. Zane was right there…close enough to touch. What would happen if she did something? Would he be shocked? Embarrassed? Would he let her down gently or would an answering desire flare in his eyes? Had he ever thought of her as something other than his friend?

There was only one way to find out, but Nicki didn't think she had the guts. Yeah she was empowered and women were equals and all that but she was just plain scared. If Zane rejected her, it would change their relationship. Was she willing to risk not being his friend anymore?

The last question was easy to answer. She wasn't. So she looked at the screen and did her best to ignore Zane.

The scene shifted, the music swelled and the screen filled with the two lovers. Nicki allowed herself to get lost in the moment and forget about her own needs.

"Movie kisses are the best," she murmured without thinking. "Sometimes better than the real thing."

Zane had been drinking and he nearly choked. "Then Brad has been doing it all wrong."

She looked at him. "Boyd does it just fine. That's not the point. Movie kisses are often highly romantic. That's important. Not that you know much about romance."

He set down his drink. "I know plenty about bodies and that's what kissing involves."

"It's not just a function, like sneezing. It can be spiritual. The mind, the body, the heart are all engaged."

"You think too much."

"You don't think enough."

"Maybe not, but I sure as hell know how to kiss."

Nicki opened her mouth to shoot off some snappy retort when Zane suddenly shifted toward her. Before she could stop gasping like a fish, he wrapped his arms around her, pulled her closed and lowered his head.

She had just enough time to clamp her lips shut when he kissed her. A for real, skin on skin, bodies pressing, heat generating oh-my-is-this-really-happening kiss.

It was heaven. It was five kinds of wonderful and if she died right this second, her life would end on a really high note.

He pressed his mouth against hers with a firmness that spoke of confidence and authority, but with enough gentleness for her to know that he wanted to share, not just take. His scent surrounded her, allowing her to get lost in the moment as she breathed in the essence of the man.

His lips brushed against hers, exploring, teasing, before settling in place. She was still caught up in the wonder of what exactly was happening when he touched the tip of his tongue to her lower lip.

Heat exploded inside. Funny how that tiny point of contact could make her body go up in flames. She was aware of her breasts, her legs and that suddenly wet and swollen place between her thighs. She wanted Zane with a desperation that made her catch her breath. She supposed it came from fantasizing about him for so long…not to mention close contact with a man who knew how to excite a woman.

He traced the curve of her lower lip in a slow, delicious movement that made her mouth part. When he slipped inside and lightly stroked her tongue with his, her entire body clenched. Then he angled his head and deepened the kiss.

He touched and tasted and explored all of her. With each movement of the dance, she found herself melting into a puddle of desire. She didn't want to stop him—if anything she wanted to beg him to kiss her forever. But even if she'd wanted to put the brakes on, she was incapable of speech or movement or breath. She could only feel and savor those feelings.

His hands rested against her back. As the kiss continued, he began to slide them up and down her back. Strong fingers stroked against her. When he dipped lower and cupped her hip with his palm, she pressed into the contact.

She ached everywhere. The wanting grew until it was all she could think about. Need spun through her like a tornado; powerful, all-encompassing, overwhelming.

He shifted slightly and broke their kiss. Before she could protest, he pressed his mouth to her jaw, then along her neck. Hot tingles shot through her. At the same time he slipped his hand from her hip to her waist, then higher still. Anticipation made her cling to him. She dug her fingers into the tight, honed muscles of his shoulders and arms.

More. She needed more.

He pressed an openmouthed kiss to the sensitive skin just below her collarbone at the same time his hand closed over her breast. She sucked in a breath as his gentle touch soothed her aching flesh. His thumb brushed against her nipple and she gasped as fire jolted through her. Exquisite pleasure joined the out-of-control need. Between her legs, she melted, swelling, readying, wanting.

What had started as a simple kiss turned into something more. While Nicki wanted to lose herself in the moment, a persistent voice in her head screamed a single question over and over.

"What on earth are you doing?"

Did she want to be sensible and stop this? Did she want to ask Zane if he knew what he was doing? Not "did he know he was making love?" but "did he know he was doing it with *her?*" Never once in two years of friendship had he ever hinted that he saw her as someone other than a buddy. So why was he suddenly acting as if he knew she was a woman? And did she really want to know?

As if sensing her internal confusion, he sat up and stared at her. Passion darkened his eyes to the color of midnight. His mouth was damp and swollen, his hair slightly mussed. He looked so good that had he been a magazine ad, she would have assumed he'd been digitally enhanced.

The sound of a jet taking off cut through the silence. Zane turned, grabbed the remote and turned off the movie. Then he moved his hand from her breast and rubbed his thumb across her lower lip.

"Still think movie kissing is better than the real thing?" he asked softly.

Despite her questions and uncertainty, she smiled. "No. Doing is better than watching."

"Told you." He put his hand on her leg, then groaned softly. "Your legs are bare. I noticed when I lifted you into the SUV. It's been driving me crazy."

Wow. Really? Did he mean that? "You try putting on tights while sitting down. It's a pain."

He stroked her thigh. "I'm not a tights kind of guy."

She chuckled. "How awkward things would if you were."

He didn't smile. Instead his already serious expression turned intense. "I didn't plan this Nicki. I don't make moves on women involved with other guys."

Other guys? Oh. "Boyd?"

"Yeah."

"I'm not..." She cleared her throat. Discussing this was difficult enough without the distraction of his hand moving up and down her thigh. "We haven't… That is to say things never got this far with him."

Zane's eyebrows lifted slightly. "If you tell me that you were willing and he held back I'm going to have to nominate him for stupid guy of the year."

The compliment delighted her. "I'm not sure either of us were interested."

"So I'm not trespassing?"

She shook her head, then nearly fell over from shock. They were talking about this whole thing as if they were going to keep going. As if it hadn't all just ended with a kiss.

Before she could ask, not even sure she wanted to know, Zane pressed his mouth to hers again. The kiss was long, slow, deep and impossible to resist. She surrendered to the feelings surging through her, to the taste and scent of him, to the hands roaming over her back and sides. When he slipped them up her ribs to her breasts, she could only breathe her pleasure.

He cupped her curves, then gently stroked her nipples with his fingers. She thrust her chest forward, silently begging for more.

When he responded by moving away, she moaned in protest. Against her mouth, he smiled.

"Impatient, aren't you?" he murmured. "I'm not going anywhere."

When he reached behind her, she understood his intentions and shifted so he could more easily reach the zipper of her dress. He pulled it down and slipped the silky fabric from her shoulders.

"Better," he whispered when he'd dragged the material to her waist. Expert fingers unfastened her bra.

She had a brief moment of concern, wondering if he

would find her more modest charms interesting, but when he lowered his head and pressed an openmouthed kiss to her already sensitized flesh she found she didn't care about anything but making sure he never stopped.

He licked her breast, then drew her nipple into his mouth. While his hand mimicked the movements on her other breast, she dug her fingers first into his shoulders and then ran them through his hair.

"Zane," she breathed.

Wanting filled her. The intensity of her reaction should have frightened her but thinking about it took a level of rational thought she no longer possessed. She squirmed to get closer, then pressed herself against him. He was aroused. She could feel his hardness against her hip. Unable to stop herself, she dropped her arm to her side and reached between them so she could touch him there. At the first brush of her fingers, he swore and stiffened.

When he raised his head the fire in his eyes had been dampened slightly by questions.

"Nicki?"

She pressed her lips together, not sure what he wanted to hear and what she wanted to say.

"I want you," he breathed. "If you're waiting for me to be sensible, hell's going to freeze over first. But I'll listen if you tell me to stop."

Stop? Was he kidding? She smiled, then brushed her fingers against his cheek.

"I would like it very much if you would stay."

Zane hadn't realized he'd been holding his breath until he released it. He hadn't planned to start kissing Nicki and he'd never intended for things to go this far. Had he thought it through, he would have assumed she would slap his face and toss him out on his butt. Yet if the warmth of her smile, not to mention her sensual reaction was anything to go by, she was more than interested.

He was smart enough not to question his good fortune, or risk the mood by considering the consequences. Instead he returned his mouth to her breast, while trying to stay focused enough to consider logistics.

He knew she wasn't a virgin. They'd talked about their dates enough over the past couple of years for him to know that while she was particular about who she invited into her bed, she did sometimes issue the invitation. He also knew that despite the lack of strength in her legs, she could feel everything.

He had a brief debate about moving things to the bedroom or continuing them right here, and decided the sofa would work just fine.

That decided, he closed his mind to everything but the pleasure in touching her, pleasing her, and brought his hand up to her breast.

She tasted sweet. The flavor of her lips, her mouth, her skin all lingered on his tongue like fine wine. As he licked her tight nipple and felt her body shiver in response, he focused on the feel of her warm skin and how soft she was.

He brushed his fingers against her nipple, then gently teased it with his thumb. Her hands stirred restlessly along his back. Her nails scratched erotically. Heat swirled between them, enchanting his senses, making him want more.

He'd been hard since ten seconds into the first kiss and was getting harder by the second. The trick was going to be staying in control.

While he continued to lick and suck her breasts, he worked the bottom of her dress toward her waist. It was a dirty job, he thought humorously as he was forced to slide his hands against the silky smoothness of her thighs, but he was man enough to see the task through to the end. When there was nothing between himself and paradise but a pair of very skimpy bikini panties, he raised his head from her chest and shifted until he knelt on the floor.

Nicki opened her eyes and smiled at him. "Is this the part where you promise to be my devoted slave for the rest of your life?"

He smiled. "Would you like that?"

"Maybe. What duties come with that sort of servitude?"

He put his hands on her hips and eased her into a half-seated half-lying position. "I guess I'd have to be responsible for your sexual satisfaction."

As he spoke he pressed a kiss to the inside of her right knee. Thin scar lines crisscrossed her skin. He followed the trail they made all the way up her thigh.

She sighed. "I guess you deserve a tryout."

"Did I say I was applying?"

She raised her eyebrows. "Your position would say you were."

"Yours would say you wanted me to."

Her green eyes darkened. "You're right."

Their gazes locked. Blood heated and surged. It was all he could do to keep from unfastening his slacks, ripping off her panties and plunging home. But he'd given up one-sided sex about the time of his nineteenth birthday. These days he wanted his partner arriving at the finish line along with him. Which meant he had to get control.

Watching her watch him, he moved his hands up to her hips and hooked his fingers around her panties. Moving slowly, deliberately, he drew the scrap of silk down, down, down until he could peel it away. When she was bare, and still watching, he moved close and parted the slick, swollen folds of her feminine flesh. Then he opened his mouth and tasted her.

Paradise, he thought with the first flick of his tongue. His mind split neatly in two with one half wanting her climaxing so he could take his own release. The other half urged him to wait, to hold back, so he could taste and tease and pleasure her long into the night.

She groaned low in her throat and lightly touched his head. "I can't believe how good that is," she whispered. She pulled her knees back toward her chest. "Oh, Zane."

If was as if he could read her mind, Nicki thought hazily. Maybe he could. That was the only explanation for how he knew to go faster, then slower. He touched her with an attention to detail that left her unable to do anything but respond.

Within a minute, she was shaking. Within two she was panting, begging and on the verge of climaxing. Within three minutes…

Tension grew and grew until there was nothing in Nicki's world but the pleasure he created with his mouth and tongue and the ache filling her. She strained toward him, urging both of them on and found herself caught up in an orgasm that ripped through her like a hurricane.

Tossed, tumbled, set free and finally settling back onto the sofa, she needed a second to catch her breath. When she resurfaced, she found Zane staring at her intently. Need tightened his features, but smugness curved at the corners of his mouth.

"Not bad," she murmured.

"You're welcome to write a response card," he teased. "All compliments welcome."

She would have plenty of those. She couldn't remember the last time she'd been able to let go so easily. Even several minutes after the fact, tremors rippled through her body. Maybe because although he'd pleasured her, he still hadn't claimed her.

She tugged on the sleeve of his shirt. "One of us is a little too formally dressed."

She saw she didn't have to ask him twice. The words had barely formed before he went to work on his shirt. His shoes, socks, slacks and boxer shorts followed until he was naked and very, very ready.

He bent over her, moving her gently, positioning her lower body so he could ease himself between her thighs. The sight of his arousal made her own need roar back to life and when he knelt on the sofa, she reached for him.

"Be in me," she whispered.

He surged forward, filling her, stretching her, making her cry out in pleasure. His gaze locked with hers, allowing her to watch him take her.

His breathing increased with each stroke. He groaned her name over and over. The pace quickened and she felt herself losing control. Contractions rippled through her, making her cling to him, urging him on. He plunged inside of her, taking her to the edge, then flinging her out into the cosmos where she lost herself into glorious release before finding her way back.

When they had both recovered enough to breathe normally, Zane raised his head and smiled at her.

That was it. He didn't say anything, he simply smiled. And she smiled back because this felt good—right. Something she would never have guessed.

Then he stood in all his naked glory, scooped her up into his arms and carried her into the bedroom.

When they were both under the covers he looped an arm around her and pulled her close.

"Good night, Nicki," he mumbled.

Good night? He was staying? He never stayed. She knew that for a fact. He made it a point to cut and run after he'd had his good time. A thousand questions filled her mind, but before she could ask even one, she heard the quiet sigh that indicated he'd already fallen asleep.

She shifted so that she could study him in the dim light. She lightly traced the shape of his jaw, then pushed a lock of dark hair off his forehead.

The questions could wait, she told herself. For now this was enough. More than enough. It was more than she'd ever thought she would have.

Sunlight made a brutal alarm clock, Nicki thought the next morning when she opened her eyes and instantly had to squint. She started to turn to find out what time it was only to realize she was pinned under a strong, warm, heavy arm.

At that same moment, she realized she was naked, and that Zane was in her bed. Oh, and in case that wasn't enough, they'd made love. Not just the one time on her sofa, but also later. Here. In her bed.

Second thoughts arrived and they brought friends. What had she been thinking? Making love with Zane? Was she insane? Wasn't it bad enough that she had a completely foolish crush on him? Did she have to go and make it worse by bonding through intimate physical contact?

"I'm second cousin to the moron twins," she murmured, wishing she could simply duck and run. Unfortunately escape wasn't going to be that easy.

Her wheelchair was still in the living room. There weren't even any braces close by. Which meant she had the choice of waiting for Zane to bring her the chair or she could roll out of bed and drag her naked self across the hardwood floor. Given the two choices, she decided to wait.

Unfortunately there was the pressing problem of embarrassment, regrets and a rapidly filling bladder.

"Morning, good-looking."

She turned toward the voice and saw Zane was awake. Awake and smiling, which she couldn't believe. Like he was happy. Like they hadn't just made a huge mistake.

She offered a tight-lipped smile of her own. "Would you please get my chair and my bathrobe?"

"Sure thing."

He dropped a kiss on her nose, then rose. Once standing, he stretched his arms toward the ceiling. Apparently the naked thing bothered her a whole lot more than it bothered him. Of course his body was damn near perfect, so why would he care if she was looking? And look she did. At the lean muscles, at the dusting of hair on his chest and legs, at the shape and size of his maleness, impressive even at rest.

When he turned to leave the room, she admired the curve of his rear and the way his legs moved so easily.

He returned with her chair. While he was in the closet getting her robe, she pushed herself into a sitting position. After putting on her robe, she started to move into the chair. Zane lifted her into place.

"I can do it myself," she snapped.

He stepped back and raised his eyebrows. "I always thought you were a morning person."

"I am." She usually was. But this morning she felt out of sorts. Everything was confusing and more than a little scary.

"Come on," he said, jerking his head toward the bathroom. "Let's take a shower."

She couldn't believe it. "Together?"

"Sure. It's a great way to start the day. You wash my back…" His voice trailed off as he winked.

Oddly enough the suggestion made her more sad than annoyed. Her body went on instant alert at the thought of her up close and naked with Zane. But even as she considered the possibility, the logistics involved doused her like a face full of cold water.

Getting in the shower was more of a production for her than most people. She remained seated, she had special hold-bars and nonskid surfaces. Not the least bit sexy or appealing. She would imagine that Zane had pictured something along the lines of her up against a wall while he moved in and out of her, and that was so not going to happen.

"I have a lot to do today," she said at last. "If you want to shower, that's fine. There's a guest bathroom down the hall."

What she really meant was a regular bathroom. One that hadn't been modified for her personal use.

His dark gaze never left her face. For a second she would have sworn she saw a flicker of hurt, but she dismissed the possibility and told herself he was as anxious to leave as she was to have him gone.

The thought tightened her throat. Everything was different. In one night, two years of friendship had been materially changed and she wasn't sure she liked the differences. She felt awkward and vulnerable. And Zane…well, she didn't know what he was feeling.

"No problem, Nicki," he said and headed for the door. "I'll get out of your way."

She watched him walk out of the bedroom. Far more quickly than she could have imagined, he was back—fully dressed and acting as if nothing strange had happened.

"I'll call you later," he said as he bent down and lightly kissed her cheek.

She nodded because what she really wanted to say was that he didn't have to bother, but she didn't know how to speak the words without them coming out wrong. She wasn't trying to be mean. Instead she wanted to tell Zane that he wasn't obligated in any way. At least not to her.

He gave her a quick smile, a wave and then he was gone. As she sat in her chair, in her bedroom and stared at her rumpled bed, she heard footsteps, then the sound of the front door opening and closing.

Part of her wanted to call him back. Part of her never wanted to see him again, and most of her wanted to go back in time and rethink the decision to spend the night with him.

They were lovers now, at least they had been. But for how long, and what would happen when that part of their relationship ended? Zane didn't do long-term and she didn't do affairs. There was also the matter of their friendship and what impact this would have on that. Not to mention her feelings. How much had their intimacy caused her to bond with him?

Nicki sighed and headed for the bathroom. This situation was going to take a whole lot more than a shower and a couple of hours to figure out, but right now she didn't have anything close to a better plan.

# Chapter 5

Neither the shower nor time helped. By noon Nicki was restless and practically itching to do something—but what? Maybe it didn't matter, she thought as she tried to concentrate on sorting laundry. Maybe she just needed to occupy her mind so she didn't have so much time to think. Because she'd been thinking all morning and all she'd achieved was to give herself a massive headache as she wondered why on earth she'd slept with Zane.

Last night had been amazing. More than amazing. It wasn't just that Zane knew his way around a woman's body, although that was nice, too. It was that despite her limitations, she never once felt less than normal. He'd found positions that allowed her to move and be a part of things. He'd taken her suggestions and incorporated them into their lovemaking in such a way that she'd been able to lose herself in the experience of being with him.

He'd made her feel good—not just with an assortment of

orgasms but by laughing with her and treating her like his best friend with whom he just happened to be having sex.

Just thinking about their night together made her long for him. Which terrified her. Longing wasn't allowed. Longing implied a level of connection on her side of things that went way beyond her crush. She'd known from almost the first moment she'd met him that Zane wasn't a forever kind of guy and her long-term goals included marriage and a family. If he wasn't going to be a part of that, it was really dumb to waste her heart on him.

But could she choose who she cared about? It had been relatively easy to keep her feelings in check before, but what about now? And why didn't Zane want more than a series of short-term flings? What was it about him or his past that caused him to walk away? And why on earth had she slept with him?

"Stop it," she commanded herself. All this circular reasoning wasn't accomplishing anything. Maybe she should go for a drive or something.

She rolled toward the front of the house where she kept her purse and her keys. As she passed through the living room, the phone rang.

Nicki froze. While there were several people who *could* be calling, she knew exactly who was on the other end of the line. The certainty made her hesitate before picking up the receiver. What finally got her moving was the reminder that she'd long ago learned there was no point in avoiding the inevitable. Putting it off only made it worse.

"Hello?"

"Hey, gorgeous," Zane said, sounding cheerful and friendly. "How you doing?"

"I'm okay," she said cautiously.

"Just okay? You should be wonderful. Last night was pretty great. I do have all that practice."

His comments were no more outrageous than usual. In the context of their friendship, her move was to make some witty response that firmly put him in his place. Or if she was to go into lover mode, she would agree that last night had been wonderful and so was he. But she couldn't seem to find any words and when she did, her mouth wasn't working right.

He stepped into the silence. "I thought I'd swing by later and we'd go out."

That single sentence was almost as stunning as the previous night. "What?"

"Catch a movie, have some dinner. You'll need to drive because I had to return Ashley's SUV, but I'm tolerant of your feminine inadequacies behind the wheel so don't sweat it."

Dinner and a movie? Like a date? Was he kidding?

"I don't understand," she told him.

He sighed theatrically. "I'll speak more slowly then," he said as he demonstrated by leaving a noticeable pause between the words. "It's the weekend. We should go out and have fun."

Nicki closed her eyes. Her chest felt tight and she wasn't sure why. Suddenly everything hurt, most especially her heart. If she gave in to the feeling, she could be in tears in less than a minute.

He was asking her out. She didn't know what it meant, but there was no way she trusted him. Or what he was doing. She wanted to yell at him. She wanted to yell at herself. Neither made sense.

"Nicki?"

"I'm here," she murmured.

"What's going on?"

"Nothing."

Everything. He wanted to make plans. She thought of her laundry piles and the fact that she had to call Boyd and break things off officially. Not that he was going to be heartbroken. Based on how he'd been canceling dates lately, he'd been having some second thoughts of his own.

But with Boyd there had been possibilities. Promise. And with Zane there was nothing.

"I can't," she told him. "I have things I need to get done. But thanks for asking."

Then, before he could say anything else, she hung up and started to cry.

Zane stared at the phone and wondered what the hell had just happened. Obviously Nicki was upset, but why? She'd enjoyed last night. Every time he'd reached for her, she'd been wet, willing and doing her own fair share of grabbing. They'd made love into the hours before dawn, then had slept entwined. He didn't usually like to spend the night, but with Nicki it had felt right. There hadn't been any sense of being trapped by expectations.

So what was up with her this morning? His first instinct was to go see her and demand an explanation. But he was unsure of his welcome—something that had never happened before with Nicki. He didn't like it.

Restlessness stirred him. He wanted to run. Literally.

He moved through the living room to the bedroom and emerged a couple of minutes later in shorts, running shoes and an old T-shirt. A minute after that, he was out the door, so he wasn't around when the phone began to ring.

Nicki knew she was slime. Maybe even worse than that. Whatever had happened between Zane and herself, she didn't have the right to blow him off when he called. She'd been raised better than that and certainly considered herself a nicer person than she'd shown by her behavior. More importantly, he was her friend and she'd treated him badly. An apology was in order, which explained why she was now navigating a part of the city that made her uncomfortable…the marina.

Zane lived on a houseboat in a neighborhood made famous by the movie *Sleepless in Seattle.* His houseboat sat along a dock in Lake Union. She'd been to the two-story home a couple of times before and each time had been reminded that this area was not wheelchair-friendly.

The ramp down to the dock had crossbars every couple of feet. She understood the purpose was to keep people from slipping when the ramp was wet—something that happened frequently in the Seattle rain. But each bump meant slow going for her. The railing looking sturdy enough, but was at such a height that if she fell out of her wheelchair, she would slip between the rails and fall into the chilly lake below.

Once she reached boat level, there was the dock movement to contend with, followed by an impossibly high step entrance onto Zane's houseboat. Which meant she couldn't roll up to the door and knock. Instead she was forced to pause on the dock and call him from her cell phone.

"It's me," she said when he picked up. "I'm right outside your front door."

Seconds later the door in question opened and Zane stepped out into the afternoon sunlight.

He looked good, she thought as her stomach clenched and her heart rate increased. Too good. Clean shaven, freshly showered and just a little wary. She couldn't blame him for the latter, even though it made her feel like slime.

"What's up?" he asked as he approached.

She managed a smile. "The four most horrible words known to your gender. We have to talk."

He grinned. "I can handle it."

She was glad one of them could.

He stepped onto the dock and scooped her into his arms. "You didn't have to come here," he said. "I know you don't feel comfortable in the houseboat. I would have come to you."

"That would negate the power of my groveling."

They were close enough that she could see his individual eyelashes and feel the beat of his heart. Her body reacted to the nearness by heating up while her mind seemed in danger of shutting down.

He looked at her. "Are you groveling?" he asked.

"I plan to."

"Lucky me. I'll be in the front row."

He set her on the sofa, then went outside to bring in her wheelchair. When he returned, he moved a few pieces of furniture out of the way and rolled up a rug.

While he worked, she glanced around at the small, tidy space. The beauty of houseboats was life on the water with more room than on a traditional boat. Huge windows offered impressive views of the lake and the rest of the marina. Low bench seats hugged the walls, providing extra space for guests and storage underneath.

The color palette—teals, blues and greens, with gold and burgundy accents—had been provided by the previous owner with a flare for decorating. While Nicki enjoyed the elegant touches, such as the refurbished nineteenth-century light fixture over the dining room table and the parquet floor, she sensed that Zane would have been just as happy in a house of beige.

When he put her back in her wheelchair and took a seat in a club chair, she knew it was show time. Funny how in her van on the way over she'd known exactly what she was going to say and now her mind was a complete blank.

"I called you back but you didn't answer," she said by way of a stall.

"I went for a run."

She nodded and tried to figure out what he was thinking. Did he seem wary, or was that just guilt on her part?

She sucked in a breath and cut to the chase. "I'm sorry I hung up on you. I was…upset."

He frowned. "Why?"

"Because of last night…and this morning."

"Didn't you want us to make love?"

How like him to go for the heart of the matter with one simple question. Had she wanted them to make love?

"Yes and no."

"That makes it clear."

He spoke with just enough amusement that she knew he wasn't mad. Relief filled her, making it easier to tell him the truth.

"Zane, we're friends," she said earnestly.

"I know. I like us being friends."

"Me, too. Our relationship is important to me and I don't want to mess it up."

"I agree. But what does that have to do with last night?"

"Everything. Friends don't sleep together."

"Why not?"

She stared at him. "You have got to be kidding. There are a dozen reasons why not."

"Give me three."

Of course her mind went blank that instant.

"Because."

"That's not a good reason," he told her.

She already knew that, but it was the only reason she could think of that she could tell him. She couldn't say if they slept together, he would start to matter too much. Her crush could turn into something else. Something she didn't want to think about because one of these days she was going to lick the Zane problem and actually fall in love with a guy who would want to love her back.

"I liked things the way they were," she said instead.

He looked genuinely baffled. "But the sex was great."

"Agreed."

"Then why wouldn't you want to keep doing it?"

Did he have to be such a *guy?* "Because eventually you won't want to have sex with me. Then what? I don't think we can end things as lovers and still be friends. You don't do long-term and I don't do affairs. So we're at an impasse. Honestly, as good as it was last night, I would rather be friends than lovers."

He rose to his feet and crossed to the window. She watched his movements, as always taking pleasure in his body. He was graceful and athletic in everything he did. She knew he took his mobility for granted, as most people did.

He turned to face her. "But we…" He shook his head and swore. "You're being sensible."

Relief settled over her. He might protest, but he didn't fundamentally disagree. She'd been afraid that he would think the sex was more important than their friendship, which would have been fabulous in the moment, but tragic over time. As friends, they could be there for each other indefinitely, but as lovers, there was a ticking clock until things ended.

"I don't agree with this," he told her.

"Yes, you do."

His mouth twisted. "I don't like it, then."

"I'm with you on that. Last night was amazing and I would be more than happy to jump back into bed with you right this second."

His expression turned predatory as he took a single step toward her. She held up a hand to stop him.

"You know it's far better to just be friends. You have plenty of lovers, Zane, do you really need another one?"

"You don't have any."

Good point, and something she didn't want to think about. "I'll get one, eventually. Until then, can't we have things the way they were before?"

He shrugged. "Sure. If that's what you really want."

"It is."

But oddly enough, she didn't sound convinced, and when he continued to look at her with his dark eyes, she was suddenly aware of the subtle movements of the houseboat. They made her wonder what it would be like to make love on the water, with the sounds of the lake all around and the sunlight illuminating Zane's perfect body.

"You're thinking about it," he said.

"I'm not," she lied, then knew it was foolish to deny the truth. "Okay, maybe a little, but that doesn't matter. Maturity is important. Think of this as building character."

He didn't say anything. Instead he continued to watch her, which made her wonder if he was going to ignore her request that things go back to what they had always been. If Zane swept her up in his arms and carried her to his bedroom, there was very little she could do to stop him. So she would have to give in and it wouldn't be her fault.

Don't go there, a voice in her head screamed. Making love with Zane again would put her too close to falling in love and then what? She would have completely fallen for him and he would be itching to walk away. Better to ache with wanting than bleed from a broken heart.

"What is this supposed to be?" Nicki asked the next afternoon as she stared at the array of large boxes loosely connected by twist ties and staples. Ashley Ritter laughed at the question.

"It's a carnival booth. Can't you tell? For Maggie's school. They're having a fall festival as a fund-raiser. I volunteered to decorate one of them and when this was delivered, Jeff instantly went into macho 'I can build better.' It was all I could do to keep him out of the garage. He would do anything for his daughter."

Nicki smiled at the softness and love in Ashley's voice and did her best not to feel envious of her friend's happy marriage. Not that Nicki would want Jeff for herself, but someone who adored her with Jeff's devotion to his family would be nice.

"He's been making me crazy for the past couple of days," Ashley continued, "which is why I sent him off to the movies with the kids. I knew there was no way this was going to get finished otherwise." She smiled. "You're so sweet to offer to help me with it."

"How could I resist?" Nicki teased as she picked up a length of crepe paper. Besides, it beat being at home trying not to think about Zane, while being unable to think about anything else.

"How are you feeling?" she asked, nodding at her friend's still flat midsection.

"Okay." Ashley plugged in the glue gun and dumped a bag of cut-out leaves in fall colors onto the kitchen table. "The all-day sickness is fading, thank goodness. The bad news is once it's gone completely I'll start eating for twenty and pile on the pounds. As I'm a couple of years older this time, I'm guessing they won't come off as quickly as they did with Michael."

"You look great," Nicki told her friend.

Ashley laughed. "Your gentle spirit is one of the reasons I love you."

Nicki rolled her eyes. "I'm many things, but I don't know that gentle would make the list." She thought of how she'd freaked out the previous morning with Zane. Crazy fit. Or in need of serious counseling. Or a brain transplant. Maybe that would help her get over the man.

Ashley handed her the glue gun and the paper leaves. "Want to talk about it?"

Nicki stared at her. "Talk about what?"

Ashley unrolled crepe paper. "Whatever has you so unsettled. You've been jumpy since you arrived."

Nicki spent three seconds figuring out if she was going to tell her friend the truth, then knew there was no way she could lie.

She glanced around the spacious black-and-white kitchen before realizing that looking for an escape route wasn't going to help her, either. Then she took a deep breath and came clean.

"You know Zane and I were together at the party Friday night," she began.

Ashley nodded. "I was stunned at first, but excited. You've been in love with him since the second you laid eyes on him."

"It's a crush," Nicki corrected.

"If you say so," Ashley said, not sounding convinced.

Nicki ignored that. She was already in so much trouble, she didn't need to go looking for more.

"After he drove me home, he came inside. We were talking about movies and he complained that all I have in my DVD collection is romantic comedies."

Ashley leaned toward her. "Would you quit stalling and cut to the chase. What happened?"

Nicki shifted in her chair. "We started kissing and one thing led to the other and he spent the night."

"Are you talking about sex?" Ashley asked, her voice loud and high-pitched. "I can't believe it. You had sex with Zane?"

Nicki set the glue gun down, then covered her face with her hands. "I know. I can't believe it, either."

"Sex?"

She straightened. "Could you stop saying the *s* word, please?"

Ashley laughed. "I don't know. I'm stunned. More than stunned. In complete shock. How was it? I mean I'm sure Zane has more than enough experience to make things go smoothly, but I know it can be awkward for you the first time."

Nicki nodded. "Usually it is. I have to explain what I can feel or what I can or can't do, but not with Zane. He and I have talked about my legs enough that he knew most of that stuff already." She sighed as she recalled their close encounter on the sofa.

"He was perfect. Passionate, exciting, gentle. I forgot about everything but being with him. It was great."

Ashley's hazel eyes widened. "Wow."

"That pretty much describes it."

"So what's the problem? Why are you obviously unhappy and why on earth are you here, instead of out doing the wild thing with him?"

That was the more difficult question. "I don't know," she admitted. "I guess the truth is I'm scared."

Ashley's humor faded and she touched Nicki's hand. "Of caring too much?"

Nicki nodded. "Zane doesn't take any romantic relationship seriously. There's no reason to think I would be any different. I decided I would rather be his full-time friend than his part-time lover."

"I understand your reasoning, but between your feelings for him and things being great in bed, that can't have been easy. Weren't you tempted to at least try things out with him?"

"Sort of," Nicki murmured. "Okay, yes. I was very tempted. But it would be crazy."

"It wouldn't be boring," Ashley said.

"You're not encouraging me to pursue an affair with Zane are you?"

"Of course not," Ashley said, but Nicki wasn't convinced.

"Do you know how much I could be hurt? If I fell in love with him, it would be devastating."

"I know. You made the sensible choice."

"Why don't I believe you think that?"

Ashley shrugged. "Because you might not believe it yourself. You've had it bad for Zane from day one and you've yet to get over him. You finally get him into bed only to find out it's even better than you thought. Of course you're ambivalent. Who wouldn't be?"

Nicki tried to smile. "You're supposed to reinforce my decision, not make me question it."

"Sorry. I don't mean to make you more confused. You were right. Why would you want to have an ongoing physical relationship with the only man to make you practically glow when you could continue to be friends and die a slow death of frustration from wanting him?"

"He would get tired of me and dump me."

"You don't know that."

"He's never done anything else with a woman."

"He's never slept with you before."

Nicki opened her mouth and closed it. "You're not helping. Friends is better. Trust me. I've thought this through. I'm making the sensible decision. It will be better for both of us."

"If you say so."

"I do."

Nicki knew she was right. The sensible path was always the right one. And in time, she would even start to believe that herself.

# Chapter 6

Monday morning Zane arrived at the office at his usual time. He could have gotten there about three hours earlier because he hadn't slept much the night before, but he'd been too busy pacing the length of his houseboat to come into the office.

Everything was completely screwed up and even though he could say why, he didn't understand what was wrong. He hadn't planned on sleeping with Nicki. He'd asked her to the party because neither of them had a date and they enjoyed each other's company. They always had fun together. He figured the party would be more of the same.

As for picking her up and treating her like she was his date—he'd liked that. He enjoyed the company of beautiful women and when they were also funny and challenging like Nicki, how was he supposed to resist?

She'd blown him away with her combination of elegance,

humor and style. Not to mention how she'd made him feel in bed.

Lying down together meant her legs weren't an issue. There was no body weight to support and she'd moved with a sensuality that had left him breathless. He wouldn't have cared if she'd needed things to go differently, but what had excited him had been her abandon because *he'd* wanted her with a desperation that had stunned him.

He'd thought she wanted him as well. But she'd sure as hell been quick to put the brakes on. One minutes they'd been lovers, the next...friends.

He walked into his office and turned on his computer. But his mind was still on Nicki. On what had happened and what she'd said. Of course they had to be friends, he thought irritably. She was his best friend. And in theory staying away from each other made sense. But he didn't want to stay away from her and he hated that she was disconnected enough to see the logic in playing it safe. He wanted her to be so swept away by passion that she couldn't think.

"Not working out?" Jeff asked as he paused in the doorway to Zane's office.

Zane shook his head. "I ran this weekend."

Jeff nodded and left. Zane sank into his chair. He'd done more than run. He'd doubled his usual distance, pushing himself until his body screamed for him to stop. He'd run until he'd been so exhausted he'd been sure he wouldn't be able to think...but he had. He'd thought about Nicki.

"Mr. Sabotini has decided it would be better for him to make the trip here," Jeff said at the staff meeting Monday afternoon. He glanced at Zane, then at Nicki. "Sorry guys. Looks like your trip to Italy is off."

Zane said something noncommittal while Nicki could

only sigh in relief. The last thing she needed right now was long-distance traveling with Zane. She didn't want to be in the same room with him, let alone trapped on a plane with him for several hours.

Just sitting across the conference table from him was enough to get her blood pressure into the danger zone. It had been bad enough before when she could only wonder what it would be like to be the center of his universe, if only for a few hours. Now that she knew the unique combination of pleasure and unwavering attention, she found herself unable to think of anything else. Not even work.

"Once he finalizes his travel plans," Jeff continued, "we'll set up a meeting. He thinks it's going to be in L.A. or Chicago."

"Either works," Zane said.

"Fine," Nicki agreed.

Jeff frowned slightly, then shrugged and continued with the meeting.

There were bodyguard staff to assign, new clients to research and ongoing operations to be updated. Nicki followed along, making notes on the items that she would have to get involved with. Brenda, Jeff's assistant, made another stab at being allowed to test for a field operative. Without thinking, Nicki glanced at Zane and smiled.

He was already looking at her. Their gazes locked but that friendly connection quickly spiraled to something much more. She felt the heat from clear across the large table. Need flared inside of her. She wanted to be anywhere but here, as long as she was alone with Zane. She wanted to be naked, begging, pulling him closer, having him suck in his breath as he lost himself in her body.

Startled by the intensity of the flashback, she jerked in her seat and turned away. Embarrassment heated her cheeks. Work, she told herself. She was physically at work and she needed to keep her brain there as well.

When the meeting wrapped up, Nicki stayed in place until the room cleared. It was her habit, and usually Zane kept her company. But today he was one of the first people out the door, while Jeff remained seated at the head of the table. A knot formed in her stomach when he got up and closed the door behind the last person.

"What's up, Nicki?" he asked when they were alone. "You're not yourself."

She thought about asking who he imagined her to be but didn't think he would appreciate the humor. "I'm okay."

Jeff came around and took the chair next to her, angling so he faced her. His expression was kind.

"There was a lot of tension between you and Zane," he said. "Normally I can't get the two of you to shut up and pay attention. Today you weren't talking."

She ducked her head. Obviously Ashley had chosen not to tell her husband about what had happened between Nicki and Zane. While Nicki appreciated her friend keeping the confidence, she didn't know what to say to Jeff about the situation.

"We'll be fine," she murmured at last.

"Why don't I believe that?"

She looked at him. "I won't let any personal issues interfere with my work."

He smiled. "I know. You're too good at what you do. That's not why we're talking. You're important to the company, but you're also a friend."

She liked Jeff, but being friends with him was very different from being friends with Zane. Despite Jeff's blond good looks, she'd never once thought of him as anything other than her boss and Ashley's husband.

"Have you two had a fight?" he asked.

She shook her head. Not at all. Instead of arguing, they'd gotten too friendly and now Nicki didn't know how to return things to their normal footing.

"Please don't worry, Jeff."

"Hard not to, but I'll do my best." He paused, then smiled at her. "Did I ever tell you that my first wife's name was Nicole?"

"No. Does she look like me, too?"

"Not even close. You're nothing like her in any way. After we split up, I learned that some things can't be changed and some things can't be undone. My door is always open, Nicki, and I want to be there for you. My advice about all of this is to remind you that you can only do what's right for yourself. You can't control anyone else."

She knew he was talking about Zane, but she had no idea what he was trying to say. Was he warning her away from a personal relationship with his partner or telling her to go for it? Not that it mattered. She'd already made her decision. She was going to do everything she could to turn back time so that one glorious night was forgotten and she and Zane could be friends again. That was the best course of action for both of them.

She only hoped it wouldn't take a miracle.

Zane left his office and headed for Nicki's. He was willing to accept that things were going to be awkward between them for the first couple of days, but she was taking things too far.

He rounded the corner and stalked into her office. She looked up as he entered, saw his expression and frowned.

"What's wrong?" she asked.

He dropped the copy of the e-mail on her desk. "This."

She glanced at the paper, then at him. "You can't make it?"

"No. You asked if I was still coming with you."

Her green eyes darkened with confusion. "Yes, I know. I sent the e-mail."

He paced the length of her office, pausing as he turned to glare at her. "That's my point," he told her. "You asked. Dammit, Nicki, why are you doing this?"

"What?"

"Acting as if everything has changed. I've been helping you with your demonstrations on the first Monday of the month for over a year. Why would this be different?"

She pulled off her headset and leaned back in her chair. "I know. I'm sorry. It's just…"

He knew what it was. They'd become lovers and in her mind, that had changed everything. It had changed things for him, too, but he'd been willing to work through those differences, while spending some quality time in her bed. She didn't want that.

"You want us to be friends and nothing more," he said. "I respect that. So why are you the one acting as if we barely know each other?"

Color stained her cheeks. "I don't mean to do that. I feel awkward around you."

Awkward? "Why?"

"Because."

There was an answer. He pulled up the chair in front of her desk and dropped into the seat. She felt uncomfortable and probably wished the whole thing hadn't happened while he… He wished they'd never stopped being together. It wasn't just that he wanted to keep making love with Nicki, although he did. But what he really missed was the connection.

As soon as the thought formed, he pushed it away. No

connections, he reminded himself. No bonding, no caring, beyond what they already had. That was his rule and he'd lived by it for a long time.

"It's the naked thing," she said without looking at him. "Weird things happen to women when they get naked with a guy."

"Things other than sex?"

She glanced at him and smiled. "You're making fun of me."

"Only a little."

She rested her forearms on the desk. "I know it was really great and everything, but I can't help wishing we'd never done that. Don't you?"

He couldn't answer the question, not honestly. Nor did he allow himself to have an emotional reaction to her statement. She had regrets. Fine. He could live with that.

"I'll be there tonight," he said stiffly. "We'll pretend Friday never happened."

She winced. "I didn't mean that, exactly. I had a really good time."

"Sure." Why not? He was pretty decent in bed. He'd received enough compliments to have faith in his abilities. "I gotta get going," he said as he stood.

"Zane, wait. Let's have dinner tonight. After the demonstration."

He looked at her beautiful face, at the cascade of red hair that fell over her shoulders. He'd buried his hands in her hair as he'd made love with her. He'd touched her and kissed her and laughed with her. He'd wanted her, when he wasn't supposed to allow himself much more than scratching an itch.

He thought about the phone message he'd listened to on his voice mail. The call he'd yet to return.

"I can't make it," he told her. "Heather left me a message. She's in town for a couple of days and asked me to meet her for dinner. Maybe another time."

Nicki's smile never wavered. "No problem. See you tonight."

He waved and left the room.

Nicki watched him go. She managed to maintain her composure for all of twenty-seven seconds, then she slumped in her seat and had to blink back tears.

"I refuse to cry over him," she whispered fiercely. "Dammit, I'm the one who told him we were going to be friends and I meant it. So I refuse to care that he's having dinner with Heather."

Oh, but it hurt, she thought, feeling more miserable by the second. It hurt so much she could barely breathe.

Her phone rang and she considered not answering it. Then she reminded herself that she couldn't let her personal life interfere with her job.

"This is Nicki," she said after she clicked on her headset.

"Hey, it's me." Ashley's gentle voice came over the phone line. "I wanted to see how you're doing."

Her friend's concern nearly undid her, but she managed to keep from bursting into tears.

"I'm okay."

Ashley sighed. "You're lying. I can hear it from ten miles away."

Nicki swallowed. "It's just so stupid. I mean Zane wanted us to hang out and do stuff and I'm the one who said no and now things are weird, only I know they're not weird because we're not hanging out but because we had sex and I told him I wished we'd never done it and I think that hurt his feelings and now he's having dinner with Heather."

"Impressive," her friend said. "I think you got that out in one breath."

Nicki sniffed. "You're making fun of me."

"Not really. I'm trying to lighten the situation. Is it working?"

"A little."

"I am sorry, if that helps. And I've been worried about you."

"I appreciate that. You also didn't say anything to Jeff."

"How do you know?"

"He stayed to talk to me after the staff meeting because he'd noticed something was wrong between me and Zane. But he obviously didn't know what."

Ashley chuckled. "I thought the information would be more than he would want to know. So I kept quiet." She exhaled. "*Are* you having second thoughts about being only friends?"

"No." Nicki knew the danger inherent in wanting more with Zane. She would get her heart broken and getting over him would take forever. She had other plans for her life.

"I know I made the right decision. But why is he having dinner with Heather?"

"Because he's not having dinner with you?"

"Maybe." Nicki wasn't sure. "I wouldn't mind so much if she was like all the others, but Heather is smarter. And she and Zane went out for a really long time. What if she wants to start things up with him?"

"Why do you care?" Ashley asked.

"Good question. I shouldn't, huh?"

"If you're his friend, you should be thrilled he's found someone."

Nicki wanted to say she was happy, only that would be lying, too. "I want to scratch her eyes out."

"I sort of figured that."

Nicki closed her eyes. "Does that mean I've already fallen for him?"

"You don't want to know what I think," Ashley told her.

"Probably because I already know the answer. If I'm feeling jealous of Heather, it could be too late."

"I'm not the one saying that."

"You don't have to. I can figure it out for myself."

Had she fallen for Zane? And if she had, what was she going to do about it?

"There has to be a solution," Nicki said.

"You could always try the 'fake it until you make it' school of thought. Act as if everything is fine until it is fine."

"You think that will work?"

"Sure."

But Ashley's bright, cheerful tone didn't fool Nicki. Her friend thought she was already in trouble and that the worst was yet to come. Nicki hoped she was wrong.

"Whoever is attacking you isn't going to expect you to fight back," Nicki said that evening as she addressed the small group of people in the community center.

She grinned as she spoke. "Surprise is your friend and I'm going teach you how to take the element of surprise one step further."

Zane listened to the familiar speech. He and Nicki had been traveling around the Seattle-Tacoma area for over a year, talking about staying safe and self-defense for those with a physical disability. She talked tactics and demonstrated moves, while his job was to be the bad guy.

Tonight's group included a couple of elderly women in wheelchairs, an older man who used a walker and two kids in wheelchairs. There was also a teenage boy in a wheel-chair, but he wasn't part of the group. Instead he sat at the far end of the room and stared out into the twilight.

Zane returned his attention to Nicki. For the demonstration, she'd dressed in sweatpants and a loose T-shirt. Her hair was pulled back into a braid. Whatever had bothered her earlier in the day seemed to have faded, leaving her looking happy and gorgeous.

He, on the other hand, felt restless. He hadn't seen Heather in nearly a year and he knew he should be anticipating their evening together. Instead he found himself wishing he was going out with Nicki instead.

Really dumb, Rankin, he told himself. She's not interested.

Nicki finished with her lecture and he took his position up behind her. She'd placed a large handbag on her lap. At her signal, he strolled toward her, then reached down for the bag.

As he grabbed it, she screamed and tugged on the opposite end of the handle. Even though he knew it was coming, he was still surprised by her sudden release. He stumbled slightly. She took advantage of his moment of being off balance and slammed into him.

Nicki might weigh about a hundred and twenty pounds, but she could generate some force with her wheelchair. As he stumbled back, she kept moving forward. When he tried to sidestep, she banged into him again, this time not so dead on. He two-stepped, turned and found himself slipping.

While he struggled to regain his balance, she grabbed the purse and took off across the room. He knew her top speed beat his and didn't bother trying to chase her down. The audience applauded.

They went through the exercise a second time, this time

moving slowly, with Nicki explaining why she moved in, how to throw him off balance and when to run. He attacked her from behind, then tried to pull her out of her chair.

The latter move was the only one to have a chance of success, but he wasn't always able to dislodge her. He could physically lift her out of her chair, but that required getting in close and Nicki had several self-defense moves to make that a poor choice.

The entire lecture and demonstration took about ninety minutes. By the end, she'd won over the group. One of the things Zane liked best about working with her on these demonstrations was the change in attitude of those attending. At the beginning of the meeting, they were self-conscious and already convinced they were simply victims on wheels. Nicki showed them what was possible and allowed them to believe in themselves.

After the meeting ended, there was time for coffee and conversation. Zane glanced at his watch. It was about seven-thirty and he was due to meet Heather at eight. But instead of leaving, he collected a cup and chatted with those attending.

"Zane, good to see you," a white-haired woman said as she joined him.

"Betty." He smiled at the center's director. "We have a full house."

"Always. You and Nicki are some of our most popular speakers." Betty patted his arm. "She gives them hope."

He followed her gaze and saw Nicki in the corner with the teenaged boy in the wheelchair. He was no longer solemn and isolated. Instead he watched Nicki intently as she showed him how to balance on two wheels and spin around.

"Nothing his mother will want him to learn," Betty said dryly, "but probably the best thing for his spirit."

"She's good at that."

One of the older ladies wheeled over to him and smiled. "You and your wife did a wonderful job," she said. "She's a lovely young woman and you're a very special man."

Zane nodded and thanked her. Ever since he and Nicki had started doing this together, he'd had at least a dozen people come up and talk about his "wife." He'd given up correcting them—it took too long and they were always disappointed.

Betty waited until the woman had left, then shook her head. "You might as well go ahead and propose, Zane. It seems to be your destiny."

He chuckled, then excused himself and made his way to Nicki.

"I'm heading out," he said.

She frowned. "I bumped into you harder than I meant to earlier. Did I bruise you?"

He raised his eyebrows. "I'm a macho guy. Girls don't bruise me."

"Girls in metal wheelchairs can leave a lasting impression."

"I'm fine," he told her. It was his cue to leave, but somehow he couldn't make his feet move.

She poked him with her foot. "Zane, it's getting late. Heather's waiting."

He stared at her green eyes, at her easy smile and the relaxed pose of her body. Had they made their way back to the friendship she wanted? Wasn't it for the best if they did?

Comments from little old ladies aside, they weren't married and they weren't going to be. He had no claim on her. But if they were friends…

She was important to him. So important that he was going to walk away before he did something stupid.

"See you tomorrow," he said.

"Have fun."

He turned and walked out of the community center. As he put the key in the driver's door of his car, he had a last thought about canceling dinner with Heather and going out with Nicki instead.

No, he told himself as he slid onto the seat. She was right. No more dinners, no more nights into mornings. Not for the reasons she thought, not because he couldn't do a relationship but because he chose not to. He'd killed the last woman he'd loved. He wouldn't ever risk that again. Not with anyone and certainly not with Nicki.

## Chapter 7

By Thursday Nicki knew she had to get over the whole
Heather thing or she was going to collapse from lack of
sleep. She'd fretted for the past three nights, knowing Zane
was out with the woman and possibly staying until dawn.
Telling herself she'd been the one to send him away didn't
make her feel any better. She'd vacillated between polish-
ing her resumé, picking up the phone to invite him back
into her bed and signing up for online dating.

She'd settled on a couple of nights with too much ice
cream and a good cry over a romantic movie.

At three the previous morning, she decided to give herself a virtual slap upside the head. If that didn't work, then
she was going to get serious about finding a different job.
If being around Zane made her miserable, then it was time
to move on.

Feeling mature and in control, she drove to the building
about ten miles from the main office where she would help

train new bodyguard recruits. She always enjoyed these exercises and looked forward to the action. Her confident mood lasted until she pulled into the parking lot and saw Zane waiting by the back entrance. At the sight of his dark good looks her heart fluttered, her thighs heated and her stomach began to hula. So much for being in control.

He waited until she'd lowered herself to the ground and wheeled away from her van, then he strolled over and handed her a coffee from Starbucks.

"Brenda's bringing doughnuts," he said. "I told her to make sure there were plenty of glazed."

"Thanks." She took the coffee and sipped. "Exactly how I like it. Very thoughtful."

He shrugged. "I'm a thoughtful kind of guy. How was your evening?"

"Uneventful."

She'd finally met with Boyd and had officially ended their rapidly dying relationship.

"Yours?" she asked.

"Takeout pizza and baseball."

"I don't remember Heather liking sports."

"I didn't see Heather. She went back to Dallas."

"Oh."

Nicki told herself the information was mildly interesting at best, but that didn't stop her from feeling relieved. Zane bringing her coffee and waiting to escort her inside reminded her of the old days. B.N.—before naked. Were they finally on their way to returning to normal?

"You ready for today?" he asked as they moved into the building.

"I think so."

He glanced at her white shirt. "You sure you want to wear that?"

She grinned. "It's more dramatic."

"If you say so."

By ten that morning, the six new recruits were seated in front of computer terminals and learning about the basics of hacking.

"Time is always an issue," Nicki said from her place at the front of the classroom. "Even with our sophisticated password programs, you're unlikely to get into a hard drive in seconds. If the information is vital and you have a clear way out, sometimes it's simply easier to take the damn thing with you."

Several of the students laughed.

She smiled. "Especially if it's a laptop. But the real trick is when you need to get information without the person knowing you were there. Obviously then a little thievery is not going to work."

There was another appreciative chuckle.

"Okay, let me explain the basic premise of the program," she continued. "Any password is nothing more than a string of characters, be they letters or numbers or symbols. If you can—"

The classroom doors burst open. Four people tore into the room and aimed rifles at the students.

"Nobody move," one of the men yelled. "Nobody breathe. Stay in your seats."

Nicki wheeled toward the man talking. "What do you want?"

He aimed his gun at her chest. "Shut up, sweetheart, and no one gets hurts."

"Take out your wallets and cash," a woman said. "Slowly."

Nicki glanced at her purse on the floor. "I have to move to get mine," she said.

The man swung around and shot out a light. One of the students screamed.

"This is ridiculous," Nicki told the man, her voice loud and heated. "You can't just burst in here and rob us. I won't—"

But she didn't get to say what she wouldn't do. The man returned his attention to her, dropped the rifle to his side, pulled out a handgun and shot her.

Nicki felt the thud against her chest, then spreading wetness. She glanced down and saw a red stain blossoming against the front of her blouse.

The sight of it was enough to make her woozy. She glanced back to the man, then leaned forward and toppled onto the ground. There was screaming and the sound of tussling. Then footsteps as the group grabbed purses and wallets and fled.

The lights went out. There was more yelling and screaming, then the lights flipped back on and Nicki heard Zane's voice.

"Stay calm, people," he said as he crouched next to her.

She raised her head. "I hit my elbow when I fell."

He helped her into a sitting position, then lifted her back into her chair. "You okay?"

She rubbed the spot. "Sure. I'll have a bruise, but that's the price one pays for drama."

He chuckled. "You always make it look so real when you tumble to the floor."

"I don't have that far to go, so it's easier for me to relax."

He looked at her blouse and winced. "Is that going to wash out?"

"It always does."

Nicki unbuttoned the blouse and shrugged out of it, then pulled off the fake blood pack and the plastic protecting her lightweight sweater underneath. After stuffing it all in a bag, she glanced at the students.

They looked shell-shocked and more than a little stunned. Good. They were supposed to be.

"Ready?" Zane asked.

She nodded and wheeled back to her computer terminal.

"All right, people," he said taking his place in front of the class. "Take a deep breath and get focused. I want each of you to think about what just happened. Yes, it was unexpected, but attacks usually are. You have to stay alert in every circumstance. Now Nicki is going to take you through a series of questions. The purpose is to figure out what you think you saw versus what really happened." He glanced at her. "Go for it."

She nodded and typed a few keys. The large screen behind her illuminated as it displayed what was on her laptop. She scrolled to the beginning of the list of questions.

"We'll take these one at a time. Go through the questions and write down your answers. Be as thorough as possible. Impressions, feelings and details. When you're finished we'll compare notes, then we'll go through the scenario again, this time more slowly." She grinned. "And while I'll get shot a second time, there won't be any blood."

The students chuckled, then went to work. As they wrote Zane moved close, then crouched in front of her.

"Lunch," he said. "Mexican. You're buying."

"But I was just shot."

"Right. And you're so excited to still be alive, you want to buy me lunch."

She grinned and nodded. The last of the tension inside of her faded away. After stumbling through some awkward moments, she and Zane were back on their regular footing. They were friends who cared, who teased and that was how she wanted things to stay. Better to be his friend in the long-term than his lover for a couple of weeks. Now she simply had to work on getting over her crush so she could move on with her life.

Two weeks later Nicki pulled her luggage to the back of the van and prepared to lower both it and herself to the ground.

"We need to talk about a ramp," she said to Zane as he waited for her to come to a stop.

"How about some kind of hoist?" he asked. "We could load you like a bag of rice."

She rolled her eyes. "I'm in a wheelchair, Zane. You could be a bit more delicate."

He considered her statement then shook his head. "Where's the fun in that?"

"Oh, yeah. This is a real thrill a minute."

She rolled off the van's ramp and let Zane take possession of her luggage. While she raised the ramp and locked her van, he carried the suitcase to the private company jet they would use to get to Los Angeles.

After pocketing her keys, she headed for the gleaming white plane. When she'd locked her wheels, Zane swept her into his arms and carried her up the stairs.

"Watch my head," she told him. "Last time you crashed me into the doorway."

"I did not. Your hair might have lightly grazed the edge—"

She cut him off with a laugh. "I nearly had a concussion."

"If your mother knew how much you lied to me, she would be desperately disappointed."

"If she knew you'd nearly killed her only child, she'd slap you silly."

His only response was a shake of his head as he stepped into the plane.

Nicki knew Zane was right—her hair had barely brushed against the door frame, but she wanted the distraction of them teasing so she wouldn't notice how good he looked... or smelled. There was also the thrill of being in his arms as he carried her into the plane and set her carefully in a plush leather seat.

"Oh, to be rich," she murmured as she stroked the smooth covering. "Were these upscale seats standard or did you pay extra?"

He sat across from her and stretched out his legs. "When you drop twelve million on a plane, they throw in the leather."

"How nice."

The copilot walked back. "You two ready?"

Zane looked at Nicki who nodded. "I'm braced for air flight," she said.

"Then we'll head out."

"Are you going to do the in-flight announcements?" she asked Zane.

"Keep your seat belt fastened or I'll toss you off the plane."

She wrinkled her nose. "You need to work on your people skills."

"All my skills are in excellent working order. That's why I'm going to meet with this very important client. I'll dazzle him."

"I didn't think guys were your style."

"I'm ignoring you," he told her.

"Maybe I should do the dazzling," she said.

"Did you bring your braces?" he asked. "Then you'd be upright and he could pinch your butt."

"That *does* sound thrilling." She pretended to consider the opportunity. "Maybe later."

"Speaking of fun, how's Brad?"

She'd wondered if he would get around to asking about him. "Boyd is probably fine, but I don't know for sure. We aren't seeing each other."

She braced herself for teasing or questions, but there wasn't, either. Instead he slumped down in his seat.

"His loss," he said quietly.

The plane taxied to the end of the runway, then turned and moved forward. When they were airborne, the captain's voice came on over the loud speaker and gave them an estimated flying time.

"We'll be landing at the Santa Monica airport. The limo is already confirmed."

"Limo?" Nicki raised her eyebrows. "How very upper class."

Zane tossed a magazine at her. "Quit acting as if all this is a surprise. We've used a limo before."

"I know but it's fun to tease you."

"Actually Mr. Sabotini is the one providing the limo, and we're staying in his hotel."

Nicki was surprised. "I've never met anyone who had his own hotel."

"I believe he's part owner in the chain. Don't get too excited. There's a Mrs. Sabotini."

"Bummer. How about sons?"

"The oldest is about sixteen."

"Hmm, for part ownership of a hotel chain, I could hang around for a couple of years until he comes of age."

Zane grimaced. "Not funny."

"Oh, sure. Because it's a woman showing interest in a younger man. But if you had an eighteen-year-old woman hovering around…"

He shook his head. "Too young. Despite your low opinion of me, I actually like to have conversations now and then."

Nicki sensed they were heading into dangerous territory. She didn't want to think about what had happened between Zane and herself, let alone talk about it. Time to change the subject.

"Mr. Sabotini seems to have gotten himself into a little bit of trouble," she said.

"Agreed. International banking can be difficult at best, but when he inadvertently financed some nasty business in the Middle East, all bets were off. There have been multiple death threats on him and his family. The police are involved, but he wants something extra. Which is where we come in. Coffee?"

"Sure."

While Zane walked to the small galley, Nicki leaned forward and grabbed his briefcase.

"Okay if I get out the files?" she asked.

"Help yourself."

She withdrew the thick folders on Mr. Sabotini, then flipped open to the presentation Zane and Jeff had worked up.

"Is he going to agree to pull his kids from their school?" she asked.

"I have no idea, but if he doesn't, he's a fool," Zane said. "These people don't play around."

He returned with two cups of coffee and set one on the small table next to her seat.

"Jeff briefed you on the plan before we left, right?" he asked.

She nodded. "I think it will work, if our client cooperates."

"That's part of our job. To convince him that we're the right company and to remind him that cooperation on his part means staying alive."

The limo pulled up in front of an elegant white building just off Rodeo Drive. Nicki glanced around at the exclusive shops and familiar designer names.

This area wasn't exactly in her price range, she thought, but if there was some free time, she wouldn't mind looking around.

She studied the level sidewalks and wheelchair accessible curbs. At least she wouldn't be dependent on Zane to cart her from place to place. Unlike getting in and out of the limo. As they pulled up to the hotel, she waited patiently while he went around back and collected her wheelchair, then set it next to the rear door.

While she couldn't complain about his attentive service, she had to admit that she didn't like being dependent on him. Yes, being held in his arms got her hormones dancing, but that charming reaction didn't override the sense of being helpless and a bother. Nicki much preferred to make her own way in the world, which was why she'd designed her life so that was possible. Unfortunately situations during business travel weren't always within her control.

There was also the underlying uneasiness from their recent intimacy. She'd traveled with both Jeff and Zane, but always in the capacity of an employee and friend. Never as an ex-lover. She didn't want things to be different between them but she couldn't help sensing that they were.

"Ready?" Zane asked when she was settled in her chair.

She tucked her small handbag next to her hip and nodded. "What time is our meeting this afternoon?"

"Two. We have a couple of hours to get settled. Want to order room service for lunch?"

"That would be great."

She could use the extra time. While specially equipped handicapped rooms made travel easier, there were still problems that had to be worked through.

They approached the front desk. Nicki was pleased to see it was low. Most were so high, she couldn't see the person she was talking to. Either she had to go around to the end, or the person assisting her had to hang over the front.

"May I help you?" a young woman in a navy suit jacket asked.

"We have reservations." Zane gave their names.

The woman touched several keys on her computer keyboard, then raised her eyebrows. "Of course. You are both special guests of Mr. Sabotini. We are delighted to have you staying with us."

Nicki glanced around at the elegant decor of the spacious lobby. In this kind of place, everyone received excellent service. However as she and Zane were "special guests," she had a feeling they were going to be overwhelmed with attention. Not bad duty.

"If you'll sign the registration cards, please," the woman said.

Nicki took hers and glanced at it. "This doesn't say anything about the room being wheelchair friendly," she said. "I want to confirm that it is. I made the request last week."

The woman stiffened. "I'm aware of that, Ms. Beauman, but there isn't a handicapped room available. I'm so sorry. We're happy to upgrade you into something much nicer."

Nicki swallowed panic. "I don't want nicer," she said, keeping her voice calm. "I didn't ask for the room on a whim. As you can see, I use a wheelchair. I require the amenities that come with the room."

The woman nodded and picked up the phone. Zane initialed his form and passed it back.

Nicki held onto hers. Hotel rooms were not her friend. The walking areas were often narrow and littered with obstacles. The vanities were too high, the toilets a nightmare to get on and off of. She could never use the closets because the racks were well above her reach. Then there was the horror of a regular tub, which meant having to step over the side—something she couldn't do.

Looking distraught, the woman hung up. "I'm sorry, Ms. Beauman, but we only have two such rooms in the hotel. The first is occupied by a guest who also requires special amenities. The second had a pipe break and was flooded. It is currently under repair, but is not habitable at this time."

For the most part Nicki was able to ignore her condition. It simply existed and she lived her life, doing pretty much what she wanted. But every now and then circumstances conspired to make her life complicated. This was one of those times.

"A regular room won't work," Nicki said, trying not to panic. "My wheelchair won't fit between the pieces of furniture. There's no way I can step over a regular tub. Or use a closet. I can't reach that high. Even with my braces, I'd find the room a hazard."

Zane listened quietly. He'd never considered the difficulties Nicki experienced when she stepped out of her routine. For him, one hotel room was like another. But for her...

He thought about her house. The hardwood floors, the heavy furniture spaced far enough apart that she could easily wheel around it. He'd never used her private bathroom, but he didn't doubt it had been modified, just like her kitchen.

He knew they could change hotels. While he would normally suggest that, in this case there was the problem of their client.

"Give us a second," he told the clerk, then led Nicki away from the desk.

"What if I helped?" he asked. "It could be fun. You like bossing me around."

She shook her head. "There's no way I'm going to phone you every time I need to move around my room."

"I was thinking more along the lines of us sharing a suite. I'd be there to fetch and carry. You could just lie back and give orders."

She didn't smile, which he'd kind of hoped for, but her tension seemed to ease a little.

"You're not my servant."

"Agreed, but admit it. There have been times you'd like me as your slave."

One corner of her mouth quirked, then stilled.

"There are personal things involved, Zane. Things that are outside of the bounds of friendship."

He leaned close and lowered his voice. "Nicki, I've not only seen you naked, I've pretty much had my tongue and mouth on every inch of you. How many mysteries could there be?"

She shifted in her seat. "Okay, you might have a point there. But the whole idea makes me uncomfortable."

"I don't want that." He touched the back of her hand. "I'm happy to share a suite with you and do whatever needs doing. Under normal circumstances I wouldn't suggest it."

She sighed. "But Mr. Sabotini owns the hotel and he'll be offended if we stay somewhere else."

"Not if we tell him why."

She grimaced. "I don't think I want to have that conversation." She looked at him. "This could be very weird."

He winked. "Yeah, but I get to see you naked."

He waited for her remind him they were just friends and that nothing was going to happen. Instead she rubbed her hands against the wheels of her chair.

"I don't want you seeing me like that to change anything."

He stared at her, at her big green eyes and the slight quiver of her mouth. He'd seen Nicki gloating, laughing, angry and wild with passion, but he couldn't remember ever seeing her vulnerable before. Something inside of his chest tightened.

He leaned close and touched her cheek. "I have always admired you. Nothing abut that is going to change. I swear."

She swallowed. "If you're lying, I'll run you over."

He grinned. "It's a deal."

They returned to the front desk where the young woman was delighted to give them a large two bedroom suite. A bellman took up their luggage, and Zane and Nicki followed.

The suite was on a high floor, with huge windows and a north-facing view. Several Oriental rugs covered a marble floor. Sofas and chairs formed conversation groups, while a black lacquered table and chairs sat up on a dais by the window.

Nicki glanced around the room. "The rugs will have to go," she said.

The bellman pulled a small notepad out of his pocket and wrote down the instruction. "Anything else?" he asked.

She wheeled through the room and pointed to an end table, a small desk and two chairs. From there she went into the master bedroom.

Zane ducked into the second bedroom which was nice, but not nearly as opulent as the living area. He checked out the bathroom and bedroom, then walked into the master.

The bed was on a platform, but there was plenty of open floor space. He found Nicki in the bathroom. Again there was plenty of room for her to maneuver around. The large glass shower had a built in bench.

"I'll take the other bedroom," he said. "You'll be able to get around in this one."

She hesitated, as if she were going to protest, then nodded. "Thanks."

"No problem."

She had the bellman take up the small rugs in the bathroom, then returned to the living area.

Two men had already arrived and were removing the unwanted furniture. When they'd finished, Zane glanced at his watch.

"Let's order room service and then unpack," he said.

"Okay."

She picked a salad off the menu. Trying not to gag at the thought of lettuce for lunch, he ordered her meal, then got a burger for himself, with extra fries because he knew she would be stealing his. Then he carried her suitcase into the master bedroom and set it on the bed.

He'd already seen the closet so he knew there was no way she could reach up and hang her own clothes.

"Tell me what you want where," he said as he flipped open the top of the case.

She had him hang her two suits and blouses, then put lingerie, a nightgown and stockings in a drawer.

She didn't look at him as she spoke and he could tell she wasn't happy about the situation.

He dropped to his knees in front of her and took both her hands in his. "I don't know how to make this better for you," he said.

"That's not your job."

"Sure it is. We're friends." He squeezed her fingers. "Nicki, you're damned independent most of the time, which is all any of us ever get to say. Sometimes we need a little extra help."

"I know that in my head, but it still bugs me. I don't like you doing all this extra work."

"I know how you can repay me."

Her expression turned wary. "How?" she asked cautiously.

"Let me rub your panties all over my body."

She jerked her hands free of his. "That's too disgusting for words."

He grinned. "I'd let you watch."

"Don't even think about it."

Now that her good humor had been restored, he told her the truth.

"I think you're amazing," he said quietly. "You're smart, beautiful and not half-bad in bed."

She smiled. "Gee, thanks."

"None of that is about you being in the chair. I don't mind helping out. You'd take care of me if the tables were turned."

"I know, but they aren't. Nor are they likely to be."

"Next time I have the flu I'll call you over to fix me soup."

"Actually you'd have to come stay at my place."

"Even better." He winked. "You can give me lots of sponge baths."

She rolled her eyes. "Is everything about getting naked with you?"

"Pretty much."

"That is just so typical."

"Can I help it if women find me irresistible?"

"Not all women."

"Enough do."

He wanted to tell her that she was one of them but didn't want to hear her say she wasn't. After all, Nicki had been the one to put the brakes on their physical relationship, not him.

"Thanks," she said, squeezing his fingers. "For all of this. And for making it easy. Now why don't you go unpack before our lunch gets here? Did you order extra fries?"

"Of course."

"Good."

She smiled.

For a second they just looked at each other. Something hot and bright flared between them. Zane thought about leaning close and kissing her—for two reasons. Because he wanted to and because at that moment he knew she would kiss him back. But he didn't. There was a fragile peace between them that he didn't want to shatter. For reasons he couldn't explain, having Nicki need him was somehow more important than having Nicki want him.

# Chapter 8

"Nicole," Mr. Sabotini said at the end of their meeting. "I want your promise that you'll be serving as, how do you say, backup?"

She smiled. "I'll be there making sure they get it right."

"Excellent."

He took her hand and lightly kissed her knuckles. "You have impressed me."

Okay, so the man was smooth and probably only meant about thirty percent of what he said, but Nicki didn't care. She liked hearing the flattery and the compliments. After all, how often did an elegantly dressed Italian man stare adoringly at her? She couldn't think of a single incident.

"You've made the right choice with our firm," she said as she disentangled her hand. Flattery was one thing, but while Mr. Sabotini might not be thinking of his wife, Nicki was very clear on her existence.

Zane stood and collected their files. "I'll phone the office and have the contracts drawn up."

Mr. Sabotini rose. "I would like the team in place as soon as possible."

"We'll overnight the contracts. Once you sign them and provide the retainer, we'll move into place." Zane shook the man's hand. "Two of our best child-protection agents have just finished an assignment. They're already making arrangements to fly to Italy."

"Good. I worry about my boys." He smiled at Zane, then turned to her. "Nicole. You must tell me the next time you visit Italy."

"You'll be the first," she murmured, then wheeled toward the exit.

They left the spacious suite only two floors above their own and headed for the elevators.

"That went well," she said.

Zane chuckled. "Yeah. I want to say we sold him on our reputation and the quality of our bodyguards, but I think your legs were a good part of the appeal."

"He was being polite."

"He was drooling."

She smiled. "Mr. Sabotini likes women. As I was the only female in the room, I received all of his attention."

Zane shook his head. "Sorry, kid, but you don't get off that easily. I think there could have been ten women in the room and he still would have focused on you. I couldn't decide if I should offer to leave you two alone or take him out back and beat the crap out of him."

She would love to think that Zane was jealous but her imagination wasn't that good. Their client's attention had been just the ego boost she needed and she refused to apologize for that.

They reached the elevator lobby, but instead of pushing the down button, Zane pushed up.

"Where are we going?" she asked.

"To the rooftop restaurant. I made reservations for us so we would have somewhere to celebrate."

"And if we hadn't closed the deal?"

"Hot dogs and beer."

She was still laughing when the elevator arrived.

The rooftop restaurant offered a gorgeous view. It was clear in Los Angeles, warm, with a soft breeze. To the west, the sun slipped toward the horizon.

She was shown to a table on the edge of the patio. Several tall potted trees provided privacy, while a tall gas heater stood by in case the evening became chilly.

The waiter had already whisked away a chair, so Nicki was able to glide into place. She placed her napkin on her lap then picked up the menu. Zane was still by the front podium, calling Jeff to let him know what happened.

"I told him we want a raise," he said as he approached a few minutes later. "And that we were brilliant. Mostly me, of course, but I gave you some of the credit."

"Gee, thanks."

"No problem." He pulled out a chair and sank down on the seat. "So what looks good?"

They discussed various menu choices, had a conversation with the waiter about wine, then picked entrées and a bottle of cabernet sauvignon.

"The only thing that would make this day any better would be you telling me you want me to run you a bath later," Zane said with a grin.

Nicki knew he was kidding, or at least teasing. And she really appreciated his help while they were staying at the hotel. But she couldn't help wishing—just for a second—that she didn't need it.

"What?" he asked, leaning toward her. "You got quiet and sad."

She shook her head. "I'm being silly."

"I'll be the judge of that."

She debated changing the subject versus telling the truth. Funny how of all the people she knew in the world, outside of her parents, he was the only one she could imagine confiding in.

"Sometimes the limitations get me down," she admitted. "I try not to go there and most of the time I succeed, but every now and then…" Her voice trailed off.

"Like when you have to maneuver through strange hotel rooms?"

"Yeah." She shrugged. "Plus I hate you seeing that I'm not perfect."

He grinned. "Nicki, I've never once thought of you as perfect, so this isn't a revelation for me."

She chuckled. "You know what I mean."

"I do. You're not in control and no one likes that. You weren't born this way. You can remember what it was like not to deal with the chair." He glanced around as if making sure they were alone. "If you ever repeat this, I'll deny saying it, but I think you're a hell of a woman."

The combination of sincerity and teasing nearly brought tears to her eyes. Trust Zane to get it exactly right.

"You always make me feel good about myself."

He nodded. "I'm a pretty spectacular guy. And modest."

"Especially modest." She touched his hand. "I could have used someone like you around when I first had my accident."

"You were what, fourteen?"

She nodded. "We were on a skiing vacation over the holidays. Neither of my parents had any family and before I was born they'd gotten in the habit of traveling over Christmas. When I came along, they kept up the tradition."

She smiled as she remembered how happy those trips had been. "No matter where we were, they always made Christmas special."

She'd been a miracle baby, born three days after her mother's fortieth birthday. Her mother had always joked that if she'd received Nicki for turning forty that she couldn't wait to see what fifty would bring.

"The resort had dug out a couple of trees that had been knocked over by high winds, but they hadn't gotten around to filling in the holes. Whatever signs they'd put out had disappeared. I came tearing down the mountain right into a ten-foot pit."

Zane winced. "That had to hurt."

"I don't know. I hit my head, so I was unconscious until we got to the hospital. By then I was in shock and spacing out. It took a couple of days and two surgeries before I knew what was going on."

The waiter appeared with their bottle of wine. While he opened it, someone else brought bread and their salads.

Zane tasted the wine and nodded his approval. When they were alone, he raised his glass to her.

"To staying strong," he said.

She nodded and sipped.

"After a few days my parents were told my left leg would never heal right. There were too many breaks and there was no way to put it all together. I was okay with that. I figured I could survive a limp."

Zane didn't think he would have survived the same experience with Nicki's faith in life and good spirits.

"Then you came down with the bone infection," he said.

"Exactly. That was tough. They had to open me up again, scrape stuff out. I was on so many antibiotics I practically glowed. My parents were frantic with worry."

"You pulled through."

"But the bone was weakened forever." She picked up her fork. "I went into physical therapy. Once there I learned I wouldn't be walking again. Not without braces and a walker. It was a real down time. I thought…" She glanced at him, then away. "I really thought about killing myself."

"Makes sense."

She looked surprised. "But that's the easy way out."

"Nicki, you were what, fifteen? Your entire life had been shattered. Of course you'd think of ending it all. Who wouldn't?"

"I thought everyone else would be stronger than me. I've dealt with a lot of guilt over my plan." She smiled slightly. "I have to say being underage and in a wheelchair made the 'how' pretty difficult. Then one night while I was sitting alone in my room, I heard a voice."

He stared at her. "What kind?"

"I don't know. It was in my head. I'd never heard it before or since. It wasn't my voice or my folks. It wasn't anyone I knew. But it told me I was an idiot. I had parents who loved me, unlimited opportunity and if I ended my life over something as foolish as not being able to walk then I was too stupid to live anyway."

She shrugged. "I figured if I was hearing voices, I'd better listen."

Over the past couple of years he'd learned various details about her injuries and subsequent recovery, but he'd never heard this.

"What happened?" he asked.

"I made the decision to get over myself. I threw myself into physical therapy and went back to school. Once I figured out I could still play sports and have a life, I did the best I could and never looked back."

"Any more voices?"

"Not even one." She took a bite of her salad and chewed. "Once I accepted myself, I found all my friends were more than ready to accept me."

"I'll bet." He imagined a sixteen-year-old Nicki. "You broke hearts on a weekly basis."

"I don't know about that, but I did have boyfriends. I told you before that I wore my braces to the prom so I could slow dance."

He didn't want to think about that—about some high school senior carrying her out to the dance floor and holding her close.

Crazy to be jealous of a ghost, he told himself. Maybe if he didn't still want her, he wouldn't mind so much.

"You showed them all," he said. "Even yourself."

"I learned I'm a survivor. I think that's an important lesson."

He agreed. But Nicki had done more than survive. She'd thrived.

"Have you—"

But whatever he'd been about to say got lost when he looked up and saw her watching him. There was something in her eyes, something bright and hot and passionate.

Heat exploded inside of him. In less than two seconds he went from interested to hard. His chest tightened, his hands curled into fists and damn it all to hell, he couldn't seem to catch his breath.

"You said friends," he reminded her when he could finally speak.

"I know."

Her voice, more murmur than whisper, made him think of being naked with her. Of tangled sheets and soft cries and the thrill of pleasing her.

He wanted to tell her they couldn't do this. That he understood her reasons for wanting them to be only friends and he respected them. But he couldn't seem to say the words. Maybe he just didn't want to.

"I know I'm changing the rules," she said. "Is that okay?"

He managed a smile. "You think I'm going to tell you no?"

She smiled. "Then I guess we should get dinner to go."

It took a few minutes to settle things with the waiter and collect their takeout boxes. Nicki tried to keep her mind perfectly blank because if she thought too much about what she'd said, about what they were going to do, she would start to hyperventilate.

She knew this was crazy, that *she* was crazy. She had very logical, sensible reasons for keeping things on a "friend's only" footing with Zane. She didn't want to get her heart broken, she didn't want to lose him. She wanted to be free to fall for someone else and get started on her happily ever after. But she couldn't seem to not want him.

She'd just told him her deepest darkest secrets and instead of running for the hills, he'd looked at her as if she were his hero. How was she supposed to resist that? Plus he'd been so sweet about them sharing a room. He'd made jokes and gone out of his way to make her feel special and normal. That, combined with spending time alone with him, had apparently undone her good intentions, leaving her little more than a liquid puddle of longing.

The elevator ride to their floor was short and silent.

Nicki didn't know where to look and when her gaze accidentally landed on Zane's face, she nearly fainted at the desire she saw etched there. Whatever doubts she might have about the foolishness of her decision to make love with him again were overshadowed by the fact that he wanted her just as much as she wanted him.

When the elevator doors opened, they exited and moved directly to the suite. Zane already had the key out. He pushed opened the door and she entered. He was right behind her. She heard the slap of the takeout containers hitting a table, but she was already heading for the bedroom. As she rolled, she reached down and pulled off her shoes, while shrugging out of her suit jacket.

That was as far as she got. Zane caught up with her halfway across the bedroom and knelt in front of her wheelchair. Then his hands were on her face and he was kissing her with a desperation that made her heart break.

His warm, firm lips took as much as they offered. She tasted wine and a hint of the man himself.

At the first brush of his mouth, her breathing caught and she parted her lips for him instantly. When his tongue swept inside, touching her, teasing her, making her want with a force that should have terrified her, she ceased to need breath. As long as she had this man, as long as he touched her and allowed her to touch him, she would survive. This moment was enough. This world in which they were lovers was paradise.

"I want you," he breathed as he kissed her cheek, her nose, her forehead. He cupped her head and gazed into her eyes. "Nicki."

The sound of her name was as erotic as a touch. She shivered in anticipation of what was to come. Of how they would be together. She was already damp. She could feel the wetness on her panties. Her breasts had swollen, as had that most intimate part of her.

"Zane," she whispered as she ran her fingers down his cheeks.

He wrapped his arms around her and drew her out of the chair and onto his lap. Leaning up against an oversized chair, he cuddled her close and kissed her.

These were slow, deep kisses. Kisses of preparation and exploration. Waves of sensation crashed through her as she struggled to get closer and closer. If only she could crawl inside of him, everything would be all right.

He kept one arm around her. His other dropped to her lap where his hand began a lazy exploration of her legs. While he nibbled on the corner of her mouth, then sucked her lower lip, he tickled the inside of her knee and slowly began to drift up her thigh.

For her part, she explored his broad shoulders, then began to unbutton his shirt. She wanted to feel bare skin against her own. She wanted to make *his* breath catch as much as her own.

"So beautiful," he whispered as he rained kisses down her throat and across her collarbone. "So—"

The hand on her thigh froze. She felt a little jolt of her own as he crossed from the top of her stocking to skin.

He raised his head and looked at her. "What the hell are you wearing?"

She couldn't help smiling at his tone of outrage. "What I always wear when I have to put on stockings. A garter belt."

He swallowed, swore, then swallowed again. "You're kidding?"

She shook her head. "Pantyhose aren't really a thing anymore, thank goodness. It's just about impossible to put them on while seated in a wheelchair. I can't stand up, and all the wiggling in the world isn't going to pull that waist-band into place. I gave up years ago. Actually the whole stocking thing is the reason I prefer pants. But for business meetings, I'll put on thigh-high stockings and a garter belt."

Heat flared in his dark eyes. "You mean to tell me that every time I've been in a meeting with you and you've been in a skirt, you've had this on underneath?"

As he spoke he caressed her thigh and the garter belt clasp.

"Sure."

He groaned. "Thank God I didn't know."

She looked at him. "What's the big deal? It's just underwear."

"Nicki, it's a whole lot of things, but 'just underwear' isn't one of them."

He shifted onto his knees, then still holding her, stood and walked to the bed.

"I'll admit it's completely adolescent, but I have to see," he murmured as he placed her on the mattress and reached for the side zipper of her skirt.

The garment slipped off, and he stared at her. Nicki raised up on one elbow to see what all the fuss was about. To her the view was what it always was. Garter belt, panties and stockings.

"I don't get the big deal," she began, right as Zane bent over and pressed an openmouthed kiss to the top of her thigh.

Instantly overcome by need and weakness, she sank back onto the bed. Maybe it didn't matter if she understood why it worked for him. Maybe the important information was that it *did*.

He nibbled higher, making her squirm when he tickled her tummy.

As he kissed his way north, he also reached for the front of her blouse and went to work on the buttons. Seconds later, he flipped open the front catch on her bra and took her right nipple in his mouth.

Glorious didn't begin to describe the sensations filling her body. While he used mouth, lips and tongue to tease her into a frenzy, his hand matched the movements on her other breast. She gasped and writhed, clung to him, pressed closer and begged for more.

There seemed to be a direct connection between her breasts and that place between her thighs. Her legs fell open. She ached and wanted, even as she held him in place.

It was better than she remembered, which she didn't think was possible.

They were both breathing hard. Nicki felt Zane tremble as he continued to touch her and she didn't think she could hold out much longer.

"Get naked," she whispered.

He didn't need to be told twice. He stood up and grinned, then went to work on his clothes. Seconds later he stood before her, undressed and aroused.

She stared at his broad chest, at the pattern of dark hair that led down to his flat belly and the thick maleness jutting toward her. Had she been standing, she would have gone weak in the knees. As she was lying down, she was able to stay relatively in control.

She shifted back on the bed while he moved next to her. Then their hands were all over each other. While he traced the curve of her hip and the length of her leg, she stroked his back, his rear and the top of his thigh before settling her hand on him.

She rubbed back and forth, then slipped her thumb over the soft, velvety tip. His breath caught in a ragged gasp.

"So you want to play that game," he whispered just before pressing an open kiss on the sensitive skin below her ear. His tongue flicked back and forth, causing goose bumps to break out on her arms.

At the same time he slipped a hand between her legs and moved his fingers through the swollen dampness. Now it was her turn to gasp, then writhe as he searched for and found that one place of pleasure.

Electricity jolted through her. She couldn't do anything but close her eyes and let him please her. It was too much—it would never be enough. More, she thought desperately, unable to focus enough to speak the words.

Fortunately, Zane was able to read her mind. He shifted his hand so his thumb pressed against her most sensitive spot and his finger dipped inside. Then he moved both, delighting her, making her hips buck, her head fall back and her entire body tense in anticipation.

She was already so close. Too close. She wanted to tell him to wait, to let her savor the moment. She wanted to take her time. But it was too late.

As his thumb circled and his finger mimicked the act of love to follow, he claimed her with a kiss that touched her soul. Mouths pressed, breaths exchanged, she lost herself in the pleasure. Her release swept through her, a violent storm that battered her senses and left her shaking with ecstasy.

Zane continued to touch her, lighter and lighter until he barely brushed against her throbbing flesh. When she was able to finally open her eyes, she found him looking at her. Not smiling, not speaking, just watching.

"Thank you," he murmured at last.

His tender words made her eyes burn, but she blinked away the tears and reached for him. When he was inside, stretching her, filling her, making her reach again for the moment of release, she found that it was her turn to watch him. Even as pleasure claimed her a second time, she saw the tension in his face, the near grimace of his mouth as he pumped in and out, reaching for his own climax.

At that crucial moment, when they were both lost in the wonder of what their bodies could do together, their gazes locked. She saw down to his very essence and knew he had the same view of her.

For a split second, time stood still. Shy, bruised and lonely souls kissed in a moment of connection so profound, she had no words. This wasn't just making love, Nicki thought, this was two becoming one.

They clung to each other until their bodies returned to normal. Then Zane rolled on his side, pulling her with him.

She braced herself for his casual response to what she'd considered a life-altering experience, but he didn't speak. Instead he maneuvered them both under the covers, then pulled her close and stroked her hair.

Nicki knew it was crazy, but she had the overwhelming need to cry. She wasn't sad—if anything she was more content than she'd ever been. But she was also terrified.

Something had happened. Something more scary than when she'd broken her legs and been told she wouldn't ever walk again. Even as she lay there, safe in Zane's embrace, she could feel something shifting inside. It was as if her heart were physically opening up and allowing him to be a part of her.

She hadn't wanted to fall in love with him, but what if it was too late? What if she already had?

If she loved him, she would want him to love her back. If she loved him, then leaving and starting somewhere else wasn't possible. Loving Zane would mean needing him as much as she needed air or food or sleep. He would weave himself into the very fabric of her being and then what? Would he love her back? And if he didn't, how long would it be until he left and she had to learn to survive without him?

*I love you.*

The words hovered on her lips, but she didn't speak them. Not yet. Maybe not ever.

Loving Zane. Could she be more of a fool? He was a man who never committed. He didn't do long-term or forever. He did temporary and meaningless.

He kissed her forehead. "I want to stay here with you tonight."

She nodded because speaking would mean saying what she was thinking. What she was feeling.

"Are you hungry?" he asked. "We have those dinners."

She shook her head.

He sat up and looked at her. "What's wrong? Are you okay?"

She was far from all right, but she wasn't going to tell him that, either.

"Hold me," she whispered.

"I am."

"More. Hold me more."

He slipped back down onto the mattress and wrapped both arms around her. She turned so she could lean her head against his shoulder and breathe in the scent of him.

"Shh," he murmured. "I'm right here. I'm not going anywhere."

She believed him. For tonight. But what about tomorrow and the rest of her life?

# Chapter 9

Nicki managed to get some sleep that night. By the next morning, she'd convinced herself that worrying about being in love with Zane was a subject best explored in the privacy of her own home...when she was alone. So when she felt him lightly tracing the length of her spine, she was able to turn toward him and smile.

"You snore," he said as he kissed the tip of her nose.

"I do not."

"Okay, you don't, but you breathe deeply when you're asleep. I'll bet you're going to snore when you're an old lady."

"Is this your idea of sweet talk the morning after?"

"Yup." He grinned and got up. "So here's the thing," he said as he stretched. "It's Wednesday."

She admired the view of his very naked self and leaned back to enjoy the show. "I was aware of that, but thanks for sharing."

"You're welcome." He plopped down on the edge of the bed, on her side. "We're supposed to go back to Seattle this morning."

"I know that as well."

He was so close, she couldn't resist tiptoeing her fingers across his bare leg. As she got closer to the promised land, the body part in question seemed to notice. There was a slight stirring, then it began to grow.

Zane glared at her. "I'm trying to have a serious conversation."

"Oh, and we can't do that if I'm doing this?"

She took him in her hand and moved back and forth along the rapidly hardening length. Then she fluttered her eyelashes at him.

"Not enough oxygen going to your brain?" she asked.

He closed his eyes and gave himself up to the caress for a couple of minutes, then grabbed her wrist. "I thought we'd save that for after breakfast."

"Interesting plan, but we have a plane to catch."

"Which is my point. I have a business trip on Friday. I have to fly to New York to meet with the prince and princess of El Bahar. They're planning an extended trip to the States with their three children and they want to have local security to supplement whatever palace guards they're bringing."

She was having a little trouble tearing her attention away from his arousal. She couldn't help thinking how much more pleasant this conversation would be with him inside of her.

"I fail to see how your business trip has anything to do with us doing the wild thing again." She teased the very tip of him with her finger.

He sucked in a breath. "My point is I want to call Jeff

and tell him we're staying an extra day. The plane isn't needed back. I don't have anything pressing on my calendar, do you?"

One more day with Zane? One more night in this beautiful hotel before heading back to the real world?

"I like a man with a plan," she said. "My calendar is blissfully empty."

"Great." He rose and collected bathrobes from the closet, then tossed her one. "You call down for room service while I check in with Jeff."

He shrugged into the robe. After pushing her wheelchair to the edge of the bed and locking it into place, he picked up his jacket and dug around for his cell phone.

Nicki had a sudden thought. "What are you going to tell him?" she asked.

"That we want to celebrate the new contract by staying an extra day."

She felt heat on her cheeks. "You can't say that. He's going to suspect something."

"Like what?"

"Like we're doing it."

Zane grinned. "I swear that my business partner never wants to think about me doing it. Even if he were to find us naked on your desk, he wouldn't want to think about it. Trust me. It's a guy thing."

That may be true, Nicki thought as Zane dialed the office, but what about Ashley? She knew what had happened before and if Jeff told her that Nicki and Zane had spent an extra night in L.A. she would be able to put all the pieces together.

"Please don't share the completed puzzle with your husband," Nicki whispered as she shifted into the chair, then wheeled to the desk for the room service menu.

* * *

As they'd both skipped dinner, they were starving by the time the breakfast cart was wheeled into their room. Zane signed for the charge while Nicki poured coffee and pulled lids off of dishes. There was very little conversation for the first few minutes, until they took the edge off their hunger.

Nicki took in the view, which included Zane and the open French doors behind him. It was a clear morning, with a brilliant blue sky.

"So Jeff didn't want to know why we were staying?" she asked.

"He said we'd done great and to have a good time."

She wasn't sure she liked that. "What was his tone of voice? Was he joking?"

Zane pushed back his plate and reached for his coffee. "I have no idea about his tone. He was fine, we're staying an extra day, so let it go."

Easier said than done. She didn't usually skip workdays, which meant she had tons of vacation time built up. But as they were already here, she might as well enjoy herself.

"Come out onto the balcony," he said. "We can sit in the sunshine for a few minutes."

He led the way, then settled on a big cushion he'd brought out and leaned his shoulder against her legs. She held her coffee in one hand and stroked his hair with the other.

She wasn't any less terrified than she'd been the night before, but she was learning to cope with the feeling of impending panic. When they returned to Seattle and she had a few days to herself, she would work out a plan. In the meantime, she would simply enjoy their time together.

Something soft brushed against her knee. She glanced down and saw Zane tracing the line of the scars on her leg.

"Do they ever hurt?" he asked.

"Not the scars. There are some achy places inside. If I exercise too hard, or use my braces for too long I can feel it."

He turned and grinned at her. "These aren't all that impressive."

"Oh, you think not?"

He shrugged out of his robe and exposed his back to her. "Now that's a scar," he said.

She studied the long narrow line slicing by his shoulder blade. "A knife?"

"Wicked, huh?"

"Very nice." There was another scar by his rib cage. "Gun shot?"

"Uh-huh."

"Did you get these while you were in the Marines or are they from your previous life?"

He pulled the robe back over his shoulders and turned to face her. "I got them in the service."

He didn't talk about his past much, which made her wonder why. "Can you tell me what you did?"

His eyes clouded. "I was a sniper."

Four simple words, yet they stunned her into silence. A sniper? She had a feeling that was a polite way of saying he'd killed people. But who and where? And who had shot back?

So many questions. Rather than ask them and spoil the day, she shifted to another topic.

"So you went into the military to get yourself straightened out, right? I remember you saying you got in trouble for stealing a truck."

"Not just a truck," he corrected with a grin. "A truck filled with stolen televisions."

"Not exactly a smart thing to do."

"It was only dumb when I got caught. As it was my first offense, the judge sent me to one of those boot-camp reform schools instead of prison. I found I liked the discipline of the service and enlisted when I turned eighteen."

She thought of her own happy childhood, of the parents who had doted on her. "Where was your family?"

He shrugged. "Gone. I never knew my dad. My mom took off when I was three or four, so my grandmother raised me. She wanted more for me than life in the streets or dying young in a gang. I didn't know any other world. So in some ways, getting caught was the best thing that ever happened to me."

"You've come a long way."

"Up and out."

"Why did you leave the Marines?"

The shadows returned to his eyes, and with them came a stiffness to his body. She could feel the ghosts circling them and wondered if they belonged to the living or the dead.

"You don't have to tell me," she said.

He shrugged. "I got hurt pretty bad. I knew that if I kept doing what I was doing I'd end up dead. One day I didn't want that, so I left. I met up with Jeff about two weeks later and we started the company."

She wanted to know where he'd been when he'd been hurt and why he'd thought dying was better than living. She wanted to know what had changed his mind.

Before she could decide on what questions to ask, Zane took her coffee cup from her hand and set it on a small glass table, then swept her into his arms. She shrieked.

"Where are we going?" she asked.

He nuzzled her neck. "To take a shower. I noticed there's a very interesting bench in the master bath and it's at just the right height."

She looped her arm around his neck and smiled. "The right height for what?"

"I'll show you."

Zane deposited Nicki on the counter, then dropped his robe to the floor and walked into the spacious shower to start the water. When it was the right temperature, he turned back to collect her, then had to stop dead when he saw that she, too, had shrugged out of her robe.

The white terry cloth pooled at her waist, exposing her breasts to view. She might not be as well endowed as most of the women he'd taken to bed, but she was still perfect. Her sweet curves begged to be touched, explored and tasted while the peach-colored nipples pointed right at him in a saucy "come and get it" kind of way.

In the three steps it took to cross to her, he was already hard. It took every ounce of self control to keep from burying himself into her waiting warmth. But he had plans for their shower, so instead of giving in to what he guessed they both wanted, he carried her into the steamy shower and set her on the bench.

"What do you think?" he asked as he knelt in front of her and let the water dance over both of them.

She smiled. "This could be interesting."

"More than that," he promised.

Humor brightened her eyes, and passion. She wanted, just like he did. For a second, the past had threatened. He knew better than to talk about it, but being around her had somehow lulled him into lowering his guard. It wouldn't happen again, he told himself. It couldn't.

He brushed those thoughts away and reached for the soap. After lathering it between his hands, he touched her everywhere, as much to excite as to cleanse.

He stroked the length of her arms and her back, then

cupped her breasts. He slid his hands down her belly, along her legs, then returned to slip them between her thighs. When her breathing was ragged and he could feel her pulsing toward him, he shifted out of the way so the spray could rinse her. Then he lowered his head and tasted her.

The intimate kiss made her gasp. She clung to him, digging her hands into his shoulders. Her legs parted more as she moaned. Water washed them both, while steam surrounded them.

He tasted her, drank of her and the water. When he inserted a single finger into her waiting slickness, she arched back and convulsed around him. He felt the spasms of her orgasm as he continued to flick his tongue against that single point of pleasure. He drew out the contact until she sighed her completion. Only then did he straighten and smile at her.

Her eyes opened slowly. She looked deeply relaxed and satisfied.

"Talk about a great way to start my day," she said. "Wow."

He grinned and reached for the soap.

"I'll do that," she said and proceeded to wash him down.

She had him stand and turn away so she could do his back and the backs of his legs. When he faced her again, she had a gleam in her eye that told him there was about to be the best kind of trouble.

"Ready?" she asked as she lathered her hands again.

He already knew, but he couldn't help asking, "For what?"

She dropped the soap and put her hands on his hardness. The slick pressure was erotic and mind bending. He felt his knees give way and he had to lock them in place.

Back and forth, back and forth. Pressure built at the base

of his arousal. He'd planned on sitting down and having her straddle him but right now he couldn't imagine moving.

When she pushed him back into the spray, he didn't understand, but when she pulled him close and leaned forward, everything clicked into place.

As her mouth settled over him, he braced himself against the shower walls. The water pummeled his back while her lips and tongue worked magic between his legs.

Need built. He swore. He groaned her name. Then he lost control in the best way possible.

"You can't be serious," Nicki said late that morning as she wheeled across the parking lot.

"Why not? We want to hang out and have fun," Zane told her. "What better place?" He tugged on a strand of her hair. "The park is completely wheelchair accessible. I spoke to the concierge at the hotel and she assured me they have a sterling reputation for that sort of thing."

"I know, but Disneyland?"

Nicki stared at the castle rising against the blue sky and the white mountain where three climbers made their way to the top. She could hear the excited conversation all around her.

Zane looked at her. "Don't you want to go?"

She bit her lower lip, not sure how to explain that she'd only been once—the year before her accident—and that she'd always wanted to go back. But somehow she'd never made the time and now they were here and the fact that Zane had been the one to think of it made her want to burst into tears. Or do it with him right there by the entrance.

"I'm delighted," she said when she was sure she could speak without her voice cracking.

"Good."

They had a heated discussion about which ride to go on first, then agreed to alternating picks with a coin toss to determine who went first. The resulting schedule meant dashing from one side of the park to the other—perhaps not the most sensible plan, but one that was lots of fun.

"Hurry," Nicki called as she maneuvered through the crowd on her way to the Haunted House. "Jeez, Zane, you're such a slowpoke."

He caught up with her by the entrance. "You're too fast on those damn wheels."

"Zane was beaten by a girl," she said in a singsong voice.

He bent low and kissed her. "Sugar, you can beat me any time you want…just so long as you're wearing black leather."

Black leather? Her eyes widened and she had a feeling she looked stunned. But before she could pursue that line of conversation, they were moving toward the front of the mansion and surrounded by children.

"I'll be bringing that up later," she told him.

"I'm counting on it."

The helpful staff took possession of her wheelchair while she sat through the charming ride. At the end, when a ghost "tried to follow them home" Zane put his arm around her and told the green visitor that, "No one is going to get my girl."

Nicki tried not to read too much into the words. She and Zane were hanging out together, and she knew that he liked her, but that was a long way from what *she* was experiencing. Still, his possessiveness made her feel all warm inside.

They headed toward Main Street. They still had about a half hour before heading for the Blue Bayou Restaurant and their dinner reservations.

"Let's go in here," he said, pointing her toward one of the big shops that lined the street.

Once inside, Nicki found herself wanting to buy one of everything. There were stuffed animals, watches, T-shirts, collectible cartoon cells.

Zane made her laugh when he tried on mouse ears, then picked up three glowing rubber balls and started to juggle. Talk about another surprise—he wasn't half-bad.

"Betcha Brad can't do this," he said as he caught the third ball and dropped them back into the counter.

"You're right."

There were a lot of things Boyd hadn't been able to do. The biggest had been to help her get over Zane. Now it was too late. Watching him move through the store, joking with the sales staff, offering to buy her everything from a stuffed Simba to mouse ears of her own, she felt her heart tighten with love. Zane was everything she'd ever wanted. And for this moment in time, he was hers.

She studied a collection of postcards, then decided to pick several to help her remember the day. A burst of laughter caught her attention. Turning, she saw three young women hovering around Zane. They stared at him with obvious interest.

Nicki allowed herself a moment of envy for their easy walks and long, healthy legs. Then she shook off the feeling and reminded herself that her life was exactly what she wanted it to be.

A minute or so later Zane walked away from the women. His gaze settled on her and when he smiled she knew he was thinking about last night and this morning. Those young women had never even registered.

Happiness bubbled inside of her. When Zane approached, she grabbed his shirtfront and pulled him down so she could kiss him…thoroughly.

When she released him, he crouched next to her and smiled. "What was that for?"

"No particular reason. I just wanted to connect."

"Good."

He pulled something out of his shirt pocket. A small box. When he opened it she saw he'd bought her a gold charm bracelet decorated with a pair of mouse ears.

"So you can remember our day together," he said as he fastened the catch.

As if she could ever forget. "Thank you, Zane."

He touched his index finger to the tip of her nose. "You're welcome."


The plane landed shortly after eleven the next morning. Zane carried Nicki down the steps and set her into her wheelchair while the copilot collected their luggage from the hold.

"You said you're taking the rest of the day off," Zane said as he followed her to her van. "You need to get some rest."

She smiled at the worried tone of his voice. "You slept as little as I did." They'd both been up most of last night, making love.

He shrugged. "I'll catch up tonight and on the plane tomorrow."

That was right. His New York trip. She would miss him, but wasn't sure if she should tell him.

She clicked the remote unlock button. "I promise to get plenty of rest, both today and tonight."

"I'll call you from the hotel," he promised. "You know. Just to check in."

She liked that he wanted to check in, even as she told

herself it didn't mean anything. Zane was being nice, nothing more. As for what was going on between them…she'd already decided that would stay undefined until he got back from his trip. Then she would have a talk with him. Well, assuming she had the courage. There were times when she thought it was better not to know what he was thinking about them.

The copilot set her luggage on the ramp and she thanked him. Then she wheeled onto the ramp and pushed the button to raise it.

When she was level with the rear of the van, she looked at Zane. "Have a good trip."

He moved close and kissed her. "I'll miss you."

His words made her chest tightened. "Me, too."

He tucked her hair behind her ears. "What happens if Boyd calls while I'm gone?"

"Jealous?" She chuckled. "Not to worry. I told you, we broke up."

"Just see that it stays that way."

A delicious thrill shot through her. Maybe this time was different. Maybe Zane was interested in more than temporary and short-term.

He gave her another quick kiss. "Drive safe," he said.

She nodded and headed for the front of the van.

Less than forty minutes later, she was in her house with her suitcase open on her bed. As she unpacked, she found herself humming softly and smiling for no reason at all.

Okay, she had it bad. Worse than bad. She was a woman in love and was there anything sappier than that?

As Nicki picked up the shirt she'd worn to Disneyland, she recalled their romantic dinner with a view of the water. Okay, most of the plants had been plastic and there had been noisy kids all around them, but the room had also sparkled from the white lights and Zane had stared at her as if she were the most precious woman on the planet. He'd made her feel special and whole and normal.

She collected another blouse and dropped them into her laundry basket. She supposed that was Zane's greatest gift—his ability to see her as just like everyone else.

She'd been nervous about sharing a room with him, but he'd made everything so easy. She'd never remembered to be embarrassed. If a moment had threatened to turn awkward, he'd distracted her with a joke or a kiss, or both. While she'd had lovers before, she'd never been that *intimate* with a man.

Nicki picked up her makeup case and carried it into the specially modified bathroom. There wasn't a tub. Instead an oversized shower stood in the corner. It was designed so that she could wheel right in. There was a wide bench, grip bars and a nonskid floor. In the past she'd always hated her shower, seeing it as a symbol of what she couldn't do. Now remembering making love in the hotel shower, she saw the shower as filled with possibilities. Most of them sexual.

It didn't matter if she never had sex in her modified bathroom; she knew she could. Another gift Zane had given her.

As she unpacked her makeup, she watched the movement of the mouse ears on her bracelet. Light bounced off the curved gold and danced on the walls. Smiling, she bent down to set her cosmetics on their shelf. Her gaze landed on the pink box of supplies for her period.

It was one of those odd moments in space and time when the world seemed to stop turning. She moved, she breathed and yet nothing was as it should be. As if from a great distance, she reached out to touch the box. Her fingers barely grazed the front, then her hand fell to her side. Bone-cold panic seeped into her midsection.

In that heartbeat, Nicki knew.

She told herself it wasn't possible, even though it was. She told herself no one was that stupid, even though she had been.

That first night she and Zane had made love on her sofa, then later in her bed. How many times? Two? Three? They'd made love without protection and she'd never once considered the potential disaster.

Why? Where was her brain? She was always careful. Usually she was on the Pill. Just not in the past few months.

There'd been that night, then the past couple of days. Not once had birth control crossed her mind. How could she have been so irresponsible? Or dumb?

Closing her eyes, she did some quick calculations. She was late. More than a little late. She was late by at least ten days.

After dumping the rest of her makeup into the sink, she turned and raced to the front of the house. She collected her purse and her keys, then made her way to the van.

It took thirty-seven minutes to drive to the drugstore, make her purchase, return home and pee on a stick. Thirty-seven minutes after which her life changed forever.

She was pregnant.

# Chapter 10

Nicki didn't sleep that night, and she hadn't slept the previous two nights in Los Angeles, so she was pretty much a basket case by the time she pulled into work the following morning. She considered calling in sick, but she knew Zane would get word of that and demand to know what was wrong. As she hadn't quite figured that out herself, she didn't know how she was going to have the conversation with him. No, better to muddle through the day and head home early.

Complicating matters was a headache she knew was only going to get worse. If she was pregnant there were no more cups of coffee in her immediate future, which meant she was going to suffer with caffeine withdrawal. After all she had to do what was right for the baby.

Baby! She still couldn't believe it. Of course she only had herself to blame. Previously she'd been on the Pill whenever she'd been sexually involved with a man, and she'd always insisted he use protection. With Zane… She locked her van and headed for the building. She'd just plain forgotten to take care of things.

She knew he wasn't like most people who assumed that because she was in a wheelchair she couldn't get pregnant. How many times had she had to explain that nonworking legs didn't mean nonworking ovaries. Zane knew she was on the Pill. He teased her about it. So it would never have occurred to him that she wasn't safe.

"Complications to mull over another time," she told herself as she entered the building. Now that she was here, she would do her best to focus on her job and push the rest of it out of her mind. There was nothing she had to do about the baby today, and with Zane gone, no one she had to tell.

She made her way into her office where she found stacks of paperwork and phone messages waiting for her. She'd barely finished organizing her in-basket when Jeff stopped by to see her.

"Great work," he said, taking the chair across from hers. "Mr. Sabotini couldn't say enough good things about you."

She smiled. "He was very charming, and very worried about his children."

"We already have the team in place." Jeff tossed another file on her desk. "This job is going to bring us a lot more work. The company will grow and you'll be a part of that."

Nicki knew that Jeff and Zane rewarded employees who worked well and she didn't doubt she would find something extra in her next paycheck. For a second she thought about asking for extended maternity leave instead, but reconsidered. Jeff might not know that she and Zane were more than friends, but he wasn't an idiot. He would put things together fairly quickly and then who knew what would happen. Better for her to be the one to tell Zane he was going to be a father.

She must have paled at the thought because Jeff leaned toward her and frowned.

"You okay?"

No. Not even close. She sighed. "I'm fine. Just the rigors of travel catching up with me."

Jeff grinned. "Zane said you went to Disneyland yesterday. How rigorous could it have been?"

She chuckled. "Hey, there was a lot of walking."

"Very funny." He rose. "Why don't you head out early today? Consider it part of your reward for a job well done."

"That would be great. Thanks."

She waited until Jeff left, then picked up the phone. There was only one person she could think of who could possibly understand what she was going through.

She waited until Ashley was on the phone. "It's me," she said. "If I leave work early this afternoon, would you have time to talk?"

Zane had dealt with a lot of rich people over the past few years. In his business, they were usually his clients. But the prince and princess of El Bahar were his first shot at royalty. He was pleasantly surprised by how the meeting was going.

"El Bahar is neutral," he said to the royals, "but terrorists don't care about things like that."

Prince Jamal nodded. "I agree. Heidi and I are concerned about striking a balance between relative normalcy and overprotection. We also have the children to consider."

Princess Heidi, an American who had married into the ruling family of El Bahar, smiled at him. "Jamal and I thought people more familiar with the lay of the land, so to speak, would be assets to our existing security team."

"We often have to work with a team in place," Zane told her. "Our personnel don't have a problem with that."

"Good."

Despite the designer clothing and impressive jewels, Princess Heidi seemed like a down-to-earth person. When her husband left to make a call, she smiled at him.

"I understand you're from Seattle," she said. "It's a very beautiful part of the country."

He nodded. "A lot of green. Nothing like El Bahar."

"True. We're a desert nation, but when we get the rains, a surprising number of plants seem to spring to life overnight."

He'd never spoken with royalty before, so he wasn't sure what was allowed. Still, he knew Nicki would be interested in his encounter with a real live princess, so he decided to risk the potential protocol breach.

"You're American."

The princess grinned. "Technically I'm a citizen of El Bahar. Marrying one of the princes makes that a requirement. But in my heart, I belong to both countries. That's one of the reasons I want us to spend more time here. So our children can see what life is like in the West." Her smile faded. "While the people of El Bahar have always welcomed those from other countries, there are extremists in nearby nations who don't share those liberal beliefs."

"Both El Bahar and Bahania are excellent examples of the peace that is possible in the Middle East," he said.

"True and a good thing, what with all three of the El Baharain princes marrying Americans." Her smile returned. "It was something of a scandal."

He chuckled. "And now the same thing is happening in

Bahania. I understand that one of the king's sons married an American."

"You're right," Heidi told him. "In fact Princess Cleo is from your own Washington state."

Prince Jamal returned to the hotel conference room and sat down. "Where were we?" he asked.

When the meeting concluded, Zane collected his papers and an extra copy of the proposal. After closing his briefcase, he pulled out his cell phone and dialed the office. He was put through to Jeff.

"I want a big raise," he said by way of greeting.

"And here I thought it was my job to bring in new clients while you were busy risking your life on the job."

"Send me back out in the field," Zane said easily.

"Maybe not. I already heard from the El Baharian office of royal security. We've been retained."

Zane detailed the high points, then waited while Jeff put him through to Nicki.

"You should have been here," he told her.

"Really?"

"Sure. I just sat across from a genuine princess. Pretty cool, huh?"

He heard the smile in Nicki's voice as she said, "So you head off for the east coast and less than twenty four hours later, you're infatuated by a princess? What kind of loyalty is that?"

He grinned. "Don't sweat it. Even if I didn't think you were hot enough to be irresistible, she's married. And her husband looked like the kind of guy who would throw anyone messing with his wife into shackles for a couple hundred years."

"Was she nice?"

"Very."

"Attractive?"

"Sure, but not my type." Especially not when he couldn't get a certain redhead out of his mind. "Want me to see if I can steal a couple of pieces of her jewelry?"

"I doubt it's my style. I'm a simple girl at heart."

"Simple tastes or simple-minded?"

She laughed. "Very funny." The humor faded. "When are you coming home?"

"In a couple of days. I have meetings with their security people tomorrow and Monday morning. I have a flight out early in the afternoon."

"Okay."

He straightened. There was something about how she said the word. Something that made him wonder if everything was all right.

"What's going on?" he asked.

"Nothing."

"You okay?"

"I'm fine. I swear." She cleared her throat. "Why don't you come to dinner Monday night? You can tell me all about the princess."

"Sure. I'd like that."

There was a brief pause. For a second Zane thought about telling Nicki that he missed her, but he stopped himself before he said the words.

Wanting, he reminded himself. Not missing. Missing wasn't allowed. He'd made it a point to never get involved with someone he *could* miss. Had Nicki changed that? He'd always cared about her, but things were different now. Confusing.

Still he knew the danger of getting too involved. No way that was going to happen.

"You going to be around on Sunday?" he asked.

"I think so. Why?"

"I thought I might give you a call."

"That would be nice."

"Great. I'll talk to you then and I'll see you on Monday. I'll bring wine."

Nicki hesitated, then said that would be fine.

When he hung up, he heard a sound and turned. Princess Heidi stood in the doorway of the conference room. She smiled sheepishly.

"Okay," she told him. "I was shamelessly eavesdropping. I can't help it. I'm a sucker for couples in love."

"No problem," Zane said with a casualness he didn't feel. In love? Not even on a bet. He didn't do love. Not ever. He knew the price of loving…and losing, and he'd vowed to never pay it again.

Ashley walked back into the living room and collapsed on the sofa. "I'm sure he's finally asleep," she said and sighed. "He's only eighteen months old. The terrible twos aren't supposed to start for another six months, but he's already making trouble." She checked her watch. "Maggie won't be back from her play date for another hour and half, so we're on our own."

"Great."

Nicki fingered the hem of her sweater, then shifted in her chair. She'd been the one to request the meeting with her friend, so it was up to her to get things started. It wasn't as if Ashley knew what was wrong.

But she didn't know what to say, which led to an interesting dilemma. If she couldn't say the words to her best friend, how on earth was she going to tell Zane?

A bridge to cross when she next saw him.

"I'm—" She closed her eyes, then opened them.

Ashley tilted her head. Concern darkened her eyes. "Are you sick or dying?"

"No, I'm perfectly healthy." Pregnancy was a condition, not a disease, right?

"Good." Ashley smiled. "I was a little worried. You sounded so serious on the phone and you haven't been yourself since you arrived. What's going on? Is it Zane? Jeff told me you two spent an extra day in L.A. I thought that might mean things had started up again."

"They did, but that's not really the problem." She reconsidered the statement. "Okay, it's part of the problem, but not the big part."

"That's clear." Ashley leaned toward her. "Just start at the beginning or blurt it out. I can't think of a single thing you could tell me that would be the least bit shocking."

Nicki swallowed. "I'm pregnant."

Ashley blinked. "Okay. Except for that. Pregnant? Are you sure?"

"I used four different home pregnancy tests. They were all positive."

"Okay then. You probably are. Wow." Ashley grinned. "Are you happy? I know it's unexpected, but still, a baby. That's so wonderful."

Nicki opened her mouth to protest, then closed it. Ashley was right. A baby *was* wonderful. And amazing. Funny how she'd been so busy mentally ranting about how stupid she'd been to not use birth control that she'd never stopped to consider that there was a precious life growing inside of her. She'd always wanted kids. Maybe not this way, but that was okay.

She smiled. "It is great, isn't it?"

"I'm guessing Zane's the father."

"He's the only one I've been sleeping with."

Ashley shook her head. "I take it he doesn't know."

"Not yet. He's in New York and I didn't want to tell him over the phone. He's coming to dinner Monday night. I'll spring it on him then."

"Any idea what he's going to say?"

Nicki had been doing her best not to think about that. "Not really." She wasn't sure she wanted to know.

Ashley rose and hugged her. "I think this is fabulous. You'll be a great mom."

Nicki hugged her back. "I hope so. I never thought about doing it on my own. How did you manage all those years with Maggie?"

Ashley resumed her seat. "It was a struggle," she admitted. "I didn't have your education or health insurance. Honestly, there were times I could barely keep food on the table. I was working nights, going to school during the day. The only thing that kept me going was how much I loved Maggie and that light at the end of the tunnel. I knew when I finally finished my degree, life would get easier for both of us."

"Then you met Jeff and he swept you off your feet."

Ashley's expression softened. "Something like that. He was scary at first. A little distant. Maggie won him over right away. I think watching him fall for her made me start to fall myself." She raised her eyebrows. "But there is definitely something in the water at that company."

"What do you mean?"

"I was pregnant before Jeff and I married. In fact he'd told me he couldn't have children." She waved her hand. "It's a complicated story. Anyway, there I was pregnant. And here you are. You're definitely keeping the baby, right?"

Nicki nodded slowly. "Now that you mention it, I never

considered any other option." She couldn't give up her child. "I'll spend all my time terrified, but I can raise a baby on my own. I have resources."

"Me, for one."

Nicki glanced at Ashley's stomach. "Right, because with two kids and a third on the way, you'll have so much free time."

"I can at least give you advice."

"I'll need plenty of that. I have money. Not just my salary, but money from the settlement."

"What settlement?"

"When I broke my legs." She explained about the accident at the resort. "I don't know if my parents would have sued them or not. Before any decision was made, the owners offered a large settlement. My folks accepted on my behalf."

Ashley grinned. "So you're secretly rich?"

"I have a nest egg. My parents' insurance covered most of my medical expenses so very little of the settlement got used for that. They invested the money and it did well. I spent some of it remodeling my house but the rest just sits there. Between my salary and my savings, I shouldn't have to touch it, but it's nice to know it's there."

"More than nice," Ashley told her. "It's one less thing to worry about. Are your parents going to freak out?"

Nicki considered the question. "I don't know. They always wanted me to get married and have a family. I think they'll be happy about the baby, even if they're worried about me." She smiled sheepishly. "I checked our insurance coverage. I'm entitled to eight weeks maternity leave with pay and six weeks without for maternity leave. I was thinking I could even work from home."

"If Jeff doesn't agree to that, you let me know."

Nicki laughed. "Because you'll take him on?"

"You bet." Ashley leaned forward. "You'll need to start looking for day care. What about having someone come in and stay with you?"

"I would like that. I'm sure my folks will come up for the first few weeks, while I'm still in the panic stage."

"You know, we've talked about everything but the baby's father," her friend said. "Are you scared about telling him?"

"Wouldn't you be?"

"Sure."

Nicki touched her stomach. "I don't know what to say. I guess there isn't a good way to break it gently. At the same time I want him to understand that I'm perfectly capable of raising this child on my own."

"Is that what you want?"

"It's what makes the most sense. Zane isn't going to be interested in having a family. He's just not that kind of man."

"He could surprise you."

Nicki knew it was too dangerous to have those kind of hopes. But in her heart, that was what she wanted. For him to be thrilled by the news and instantly confess his undying love for her. Then they could get married and live happily ever after. The thing was, she had a feeling life wasn't going to be that tidy.

"Zane doesn't do permanent commitments," she said. "He's not going to want to be a father. I doubt he'll want to be involved at all."

Ashley shook her head. "I think you're wrong and that he'll surprise you, but we'll have to wait and see. You said he's coming over Monday night?"

"Right. For dinner."

"I have a word of advice."

"What?"

Ashley smiled. "Before you tell him, get him a drink. A really big one. He's going to need it."

# Chapter 11

Zane arrived at Nicki's house about fifteen minutes early. He'd brought roses and a bottle of wine. The flowers weren't his style, but when he'd driven by a florist on the way over, he'd found himself pulling into the parking lot. Once inside the store, he'd seen peach-colored roses that he'd had to buy. Which made him feel like some high-school kid taking out the prom queen.

But anticipation was stronger than his chagrin. Maybe he shouldn't have missed Nicki, but he'd spent the past four days counting the hours until he saw her again. She'd invited him for dinner and he was hoping she planned to keep him around until breakfast.

When he knocked on the front door, she called that it was open. He stepped inside.

"What if I'd been a serial killer?" he asked as he closed the door behind himself.

Nicki sat in her chair in the entrance to the living room. She smiled. "Then you wouldn't have knocked."

He crossed toward her. "You work for a security company. You know better."

"You're right."

He grinned. "My favorite two words in the world." He set the wine on the floor, the flowers on her lap, then bent down and cupped her face. "Hi."

"Hi, yourself."

Makeup accentuated the wide shape of her beautiful green eyes. Her mouth was full and inviting. She smelled exotic and sexy. Her casual dress fell to the knee and left the rest of her legs bare. He noticed she wasn't wearing stockings, which was probably for the best. Knowing about her garter belt would have made it impossible for him to concentrate.

He pressed his mouth to hers, meaning the contact to be a friendly greeting. But the second their lips touched, his blood heated and he wanted more. He leaned in a little. Nicki touched his cheek, then shifted her head slightly.

"The flowers are beautiful," she said. "Thank you."

Zane straightened. "You're welcome."

Was it his imagination or had she just pulled away from him? He studied her, searching for clues. He couldn't find even one. Her smile seemed genuine, her gaze was steady.

"I need to get them in water," she said as she turned and wheeled toward the back of the house.

Zane picked up the wine and trailed after her. "What's for dinner?"

"Lasagna. My mother's recipe."

"I'm impressed."

"You should be. I had to dirty nearly every pan I own

to make it. The good news is it freezes well, so I'll have many meals from it."

She stopped in the center of the kitchen and pointed to one of the few tall cabinets. "Vases are in there."

"I remember." He pulled out a glass one and filled it with water. Nicki unwrapped the cellophane and placed the stems into the vase.

"Should I put them on the table?" he asked.

"Sure."

The dining room had already been set for two. He liked how the place settings were so close together. Obviously she had an intimate meal planned. He must have been imagining things with the kiss.

He took a step toward the living room, then paused. Unless Nicki had regrets about what had happened in L.A. The first time they'd made love, she'd asked that things return to a "friends only" footing. While he hadn't been excited by the idea, he'd agreed because he hadn't wanted to push her. But things were different now. Somehow he was going to have to convince her of that.

He walked into the living room and found her by the sofa. He took a seat close to her.

"How was your flight?"

"What's going on at work?"

They spoke at the same time. Nicki smiled. "You first."

"How's work?" he asked.

"Good. Everyone is very excited about the contract with the prince and princess. Jeff said Ashley is already talking about vacationing there."

"With three kids?"

"I don't think it's a thought out plan at this point."

"They're nice people."

She raised her eyebrows. "The prince and princess?"

"Yeah. She's American. Sensible."

Nicki laughed. "You mean exotically beautiful."

"That, too, but I barely noticed." He shifted closer, suddenly wanting to tell her that while it probably wasn't a good idea, he *had* missed her. "Nicki, I—"

She cut him off. "I haven't offered you anything to drink. What would you like? That wine you brought? Does it need to breathe?"

There was something about the way she spoke. Something about her body, as if she were stiff all over. Zane hadn't wanted to see the signs, but as he looked more closely, he saw tension in the set of her mouth and worry in her eyes.

Damn. He knew exactly what was wrong. Okay, maybe he didn't want to hear it, but if Nicki wanted to end their physical relationship, he had no right to stop her. Ignoring the knot in his gut, he took her hands in his.

"I don't need a drink," he said, "but I do need you to tell me what the hell is going on."

She stared at him. "I have no idea what you're talking about."

"Something's wrong. I can sense it."

She glanced down at their clasped hands, then back at him. "You're right," she said in a low voice.

The knot turned into a vice. Zane wanted to bolt out of the room. He wanted to demand that she not try to change things. Instead he sat and waited.

"We used to be friends," she said slowly. "Just friends. I liked that. It was certainly much less complicated. Then we went to that party together and you came back here and, well, you know what happened."

"We made love."

She nodded and pulled her hands free. He tried not to

take the withdrawal personally. Not that he did a very good job of convincing himself.

"We didn't plan it," she said. "I know it just happened. I don't regret that. I can't. But it changed things."

He braced himself for her rejection. "Then we got back together in Los Angeles."

She frowned. "Yes, but that doesn't really have anything to do with this."

"What? Of course it does. You want us to go back to being friends."

Her eyes widened. "Is that what you think? No, Zane. It's not that at all." She swallowed. "What I'm trying to tell you is that I'm pregnant."

Nicki kept talking, but Zane couldn't hear anything else. He couldn't think, couldn't move. There was only that single word reverberating in his brain.

Pregnant.

Involuntarily his gaze dropped to her stomach. It was as flat as it had ever been. But if she was talking about that first night together, she was only a few weeks along.

He swore silently. The room shifted and instead of Nicki, he saw Amber. Laughing, beautiful Amber telling him that she had a surprise. Amber handing him a small box tied with a yellow ribbon. He'd opened it to find baby booties inside.

He remembered feeling elated beyond words. She was going to have a baby. They were going to be a family. Then he remembered nothing but the fiery explosion that had destroyed his world.

No, he thought as he pushed to his feet. Not again. He couldn't survive it.

"What the hell happened?" he growled.

Nicki's half smile faded. "The usual. You were here that

night. We did it more than once and we didn't use protection."

A condom. Right. He *always* used a condom. But he hadn't expected to make love with Nicki so he hadn't had one with him. Not at her place and not in L.A. For the first time in his life, birth control and protection had never crossed his mind.

"You're on the Pill."

"I was," she said apologetically. "I went off a few months ago when I was between guys. I wanted to give my body a rest. Boyd and I didn't seem to be heading into bed, so I didn't think about it." She squared her shoulders. "I didn't do this on purpose."

He knew that, he thought as he paced the length of her living room. Nicki wasn't deceitful. He believed it was just one of those things. It had happened and now they had to deal with it.

His brain flashed again on those tiny baby booties, on Amber's smile, on the heat of the explosion.

No! He couldn't do this. Not again. Not ever. What if Nicki died?

Panic swirled into fear. A fear that crawled inside so deep, he knew he would never get it out.

He looked at her, then headed for the door.

The slam of the front door echoed in the quiet house. Nicki had expected a lot of reactions, but she'd never thought Zane would bolt. She hurt as if she'd been dragged for miles. But more damaging to the pain in her body was the ache in her soul.

The timer dinged, telling her the lasagna was ready. She knew she had to go take it out of the oven. If she didn't it would burn and what would that accomplish?

She'd thought things would go better. Maybe Zane would be upset or shocked or even mad. Maybe he would yell at her. She'd braced herself for his anger, but she'd never thought he wouldn't react at all. If she lived to be a hundred, she would never forget the blankness that had overtaken his expression. She'd had no way to know what he was thinking, even though she guessed it was bad.

She had been willing to fight with him, to reason, but how was she supposed to battle an empty room?

Forcing herself to move, she headed for the kitchen. After removing the lasagna from the oven and setting it on a hot pad, she leaned back in her chair and fought a wave of nausea.

She had a feeling this upset had nothing to do with the baby and everything to do with her broken heart. Zane hadn't been delighted or confessed his undying love or wanted them to be a family. Apparently he hadn't wanted anything but to be gone.

Only now did she allow herself to admit that if her most pressing fantasy wasn't to come true, she'd hoped that Zane would at least be happy about the child. That he would want to be a part of its life. That they could be a part-time family if nothing else. Apparently that wasn't going to happen, either.

Nicki covered her face with her hands. She had to accept that she was in this alone. That Zane wasn't interested in the baby. Or her.

Tears burned her eyes. She fought them for a couple of seconds, then let them fall. What did it matter if she cried? There wasn't anyone to see or judge.

She wasn't sure how long she sat there. Eventually the tears ran out and she had to go in search of a tissue or five.

In the bright light of her bathroom, with her nose and

eyes red and her face blotchy, she was forced to face the truth.

Zane didn't love her. She'd known he wasn't into commitments or long-term relationships when she'd invited him into her bed. He hadn't changed the rules, she had. So it wasn't his fault that she was now left alone and shattered.

While the truth should have cleansed her, instead it only made her want to weep more. If she'd been unable to get over her simple schoolgirl crush on Zane, how would she ever get over being in love with the father of her child?

Zane didn't remember leaving Nicki's house, or driving, but somehow he ended up by the water. As he stared out over the sound, he saw the first wisps of fog forming and felt the chill in the air. Soon the dampness would seep into him. He welcomed the discomfort. Maybe it would distract him from the images filling his brain.

He saw Amber again—laughing, smiling. In his mind, she moved closer and spoke his name, but when he reached for her, she was gone, her presence no more substantial than the fog.

They'd been happy, he remembered, closing his eyes against the present. The clank of the sailboat riggings and the smell of the sea all faded as he recalled warm, sunny days. Happy and content days. For him, it had been a first. He'd grown up on the street. His gang had been his family, but not Amber. She'd been one of four kids, the only girl, and the only child to follow in the family tradition of a life in the military.

They'd met in officer training school, both young and excited about the possibilities of a career with the Marines. He remembered her as an erotic combination of tough and feminine. Every guy had wanted her, and for reasons he'd never understood, she'd chosen him.

He remembered Amber telling him that eventually one of them was going to have to learn how to cook. Amber insisting they shower together each morning, even when there wasn't any time and they were always late because showering led to other things. Amber inviting him to spend Christmas with her family then laughingly complaining that it had sure taken him long enough when he'd finally proposed. Amber saying she was pregnant.

Her smile, he thought grimly. He remembered that the most. That and the explosion.

He'd been there. He'd watched her smile and wave as she'd stepped onto the helicopter. He'd stood on the tarmac as the machine rose up and up, then headed east. Suddenly it had swerved and without warning it had plowed into the side of a mountain.

He opened his eyes, but the explosion didn't fade. He could see it, smell it, hear it.

He'd done it, he reminded himself. He'd killed her as surely as if he'd flown the helicopter into the mountain himself. And now Nicki was pregnant.

The fear returned and with it a metallic taste, like blood on his tongue. Guilt fed the fear until it was all he could feel.

Not again, he told himself. He couldn't go through that again. He couldn't lose Nicki, too.

But he'd been unable to keep Amber safe. How could he protect Nicki and their baby?

Ironic, he thought. His job was to protect others and yet he'd been unable to save those he cared about most.

He clutched the railing, gripping the cold, damp metal until it bit into his hands. He couldn't change the past, but he could secure the future. Somehow he was going to have to make this turn out right. He would explain—make her see why he had to be in charge. Why he had to know everything. He only knew one way to do that.

He climbed back in his car and started the engine.

When he arrived at Nicki's place, he hurried up the walkway, then pounded on the front door.

"Nicki, it's me," he called. He heard the click of a lock.

He could see that she'd been crying. While she was the kind of person who laughed easily, he'd rarely seen her cry and his chest tightened at the thought of him hurting her. He wondered if it would help to tell her *why*.

Later, he thought. First he had to get her to agree. Once he knew he could keep her safe, he could take the time to explain.

"You didn't have to come back," she said. "You made it clear how you feel about this."

"You couldn't be more wrong."

He stepped into the house, then led the way to the living room. When he perched on the edge of the sofa, she stopped several feet away.

"What?" she asked as she wiped the tears from her face. "What do you want?"

Too many things, he thought. A chance to undo what was done. A chance to change the past. As those were unavailable to him he would focus on keeping the future positive—on keeping her and the baby safe.

He rose and crossed to her, then grabbed the arm of her chair and pulled her nearer to the sofa.

Her gasp of outrage didn't surprise him. It was one thing to help her in and out of the company plane, it was another to use her wheelchair against her by pushing her around.

"I need you close," he told her, before she could say anything.

Her tight expression didn't soften, but at least she didn't yell at him.

He leaned toward her and took one of her hands in his. He half expected her to pull away and when she didn't, he took a moment to study her face. Her eyes, the shape of her mouth and her chin. Who would the baby look like? Would it favor one parent over the other, or would it be a blend of both of them? Boy or girl? Did it matter? He shook his head. All he cared about was keeping it from dying. And her.

"I want us to get married right away," he said, speaking quickly. "This week. Tomorrow. We'll get a license and make it happen. Then you'll have my name and I'll be here for you every single minute. I mean that, Nicki. I'm not going anywhere. I want to keep you and the baby safe."

She didn't speak. Her lips had parted slightly and all the color fled her face, but these weren't the kind of signs that would tell him what she was thinking.

He glanced around at her living room. "I'll move in here. I know the houseboat is too hard for you. Plus it wouldn't be safe to have a kid running around right on the water. Which is fine. There's plenty of room. I can pack up a few things tonight, then move the rest of it over the next few days. The houseboat will sell fast. They're always popular. I'll put the money into a trust for you and the baby." He frowned. "I need to get some life insurance, too. And we can start a college fund. Do you have a doctor? Have you seen one? Are you feeling all right?"

There was too much to take in at once, Nicki thought. Even though she knew she was sitting in her chair, she felt as if the room were spinning.

Zane was saying all the right things, but somehow she

couldn't believe them. Two hours ago he'd been so stunned by her announcement that he'd walked out without saying anything. Now he was back, talking about them getting married and moving in together. What had changed his mind?

Maybe she would have been a little more quick to jump at his proposal if he'd looked the least bit happy about it. Instead his expression was grim and determined. As if this was a campaign he had to win, regardless of the odds stacked against him. Obviously he wasn't happy about the baby. So why would he sacrifice himself if he—

Then she got it. And with that truth came a pain so sharp, she thought it might slice her in two. She pulled her hand free of his grasp and folded her arms in front of her midsection, as if by pressing hard, she could hold herself together.

Why Zane? She might have expected it from someone else, but never from him. He'd always acted as if the chair didn't matter. Had it just been an act?

Tears threatened, but she willed them away. She would not cry over this. Maybe over the baby and Zane not loving her, but not over this.

"Stop," she said quietly. "Just stop."

He stared at her. "My plan makes sense."

"Not to me." She sighed. "I expected so much more of you, Zane. I thought we were friends."

He stared at her. "What the hell does that have to do with anything?"

"Being in a wheelchair doesn't make me any less capable. I'm perfectly healthy. I will carry this baby to term without any help from you. Being in a wheelchair doesn't mean I can't be a good mother."

He sprang to his feet. "Is that what you think? That this is about you being in a wheelchair? It's not."

He paced the length of her living room, then turned and glared at her. "I don't give a damn about the chair. This is about you and the baby and me wanting to be a part of things. This is about protecting you."

He sounded sincere, but he wasn't making any sense. "Protecting us from what?"

"Everything."

She could see the tension in his body. Obviously he wasn't kidding about all of this, but she didn't know what he was talking about. There was no "everything" to keep her or the baby safe from. Which meant his worries were about her abilities. There was no other reason for him to want to move in and take care of her.

Ever since she'd met Zane, she'd thought he was one of the good guys. That he saw her as a regular person who happened to use a wheelchair to get around. But it wasn't like that at all. She'd based her relationship with him on a lie. He was just better at hiding what he thought than most people.

The truth hurt in ways she couldn't yet define, but this wasn't the time to deal with that. Later, when she was alone, she would curl up and lick her wounds, but not until then. While he was around, she would make sure she stayed strong.

"Let's come at this from a different direction," she said quietly. "Here are the facts. I'm pregnant and you're the father. Honestly, I didn't think you'd have any interest in a child, but I can see I was wrong about that. I'm glad you want to be a part of the baby's life. I'm willing to work with you to come up with some kind of a plan so you can be a part of things. Please understand that I don't want to exclude you at all, but none of this is an invitation for you to move in here with me."

She wasn't going to say anything about his proposal,

mostly because she didn't think she could get the words out without her voice cracking and she didn't want Zane to know how much he'd wounded her.

Zane shook his head. "We have to get married."

Not "I love you." Not even "You really matter to me." Just a bald statement of what he saw as fact.

"Why?" she asked.

"It's necessary. A child needs two parents."

"Our baby will *have* two parents."

He frowned. "You know what I mean. Two parents who live together."

"You didn't have that and you turned out fine."

"I want more for our child. I want…" He paced to the window and looked out. "Marry me, Nicki. Just say yes."

If only he knew how much she wanted to agree. She loved him and spending the rest of her life with him was her idea of perfect happiness. But not like this. Not as an obligation. If he'd said he cared, that she mattered, she might have been willing to wait for deep friendship and respect to grow into love. But now she wasn't even sure about that. Did Zane respect her? How much did he care and why?

"No," she whispered.

He turned back to face her. "Then I want to move in."

"No. You have your house and I have this one. When the baby comes—"

He cut her off. "I don't want to wait that long. I want to be a part of things now."

"There's nothing going on. The baby isn't even the size of a rice grain. What do you want to do?"

He shook his head, obviously frustrated. She didn't know what to say, either. Because none of this was what she'd expected for her life. A baby before a husband? That hadn't exactly been her master plan.

He exhaled. "You win, but only for now. I'm not giving up on this."

"Fine. I'm not changing my mind." Not unless he could come to her and tell her he loved her.

He crossed to the front door and let himself out. She watched him go.

When she was finally alone, she covered her face with her hands and gave in to the tears again. Nothing about their conversation felt like a victory to her. Instead she was left feeling empty and alone, and in love with a man who was willing to marry her for the sake of a child, but not for herself.

# Chapter 12

Midmorning Tuesday Zane walked up the front path to Jeff's house. He knew his partner was in an all-day meeting, which was fine. Zane had come here to talk to Ashley.

He knocked on the front door and waited. When she appeared, she had eighteen-month-old Michael on her hip and a sippy cup in her free hand.

"Zane? Hi. What's going on?"

He shrugged. "I just…" He ran his hand through his hair. "I need to talk to you. Is this an okay time?"

"Sure."

She stepped back to let him enter. Zane followed her to the family room where she set Michael on a play mat. There were all kinds of toys surrounding the kid and when he picked up a brightly colored plastic dog, various musical notes blared out.

Ashley offered Zane something to drink, which he declined. He sat on one end of the sofa, while she settled on the other. She was close enough to Michael that she could offer him a set of baby-size workshop tools.

Zane studied the baby. Michael was sturdy-looking, with sandy-colored hair and hazel eyes. He was a blend of both his parents. Outgoing, bright, friendly. And so damn vulnerable it made Zane break out in a sweat.

He sprang to his feet and walked the length of the large family room. Pictures, toys and books covered all the tables. The room was bright, lived in and felt happy. As if lots of good times happened in this space.

He stopped in front of the sliding glass door and turned back to Ashley. She still sat on the sofa, but her expression had turned from curious to concerned.

"I need to talk," he told her.

"I figured that much out."

"It's just…" He swore silently, not sure how much to tell her. What was she going to think, to say? Did Nicki want people to know? Hell, they would find out eventually.

"I can tell from the track you want to wear out in my carpet that Nicki told you she was pregnant," Ashley said calmly.

Zane stared at her. "You knew?"

"She found out shortly after you two got back from Los Angeles and told me over the weekend." Ashley slid onto the floor and rubbed her son's back. "I told her it was something in the water over there at the office. First Jeff got me pregnant, then you do the same with Nicki." Humor brightened her voice. "Haven't either of you guys ever heard of condoms? They're these neat latex devices that fit over your—"

He cut her off with a shake of his head. "Yes, I know what a condom is." As for Jeff getting her pregnant, that wasn't anything similar. Jeff had been eighty percent gone before he'd ever slept with Ashley and making love with her had made him fall hard. It had taken Jeff a few weeks to figure out the truth, but Zane had known it all along. This situation was completely different.

"She doesn't understand," he said as he paced to the entertainment center on the far wall. "This was a shock, but I'm dealing with it. The thing is, I want to be there for her. I want to take care of things." He paused and looked at her. "I want to marry her, but she refused. I can't let her do that. I need to be there to keep her safe. And the baby. What about the baby?"

Ashley studied him. "You have it bad."

He did, but not in the way she meant. The fear was with him every second. The past lurked. How the hell was he going to keep it at bay? How was he going to have this turn out differently? He couldn't lose Nicki and their baby—not and survive. Why couldn't she see that?

"Tell me what to do," he said.

"Mother Nature has made sure there's not much you *can* do until the baby is born. Zane, take a deep breath and relax. Nicki is perfectly healthy. There's no reason to think her pregnancy won't progress like millions of others. She'll have good days and bad days. She'll swell up like a balloon and get stretch marks and eat right and take vitamins. In nine months, give or take a few days, she'll give birth. That's when she's going to really need you. But until then, just let nature take its course."

She wasn't helping. "How do I get Nicki to marry me? I need to convince her."

"Why?"

"I have to be there with her. I want to take care of her. I can't do that from fifteen miles away."

"Not a very good reason to marry someone."

He knew what she meant. That most couples married for love. Because they cared. Because they wanted to build a life together.

He'd wanted that once—with Amber. He'd seen their future, their kids, their life after the Marines. He'd known he would grow old with her. Right up until the day he killed her.

He sank into a recliner. He couldn't love Nicki. He'd vowed to never love anyone again. He couldn't stand to go through that again. Not ever.

"She's important to me," he said at last.

"Wow. Words to warm a woman's heart for sure," Ashley told him. "No wonder she didn't jump at your proposal." She pulled Michael onto her lap and stroked his hair.

"Here's the thing, Zane. You have eight-plus months until the baby arrives. Why don't you simply accept Nicki's ground rules for now. Live with them, see if they work. If, as the time for the birth gets closer, you still feel this strongly about getting married, then ask her again. In the meantime, I suggest you look at what's going on and think about whether or not there's a way to be a part of both of their lives without living together. Other couples have made it work."

He nodded because that was what she expected. But he hadn't found the information he'd been looking for. The magic sentence that would make Nicki say yes.

He thanked Ashley for her time and left. On his way back to the office, he decided that that he would go into a "wait and see" mode. He would study the situation and look for weaknesses on Nicki's part. There had to be some way to convince her and he would find it. In the meantime, he would do everything in his power to protect her and his unborn child. He was a trained expert. He had skills and he intended to use them.

\* \* \*

Nicki pulled the lunch cooler she often brought to work out from under the desk. It was like opening a can of tuna with a hungry cat in the house. Somehow Zane heard the noise from the other side of the office and suddenly appeared in her doorway.

"What are you eating?" he asked.

Before she could answer, he took the container and unzipped the top. As she watched in a combination of amazement, amusement and horror, he laid out her sandwich, the salad she'd made and the piece of fruit. Then he pulled a small notebook from his shirt pocket, flipped it open and noted her choices.

"How much protein on the sandwich?" he asked as he wrote.

She considered the question. "I used a couple of slices of ham."

"Any in the salad? Beans, chicken, cheese?"

"No."

He didn't look happy with her answer. "You're not getting enough protein, Nicki. And don't use lunch meat. You want something more high quality than that."

"What I want is to be left alone in peace," she told him. "Zane, it's been all of three days and you're driving me crazy. You check on my breakfast. You call me at home to find out what I'm having for dinner."

His dark gaze never left her face. "So?"

"So, it's nuts. I eat a healthy diet about ninety percent of the time. I think that's fine."

He frowned. "Not while you're pregnant. I'm going to Pike Place Market after work. I'll pick up some fresh fish and produce and drop it by."

She knew his heart was in the right place, but if he kept

this up, she was going to have to get a restraining order against him. Worse, while he was trying to be caring and supportive, he was breaking her heart about fifteen times a day. Like just now. He'd told her he was buying her food, but he hadn't mentioned anything about staying with her to enjoy it. He didn't seem to want to come over to dinner or talk or anything.

"I should have the food chart ready by then," he said.

She winced. "I thought you were kidding about that."

"No. I'll print out the spreadsheet, seven copies at a time. All you have to do is fill in the foods you eat. The chart will show how many of the various food groups you should have and the quantities. You can pick anything you like within that category."

"How generous," she murmured.

"Your nutritional needs have changed," he said. "And they'll continue to change with each trimester. Research shows that vital elements of the baby's neurological system are being formed even as we speak."

Zane had devoured several books on pregnancy in the past couple of days. Nicki was still in the first chapter of the one she'd bought.

"I appreciate the need for good nutrition," she said. "But I'm not sure my doctor expects me to be this regimented."

As soon as the *D* word passed her lips, she wanted to call it back. Zane slapped the notebook closed and tucked it back in his shirt pocket.

"The appointment is still next Wednesday, right?" he asked.

She nodded.

"I'll be there."

Hardly news, she thought. Zane might not have moved in with her, but he was sticking about as close as a tick. Just this morning he'd wanted to talk about her fiber intake. Of course he'd insisted on accompanying her to the doctor. His list of questions had reached two pages.

While Nicki could handle his worries about the baby, it was the other questions she didn't want to hear. Like the ones where he asked the doctor how her disability would impact fetal growth and delivery.

In the past couple of days she'd ceased to be a person to Zane. Instead she was the woman responsible for his baby's gestation.

"Want to come over and watch the game on Saturday?" she asked. "The University of Washington is playing UCLA. I'll even give you points."

He shook his head. "I would like to meet to discuss future modifications of your exercise program."

Nicki slammed her hands against the desk. "Dammit, Zane, back off. I mean it. You're making me crazy with your micromanagement of my life. I'm fine. The baby's fine. Go live your life. If you don't want to hang out with me, then find another bimbo and have at it. I will be your friend, or your lover or both. But I will not be some science experiment. Whatever your problem is, get over it. Do you understand me?"

She'd raised her voice with each sentence so that by the time she finished, she was practically shouting. Her last words echoed in the still room.

For a second she thought she'd gotten through to him. Zane nodded and even gave her a slight smile. But when he spoke, hope died.

"You're starting to feel the mood swings. I read about them. Don't worry, it's just hormones. Things will get more even in your second trimester. As for me backing off, it's not going to happen. You might not understand what's at stake here, but I do. And I'm never going to forget it."

Nicki spent the weekend trying to figure out how she was going to tell her parents she was pregnant. She knew they would be very excited about being grandparents, but they also had big plans for a wedding. Despite the fact that she'd told them she didn't expect them to pay for her trip down the aisle, they'd been saving for years. Every few months, her mother sent her pictures of bridal dresses or cakes. Just for Nicki to look at.

They loved her, she thought Monday morning as she wheeled through the quiet office and headed for the company gym. They wanted her to be happy. Unfortunately she was about to disappoint them in a huge way.

Oh, they wouldn't say anything. They both adored Zane and would welcome him to the family. But having a baby without first being married wouldn't make them proud.

Although right now her folks were the least of her problems, she thought as she entered the workout room.

"Nicole," Ted called from his place at the chest press. "You're looking especially lovely this morning. Ever consider the value of working out naked?"

The familiar banter with her co-worker eased her tension. She grinned.

"You're a sexist pig, Theodore."

Ted finished with his exercise and sat up. He was tall, muscular and could have squashed her head like a bug. "I like naked women," he said without the least bit of remorse. "So sue me."

"I just might have to do that."

"What if I offered to take my clothes off, too?"

"Nobody wants to see your hairy butt," Rob said as

he strolled into the room. "Least of all a classy chick like Nicki. What's going on, kid?"

"I'm good," Nicki said. "Why aren't you in New York with the royals?"

"They headed home. This was all just preliminary work. The real trip starts at the end of the month." Rob headed for the treadmills. He'd tied his long, blond hair back in a ponytail. As he stepped onto the machine, he flipped his towel on the side bar.

"Yup, just me, the princess and the New York skyline."

Nicki laughed. "Oh, what about her husband? I've heard that El Bahar men are very hot-blooded."

"You wouldn't want to lose your head," Ted joked.

Rob ignored them both and punched in the program on the machine.

Feeling better than she had in a week, Nicki made her way to the recumbent bike and shifted onto the seat. After strapping her feet in place, she started her workout.

There were several programs to choose from on the bike, along with intensity levels and adjustments to time. She punched in her favorite and set the difficulty level for five. After setting the clock for thirty minutes, she began to cycle.

Her muscles were slow to warm up. For the first half mile there were an assortment of aches and pains that finally gave way to a sense of strength. She picked up the pace.

Twelve minutes and thirty-seven seconds into her workout, the door to the gym burst open and Zane stalked in. He looked so annoyed that neither Rob nor Ted called out a greeting. Nicki ran through her activities for the past twelve hours, which was about how long it had been since Zane had checked in with her, and couldn't figure out what rule she could have violated.

She'd eaten a snack before coming in, blending the protein-carb ratio perfectly. She was already into her second eight-ounce glass of water. She had a healthy breakfast waiting for her in her office and…

"Wait just one darn minute," she said as Zane stopped next to her. "You're not my mother. If you can't be pleasant to me and our co-workers then you can leave right now."

"I'm pleasant," he snarled. He turned to the two bodyguards. "Good morning." It sounded more like an order than a greeting. His attention swung back to her. "You're not wearing a heart monitor."

"What?"

"A heart monitor. I bought you one."

Sure enough he pulled the equipment out of a box and handed it to her.

"Why on earth do I need this?"

He looked at her as if she had an IQ of sixteen. "So I can monitor your heart."

He thrust the band that would wrap around her chest toward her. She took it and stared at the strip of rubber and elastic.

"No way," she said, but Zane was already strapping the display unit on his wrist.

She actually yelped. "You are so kidding," she told him, her temper flaring to the point of spontaneous combustion. "There is no way in hell that you're going to put a heart monitor on me, then keep the display for yourself."

"I'm the one who's interested."

"You're the one who's crazy."

They glared at each other.

In the background she heard scuffling noises. She turned

her head and saw both Rob and Ted heading for the door. She knew it was more about them escaping from the fight than any desire to give them privacy.

She returned her attention to Zane, determined to win this battle. He blinked first.

"I really want this, Nicki," he said, his tone slightly more reasonable. "It's important to me."

She could understand that. Respect it even. But not at the price of her privacy and well-being.

"Zane, you have *got* to stop. Women have been having babies since the beginning of time and I'm going to guess almost none of them wore heart monitors. Okay? So back off."

She held out the band. After a couple of seconds, he took it.

"Would you wear it if I let *you* have the display?" he asked.

"No."

He nodded and shoved the unit back in the box, then he turned and left the room.

She was alone. After a couple of seconds, she began peddling again, even though she was no longer in the mood to work out. Everything was different, she thought sadly. Just a couple of weeks ago their time in the gym had been fun and sexy. She and Zane would talk and joke. He helped her with her exercises and she watched his long-legged strength and grace. Now all that was lost.

She missed him. She missed *them*. And she didn't know how to get everything back the way it was.

"Just perfect," Dr. Sheri Grant said with a smile. "I'm going to let you get dressed, then we'll meet in my office.

I'm sure you have a lot of questions. I have answers, and some information I'd like to give you."

The poor woman had no idea what she was getting into, Nicki thought as she sat up and watched her doctor leave the examining room. Zane had been surprisingly quiet during the physical exam. After introducing himself, he'd taken a seat in the corner of the room and had simply observed.

Nicki had a feeling that was all going to change when they moved on to the next stage of the appointment. The previous afternoon Zane had given her a typed list of his questions, along with the offer to add hers to his. As he'd come up with things she'd never thought of, she'd done little more than read through the three pages and shake her head.

Now she waited while he came over and lifted her down to her wheelchair.

"I did some research on Dr. Grant," he said while he settled her in place.

"I don't doubt that."

"She's very experienced, well respected and has a pleasant bedside manner, which will be important to you. From what I can tell, she favors open communications with her patients."

Nicki cared less about his recitation than the fact that she wasn't wearing anything but a thin cotton robe. Hadn't Zane noticed her bare skin when he'd lifted her up to the table or back down into her chair? Did he want to pause and feel the warmth of her body so close to his? Didn't he find any of this a turn-on?

Apparently not, as he told her he would wait outside in the hallway while she dressed.

Five minutes later they were in Dr. Grant's office. Zane tried to hand her the small lunch bag he'd brought.

"You should eat something," he told her.

"I'm not hungry." Okay, if she were to tell the absolute truth, she felt a slight gnawing in her stomach, but there was no way she was going to encourage Zane by taking the food he'd insisted on dragging to their appointment.

"You had breakfast at eight," he said. "It's nearly noon. You need food in your system."

She sighed. "What I need is some quality time with a normal person."

He ignored that. "I have string cheese and some grapes."

He opened the bag just as Dr. Grant stepped into the room. Nicki grabbed the lunch sack and shoved it into her purse.

Dr. Grant, a tall, slender woman in her mid-forties, settled behind her desk.

"New mothers and fathers-to-be always have lots of questions," she said with a smile. "I want to answer all of them. We have plenty of time, so don't be shy. Oh, let me give you this first. I don't want to forget."

She handed over a thick envelope filled with brochures and booklets on everything from weight gain to cloth versus disposable diapers. Nicki took it and pulled out the first sheet while Zane launched into his questions.

"I understand that Nicki will need to take extra vitamins. Now the prenatal variety offer extra supplements, but what about a regimen we put together ourselves? I've done some research—"

At that point he actually pulled out a chart. He had two copies, one of which he passed over to Dr. Grant.

"I've listed the makeup of the three most popular prenatal vitamins currently used. As you can see, the second column lists all known requirements for a pregnant woman. And while we're on the subject of supplements and nutrition, I've been reading about the advantages of more fish for pregnant women."

Nicki winced.

Dr. Grant sat back and shook her head. "Zane, did you print out the questions you'd like me to answer?"

"Sure. If you prefer to handle it that way."

He passed over his multipage list.

She scanned the material. "I see you're concerned about sleep, exercise. Aha. Oh, imported fruits and vegetables. I don't usually get asked that one."

Nicki looked at him. "When did you add that?"

"Last night. There was something on the news about the fact that we're getting close to winter. Soon our fruits and vegetables will be coming from the southern hemisphere. Is that all right?"

"Of course it's all right," she snapped. "If not for those imports, we wouldn't see so much as a grape until spring. You are *not* keeping me from eating fruit for this entire pregnancy."

"Of course I want you to eat fruit. That's the point." He turned back to the doctor. "You understand my concern."

"Of course." Dr. Grant read off a few more items. "Is it all right for Nicki to be in the house while the cleaning service is there? What about exercise? Oh, I see you've included her workout schedule." She smiled at Zane. "You're very thorough."

"You have no idea," Nicki muttered.

"I do. I've seen this before." Her expression turned sympathetic. "The good news is it gets better."

Zane didn't look pleased to be discussed in this way. "What gets better?"

"The obsession," Dr. Grant said. "You want to do everything in your power to keep Nicki and the baby safe."

Zane stiffened. "How did you know?"

"It's not an uncommon reaction. Especially for a first-time father. You're not physically a part of the baby the way Nicki is. You're excited, terrified and want to put Nicki in a plastic bubble to keep her from harm. The baby, too, of course."

Zane didn't look convinced. "It's not that simple."

"I understand." She set the list on her desk. "Zane, Nicki is healthy, you're healthy, there's no reason to think this pregnancy will be anything but completely normal. Monitoring every detail of her life isn't going to change anything, but it will increase her stress level. You think you're helping, but in this case, you're creating a problem where one doesn't exist."

Nicki reached out and touched his arm. "She's right. I want you to be a part of things, but you can't monitor every speck of food I put into my mouth."

He looked as if he wanted to ask why not. She supposed that she could see his point. His job was to keep people safe. Of course he would feel that more intensely about his child. If she were in—

She froze in her chair as her brain clicked over a few important pieces of information. Zane's list of questions. The ones that had embarrassed her and frustrated her and made her want to shake him were all about her health. What she was eating, how much she was sleeping, vitamins. Nothing on those pages was about her being in a wheelchair. He'd never mentioned it even once.

She shook her head and called herself fifteen kinds of idiot. Zane hadn't been lying when he said it didn't matter and she hadn't believed him. Because it was the easiest place to go. Talk about dumb.

She wanted to take a few minutes to dwell on her realization but this wasn't the time. However, the information did give her the impetus to see things from his point of view.

"How about if we make a deal," she said. "You can monitor me until you start to make me crazy. I'll make a serious effort to be patient and you'll promise to back off when I tell you to. Then we'll see how it goes and hope Dr. Grant is right, and that this will all calm down in a month or two."

Zane looked from her to the doctor.

"It sounds like a plan to me," Dr. Grant said.

Zane nodded slowly. "All right. As long as you agree to eat more quality protein."

She thought about the three pounds of salmon he'd left in her refrigerator. "I'll do my best."

"Okay."

Dr. Grant smiled at them both. "All right. Now let me answer a few of the more 'normal' questions."

She reviewed the workout schedule. "Nicki, all this is fine. You may experience some days when you're more tired, so go easy if that feels right. None of your workout is weight-bearing so you won't have to change it as you get closer to term. You're biggest problem will be dealing with your increasing midsection. I'm sure Zane can help you modify your routine when the time comes."

"That would be great," she said.

Zane agreed.

"There are going to be a few considerations due to you being in a wheelchair," her doctor continued. "As you don't use your legs walking around, I want you to get in the habit of putting your feet up a few times a day. This will help with circulation."

"You're thinking of blood clots," Zane said. "I read about them."

"I'm sure you did." Dr. Grant looked at him. "This is

preventative. There's no indication that Nicki is going to have a problem."

"I understand." He turned to Nicki. "I could build something for under your desk. If it was the right height and placement, you could stretch out your legs while still in your chair."

"Perfect," she said, equally annoyed and amused. He cared, she reminded herself. Maybe he didn't love her, but wasn't his obsessive worry a twisted sign of affection? It beat not caring at all.

"All other daily activities are fine," Dr. Grant said. "Including the one that got you into my office in the first place. Some couples worry that making love will hurt the baby. That's not the truth. Most couples find that their intimacy is more special in pregnancy. It will bond the two of you, which you're going to need to survive the 2:00 a.m. feedings."

Nicki found herself unable to look at Zane. Ever since he found out about her pregnancy he'd been a whole lot less interested in her as a person. She couldn't imagine him ever wanting to make love with her again.

But she wanted to, very much. She thought about their times together, how he'd made her feel, how she'd wanted to please him, and she missed it.

Did he? Did he think about those nights and wish for more? She sighed. One day very soon she was going to have to find the courage to ask him. And if the answer was yes, then she was going to have to do whatever it took to get him back into her bed.

# Chapter 13

On the way back to the office, Zane thought about what had happened at the appointment. He knew Dr. Grant lumped him in with all the other neurotic fathers-to-be and there was no way he could explain the truth about his past. But one piece of information *had* caught his attention. That his overmonitoring of Nicki's health would cause her more stress, which would have a physical impact on her body.

Which meant he was going to have to be more subtle in his approach.

He glanced over at her. She sat behind the steering wheel, her attention on the road. When they stopped for a traffic light, he spoke.

"I'm going to back off," he said.

She turned toward him and raised her eyebrows. "I'm not sure I believe you."

He nearly smiled. Damn, but she knew him well. "I'm going to *try* to back off. Maybe shoot for twenty percent."

"It's a start."

The light turned green and she eased the van forward.

"I'll try to be more cooperative about some things, too," she said. "Like when I work out, I'll put on the heart monitor, but *I* get to wear the display unit. Fair enough?"

He nodded. He didn't care who wore it, as long as she kept track of her heart rate. Scratch that. He *did* care, but he was willing to let this one go.

"I'd like to read through the material when you're done with it," he said.

"Okay. I'll look it all over this weekend and bring it to work on Monday." She sighed. "Speaking of work, we're going to have to make an announcement at some point. We've both been acting weird, so I'm guessing everyone knows something is up, even if they don't have specifics. And in time, my condition will become obvious to everyone."

He hadn't thought about that. About people knowing. He and Amber had never reached that stage. When she'd died, he decided not to burden her family further by telling them she'd been pregnant.

"What about your folks?" he asked.

"Not something I want to think about."

"They want grandkids," he told her. "They'll be happy."

"They're more into the traditional way of doing things, and don't remind me that you've offered to marry me. I'm aware of that."

He wanted to make his case again, to tell her it was the only way to make things work, but he held back. For now.

"I can't decide if I should tell them over the phone or wait until they come up for Thanksgiving," she continued. "That's two months from now, and they might not understand why I waited so long. But they're heading out to Australia any day now, so that's a good excuse to keep things quiet for a while."

"I could tell them," he offered.

She glanced at him. "You were a marine, weren't you. Talk about stepping into enemy fire." She lowered her voice. "Hi, Mr. and Mrs. Beauman. I'm calling to let you know I knocked up your only daughter."

"I wouldn't phrase it like that."

"There are very few delicate ways to tell my parents I'm pregnant. Believe me, I've been trying to find one or two."

He felt helpless and hated the feeling. If she would just marry him, this problem, along with several others, would be solved.

She turned left at the signal, then pulled into the office parking lot.

"Thanks for coming with me, Zane."

He stared at her. "I thought you didn't want me to go with you, but you didn't know how to stop me."

She smiled. "That was true at first. But you didn't ask any embarrassing questions during the actual exam and I liked not being alone."

Suddenly he wanted to touch her. Not just to take her pulse or see if she had a fever, but because he ached for her. There was an emptiness inside him that only Nicki seemed to fill.

"I want to come to all your appointments."

"I know. I guess I'm going to let you." She pulled the keys out of the ignition. "And while we're on the subject of you helping out, I want to redo one of the bedrooms at my place. You know, paint, maybe a border print. Do you want to help?"

"Of course."

"Good, because I bought a crib and I've tried to put it together and it's just not happening."

He grinned. "You might be a computer whiz, but you're lousy with a screwdriver."

"I do okay. But the directions make no sense. I can't tell what part is what and none of them fit together right."

"I'll take a look at it. What are you doing Saturday?"

She shrugged. "Hanging out."

"How about if I pick up some paint chips and swing by? I'll work on the crib while you pick out colors."

"Works for me. There's a wallpaper store by me. Maybe I'll stop on my way home and borrow some sample books. We can look at border prints together."

"There are no words to describe my joy."

She laughed and for that second, some of the fear left Zane. They were what they had always been—good friends who cared about each other. Then he remembered about the baby and everything was different again. Everything but one.

Even though he knew it was dangerous, even though he knew it would distract him from his main mission of keeping her safe, the wanting had returned and he didn't know how to make it go away.


Zane showed up late Saturday morning. Nicki let him in, then laughed when she saw the bags, boxes and charts he carried.

"We're talking about getting a room ready for a baby, not planning an invasion of a third world country."

"Paint chips," he said as he set down a bag filled with a rainbow of bits of color. "My toolbox so I can put the crib together. The additional wallpaper books you asked me to pick up because the eight you had weren't enough, and graph paper so we can lay out the room to scale and plan where the furniture will go."

She closed the door behind him. "Of course. Graph paper. And me without a scrap in the house. What *was* I thinking?"

He gave her a mock glare.

Nicki waved toward the kitchen. "I made coffee. Help yourself." Before he could start in on her, she shook her head. "It's a fresh pot I made just for you. I already had my cup of decaf, thank you very much."

"Thanks," he said as he walked down the hall.

Nicki picked up the bag with the paint chips and carried it into the living room. She dumped the contents onto her low coffee table and started sorting through the options.

There were single color chips, strips with a dark color at each end—one flat, one gloss—with a white tint in the middle, and chips with five samples ranging from light to dark in that color family. Right away she noticed a definite theme.

When Zane walked into the living room, she turned to him. "These are nearly all blue."

"No way. There are other colors."

She searched through the pile. "I found one pink chip, three green and a handful of yellows. Are you hoping for a boy?"

He shrugged, looking more than a little sheepish. "I thought it would be fun to have a son."

"Let me guess. You're thinking sports and cars. If we have a daughter, you're going to have to learn to do the hair ribbon thing. And take her to dance class."

He barely kept from shuddering. "I couldn't do that."

"We're going to have to talk about that at some point," she said.

He sat on the sofa and picked up a blue paint chip. "Dance class?"

"The sex of the baby," she said. "Do we want to know in advance?"

Zane looked at her. "From the ultrasound."

She nodded. "I haven't decided yet. There's a part of me that says there are too few real surprises in life and that it would add to the excitement not to know. My more practical nature says if we know, we can plan the room better."

"I don't know, either."

Nicki had a feeling that his indecision came from other concerns, such as would he protect her better if he knew or if he didn't know. She wished she understood what was going on inside his head and why he was so freaked out about the whole thing. She'd honestly expected panic and indifference, not this burning desire to run her life.

Although she had to admit that he'd backed off as promised. When he'd called the previous evening to check on her, he hadn't even asked what she'd had for dinner. Of course she'd heard the tension in his voice, so she'd taken pity on him and had offered the information.

"Do you need more paint chips?" he asked. "I can get different colors."

"These are fine. I was thinking of yellow anyway. It's a cheery color on our gray days."

"Once you pick out what you want, I'll do the work."

She rolled her eyes. "Because using a brush and roller will strain me in my delicate condition?"

"Because I don't want you breathing in the fumes."

"Okay. Good point. I'll let you do the painting." She smiled. "You're going to have to do the border print anyway. I can't reach."

"Not a problem." He glanced at his coffee mug, then at

her. "You don't have to keep telling me what you're eating. I'm going to let that go."

"Really? Even if I have ice cream?"

He looked distressed, but instead of complaining said, "I'd like you to eat right about eighty percent of the time."

"That's what I want to do, Zane." She rolled close to him and touched his arm. "I'm nervous about this whole baby thing, too. I want to stay as healthy as possible. Even if I get the occasional craving for a chili cheeseburger."

"You'll want to pass on that."

"Why? Too much fat?"

"You'll get heartburn. Pregnant women are more susceptible."

"That's romantic," she grumbled.

He tugged on a lock of hair. "I live to serve. Come on. Show me the crib."

She led him into one of the spare bedrooms. She'd chosen the one that faced south for the baby's room, so it would get plenty of light in the winter, but not be too hot in the summer. A partially assembled crib lay in pieces on the floor.

Zane crouched down and picked up a railing. "This isn't new."

"Oh. Didn't I mention it was an antique? That's why I bought it. A woman brought it in to sell on consignment while I was looking around the baby furniture store. The salesperson didn't want to take it, but I was interested. The woman had a picture of what it looked like and when I saw that, I fell in love with it."

She pointed to the old photograph she'd tacked up on the wall.

"Where are the instructions?" he asked.

She glanced around at the pieces. "Over there. By the headboard. Or is it a footboard."

Zane picked them up and frowned. "They're handwritten."

"I know. Isn't it cool? I thought I'd put the crib together and make sure all the parts were there, then take it apart and strip it down and either stain or paint it."

He groaned. "You don't even know if all the pieces are here?"

"The woman said they were, but there's only one way to tell."

"And you didn't want to buy something out of a box because why?"

"I want it to be special. I love that this crib is nearly a hundred years old."

"Yeah, that's real exciting. Do you see how close together the rails are? Do you know how much work that's going to be to strip?"

"Honestly, I haven't a clue."

"Great."

She couldn't help smiling. "If it's too much trouble I could hire someone to—"

He cut her off with a growl. "Fine. I'll get it together, then take it apart and strip it down. When do you plan to decide about paint versus stain?"

"I have no idea."

He looked at her. "You're being difficult on purpose, aren't you?"

"Maybe just a little. To pay you back."

He grunted. "Sit tight," he said as he rose. "I'll be right back."

He returned with several brochures for dressers, changing tables and bassinets. "I've been doing some research."

"Of course you have."

He ignored that. "Babies need a lot of stuff. Most of it is a standard height."

He opened one brochure and set it on her lap, then crouched next to her.

"See the changing table?" he asked, pointing. "It's going to be too high for you. The dresser is less of a problem, but the top drawer can still be difficult."

She nodded but didn't speak. She wasn't sure where he was going with this.

"So I talked with this buddy of mine," he told her. "He does a lot of custom work. I explained the problem, how you'd need the table low and I'd want it to be the regular height. He came up with this."

Zane pulled a folded piece of paper out of the back pocket of his jeans and passed it to her.

"See this lever here? It will raise and lower the table to different preset heights. You'd just lift it or lower it. These steel pins would lock into place, so we wouldn't have to worry about the table shifting while the baby was on it. He told me that he'd be happy to match whatever style we want." He shrugged. "If you're interested."

Nicki looked from the sketch to Zane. Deep inside, something cold and frozen warmed enough to melt. Her heart fluttered a little.

This was the Zane she'd fallen for. The man who thought of her being in a wheelchair as little more than a fact of life. Whatever logistical problems it presented were simply challenges to be solved, nothing more. He didn't judge her. She'd been wrong to think he did. Funny how all these years after she'd made peace with her condition, that was still the first place she went when something went wrong.

Apparently the healing took a whole lot longer than she'd realized.

"I think it's a brilliant idea," she told him. "You were really sweet to think of this."

He looked at her, his dark eyes filled with concern. "You sure I'm not stepping on your toes?"

She wiggled her bare feet. "Not even close."

"Good."

He sat on the floor and picked up a piece of the crib. "At least we have a long time until the kid is going to have to use this."

"What? You can storm beaches and overthrow governments but you can't put together one little bitty crib?"

He collected a handful of screws and shook his head. "I'll have to get back to you on that."

She watched him sort through the parts. As always, he moved with a graceful ease that left her breathless. Wanting stirred deep inside. Wanting and a need to connect with him. She missed the intimacy they'd shared. Not just the lovemaking, but the friendship. From what she could tell, they were taking baby steps in that direction. How long until they were back where they had been a couple of weeks ago? Or was that lost forever?

"Do you think I'll be a good mother?" she asked.

Zane looked at her. "Of course. Why?"

"I worry. I've never been a parent before. I don't want to mess up the kid."

"Your parents did a good job with you, so you've seen how it should be done."

"I hadn't thought of that," she told him.

"I've been reading that they think intelligence is passed down through the mother. So the baby will be smart."

That made her smile. "How comforting. Now if only he or she will inherit your mechanical abilities."

He glanced at the pieces he held. "I'll get it."

"I have no doubt."

Zane knew she didn't. Nicki trusted him with a completeness that left him humble. And terrified. He couldn't believe she worried about being a good mother. She was patient, loving, funny. She knew what it was like to be part of a family. What did he know? He'd grown up on the streets. He'd belonged to a gang, which wasn't exactly like being a part of mainstream society.

He'd agreed to back off the monitoring, which intellectually he knew was the right thing, but in his gut, he sweated every second of every day.

A thousand things could go wrong. Didn't she see that? If he was around, he could protect her. He could save her—which he hadn't been able to do with Amber.

"We're going to have to talk about names, too," Nicki said. "I know this is way premature, but I suspect we're going to argue about it, so we may want to start that early."

"Because you love a good fight?" he asked.

"So I'll have more time to convince you that I'm right."

She laughed as she spoke. This morning she wore her hair loose. There wasn't much makeup on her face, but her cheeks glowed with color. She was so beautiful, it was almost painful to look at her.

Dressing for the unseasonably warm fall day, she'd pulled on shorts and a sleeveless T-shirt. He could see the perfect lines of her body. He thought her breasts might be a little fuller, but otherwise, there weren't any physical manifestations of her condition that he could see.

Still, the baby grew inside of her. His baby. Their baby.

He dropped the crib pieces on the floor and shifted onto

his knees. Cupping her face in his hands, he stared into her eyes.

"Marry me," he breathed.

Her green eyes darkened with what looked like pain. "I can't."

"Why not?"

"Because you want to control me and I want to be loved."

He dropped his hands as if they'd been burned. Love. Had she really spoken the word?

"I care about you," he said.

The corners of her mouth curved up. "I'm glad."

It wasn't enough. He could see that. But how could he convince her?

"I can't be with anyone else," he told her. "Going out with Heather was a disaster. I thought about you the whole time." He swallowed. "I don't *want* to be with anyone else."

She stroked his cheek with her fingertips. "What happened, big guy? You discover that you need a little conversation while you're doing the wild thing?"

"Yeah."

"I'm glad."

She looked deep into his eyes, as if searching for something. Zane had a bad feeling she wasn't going to find what she wanted. So he did the only thing that made sense. He kissed her.

# Chapter 14

W hat started out as a distraction quickly turned into something else. The second Zane's mouth brushed hers, he found himself caught up in a passion he couldn't control. Need flooded him, making him hard and ready in less than a heartbeat.

He swept his tongue across her lower lip and when she opened for him, he plunged inside. She tasted sweet and hot and he couldn't resist her. Not when she strained toward him, moaning in the back of her throat.

Heat exploded. He wrapped his arms around her and drew her from the chair. When she was on his lap, he slid his hand up her rib cage to her breasts and cupped the luscious curves.

"Yes," she breathed as he lightly touched her already tight nipples. "Oh, Zane, that feels so good."

He'd read that a pregnant woman's breasts could become more sensitive in the first trimester. He'd thought it would mean that Nicki could find his touch painful. Apparently in her case it just meant she was more erotically responsive. He was man enough not to mind.

He pulled off her T-shirt, unfastened her bra, then bent low to take her nipple in his mouth. As his lips closed around the taut flesh, she sank her nails into his back.

"Oh, yes," she gasped. "I can't believe it. More. Do it more."

She clung to him, panting, pleading, writhing. He sucked a little harder, flicking his tongue against her, and she shuddered.

"It's not possible," she breathed, then shuddered again.

His mind raced. Was she climaxing?

He ripped off his own shirt and laid it on the floor, then lowered her to the soft cotton. Her eyes were unfocused, her mouth slightly parted. He bent down to her breasts again.

At the first brush of his tongue, she sucked in a breath. When he closed his lips around her nipple, she grabbed his head with both hands and held him firmly in place.

He reached for the waistband of her shorts and unfastened the button. After lowering the zipper, he slipped his hand under her panties and headed south. She parted her legs and moaned.

She was damp, he thought as he eased between folds of swollen flesh. Timing the movement of his mouth with the progress of his hand, he slid a finger inside of her just as he drew deeply on her breast.

Strong muscles convulsed around him. Stunned, he moved in and out of her. She sighed her pleasure.

Zane swore and jerked off her shorts and panties, then shoved down his jeans and briefs and pushed into her.

She climaxed with each thrust. He'd never experienced such intense pleasure. The combination of heat, tightness and rippling massage made short work of his restraint. In an effort to please her as much as possible before he completely lost control, he raised up slightly and slipped a hand between them.

As he rubbed that swollen point of pleasure, she actually screamed. Her entire body surrendered. It was too much for him. He pumped in twice more, then lost himself in an explosion of glorious release.

"The problem with doing it on the floor," Nicki said a couple of minutes later, "is that there's no lingering." She sighed with satisfaction, then admitted, "My back is starting to hurt."

Zane raised his head and smiled. "Then we'll have to move to the bed."

She couldn't think of a place she would rather be. "You just want a repeat performance."

He kissed her, then sat up and drew her into a sitting position. "Are you kidding? You were climaxing with me just touching your breasts. Who knows what you're capable of if I put my mind to it."

She didn't know, either, but the thought of finding out was delightful.

"What about all the work we had planned?" she asked as he picked her up and carried her into the bedroom.

He lowered her onto the mattress and kissed her. "Tomorrow," he whispered. "Let's just spend today in bed."

"I'd like that a lot."

"We can even order takeout."

"Chinese?" she asked.

"Whatever you'd like."

Monday morning Nicki practically floated to work. The past two days had been perfect. Zane had gone home Saturday afternoon to pick up a few things, but aside from that, they'd spent every second together.

They'd talked, they'd laughed, they'd made love. Given her body's new delicious sensitivity, the latter had been exquisitely wonderful.

Now as she parked her van and waited for Zane to pull up beside her, she knew that what they'd experienced over the past two days was available to them for the rest of their lives. But only if they both had the courage to fight for it.

Nicki figured she would be the one to start the battle. She loved Zane and she wanted him to love her. For some reason he couldn't...or wouldn't, and she was going to have to find out which. Any attempts she'd made to discuss his past had been skillfully diverted, so she was on her own. Fortunately, she had some ideas and she planned to put them into effect that morning.

"How can I help you?" Jeff asked when she rolled into his office shortly after eleven.

"I need your help with some research."

Jeff smiled. "I'm surprised. You're the best."

"This is a special project. I want to find out about Zane's past."

Her boss's expression didn't change, but she sensed his withdrawal from the conversation.

"This is important," she told him quickly, before he could speak. "I don't know how much Ashley has shared with you, but I'm pregnant. Zane's the father. I'm in love with him, but while he wants to be a part of my life, he's not interested in sharing much more than responsibilities and duties. I want to know why."

Jeff was a pro. She had a feeling he hadn't known about her condition or her relationship with his partner, but not so much as a muscle twitched. His expression remained as it had been.

"Ask him," he said.

"He's not big on chatting about the past."

"Maybe there's a good reason for that."

"I'm sure there is, but that doesn't change my need to know. Why does he hold his heart so carefully out of reach?"

Jeff leaned back in his chair. "Nicki, you're a great employee and a friend. I respect you and I want to help, but Zane is also a friend."

She'd been afraid of this, but she'd had to try. "You're not going to tell me anything, are you?"

"I'll tell you what you're going to find out in your search, and I'll tell you something he hasn't told me but that I've experienced myself."

Jeff rose and crossed to the window. "Zane was in the Marines. We've never discussed his work in detail. I don't know where he was stationed, what he saw, what he knows. But I've seen the same sort of fighting. The death and suffering. It changes a man forever."

"The dark soul of a warrior," she murmured.

Jeff looked at her and raised his eyebrows. She shrugged.

"Ashley mentioned it once," she said. "That there were things in your past that she could never understand. She said you wouldn't share them with her because knowing them would fundamentally change who she is and you didn't want to burden her with that."

"Very true. Soldiers learn to disconnect. To focus on what needs to be done to the exclusion of everything else. In some ways, to be like a machine."

She heard the words, but couldn't reconcile them with what she knew about Zane. He was always joking and teasing. Jeff, on the other hand, was far more intense. Was that difference a reflection of their personalities? Or had they each picked a different way to deal with the past?

"You're saying that Zane has closed himself off," she said. "It's a survival mechanism and once turned on there may not be a way to turn it off?"

"It's a possibility."

"You were able to readjust. You're married, with a family."

He smiled. "I had the help of an extraordinary woman to guide me back to the land of the living. She didn't love me into changing. Instead, by loving her, I was able to see the possibilities."

Was the same opportunity available to Zane? If she hung in there long enough and he allowed himself to care, would he be transformed?

"That's what I know about myself and speculate may be true for Zane," Jeff said as he returned to his chair. "The other piece of information I have is what you'll find when you begin your search. He was married and his wife died. This was about five years ago. She was also a marine."

Nicki stared at her boss. She couldn't breathe, nor could she feel anything but unexpected pain. It was as if someone had taken a sledgehammer to her heart.

"Married?" she whispered.

Jeff nodded. "I'm sorry, Nicki. I know this is a surprise."

She couldn't believe it. "He never said anything."

"He doesn't talk about it to me much, either. He first mentioned her when I was within inches of being a complete moron and walking away from Ashley. Zane told me not to do it. When I pointed out he was hardly in a position to give romantic advice, he mentioned the woman from his past. Later, at the wedding, he took me aside and told me that there were few joys in life that matched those found in a happy marriage."

"I see."

The words were difficult to force out of her tight throat. She felt cold, stiff and sick to her stomach. The room started to spin and had she been standing, she would have crumpled to the ground.

"Thank you," she whispered. "I have a place to start."

"Are you all right?"

She forced herself to nod. "A little surprised, but I'll get over it."

Jeff leaned toward her. "Nicki, I think Zane is worth fighting for. He cares about you. We can all see it. This may take time, but don't give up. If there's anything I can do..."

"You're being very kind," she said as she turned and wheeled out of his office.

It took every ounce of strength she possessed to get back to her office. Once there, she closed the door and gave in to the tears that burned her eyes.

Married! He'd been married. He'd loved someone else. He'd met her, been intrigued, dated her, proposed, then married her. They'd lived together, made plans. He'd touched her, made love with her and mourned her when she died.

Nicki couldn't stand to think about it. She'd thought something had happened to make Zane incapable of loving, but maybe it was just he didn't want to love her.

When the emotional storm had passed, all that was left was the hollowness in her chest. Two sides of her brain battled. Her logical half told her that a man who had loved once could love again. Her emotional side said to give up on what could never be and plan her life without him.

The problem with that last bit of advice was that she was

still desperately in love with him. Hadn't she promised herself she wouldn't give up without a fight?

Besides, there was more going on than she realized. Zane's reaction to her pregnancy had been surprising. He hadn't been excited or upset or anything but determined to keep her safe. Why? What had happened in his past to make him the way he was?

Jeff had said he thought Zane had been married about five years ago. How had his wife died and was that the reason he couldn't allow himself to connect?

She only knew one way to find out.

It was nearly seven that evening when Zane walked into her office.

"I thought we agreed you weren't going to work late," he said as he took the chair on the other side of her desk. "It's called a compromise."

He smiled as he spoke. Nicki studied him greedily, as if she had to memorize everything about him. The shape of his eyes, the curve of his cheeks, the way his mouth moved when he talked. She wanted to snuggle up next to him and breathe in his scent. She wanted to love him, and she wanted him to love her back. Unfortunately she was no closer to making that happen than she had been before.

"I had something come up," she said, pulling a handful of sheets off the printer and stacking them with the rest.

"What?"

"I'm trying to break into military records. It's not easy."

He frowned. "It's not only tough, it's illegal. What's going on? Jeff would never give you an assignment like that."

"You're right. I gave this one to myself." She shoved the stack of papers toward him. "Tell me, Zane. What is it, because I sure as hell can't find it. Tell me the secret. Tell me if there's any hope."

"What are you talking about?"

"You."

Nicki knew she was acting out of desperation, but she didn't know where else to turn. She had to know—even if the truth destroyed her and burned away any hope.

"Tell me why you can't love me," she said quietly. "We're so good together. We laugh, we talk. We like the same sports, we argue about politics, we're good in bed. I know you want me—I've seen the proof. But that's not the same as loving me. So what is it? The color of my hair? The scent of my skin? The sound of my voice?" She swallowed. "Is it the wheelchair?"

He swore and grabbed the papers. "What the hell have you been doing?"

"Searching out your past. I want to know why and I can't find it there, so you're going to have to tell me."

He scanned a couple of sheets, then tossed them back at her. "It's not the damn chair and you know it."

"I was pretty sure, but all the women you've dated have been physically perfect and I'm not." She wheeled out from behind the desk and banged her hand against the metal frame of her chair. "This is a part of me. I am not defined by what I can and cannot do, yet it influences who I am. In some ways, I'm a much stronger person. But I can't walk or dance or run. Is that any part of it?"

"No. never." He shoved his chair back and stood, glaring at her. "It's none of that."

"Then is it about the woman you married?"

He turned away. For a second she thought he might leave, but he didn't. Instead he sank back in the chair and rubbed his eyes.

"Yes. It's about Amber."

Amber. Nicki froze. Somehow hearing the name made the other woman more real.

"Tell me," she whispered.

"You don't want to know."

"Maybe not, but I need to hear why you won't give us a chance."

He was silent for a long time. She was determined to wait him out. He was right. She didn't *want* to hear the words, but she sensed there was power in the truth.

"We couldn't have been more different," he said quietly, not looking at her but at some point on the wall behind her. "She was from a big family in the south. I was a street kid. But there was something between us from the first. I never expected her to say yes when I asked her out, but she accepted and that was it. By the second date, I was hooked."

The pain was like sharp blades cutting through her body. Nicki felt the cold steel sliding between bone and organs. Her chest constricted, her fingers were numb.

"When I met her folks, I was sure they'd take her aside and tell her it was a big mistake to hang out with me, but they didn't. They made me feel welcome. It was Christmas, and after dinner we went for a walk and I proposed. We were married that spring."

Zane leaned forward and rested his forearms on his thighs. "She was the first woman I'd ever loved. I didn't know how I'd gotten so lucky. She was tough, but feminine. Small, but feisty. We were assigned to an island near the Philippines. We worked together and it was great. Then one day she told me she was pregnant."

Nicki hadn't seen that one coming. It wasn't possible for her to feel more pain, so she simply endured the violent ripping of her dreams. Pregnant. There was nothing she could offer Zane that he hadn't already had with Amber. She was little more than second best.

"I wanted her to go home," he continued. "I was scared that she might get hurt out there and I wanted her to go stateside. She disagreed. She wanted to stay as long as possible. I held the trump card. Once her commanding officer knew she was pregnant, he would send her home. I told her if she didn't come clean, I would do it for her. So she agreed. She packed up and left."

He drew in a breath. "I stood right there while she got on the helicopter. I waved goodbye and yelled that I loved her. I was due to get reassigned in about four months, so I figured we would be together then. I'd be home for the birth of our child."

Nicki knew he was about to tell her something bad. She wanted to stop him, but knew she had to know—even if the telling hurt them both.

"The helicopter rose up toward the sky. As it moved forward, something happened. A mechanical failure. It lurched, then slammed into the side of a mountain. There was an explosion. I remember standing there, feeling the heat on my face. I couldn't move, couldn't speak. I sure as hell couldn't save her. I was the one who had insisted on her getting on that helicopter. I killed her, and the baby."

Nicki didn't know what to say. She couldn't have imagined anything like this.

"That's why I date those other women," he said, raising his head and staring at her. "Because they could never matter. I only ever wanted to love Amber."

The darkness in his eyes made her back up a few feet.

"Of course," she whispered. "None of this was about me being in a wheelchair. It wasn't about me at all."

She was little more than a bit player in a story that had

nothing to do with her. Why couldn't she have seen that before she'd fallen in love with a man who was still in love with a ghost?

# *Chapter 15*

Nicki didn't actually watch Zane leave her office. When he'd finished his story, she turned away, fighting for control. When she'd finally looked back at the chair, he was gone.

Maybe it was better. What was there to say in all this? She'd wanted to know why he wouldn't love her, wouldn't give them a chance, and now she had the information. He was in love with someone else. He always had been.

She felt cold and empty, but worse, she felt ashamed. She'd been so damn sure that she was strong and capable and in charge of her life, but at the first sign of trouble with Zane, she'd assumed it was about her being in a wheelchair. She'd emotionally hidden behind her circumstances because it was easy and convenient. She'd never stopped to consider that it might not be about that at all, which meant she wasn't as far along the road to recovery as she thought.

That wasn't going to make dealing with Zane any easier. Because she was going to have to deal with him. They were having a baby together.

She rubbed her temples and told herself she would survive this. Somehow she would be strong, because she'd been to hell and back and nothing could defeat her. Not even the realization that she'd been wishing after the moon all this time.

She'd thought there was something wrong with him. That he was just afraid of commitment or that he'd been burned by love. She'd even allowed herself to consider the possibility that he was secretly in love with her, but afraid to admit it. But no.

He was in love with his late wife. Maybe he was one of those people who could only love once. A one-woman man. Which left her exactly nowhere. Because no matter how much she didn't want it to be true, she still loved him and she wanted him to love her back.

But she couldn't make him, nor could she change the past. At the end of the day she was alone and forever linked with someone who wouldn't see her as more than a friend he liked to sleep with.

"The death threats against Mr. Sabotini have escalated," Jeff said three days later at the staff meeting. "We're going to coordinate with a multinational task force." He nodded at Nicki. "You'll be spending a lot of time at your computer until this one is resolved."

She looked up from her notes. "Not a problem. I'm already coordinating with our team in New York. When he brings his family over here, that's their point of entry. Fortunately they'll be flying a private jet and not commercial. That should cut down on some of the risk."

"Good. My contacts in Europe tell me the clues are

mounting, but so far there's not enough for them to move on," Jeff continued.

Nicki wrote down the pertinent information. While she was sorry that Mr. Sabotini and his family were in danger, she appreciated having something to occupy her mind. The intense work situation kept her from thinking about Zane and what a fool she'd been.

It wasn't just finding out that he wouldn't ever love her, it was the loss of him from her life. Gone were the easy lunches, the teasing conversation. He no longer asked about her protein intake or monitored her morning exercise. Since he'd confessed his past, he'd barely spoken to her.

Now they sat at opposite ends of the table, on opposite sides. She was careful not to look in his direction and figured he was probably doing the same. Their co-workers had noticed. Brenda, Jeff's assistant, had stopped by that morning to ask what was up with Zane.

Nicki had pretended ignorance, then had felt like slime for lying. She wasn't eating, wasn't sleeping and knew she had to find a way to function, for the sake of the baby, if not for herself.

The meeting adjourned. As usual, Nicki waited until the room was empty before rolling out into the hallway. Zane was one of the first ones out the door.

As she stared after him, she wondered what she should do. Give up? That plan made the most sense. He loved someone else, which she could handle if he also wanted to love her. But he didn't. Maybe he couldn't, maybe he wasn't interested. She would probably never know. The most sensible course of action was to figure out a way to get over him.

Last night she'd made a list of her options. She could

stay where she was and hope for the best. She could quit and find another job in Seattle. Or she could move.

Her parents hadn't been subtle in their hinting that she head down to Tucson. With her degree and her work experience, she knew she wouldn't have trouble finding a job. She might even be able to do something from home. Of course moving would mean that Zane wouldn't be much of a part of his child's life.

She headed for her office. As she settled behind her desk, she considered that. Was it fair to take the baby away from him?

Did he care about the baby?

Nicki leaned back in her chair. Did he? He was worried about her health. He wanted to keep them both safe. He'd made logistical plans about changing tables and dressers, but what about plans to read to their child? To play with it, nurture it? He couldn't get over loving and losing Amber enough to love another woman. Could he get over the child he'd lost to care about the one she carried?

She could accept loving a man who didn't love her back, but she wouldn't subject her baby to that. Not ever. Which might make the decision to leave Seattle a very simple one.

Zane paced in his house. He was exhausted, but knew he didn't want to sleep. Not when the nightmares had returned.

They were vivid, cruel and detailed. In them he stood on the tarmac, watching the helicopter rise toward the sky. It stuttered, lurched, then slammed into the mountain. In his sleep he relived every second of the crash. The heat, the smell, the horror. He always came awake bathed in sweat, and screaming.

For the first three months after Amber had died, the nightmares had come every night. Eventually they'd slowed to once a week, then once a month. Finally they'd faded. Until he'd told Nicki the truth.

There were no words to describe the ache inside. He was empty. He hadn't thought he could hurt more than he had when he'd lost his wife and his unborn child, but he did. Because this time, in addition to reliving what had been ripped from him, he'd also lost Nicki.

She was his best friend. She was his refuge. The place he could be himself. With her, there was laughter and affection and escape. They'd become friends so easily that he hadn't noticed how important she was to him until she was gone. Now he was alone and he didn't think he could face another night with the ghosts.

He grabbed his keys and walked out of his houseboat. There was only one place he knew to go.

She answered the door without asking who was there. As if she'd known it was him. As he stood on her doorstep, he took in her long red hair, the vivid green of her eyes, the perfect blush on her cheeks. He ignored the wary expression and instead saw only what they had been together. He trusted her. He didn't want to lose her. He *couldn't* lose her. But how to convince her?

"Marry me," he said without thinking. "Marry me, please. I'll do anything you want. Say anything."

She wheeled back to let him enter, then followed him to the living room.

Her steady gaze locked with his. "I'm not looking for a trained pet," she told him quietly. "If I needed someone in my life to do my bidding without question, I'd get a dog."

Her anger surprised him. Then he remembered how he'd hurt her. "I'm sorry," he told her. "I didn't mean it like that."

"Actually, I think you did." She drew in a breath. "I have a question. When the baby is born, will you care about it?"

He frowned. "Of course. It's my child."

"Will you love it?"

"Yes."

"What if we have twins?"

He stiffened. "You can't—"

She shook her head. "As far as I know, there's only one baby. Don't panic. I'm just curious. Could you love two children?"

He had no idea where she was going with this. "Sure. Why wouldn't I?"

"Because you can't love another woman. You still love Amber. So why don't you still love your unborn child?"

"That's different."

"How?"

"Isn't it obvious?"

"No," she told him. "Is it because the baby wasn't real, just like our child isn't real yet? Are you saying that you could love another child because that child hadn't been born? What if it had been? Would you open your heart to another child, having lost one?"

He shifted uncomfortably. "What's your point?" he asked, not sure what she was getting at, but more than a little wary about the direction they were taking. "I want to be a father. I want to take care of both of you."

"I appreciate that," she said. "You care about me."

He relaxed a little. "You know I do."

"And as a friend, you can love me, just not romantically."

The tension returned. He sensed pitfalls but couldn't see them. "You're very important to me."

"Nice dodge," she told him. "I'm trying to define your limits. Who can you love and under what circumstances? Because I'm not sure I believe you. That you could love more than one child. You can't love more than one woman and I don't think it's different at all. You never saw your baby with Amber, so it wasn't real to you."

He glared at her. "You don't understand. You weren't there."

"I know. And watching your wife die like that had to be the most emotionally devastating event imaginable."

He tried not to picture the explosion. "It was worse," he said grimly. "I'm the one who killed her."

"That's where I take issue with you," Nicki told him. "Unless you put a bomb on the helicopter, you *didn't* kill her any more than I did. You wanted her to leave, which made sense. There was a problem with the helicopter. It was horrible and tragic, but it wasn't your fault."

He turned away from her. "You don't know what the hell you're talking about."

"As a matter of fact, I do. It's like my skiing accident. It was awful. It changed me forever. I've been to hell and back, too, Zane. You're not the only one. The difference is I lived through it, while you're still dying every day."

"You didn't lose someone."

"I lost who I was. I lost who I could have been. I'm not saying that I don't love my life. I'm grateful I survived and that I fought back, but there was still a huge loss. I faced the demons and the fear. Sometimes they still catch me off guard. I've learned that in the past couple of days. I'll beat them down again. But what about you? Will you ever face your past? Will you ever move beyond? Because if you don't, there's no point in us continuing at all. I'm not interested in a man who lives his life ruled by fear."

Zane glared at her and swore. She didn't know. She had no right to judge him. "There isn't any fear."

"I think that's all there is. Fear that if you love again, you'll lose. It's so much easier not to try. You hide behind women who can't matter because you're terrified you'll find one who does, and then what? You'll have to risk it."

"With you?" he asked with contempt.

"With anyone." She sighed. "Ironically, knowing this about you doesn't change how I feel. I still love you. I want to be your partner, your wife and the mother of your children. But I won't be your atonement. Either you risk it all, or you get nothing. You have to be willing to take a chance."

He didn't know what to say. He couldn't think, couldn't feel. His only instinct was to run.

"I want to say I think you'll come to your senses," she said. "Unfortunately, I don't."

"I have to go," he said, rising to his feet. He headed for the door.

Before he got there, she spoke. "I'm leaving Seattle."

Zane turned and stared at her. "What?"

"I'm moving to Tucson. I can't have a real life until I get over you, and I can't see you every day at work and get over you. I'm sorry. I don't know what else to do."

Leaving? But then she would be out of his life. "When?" he asked.

"I gave my notice to Jeff this afternoon. I'm listing the house this weekend and moving in six weeks."

He reached for the doorknob. It took three tries before he was able to grasp it and escape.

He climbed into his car and headed away, driving as fast as the narrow streets would let him. Leaving. She was leaving. He tried to tell himself it was better this way. That they would get on with their lives. But he didn't believe it.

What about the baby? If she was out of state, he would never see his child, or have contact with it. Was that for the best?

He drove and drove, until he ended up by the water. Always the water. He stood at the same dock, looking out at the boats and the water. Cold seeped into his bones.

He knew what Nicki wanted, what she'd always wanted. To be someone's first choice. To be loved and cherished. But he couldn't love her. It was wrong. He still loved Amber. Amber who was…

Dead. Amber was dead.

The truth slammed into him like a runaway train. It plowed through him and over him, leaving him bent, broken and in pieces. She was dead, she was gone and she was never ever coming back. Just like their child. Just like their hopes and dreams. It was all over. It had been over for years.

But he hadn't wanted to let go, because loving her had been the best part of him. Even feeling guilty had helped keep her alive. Without her, who was he?

Staggered by the truth, he clung to the handrail. The smell of the water reminded him of a day trip he and Nicki had made to Friday Harbor. He remembered the wind tangling her hair and how she'd laughed as she rolled back and forth as the boat had rocked. That had been a good day. There had been a thousand just like them, because any day with Nicki was a good day.

At that moment Zane realized he'd been blessed twice in his life. He'd managed to find two of the most amazing women ever born and somehow they'd fallen in love with him. He'd lost one, through circumstances that weren't his fault. Was he about to lose the other because he was a horse's ass?

She deserved so much more than he could offer, but for some reason, she wanted him. How the hell had he gotten so damn lucky?

He shook his head. He'd come so close to losing her.

Now all he had to do was get his sorry hide back to her place and convince her to give him another chance.

He headed for his car but before he got there, his cell phone rang. The caller ID said the call was from Jeff.

"What's up?" he asked by way of greeting.

"Sabotini's youngest son was just kidnapped," Jeff told him. "Tim already has our gear and will meet us at the jet. Be there in twenty minutes."

Zane arrived at the airport to find the team already in place. Nicki was there with a checklist. When he walked toward her, she acknowledged him with a tight nod, then pointed to his pile of gear.

"I need you to go through that. Call out what you have and I'll note it."

He wanted to talk about something more important than whether or not he had a stun gun in his bag, but knew this wasn't the time. Whatever his personal feelings might be, or what he might have learned, Sabotini's kid was in danger and that had to be his first priority.

In less than twenty minutes, they were on the jet and taxiing down the runway.

Zane and Jeff sat together. Jeff brought him up to date on how the kidnapping had occurred. Within an hour, they were receiving information from Nicki, who had set up a command center back at the office. She fed reports from local law enforcement, as well as messages from resources Jeff and Zane had in Europe.

Two hours out of New York, Zane briefed the team. They had a good idea of where the boy was being held and would be going in to get him.

"What about local law enforcement?" Nicki asked, her

voice only slightly scratchy after being bounced off a satellite.

"Mr. Sabotini wants us to move quickly," Jeff said. "We take orders from him."

"Don't get arrested."

"That's a secondary concern."

"I know. It's just all that bail money really cuts into petty cash."

Jeff smiled. "I'll be in touch," he said and disconnected the call. Then he turned to Zane. "Want to talk about what's up?"

Zane shrugged. Normally he was the one coordinating communications with Nicki, but this time, he'd handed the headset to Jeff.

Jeff glanced back at their team, then lowered his voice. "I know she's pregnant. She told me."

Zane wasn't surprised. "We're dealing with it."

"Not very well. She resigned."

Zane's gut tightened. She'd told him she'd done it, but he'd been hoping she'd exaggerated the truth. He should have known that wasn't her way.

"She wants to go to Tucson and live near her folks," he said.

Jeff stared at him. "What do you want?"

Nicki, Zane thought. "The situation is complicated."

"When I was being an idiot about Ashley, you told me that chances like that don't come along very often. That I had the opportunity to find normal and that I should take it."

"I remember," Zane said.

"I'm going to give that same advice back to you. You loved and lost once. Do you want to love and lose again because this time you're not willing to take a chance? To find someone you can love heart and soul is a miracle."

Zane nodded. "I've figured that much out myself. The thing is…" He couldn't believe he was about to admit this. "I'm not worth it. I don't know why the hell she cares, but she does. How am I supposed to live up to that?"

Jeff shrugged. "You can't. None of us can. Those women who love us are amazing. They don't expect perfection. All they ask for in return for their love and devotion is for us to love them back. It seems to me we're getting the better bargain, but they don't mind."

It made no sense to Zane. Yet when he thought about his conversations with Nicki, all she'd ever asked was for him to love her back. It didn't seem like nearly enough, but maybe he was making this too hard.

Before he could decide, the satellite phone rang. Zane reached for it.

"What have you got?" he asked.

Nicki blinked in surprise. She'd expected to hear Jeff's voice and she really hated that hearing Zane's made her heart thunder like a herd of buffalo.

"Infrared photos from the complex," she said. "I'm sending them. I think we've found the boy and his kidnappers."

She heard Zane repeating the information, then tapping his keyboard.

"Got 'em," he said. "What's the word from local law enforcement?"

"They're unhappy that you've been called in. But Mr. Sabotini has some very influential friends. A call came from D.C. that you were to be given whatever backup you needed. I guess you won't be going to jail."

"Good thing. The food is lousy."

She heard muffled voices, then Zane spoke again.

"We're about twenty minutes from landing. I'll call back when we're on our way there."

"I'll be waiting." She hesitated. "Be careful."

"Always."

There was a click, then he was gone.

Nicki spent the next couple of hours relaying information to the team. She tapped into multiple computer systems and satellite systems, coordinating everything through her console. Most of the support staff had been called in.

By the time the team pulled up to within a quarter mile of the old abandoned grocery store, it was dawn on the east coast.

"The best time to attack," she murmured to herself. "It's when the enemy gets weakest."

She'd heard Zane and Jeff talk about that dozens of times and knew it to be true. Everything would be fine. Within an hour or so, the kid would be rescued and everyone would be heading home. Including Zane.

Nicki ached to see him—a real mistake considering how things were between them. She was supposed to be leaving town in an effort to get over him. Missing him after less than twelve hours didn't bode well for her recovery.

Nicki turned her attention back to the team and what was happening. They were all wearing headsets now, and she could listen to their conversations. She sent the latest infrared photos to Jeff's handheld console and talked with Zane about the temporary security system setup.

"I've tapped into it and turned it off," she said. "The fools actually hooked it up to the phone lines, if you can believe it."

"Good work," he said. "All right, everybody. Lock and load. Remember, stun weapons only. There's a kid in there. Nobody gets dead on this one."

Nicki swallowed. The decision had been made to not use bullets for fear of starting a gunfight that would take out the hostage. But that didn't mean the kidnappers would play by their rules.

Several voices came at once, then quieted as the team approached the buildings. She heard sounds of movement, the squeak of a door. Quiet voices murmured their positions.

When the action started, it was fast, confusing and left her shaking. Just like always. But this time Nicki listened for someone to say the boy was okay. She had a direct line to Mr. Sabotini, and would get to him with real-time information, just as soon as she had it.

"Got him," Zane said gruffly. "Jeez, he's maybe seven. Hey, it's all right."

She heard a child crying, then a babble of words she couldn't understand.

"Great," Zane muttered. "He doesn't speak English."

"I'm getting a patch," Nicki yelled, as she typed furiously. "Mr. Sabotini, Zane has your son, but he's terrified. He doesn't speak English. Tell him we're the good guys."

Nicki listened as father and son communicated. The relief in the older man's voice made her smile. She touched her stomach, knowing one day she would have a baby to hold and love. Pray God she was never put in Mr. Sabotini's position.

"Better," Zane said a couple of minutes later. "Jeff, we're ready. Is that all five of them?"

Nicki froze. "Zane, there's six. Remember? That one guy who's—"

Her words were cut off in a hail of gunfire. At the sound of the bullets, Nicki's heart froze. She knew, she just *knew* even before she heard Jeff yell.

"I've got the boy. Somebody grab Zane." Jeff swore. "He's been hit. Damn it all to hell."

There was more gunfire. The console blurred and Nicki realized she was crying. "No," she whispered. "Zane, no!"

"Nicki?"

She recognized his voice. Relief flooded her. "Zane? Are you okay?"

Ted's voice came over her headpiece. "He's, ah, fine, Nicki."

She knew a lie when she heard one. "Ted, you have to save him. You have to!"

"Nicki," Zane said, sounding more than a little shaky. "I'm really sorry. About everything. I know the timing really sucks on this, but I want you to know I love you. For real. For always."

She couldn't believe it. Her tears fell faster. She brushed them away and grabbed the mouthpiece. "You better mean that, Zane. And you'd better come back here alive or I'll never forgive you."

She felt someone crouch next to her and turned to find Brenda. The older woman pulled her close.

"I'm sure he'll be fine," she said.

Nicki nodded because she couldn't speak. The sound of a helicopter filled her headset, then she heard nothing at all.

Six hours later, Nicki was back on the airport tarmac. Jeff had called to say Zane was going to be okay and that they were heading home. The kidnappers had been arrested and were already giving the names of their leaders. The law enforcement officials figured it would only take a couple of days to round everyone up.

A grateful Mr. Sabotini had promised to visit Seattle to

thank the team in person…but not for a few days. Right now he wanted to be with his family.

Nicki could relate to that. She only wanted to see Zane. Apparently he'd insisted on flying home rather than checking into a hospital, so she knew he was conscious, but she didn't know how bad his injury was. Zane could be five kinds of stubborn.

Just in case, she had a private ambulance standing by and had already plotted the quickest route to the nearest hospital. As for herself, she was numb. His last words, that he loved her, echoed in her mind. If they were true—please God, let them be true—then she had everything she'd ever wanted in life.

It seemed like hours before the plane finally appeared in the sky, then landed and taxied to where she was sitting. The doors opened. Jeff came out first. She searched his face, hoping for some clue to Zane's condition, but her boss's features were annoyingly blank. She braced herself for a stretcher, for blood, for something really horrible, then nearly passed out when Zane appeared at the top of the stairs.

He actually walked down himself. Unaided. Her gaze narrowed as she took in the sling he wore and the flew specks of blood on his shirt.

"That's it?" she screeched. "You're barely shot at all?"

He grinned sheepishly as he approached. "I sort of got winged during the gunfight. At first it looked a lot worse than it was."

She was both furious and relieved. "You made me suffer," she told him. "Dammit, Zane, I thought you were going to die."

He walked over and crouched in front of her.

"Never," he said, taking her hands in his. "I don't want to

leave you." He stared into her eyes. "I might have exaggerated my condition to get the sympathy vote, but everything else I said was a hundred percent true. I love you, Nicki."

She gazed at him. "What about Amber? What about the past?"

"I loved her, and some part of me will always care about her. But she's my past and you're my future. I want to love you every day of my life. I want us to have children together, to be happy, to grow old. I love you, Nicki, more than I can ever tell you."

The last of her doubts and fears faded away. She leaned toward him. "Then I guess you're going to have to show me."

He smiled. "Gladly. As often as you'd like." He kissed her. "I still want to marry you, but for different reasons. I'll understand if you want a little time so I can prove myself."

"I might make you wait a day or two until I say yes."

They kissed again, slowly, deeply, ignoring the movement around them as the jet was unloaded. Finally Zane raised his head.

"Let's get out of here," he said. "Back to your place where we can have a serious reunion."

"Do we need to stop by the hospital so you can get some stitches?"

"I'm fine. More than fine." He touched her cheek. "I'll go anywhere you want, Nicki. If moving to Tucson is important to you, I'll go."

She shook her head. "I'd rather stay here," she told him. "It's where we belong."

He stood and walked beside her as she moved to her van. "So who do you like for the game on Sunday?" he asked

She started laughing. "You never learn, do you?"

He smiled. "You're wrong. I've learned the most important lesson of all. But I still believe I can beat you in a football pool."

"In your dreams, big guy. In your dreams."

# *Epilogue*

*Christmas—25 years later*

Christmas Greetings from the Rankin family. Once again, we're thrilled to bring our loved ones up to date on the happenings in the household.

Starting with the youngest member of the family—Zoe is a senior in high school. She's—if you'll excuse the pun—kicking butt on her soccer team and it looks like she's going to be offered several athletic scholarships at various colleges. She still hates math, loves history and has had seven boyfriends this year. It is a record, even for her. Zane says it's because she's as pretty as her mother. Zoe says it's because she's also very picky.

Sean is in his last year at the University of Washington where he will graduate with a degree in chemical engineering. He still plans to go on to get his Ph.D., which his sisters find really scary. Sean has a "serious" girlfriend, but says we're not allowed to talk about her in the newsletter.

When he's not studying, Sean spends his time boating and plans to crew on an entry in the next America's Cup.

April and her new husband are blissfully happy. After six months of marriage, they swear they'd do it all over again, which is lovely to hear. April is still enjoying the law and plans to make partner before she turns thirty. Charlie, her husband, has two more years of his pediatric residency left before he can hang out his shingle.

As for Nicki and Zane, we celebrated our twenty-fifth wedding anniversary with a month-long trip to Australia. The security firm is still successful and growing, although rumors that the president insisted on members of the Ritter/Rankin team accompanying her on her Far East tour are slightly exaggerated.

Nicki's computer firm has doubled in size…again.

The entire family feels blessed by the love they share. We all send holiday greetings to you and yours. May all your dreams come true.

\* \* \* \* \*

*If you enjoyed this story, we think you'll also love*
*Jeff and Ashley's story,*
Shelter in a Soldier's Arms,
*and Heidi and Jamal's story,*
Desert Rogues: The Arranged Marriage.

*Both books are available wherever ebooks are sold.*

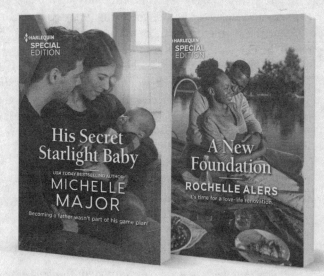

SPECIAL EXCERPT FROM

**⊕ HARLEQUIN**
**SPECIAL** EDITION

*Since she first met him months ago in Rambling Rose at the Hotel Fortune, Arabella Fortune has fantasized about sexy and sweet Jay Cross. Now she sets to find out how he'd intended to finish his last words to her: "I think you should know…"*

*Read on for a sneak peek at*
Cowboy in Disguise,
*the final book in The Fortunes of Texas: The Hotel Fortune*
*by* New York Times *bestselling author Allison Leigh!*

"I think you'd better kiss me," she murmured, and her cheeks turned rosy.

"Yeah?" His voice dropped also.

"If you don't, then I'll know this is just a dream."

"And if I do?"

She moistened her lips. "Then I'll know this is just a dream."

He smiled slightly. He brushed the silky end of her ponytail against her cheek and leaned closer. "Dream, Bella," he whispered, and slowly pressed his lips to hers.

He felt her quick inhale and his own quick rush. Tasted the brightness of lemonade, the sweetness of strawberry.

He slid his fingers from her ponytail to the back of her neck and urged her closer.

Her fingers splayed against his chest. She murmured something against his lips. He barely heard. His head was full of sound. Full of pulse beats and bells.

She murmured again. This time not against his lips.

He frowned, feeling entirely thwarted. "What?"

She pulled back yet another inch. Her fingertips pushed instead of urged closer. "Do you want to answer that?"

It made sense then. His cell phone was ringing.

*Don't miss*
Cowboy in Disguise *by Allison Leigh,*
*available June 2021 wherever*
*Harlequin Special Edition books and ebooks are sold.*

Harlequin.com

# HARLEQUIN
## SPECIAL EDITION

**Believe in love. Overcome obstacles.
Find happiness.**

Save **$1.00**

on the purchase of **ANY
Harlequin Special Edition book.**

Available wherever books are sold, including
most bookstores, supermarkets, drugstores
and discount stores.

---

# Save $1.00

## on the purchase of ANY Harlequin Special Edition book.

Coupon valid until July 31, 2021. Redeemable at participating outlets in the U.S. and Canada only.
Not redeemable at Barnes & Noble stores. Limit one coupon per customer.

52617078

**Canadian Retailers:** Harlequin Enterprises ULC will pay the face value of this coupon plus
10.25¢ if submitted by customer for this product only. Any other use constitutes fraud. Coupon is
nonassignable. Void if taxed, prohibited or restricted by law. Consumer must pay any government taxes.
Void if copied. Inmar Promotional Services ("IPS") customers submit coupons and proof of sales to
Harlequin Enterprises ULC, P.O. Box 31000, Scarborough, ON M1R 0E7, Canada. Non-IPS retailer—
for reimbursement submit coupons and proof of sales directly to Harlequin Enterprises ULC, Retail
Marketing Department, Bay Adelaide Centre, East Tower, 22 Adelaide Street West, 40th Floor, Toronto,
Ontario M5H 4E3, Canada.

**U.S. Retailers:** Harlequin Enterprises ULC will pay the face
value of this coupon plus 8¢ if submitted by customer for
this product only. Any other use constitutes fraud. Coupon is
nonassignable. Void if taxed, prohibited or restricted by law.
Consumer must pay any government taxes. Void if copied.
For reimbursement submit coupons and proof of sales directly
to Harlequin Enterprises ULC 482, NCH Marketing Services,
P.O. Box 880001, El Paso, TX 88588-0001, U.S.A. Cash value
1/100 cents.

BACCOUP20993MAX